D0198254

"A rich portrait of a country ⁣ _tail and wonder, thanks to a naturalist's eye."

—*FOREWORD REVIEWS*

"This is a novel that is, above all, about how seeing is an act of love. A profound and moving experience awaits the reader."

—REBECCA NEWBERGER GOLDSTEIN,
author of *Plato at the Googleplex*

"In clean, beautiful prose and with an environmental sensibility evocative of Stegner, *Accidentals* sings with the vibrancy of the living world . . . erudite and emotionally compelling, suffused with science and natural history."

—CHRISTIAN KIEFER, author of *Phantoms*

"An intimate family story with an astonishingly epic scope. Alive with history, politics, science, romance, and birds, it is as entertaining as it is intelligent, as beautiful as it is wise. Gabe's evolution from a passive observer to the passionate creator of his own destiny is a life-changing experience not only for him, but for readers as well."

—JEAN HEGLAND, author of *Still Time*

"This is a novel about all the things we don't yet know; all the things we know but keep hidden; and all the things we once knew but have lost. Gorgeous, smart, and surprising, this family saga takes us into the large world of nations and politics, but also the microscopic world of mud and microbes. Tender and powerful. Also with birds!"

—KAREN JOY FOWLER,
author of *We Are All Completely Beside Ourselves*

"As a conservation biologist, as well as an Uruguayan immigrant and mother of two first-generation Americans, I was as moved by the Quiroga family's layers of history, secrets, and struggles around land, politics, and love, as I was intrigued by the beautiful depictions of birds and the musings on evolution and extinction. This is a novel I would like to share with my daughters someday!"

—ANA LUZ PORZECANSKI,
Director of the Center for Biodiversity & Conservation
at the American Museum of Natural History

"A captivating novel centered around love lost, regained, and fashioned anew, a mix of cultures, and efforts to reclaim land and heritage. All this against a backdrop of discovering and recording the lives of birds in the wild with forces human- and climate-driven pressing on their survival. Deeply moving and powerful."

—SHERYL COTLEUR, Copperfield's Books

Accidentals

Accidentals

a novel

Susan M. Gaines

TORREY HOUSE PRESS

SALT LAKE CITY • TORREY

This is a work of fiction. Any resemblance to actual events or persons, living or dead, is entirely coincidental.

First Torrey House Press Edition, March 2020
Copyright © 2019 by Susan M. Gaines

All rights reserved. No part of this book may be reproduced or retransmitted in any form or by any means without the written consent of the publisher.

Published by Torrey House Press
Salt Lake City, Utah
www.torreyhouse.org

International Standard Book Number: 978-1-948814-16-4
E-book ISBN: 978-1-948814-20-1
Library of Congress Control Number: 2019936115

Cover design by Kathleen Metcalf
Interior design by Rachel Davis
Distributed to the trade by Consortium Book Sales and Distribution

This project is supported in part by the National Endowment for the Arts. To find out more about how National Endowment for the Arts grants impact individuals and communities, visit www.arts.gov.

A Sofía,
por regalarme sus locuras, sus amigas y su país.

And for Stephan,
in life, in death, in love. Forever.

1

There was nothing particularly remarkable about the birds that day. No harbingers of apocalypse. No heralds of a new age. The last summer of the millennium was fading, and the fall migrants were en route to their summer homes as if nothing were amiss, the lagoon peppered with a seasonal medley of ducks. American Wigeon, Ruddy Duck, Surf Scoter, Bufflehead, the names ticked through my head like a familiar, comforting litany. It seemed a bit early for Buffleheads, but there were dozens of them bobbing about like bathtub toys, their heads flashing white in the late afternoon sun.

I'd driven north to spend the weekend with Mom, and she'd asked me to take her birding. This was not something we were in the habit of doing together, and I should have known she had some ulterior motive, especially when I saw what an elaborate picnic she'd prepared. But I was a little slow on the uptake, if not the entirely oblivious *hijo sonámbulo* she'd accused me of being as a teenager, her sleepwalking son.

I took her to a spot in Point Reyes that my grandfather used to like, a place I hadn't been back to since he died. It was one of those rare days when the Northern California coast was simultaneously free of wind and fog, and it felt good just to be away from the city and my tedious cubicle job. The place was more crowded than I remembered, with groups of hikers scattered along the trail around the lagoon. I paused to scan the water through the binoculars, reeling off species names for Mom, who was, predictably, uninterested. She wasn't a birder, never had been. Neither was Dad, for that matter, though I learned everything I knew about birds from his father when I was a little boy. It was one of those things that skipped a generation, like the unruly Uruguayan eyebrows on the other side of the family, which had passed Mom by and landed, thick, black, and incongruous on my fair, freckled face. Grandpa Gordon took me tromping all over California, from the Sierra backcountry to the LA city dump, in search of birds. Birdwatching had been his passion, his lifelong obsession, and he'd died birding in Tuolumne Meadows, collapsed with a heart attack, binoculars in hand. That was over a year ago, just before I graduated college, but it was only recently that I'd really begun to miss him. I wasn't obsessed like he'd been, but I did have the birder gene, somewhat diluted. It was more habit than anything, something I'd been born to. You went for a walk, you looked for birds. You went kayaking, you looked for birds. You went camping, or fishing, or climbed a mountain—you looked for birds.

"I'm going back," Mom announced, ignoring my recitations.

"Already?" I scanned the dunes at the far end of the lagoon, focusing on a late-nesting Snowy Plover. I never would have spotted it from so far away, but there was a sign announcing its presence and a group of people staring at it through binoculars. Apparently, Snowy Plovers had been elevated to endangered species status since I was last here. Poor unassuming little peeps spent their lives trying to avoid notice and now here they were, the center of attention, like a display in a museum.

"Already?" Mom echoed me. "*Hace más de treinta años.* Thirty-one, actually. Summer 1968."

I lowered the binoculars and turned to Mom. "What are you talking about?"

Objectively speaking, my mother was unremarkable looking—short graying brown hair, olive skin, features that were a bit too large for her face. Thin, wiry body. Average height. But to her friends and students and colleagues, she was a beautiful alien species, blazing with manic energy and intelligence, like a comet streaking across their suburban sky. She could also explode, of course, or more likely implode, but Dad and I were the only ones who ever saw that. When I was small, she'd gone to a shrink a few times at Dad's behest, but I think the shrink just ended up joining her ranks of charmed friends. At the moment, she had a bemused expression on her face and was quietly watching a phalarope feeding in the shallow water a few yards from shore, the binoculars hanging unused around her neck. "I'm going back to Uruguay," she said.

"Oh." When I was growing up, we'd gone to Uruguay to see her family every other Christmas, the way other families went to Iowa or New York, except we got summer and beaches instead of snow. I'd stopped going when I started college, but she and Dad had gone together until a couple years ago. "That's a Wilson's Phalarope," I added. "In case you're wondering."

She shot me a look, and smiled. "I'm wondering why she does these pirouettes."

"He. It's a male. He's stirring up the crabs and bugs from the mud." I watched the phalarope spinning and dipping like a drunken ballerina. "What about Dad?" They still saw each other, after all. I even suspected they slept together now and then, though I wasn't supposed to know this. Dad used to love to go to Uruguay. And Mom's mother doted on him.

"*Tu papá,*" she sighed. "*Tu papá se achanchó.*"

Whatever the hell that was supposed to mean. Dad had turned into a contented pig? A stick in the mud? I lifted the binoculars to watch a grebe that had just popped up from an underwater fishing excursion in the middle of a flock of scoters. "Horned Grebe with very large fish," I announced. It was having a hard time getting the fish down its gullet, bouncing along the surface of the water with the tail hanging out its mouth. I glanced at Mom to see if she was watching, but she was still staring at the phalarope, missing the show.

They used to fight all the time when I was a kid, or rather, Mom fought and Dad listened implacably, mumbling the occasional platitude, which only drove her into worse frenzies. Her threats to leave him had been their marriage's refrain, cries of wolf that echoed unheeded through the caverns of my otherwise happy childhood—until the wolf arrived in truth, two years ago. I was already in college, but it caught poor Dad unawares. He thought they'd come safely round the bend to middle age and were home free. Mom, of course, had her own version.

"All your father cares about anymore is that stupid job," she said as I watched the grebe come to terms with its fish. "This American dream bullshit. What is that? Three cars and a big house with three bathrooms in a neighborhood with streets that don't go anywhere. Comfort. Striving for comfort that you already have."

She always sounded ridiculous when she cussed in English. With her perennial mispronunciation of "shit" as "sheet," she sounded like a cartoon caricature of the Latino bandit, likening the American dream to something a bull might sleep on, rather than a large pile of crap. "Dad has one car," I said. "A Honda." We'd never lived in an especially big house or had three bathrooms either, but I let it go.

We walked a little farther along the edge of the lagoon, and then headed up to the top of a grassy knoll for our picnic. Mom's rants against American materialism and suburbs were all pretty familiar. But I'd never heard her talk about Dad with such disdain before. He wrote computer software for chemists, made a good middle-class salary. I knew it wasn't the money itself that bothered her, but the idea that Dad took the job seriously, when, like my job in Oakland, it seemed to have no worthwhile purpose besides the accrual of money. Dad called this practical. He strove for comfort, got it, and was content. What was so wrong

4

with that? He ate well, worked, tossed a baseball with his son and took him camping and fishing in the summer. He read books and went to movies and the occasional play or concert, usually by some gray-haired seventies rock band. Normal stuff.

I watched Mom extract containers of food from the knapsacks, setting them out on the faded red bedspread she'd brought for us to sit on. She'd made *pascualina*, the chard and egg pie she only made for special occasions. Slices of homemade bread and ham, tomatoes and sweet peppers from her garden. All my favorites. "Dad cares about you," I said, finally. "And me."

She looked up, surprised. "*Ay Gabrielito*," she said quickly, laying her hand on my arm as if to stop the thoughts she'd let loose. "Of course he cares about you, *bichito*. He's a great father, a dear, dear man."

She'd overstepped her own boundaries, I realized then, boundaries I hadn't, until that moment, been conscious of. She'd always been sarcastic with Dad, sometimes to the point of downright meanness. But she had never, not in any of their worst moments, the myriad almost-divorces that punctuated my childhood, said anything disrespectful about my father *to me*, or to anyone else that I knew of. He was an irreproachably decent man, and she knew it, for all that she'd spent half a lifetime reproaching him. I half-shrugged, half-nodded, acknowledging what was, apparently, an apology.

"This is about *me*, Gabe. And your father never dared to scratch the surface of that." She placed squares of *pascualina* on plastic plates and handed me the one with the whole egg in the middle. "I can't stand this big monster country anymore."

She said this with such pronounced bitterness that I looked up from the tomatoes I was about to load onto my plate. I suddenly had the uneasy feeling that I'd been humming along to the wrong tune all afternoon.

"I'm going *back*," Mom said when she saw the confused look on my face. "*Para siempre, a vivir. Al paisito.*"

I stared at her. "To live? You're moving to Montevideo?"

"End of September. Thirty-four days, to be exact."

My mother had lived in California for thirty years. She was a naturalized citizen who voted in every American election and grumbled when she listened to American news. She had a gringo ex-husband—or *yanqui*, as the Uruguayans say—and a thoroughly *yanqui* son. She spoke English with a vocabulary that was more sophisticated than that of your average American. Oh, she clung to her Spanish accent, along with a few nostalgic affectations like drinking *mate* instead of coffee for breakfast, and she still scrambled up the slang. But according to her mother in Montevideo, she also spoke Spanish with an American accent. If leaving Dad had been a not-so-surprising surprise, moving back to Uruguay was a total non sequitur. "Mom?" I said. "Don't you think this is a little sudden?"

"Oh no. I've been thinking about it for the past ten years."

This was news. She'd just moved and taken a new job, teaching her favorite courses at what was reputedly one of the best junior colleges in the state—a full-time faculty member, after decades of working as a part-time adjunct. She'd left Dad with most of their communal belongings and her rented house was no bigger than a cottage, but she'd wanted it that way, or so she said. She'd fixed the place up, hung things on the walls, even framed bird drawings she'd salvaged from a calendar I made when I was twelve, a bird for every month. Evidence of the garden she'd built up in the cottage's backyard was on my plate—the homely chard, the unusual multicolored tomatoes and peppers she liked to grow.

"My father is dead," Mom said, closing her mouth around the words, as if to establish their finality. "And Mamá isn't getting any younger. I want to look after her in her old age."

It was hard to imagine Mom or anyone else "looking after" my aloof, independent *abuela*, who'd been living alone since my first memories and probably a lot longer. Mom's father had left the family when she was a kid, and he'd never been much in evidence when we visited. I vaguely remembered him as a pair of thick black glasses and wild white eyebrows, an older, more stilted version of my uncle Juan Luis. I knew he'd died earlier that year, but he was over ninety and it hadn't seemed like such a grand event, not like when Grandpa Gordon died. Mom hadn't even gone to Uruguay for the funeral.

"What about your job?" I asked.

"*Puf.*" She made one of those little sounds that could still mark her as Uruguayan, dismissing twenty years of dedicated teaching, a long list of awards, and generations of grateful students with this little blast of air and a flick of her hand. "I already resigned." According to Mom, teaching at the junior college had been her concession to motherhood—she had a master's degree in biology and would have gone on for a PhD if it weren't for me—but she was, by all reports, exceptionally good at it. Teaching, that is.

I refilled my plate with ham and bread and *pascualina*. This was Mom's weird idea of a goodbye dinner, I realized, her *adiós* to the monster country. *Adiós* to California and the great Pacific. To her *yanqui* son. I watched a wave rise and crash into a wall of frothing white almost as high as our knoll. The bank of fog on the horizon was already tinted with the oranges and reds of the approaching sunset, and it was the time of day when everyone was out looking for something to eat—a pelican dive-bombing the fish beyond the surf, a White-tailed Kite hovering like an elegant white moth above the bluffs to the south, a Marsh Hawk on cruise patrol beneath it, shorebirds dabbing at the wet sand of the lagoon's tidal flats. *We're nature's guests in paradise*, Grandpa used to say, and when I was a kid, watching a swarm of phalaropes descend on Mono Lake or creeping across these very dunes and competing for how many sand-speckled Snowy Plover eggs we could spot, I had believed him. But what had looked vast and immutable when I was small seemed diminished and

ACCIDENTALS

doomed to me now, hemmed in and outmoded, Grandpa's paradise as quaint and irrelevant as a Renaissance painting in a postmodern art exhibit. "What are you going to *do* down there?" I said, turning back to Mom.

She smiled and perked up, as if this were the question she'd been waiting for. "I'm going to grow vegetables! A real farm!"

This was the punch line? "You grow vegetables here," I said. "Remember? The biggest, sweetest, juiciest chocolate peppers in Northern California." I held out a thick slice of brown pepper, but she waved it aside, and I ate it myself. When I was little, she'd brainwashed me into thinking they really tasted like chocolate. I'd even painted a picture of them in the third grade, an ode to chocolate peppers in chalky brown tempera paint with "Hershey's Peppers" inscribed across the top.

"You remember my father's *estancia*? We went out there once, but you were pretty little."

I shook my head. "I thought he was an architect. I didn't even know he had a ranch."

"Oh yes. Really just a *chacra*, but Papá was pretentious, called it *una estancia*. It was managed by a couple of *paisanos* and their families. Three horses, a pony, and some cattle. We used to spend the summers there with all our friends."

I ate the rest of the peppers and started packing the empty food containers into the knapsacks while she went on about the estancia and the pony her father had given her. I was used to her being nostalgic about Uruguay. And I was used to her complaining about the monster country and its politics, the *yanqui* this and *yanqui* that. But these had been separate activities, two independent states of Mom—it never occurred to me that they had a common denominator, let alone that they might add up to action.

"That land now belongs to me and your *tíos*," Mom said as we folded the blanket. "And it's just sitting there, abandoned. Juan Luis is too busy to do anything with it, and he'd never get

Elsa to live out there. Rubén is in Venezuela, too buried in problems with Mariela to think about anything else. Mamá thinks we should sell it, but it's not worth much of anything. Three hundred hectares, Gabe. Good soil, plenty of water—and in Uruguay, it's not worth anything. We should be *farming* places like that, but all they can think about is cattle."

I watched her stuff the bedspread into the knapsack. She was wired, energized, about to launch off our knoll and fly south with the millennium's last migrant birds.

"I've been talking to Juan Luis and Rubén," she said. "Papá left us a little money, and I want to invest my part in the estancia. I've got some savings here. We don't need that much, to get things started."

"You're out of your mind." I turned away and cupped my hands around my mouth like a megaphone. "Forty-nine-year-old American housewife has midlife crisis!" I announced to the ducks and shorebirds below us. Mom hated being called a housewife, even though she had, in fact, managed our household and done most of the cooking and cleaning when I was growing up. I spun around to address the Marsh Hawk that was cruising our way. "Biology teacher reincarnated as Uruguayan peasant!"

"Uruguay is reinventing itself," she went on, ignoring my goading. "Everyone complains that we're too small, that we don't stand a chance, but it just takes a little imagination. *El paisito* is finally moving on, Gabe, starting over. And I want to be part of that."

We started down the steep side of the knoll, toward the far end of the lagoon, where there weren't as many people. I knew this place like I knew the inside of the house I'd grown up in. Maybe that was why it no longer impressed me.

"When you vote in *el paisito*," Mom said behind me, "you know it matters."

Theoretically, I could have been an Uruguayan citizen—I'd been born by chance in Montevideo when Mom was visiting and started labor too early. But I'd never lived there, hadn't even been to visit since I was sixteen. My memories were limited: Abuela's dark house with the grape arbor in the backyard, kicking a soccer ball around on the beach, eating massive amounts of meat and dulce de leche and *bizcochos* and the best ice cream in the world. It was a place for vacation.

"It's a dream," Mom said wistfully as we came to the bottom of the knoll. "Going home, farming that land."

It was a dream I'd never heard about before, a home I'd never thought of as her home, and a ridiculously prosaic undertaking for a midlife crisis, or so it seemed to me. I guess Dad and I had taken her gardens for granted.

I led her out to the edge of the lagoon's tidal flats and knelt in the sand, quietly surveying the scene. Red Knot, Long-Billed Curlew, all three species of peep. Spotted Sandpipers. A flock of dowitchers were peppered around the mudflat like little oil derricks, their long bills probing for treasure. Grandpa's paradise might seem diminished and passé to me, but it was still a five-star hotel for migrating shorebirds. They came from the east, from the Sierras or the Great Plains, and stayed for the winter; or they came from Canada and Alaska, fueled up on California cuisine, and continued south into Mexico, Central America, and beyond . . . to Uruguay? No one went to Uruguay.

"Gabriel . . ." Mom drawled, riding the Spanish accent on the last syllable like a hawk on an updraft, leaving my name to linger in the evening air. She had squatted down next to me in the sand, and she was watching me so closely I wanted to scurry away and disappear in the dunes with the besieged Snowy Plovers. "*¿Por qué no venís conmigo?* Just for a few months. Visit the family. Stay through Christmas and help me get the farm started."

I had the sensation that she'd been reading my mind before I'd even read it myself, a feeling I used to get when I was small: I'd be certain she was ignoring me completely, so self-absorbed and trapped by her own torments that she'd forgotten I existed, and then out of the blue she'd start up a conversation about whatever weird thing I had been thinking or dreaming about.

"You don't care about that job you're doing," she said. "*Las bobitas* you've been going out with. *Esa naba—*"

"Mom. Nicole was a pre-med student. Not exactly a dumb turnip. Not even a dumb blond." Nicole was the only one of my college girlfriends Mom had met, but she'd already decided in high school that my taste in women was problematic.

"Are you still seeing her?"

I shrugged. We'd split up over a year ago, when I graduated. Since then, I'd slept a few times with a girl I met kayaking and had an on-and-off affair with an older woman at work, but nothing to tell Mom about.

"Seriously Gabe, why not make the trip with me? You have more money in the bank than you know what to do with anyway." She laughed abruptly, and a Willet that was feeding nearby took off in an indignant flash of black and white. "You can subsidize my farm operation! Just think, Gabe, your first venture capitalist investment! In Uruguay!"

"Sure, Mom, great idea. We'll be millionaires in no time." It was the first snide remark she'd made about my job at Envirorep. In fact, she'd been disconcertingly supportive, almost like a normal mother. She'd even helped me buy clothes when, two months after graduating with a useless degree in geography and no more idea what I wanted to do than I had when I finished high school, I landed a job that paid more than she made at the JC.

"You haven't seen the family in years. Mamá was asking about you. Juan and Elsa will be thrilled. Maybe Rubén will even come from Venezuela for Christmas."

I thought about that, and about the job. I spent eight hours a day sitting in front of a computer analyzing geographic information systems data. It was simultaneously challenging, boring, and pointless—a deadly combination. But it did pay well. And they liked me there, treated me like a rising star. The seduction of positive feedback.

"You'll like the estancia," Mom said. I hadn't even looked at her, but she knew she was getting to me. "It'll be spring, summer. If you don't want to help with the farm, you can go exploring. Borrow a horse, or go hiking and birding."

I knew nothing about the Uruguayan countryside, except that it wasn't very populated, which sounded appealing. Mom was right, I had a lot of money in the bank. I could even travel if I wanted. I thought about what she'd said about Dad, the disrespect that had escaped her marginally maternal vigilance. I loved my father, I respected him. And yet, I wasn't unaffected by Mom's disdain for the normal successes and goals of life. It was part of my inheritance, after all, bound to breed confusion and discontent.

"I can't bear to see you so cynical. You're too young for that."

"I'm not cynical. The world is cynical." I was twenty-three years old, convinced that nature was fading with the millennium and I'd been born too close to the end—but I didn't think I was really cynical. Disaffected, perhaps. Ambivalent.

"Gabe. That job—"

"Yeah, okay. The job is cynical." The goal of the so-called environmental consulting firm I worked for was to keep its big industrial clients out of court and save them money. Period.

I pressed the binoculars to my eyes. Marbled Godwits, Dunlin, Semipalmated Plover, Yellowlegs, a jumble of juveniles and molting adults in every conceivable stage of plumage. Somehow they all knew where to go for the winter, how to find sustenance, when to find a mate, how to raise their young. I'd read that migration was part learned, part genetic, and yet even now, with climates changing and their habitats disappearing at apocalyptic speed—even now, when you'd think they'd be just as confused as the rest of us—they all seemed to know what they should be doing.

"*Uruguay te hará bien*," Mom said, as if I'd agreed to go. "It's a place you can get your mind around. The perfect antidote for end-of-millennium post-adolescent angst." She reached over to brush the hair back from my forehead, a triumphant smile breaking across her face.

I backed away from the caress and stood up, annoyed. "It's your middle-aged angst that needs an antidote," I said. "This is your midlife crisis we're talking about, thank you." As if Uruguay mattered. As if cynicism or ambivalence or whatever it was that infected me had a stamp that said "Made in USA," or, for that matter, "Made in China" or "*Feito no Brasil*," as if it weren't just another transnational product, without label, without recourse, *sin patria*. "I'm just going along for the ride," I said. "If I go."

2

It's funny the things you notice, or don't notice, when you're a kid. I didn't remember noticing how flat and dull Uruguay looks from the air. Flying south over the lush chaos of Brazil you see the colors fade, the greens grow paler, the land treeless, shadowless. For the last two hours of the flight, I sat with my nose pressed to the window, wondering why in the world I'd agreed to come on this trip to nowhere. That's what my mother's country looked like to me then, just an empty, stepped-on, nowhere place. I had thought I might like that, an empty place—but gazing out the plane window I suddenly realized that when I thought of empty places I was imagining wild places. Forests and rivers with whitewater rapids, granite, alpine lakes, black bears and eagles, southwestern deserts and red rock, coyotes and vultures. . . . I did not think of endless miles of grass. Cows. Horses. A few sheep. More cows.

When we'd reboarded in São Paulo for the last leg of the flight there was an odd stench on the plane—Mom said it smelled like used tampons—and the pilot, in his welcome-aboard announcement, apologized and said there were cattle up front. I leaned across Mom and looked up the aisle toward the curtains that partitioned off first class. "They have cows up there?" I asked without thinking, and the woman sitting in front of us said, to no one in particular, "*Sólo en Uruguay*," and then the man across the aisle leaned over and said to me, "They have excellent grass cocktails on Uruguayan flights."

14

You could tell the Uruguayans on the plane because they were all shaking their heads and making sarcastic remarks. Mom was laughing too hard to say anything, and I was still trying to figure out where they could put cows on a passenger jet. The stench was enough to make you want to skip lunch.

"Uruguay takes its cows very seriously," Mom said finally. "But I do think he meant in the cargo space up front."

She was laughing then, but a couple hours later she leaned past me to peer out the window and broke into tears. That's another thing I'd never noticed before, Mom overcome with emotion at the sight of Uruguay. "You okay?" I asked, and she nodded and leaned back in her seat without saying anything. Maybe, I thought, it was because she was returning for good this time.

We stayed in Abuela's house, a big gray concrete affair that my grandfather had designed in what Abuela called the "modern" style of architecture. It looked like the front half of an old industrial ship, broken off and beached on the corner, the front porch straddling it like a forecastle, little porthole windows in the side. Inside, it tended to be too dark—brown leather and dark-stained pine furniture, gray granite stairs, the walls painted beige—and Abuela was in the habit of leaving the heavy wooden blinds down all day, which made the otherwise comfortable house a bit depressing. Mom would go around opening the blinds in the morning, and then Abuela would go through and close them, until finally they compromised with half open, so at least you felt like you were in the ship's living quarters instead of its cargo hold. Mom told me there used to be lots of houses built on the ship motif, but most of them had been along the Rambla, the boulevard that followed the coast and was now lined with ugly new high-rise boxes. With everyone worried about the country depopulating—an incomprehensible worry for someone who grew up in California, but definitely at the top of the Uruguayan complaint list—and so many empty buildings, it was hard to fathom the high-rises. Tía Elsa, who lived in one, told me people liked them because they were comfortable and modern. Abuela said they were an investment, safer than the bank. And Juan Luis said it was all part of a money laundering operation for rich Argentinians. None of this clarified matters, though I did understand that it was a little like the stock market, where what mattered was the *perception* of value, rather than any innate qualities of usefulness.

At home, most news about "the economy" seemed to be relegated to the business section of the newspaper, which I rarely read. But in Uruguay, the economy was a daily component of the front page, right up there with the soccer matches and the cows. Even my effervescent tía Elsa, who's the last person in the world you'd expect to read the business section of the newspaper, grumbled in a knowledgeable fashion about the failing economy—the fickle Uruguayan peso, the boarded-up stores, her sister's son who couldn't find a job, the brain drain of young people to the United States. . . . As far as I could tell, Mom's idea that the country was trying to reinvent itself was wishful thinking that only she was party to. The United States, on the other hand, appeared to be an unsinkable economic *Titanic* in 1999, and everyone who stopped by to see Mom that first week thought she was going the wrong way. In fact, none of them really seemed to comprehend that she was there to stay—including Abuela, who was an unwitting but essential part of Mom's repatriation plan.

"Why are you working so much?" she asked Mom, on our fourth day in Montevideo. "You're on vacation, you should go to the beach and relax." Mom, it seems, was trying to make up for a lifetime of absence by fixing things up around Abuela's house. She'd already enlisted my aid to install a lock on the upstairs terrace door, which Abuela had booby-trapped with a board and a cowbell. Now we were cleaning all the junk out of the little room off the entryway that was my temporary bedroom. My grandfather had used the room as an office, and though the desk was long gone and it now contained a narrow pine bed and several layers of out-of-use objects, everyone still referred to it as "*la oficina de Papá*," nearly four decades after he'd moved out. His books and journals still occupied the bookshelves, and most of the old papers and clothes we'd been sorting through had belonged to him.

"I'm not here to relax," Mom snapped, trying unsuccessfully to heft the box she'd just filled with trash. "Gabe can go if he wants," she added in English. She hadn't spoken English to me since we got off the plane, but she was clearly trying to irritate Abuela, who didn't like to admit that she couldn't understand.

It was too cold to be lying around on the beach—September was not exactly vacation time in Uruguay—but I wouldn't have minded taking a walk down to the Rambla. It didn't, however, seem wise to abandon Mom just yet. She was mad that Abuela wasn't taking her plans seriously, but as far as I could tell, Abuela's remarks were just her odd way of showing affection—she was never exactly the demonstrative type. If anything, I figured, she was afraid to believe that Mom was going to stay, afraid of being disappointed. But Mom was always overreacting. I picked up the box she was struggling with and turned to carry it out, but Abuela was standing in the way.

"What's in there?"

"Trash," Mom said.

I leaned over so Abuela could see into the box, but she wanted to go through it so I set it back down on the floor. Perhaps it was just because I'd grown, but she seemed even tinier than I remembered, an oxymoronic cross between gnome and cherub. Her skin was otherworldly pallid and smooth, her hair a translucent halo, her round face caved in at the mouth, and her glasses were so thick and yellowed with age it seemed doubtful she could actually see through them. She was just a grandmother, a slightly eccentric old lady—but her esteem was a seriously coveted commodity in the Quiroga family.

"These are still serviceable." She extracted a pair of worn pink bedroom slippers from the carton and held them up. "Where are you taking this stuff?"

"Mom said I should leave it for the *bichicomes*, next to the dumpster across the street."

"*Mendigos*," Abuela corrected me.

Bichicomes was what people called the guys who went around the city on horse-drawn carts and picked through the curbside dumpsters for recyclables, but the word was too Uruguayan for Abuela. She was trying to teach me "proper" Castilian Spanish.

"*Mendigos* are beggars," Mom told me. "Not the same thing as *bichicomes*."

"*Bichicomes* comes from English," Abuela said, as if that explained everything—and then I laughed, realizing for the first time that the word was a perversion of the word "beachcomber." She looked into the box again and extracted a music cassette. "And what about this?"

"Mamá, it's tango. You don't like tango."

"Elsa might like it."

"Elsa has a CD player. She never listens to tapes anymore. Anyway, the tape is torn."

Abuela slipped it into the pocket of her housedress. She surveyed the room, as if trying to guess what other valuables Mom would want to get rid of. "You'd better just set things aside for me to look through," she said, and then she trundled off with her pink slippers.

"I grew up in this house," Mom fumed. "I don't want to feel like a guest here." She was tugging at a mass of extension cords, trying to untangle it. "She doesn't even like pink."

"I guess she doesn't want us to throw anything away."

"Those must have been Mercedes' slippers."

"Whose?"

"Papá's second wife."

I laughed. "How did *they* get in here?"

She looked around the room at the jumble of broken light fixtures and dishes, unused blankets and piles of old newspapers. "Juan went over there and cleaned up after Papá died. Looks like he just stashed everything in here, trash included." She gave up on the extension cords, which were all missing plugs, and tossed the whole mess into the box.

"I could take stuff out at night," I offered. "After she goes to bed."

Mom looked at me and started giggling like a conspiring teenager. "She won't even know it's gone," she said.

I could have slept upstairs in my uncles' old bedroom, the way I had when I was small. Or stayed with Elsa and Juan, where there was a computer and Internet access, not to mention Elsa's good cooking. But I liked this cramped little room off the entrance, with its two porthole windows, in the prow of the ship. The streetlamp on the corner cast a pleasant yellow glow at night, and I could hear the most intimate of conversations as people walked home in the wee hours, the comforting clip-clop of horses' hooves when the *bichicomes* made their morning rounds.

The wall across from my bed was lined from floor to ceiling with dusty old books and journals, and between helping Mom with her filial guilt projects and visiting with her old school friends and relatives in those first few weeks, I started poking around in them. I'd suddenly become self-conscious about my clunky Spanish, and I thought reading might improve it. Mom had a small library of Uruguayan books at home, but I'd never explored it beyond the tattered collections of Mafalda cartoons, and I had the literacy of a seven-year-old. Though Mom had jabbered at me in Spanish all my life, I'd been answering her in English since first grade, only really speaking Spanish during our Christmas visits to Montevideo.

At first, I forced myself to look up every word I didn't know, but that meant I spent most of my time shuffling through the wispy yellowed pages of Abuela's two-volume *Real Academia Española.* I'd look up a word, and then I'd have to look up words in the definitions and I'd end up darting from dictionary entry to dictionary entry until I lost track of my original inquiry and abandoned whatever I was trying to read. After an afternoon of this, I gave up on the dictionary and started just looking at illustrations and reading past the words I didn't know. Amazingly, it worked. If I didn't fret about individual words, I found I could read pretty much anything I wanted to. There was a certain mystique to it, pulling a book from the shelf at random, blowing the dust off, and flipping through the musty pages, pausing on whatever caught my fancy and letting my mind float free above the text, a comprehensible whole somehow emerging from incomprehensible pieces. I guess all Mom's jabbering had left a more substantial trace in my brain than I realized.

Mixed in with my grandfather's architecture books were a lot of old magazines and journals, including installments from something called the *Enciclopedia uruguaya* that was full of illustrated essays about Uruguayan culture and history. Uruguay as seen from California was so inconsequential that it had hardly been mentioned in my geography studies, but here it was center stage. I read about how José Gervasio Artigas had gone galloping across the grasslands with his wild brigades of gauchos, calling for freedom and equality, winning independence from Spain—surely a more colorful founding father than the stuffy old guys with white wigs I'd learned about in school at home. I understood for the first time why Uruguayans called themselves *orientales*, that it meant "easterners" and referred to the eastern bank of the Uruguay River, distinguishing them from the Argentinians on the other side. There was a book about the gauchos, who were the criollo offspring of surviving Charrúa and Guaraní, renegade Spaniards, and escaped slaves. They'd formed a nomadic cowboy culture, eluding colonial governments and living off feral cattle until the end of the nineteenth century, when the big *estancieros* fenced off the grasslands and the gauchos were reduced to serfdom. The book was full of reproductions of nineteenth-century oil paintings depicting life in the countryside as a paradoxical mix of bucolic and stark—Artigas and his mounted followers with dead bodies strewn casually around them, a gaucho relaxing on the grass next to his horse, another sitting on a stool with his guitar in a desolate, treeless panorama. . . . The paintings made me eager to get out of the city and see the countryside, but though the estancia was the main feature of Mom's plan, we had to wait for Juan Luis to drive us out there and it was nearly two weeks before he got around to it.

They started arguing before we even got out the door of Abuela's house.

"No one has stayed out there in years," Juan said. We were standing in the foyer, the door open on a cool, clear spring morning. "The house isn't livable."

"That's why we're going," Mom said. "To fix it up." The estancia was a four-hour drive, and she wanted to spend the whole weekend there.

"We can take a look around, have a nice *asado*, and come back tonight," Juan said.

I set down the two bags I was carrying.

"You can leave us out there." Mom picked up the bags and headed out the door. "We'll take the bus back."

We followed her out to the car and Juan opened the trunk. "Did you ever take a bus to the estancia, Lili?"

She didn't answer him. She deposited our bags, closed the trunk, and got in on the passenger side. I settled into the back seat.

Juan was laughing as he started the engine. "Lascano is as close as they get," he said. "A nice forty-kilometer walk." He caught my eye in the rearview mirror, and I couldn't help smiling.

I liked my uncle, though I sometimes found him a little intimidating. He was an agronomist—cattle, grains, that sort

of thing—not what you'd think of as a profession of intellectuals, but he spoke five languages and seemed to know everything about everything. I didn't know why he and Mom were
bickering so much that day, except that Elsa wasn't around to
lighten things up. Elsa and Juan Luis were such total opposites
that when they were in the same room together, they almost
seemed like parodies of themselves, my impenetrable uncle with
his aura of brooding, unfulfilled brilliance, and Elsa, so warm,
exuberant, and good-humored that your spirits lifted just being
in her company. She was as expansive as she was physically com-
pact, a chatterer, an enjoyer of tango, corny movies, and pretty
knick-knacks—and Mom, who didn't like any of those things,
adored her in an unconditional way I'd never seen her adore
anyone. But Elsa had no interest whatsoever in the estancia, and
we were doomed, it seemed, to a day of Quiroga sparring.

Once we got away from Montevideo, there was hardly any
traffic and not much to see, just mile after mile of empty grassland. Uruguayans say the land is undulating rather than flat,
though billowing might be a better word, as if the grass were
a blanket with the wind caught beneath it. We passed a couple
of tiny towns and the occasional ranch house, here and there
a horse-drawn cart or a bicycle in the middle of the two-lane
highway. Rocha, the regional capital, was more than an hour
and a half away from the estancia, but it was the biggest city
around—a couple dozen paved streets laid out in a grid around
a sleepy nineteenth-century plaza—and we stopped to buy fresh
bread and meat for an *asado*. Then, with Mom and Juan arguing
about the route, we headed out of town on a gravel road—the
main route across the northeast part of the country.

We drove for some fifty kilometers, through a landscape of
palm trees and grassland that seemed totally incongruous to me.
I associated palm trees with Southern California, with beaches
and shopping centers, or, in my imagination, with tropical
islands. I didn't expect to find them sprouting out of pastures

in *el país de las vacas gordas*, the so-called land of the fat cows, which was what people liked to call Uruguay when they weren't calling it *el paisito*. Off to the east we passed a large lagoon, one of a series that lined the coast from Montevideo to Brazil, and there the palms grew so thick as to form a forest, the only one I'd seen that wasn't a plantation of imported eucalyptus or pines. The palms were native to the region, Juan said, but they were almost extinct—*butiá*, he called them. They produced a small orange fruit that the locals liked to use for jam and liqueur, but which wasn't worth cultivating. The trees we saw scattered about the grasslands, he said, were all over three hundred years old, leftovers from when the Spaniards first introduced cattle, which ate all the young sprouts. The only young trees were in a few marshy patches the cattle couldn't reach, like the one by the lagoon.

We came to a junction and turned inland onto another dirt road, which we followed for about twenty minutes, and then Juan started quizzing Mom about where to turn. He followed her directions and got us lost in a maze of dirt tracks, just to prove she didn't remember how to get to the estancia. Then he backtracked to the road we'd been on and drove for another half mile before turning off on another unmarked dirt track, which we bumped along for fifteen minutes, turning at two more undifferentiated junctions, until finally, the track we were on simply ended.

We got out of the car in the middle of an unremarkable expanse of green. There was a one-story brick house and a brick barn and a concrete shed, all of which looked hopelessly abandoned. The only trees were a grove of sterile old eucalyptus along the drive to the house. It didn't look anything like I had imagined it, though now that I thought about it, I wasn't sure exactly how I'd envisioned the estancia. I guess I'd expected it to be more distinctive somehow, more of a *place*. Instead, the ranch structures appeared to be crumbling into the landscape, and the landscape itself was too mild, too flat and homogeneous to inspire much interest or respect. It was as though we had come all this way to visit an empty football field or a vacant lot. Mom, however, stepped away from the car and opened her arms to embrace the air as if she'd landed at the glorious center of the universe. She looked at me and smiled, and though we'd been driving with the windows wide open, she took the kind of deep, grateful breath that signifies release from long confinement in a stifling, airless place. She even smiled at Juan Luis, but he refused to acknowledge her mood.

"I told you it was run-down," he said. We walked over to the house and Mom struggled with the warped, unpainted door. "The only one who ever comes out here is the *paisano* who works for Caruso, to check on his cattle," Juan Luis went on. "And he doesn't care about the house." He reached past Mom and yanked open the door.

"One would think *you* would care," Mom said, leading the way inside. "At least you could have painted the place."

"*Paint*? Don't be an idiot. As if I'm going to spend my time out here painting a bunch of crumbling bricks."

Juan Luis was right. There was no glass in the windows, the thatch roof was entirely torn away in places, and there were weeds growing through the cracks in the tile floor. Mom stood in the middle of the spacious front room looking around. "I guess we need to patch this floor," she said, nudging a broken tile with her foot. "Get someone to do the windows, and maybe replace the thatch."

"I've been thinking about getting an architect to design a remodel. Or maybe just start over."

"*Bah*, how bourgeois. You don't need an architect to put in a few tiles, patch the roof. Paint."

"I don't want a bunch of *chapucería*—"

"What's so wrong with a little *chapucería*?" Mom said, walking into the next room.

"What's *chapucería*?" I asked Juan Luis.

"Ask your mother. She's an expert. Lili," he said, following her. "Translate *chapucería* for your son."

"It means jerry-rigged," Mom said as we followed her back into the big front room, a corner of which appeared to have been a kitchen.

"Slipshod," Juan Luis said, in the near-perfect English he refused to speak with me. "It means slipshod."

"A way to make something functional using what you have," Mom said. "Better," she added, switching back to Spanish and looking past me at Juan Luis, "than sitting around *thinking* about how to do it perfectly and never doing anything because it can never be good enough." She went over to the sink and turned the faucet handle, but nothing came out.

"And the electricity?" Juan Luis said. "You won't have water until we put a pump in that well—"

"What happened to the windmill?" She didn't wait for an answer, but went outside to see for herself. We followed her around the back of the house to the well—I because I was curious to see the place, and Juan Luis because he obviously wasn't about to miss a chance to rain on her parade.

The well was just a hole surrounded by a ring of crumbling bricks, and Mom's windmill was missing a few blades and obviously hadn't worked in years. She stood there looking up at it, Juan Luis standing by with his arms crossed and a smirk on his face, waiting to see what she would say. "We ought to be able to fix it," she said. "It's a pretty basic piece of technology."

"That'll get water to the house, but it isn't going to get electricity out here," Juan Luis said.

"Why not? If we can do one windmill we can do several. Or solar collectors maybe. And a solar water heater would be easy enough."

Mom's enthusiasm can be infectious, and I found myself looking around, thinking about the wind, as intrinsic to that landscape as the grasses, and imagining windmills scattered over the green, imagining self-sufficiency and sustainability, Mom's revenge and her escape. But what most people find charming in my mother seemed to have a contrary effect on her oldest brother.

"Let me know when you want to be serious about discussing the estancia," he said, and walked away.

"*Qué plomo*," Mom mumbled. Whatever she meant by that. Juan was a blob of lead? She expanded on the theme as we walked over to the barn: her brother was a tedious bore and a pain in the neck.

The barn was just a brick shell with a dirt floor and a tin roof, all intact. Mom started taking inventory of the junk inside, making notes in the spiral pad she'd been carrying around—rusty hand tools, jars of nails and screws, boxes of used horseshoes, scraps of wood and broken tiles, horse harnesses hanging on the wall. . . .

"My pony's saddle!" Mom was in the far corner of the barn, caressing the worn, dried-out leather of a diminutive saddle as if it were in fact the pony of her childhood—as if here, finally, she'd found the warm, unconditional welcome she'd been missing from her brother and mother. She leaned down to press her cheek against the scrap of yellow sheepskin that covered the seat . . . but before I could comment, she bounced back into action and continued her inventory. When she'd finished, I helped her carry some packing crates and planks back to the house, and we set up a makeshift table and benches. Then she handed me an old straw broom, and went out to collect wildflowers from the pasture. It seemed a little ridiculous to be sweeping a house that had grass growing up between the tiles, but I complied, picking up the worst of the broken tiles and piling them neatly in a corner. Mom had returned with a bouquet of weeds and was arranging them in one of the empty jars when Juan Luis reappeared.

"All those years in *yanquilandia* really rotted your brain, didn't they?" he said to Mom, who ignored him.

I looked up from pulling a clump of grass out of the floor and met his eye, caught between wanting to humor Mom and wanting to be considered sane by my uncle. I could smell the smoke from the fire he'd started out front.

"You want to do something useful?" he asked me. "Gather some more wood for the *asado*?"

"Sure." I leaned the broom against the wall and followed him out to the fire.

"We don't even have a proper *parrillero* out here," he grumbled, squatting down to comb the first coals under the grate he'd set up on the ground. He directed me to what he called *el monte*, not a hill but a big patch of brush I hadn't noticed on the far side of the pasture, behind the house and barn.

Glad for the excuse to explore a bit, I set off across the pasture. It was peaceful out there, and I realized that Mom and Juan Luis's bickering had been getting on my nerves. It was just how they talked to each other, I thought. If you had a Quiroga's skewed sense of affection, it might even be considered affectionate. I wasn't paying much attention to where I was walking, just thinking about Mom and her brother, enjoying the soft give of soil beneath my sneakers, the grass catching under my jeans and brushing past my ankles, the warm breeze on my face . . . when suddenly the field exploded in a cacophony of angry screams and my attention turned from the estancia's squabbling absentee owners to its current resident.

One of the loudest displays of avian fury I'd ever witnessed was coming from a single bird, like a Killdeer but larger and more ferocious. It had risen from the grass a few yards from my feet and flown off across the pasture, only to double back and land in its original spot, screaming bloody murder the whole time. It was a *tero*, I realized, common enough that you saw them in the grass along the Rambla in Montevideo. But I'd never seen those city birds do *this*. I squatted down in the hope it might relax, but it was no use, the thing just kept strutting back and forth across the grass with its beak open, making this god-awful alarm call, "*tero, tero . . .*," though there was no nest or other reason I could see for it to be protecting that particular square yard of grass. It had a few thin feathers sticking up from the back of its head like some kind of anemic plume, combative red spikes poking out from its wing-pits, a fierce black stripe down its face, and a bright red bill and legs. When it flew, its wings showed an audacious flash of black and white. It was one of the most common birds of Uruguay, but to me it seemed exotic.

As I continued across the grass on my wood-gathering mission, I wished I had brought my binoculars, but I hadn't even thought to unpack them from my suitcase in Montevideo. Some sort of a tanager swept past me as I neared the *monte*, but unlike any tanager I'd ever known, this one was a celestial, almost turquoise, shade of blue. There was a bird that reminded me of an oversized, overdressed kingbird calling insistently at the edge of the swathe of brush, a wheezing, inexplicably familiar, three-beat cry that was drawn out on the last note. It was making forays over the pasture to catch bugs, and it reminded me of a Western Kingbird. But the bill was heavier, the colors bolder— bright yellow breast, heavy black stripe through the eye—and it was stockier and brasher than most of the flycatchers I knew. As I moved in among the bushes to look for dead wood, it dawned on me why the call was so familiar: this was the bird whose incessant cries woke me every morning in Montevideo.

The *monte* was more extensive than I'd thought, even included some low-growing trees, and I'd almost gathered a full armload of wood before I discovered the stream running through its midst. There was no rush and gurgle of water over stone to warn of its presence, and I was standing almost at its edge before I noticed it, slinking quietly through the grass and brush, hardly flowing at all. I started back with my load of wood, and when I came out of the brush I paused to gaze out over the estancia. That's when it struck me that it wasn't as flat as I'd thought, because I was looking *over* the estancia, and I had walked up a slight incline to get to the creek, a slight lift in the land that was so gradual, so *integral* to its landscape, that it was hard to see it as a hill at all. It was pretty, I could see that then, the vibrant green of healthy grasslands tilting off to the horizon, a placid, guileless, open book of a landscape. But there was nothing spectacular about it, nothing to make me catch my breath, or raise my arms in celebration, nothing to inspire Mom's rapture.

Mom and Juan Luis were both out by the fire when I returned with my armload of twigs and branches. I had an urge to tell them about the riotous bird in the pasture, though I knew it was one of those you-had-to-be-there sort of tales, and even then no one but another birder would find it amusing. Surely Juan would think I was crazy for being excited about a *tero*. He was in the middle of another argument with Mom, brandishing an unlit cigarette and waiting for the most strategic moment to light it, while Mom stared at the fire.

"You told me you weren't doing anything out here," she said. I dumped my pile of wood on the ground and squatted down to feed the fire. The fat on the lamb was beginning to sizzle, releasing an aroma that made me want to hyperventilate. "You said the land was just sitting here, that I could do what I want."

"Papá always leased it to the Carusos for their cattle." Juan fished a burning twig out of the fire and held it up to his cigarette, inhaling slowly and dramatically.

"I want to *farm* it, Juan." She waved his smoke away and added, on cue, "Go ahead, give yourself and the rest of us lung cancer, that's what we all need."

"Liliana. Be reasonable. You're talking about a garden, a hectare or two. Out of three hundred. Manuel Caruso has been working a rice rotation on his place up the road since the mid-eighties. It's been wildly successful—"

"*Rice*? I'm trying to create an organic farm, and now you want to lease it out to grow rice? With who-knows-what pesticides and chemical fertilizers—"

"Don't come at me with your ecology nonsense, you're in the wrong hemisphere. And who says I'm going to lease it? I want to farm the rice myself. Lili, we're talking about an estancia here, this is serious business."

"Since when? Since when have you considered the estancia serious business? Look at this place—"

"Isn't this ready?" I interrupted, poking at the meat with a stick. It looked done enough to me, and with Juan Luis criticizing Mom's "*tontería ecológica*," there was no way the conversation was going to end soon. Or well.

"Probably. Juan likes to overcook it."

"You want it to be dripping blood?" He tucked his cigarette into the corner of his mouth, picked up the fork and carving knife he'd brought from Montevideo, and made a show of checking the lamb, but it was obviously ready. He sliced off chunks and pushed them to the side of the grill, and Mom and I loaded up the plates she'd brought and went inside to eat.

I wasn't sure Juan Luis was going to condescend to join us at Mom's makeshift table, but he followed us in and settled himself on one of the crates. He stared at the weed arrangement, trying to get a rise out of Mom—but she had her eyes on her plate and was furiously and single-mindedly sawing meat off of bone. We ate in deliberate silence for a few minutes, and then she looked up at Juan and threw down her best trump card. "Papá wouldn't have wanted us to grow rice out here," she said.

Juan let out a loud, sarcastic guffaw and reached across the plank for the bread. "How would you know what Papá wanted?"

I waited for Mom's retort, but it seemed that Juan had just trumped her trump.

"Papá didn't care about this place. He came out here for vacations, to go hunting, and that was it. Didn't even do that, in the past twenty years. That's why it's so run-down."

"I thought he was nostalgic about it," Mom said softly.

"Nostalgic and caring are not the same. Nostalgic is pining for something that doesn't exist. Caring is making something of what you have."

"He loved the ducks," Mom said. "The hunting."

She had always maintained that hunting and hunters were barbaric, and now she was defending her father's love for it? I opened my mouth to comment—but decided I'd better stay out of it.

"Everyone has tried to lease this land for rice," Juan said. "Caruso wanted to bring it into his rotation system, and two contract rice growers that I know of, there may have been others. But Papá said no. He wanted to have it just sitting here with a few cattle on it. It's a waste."

"Well, we agree on something. The waste. But I thought you said this place was worthless."

"It was," Juan said, but didn't elaborate. He cut himself a bite of lamb, shoved it into his mouth, then looked back at Mom. "Look, Lili," he said more gently. "Do what you want with the house, I don't care. And take a hectare for your vegetables. Or two or five—in fact take all the best land, up there behind the barn. There's about ten hectares all told, and I'll wager you'll never use more than one. Do what you want, experiment to your heart's content. I'll work up a management plan for the rest—"

"Right. When's the last time you drove out here? And now you're going to 'manage' the estancia? What, Juan, in your abundant spare time? When you retire? Why didn't you ever do that before? Why didn't you 'manage' this place for Papá if you were so hot to—"

"Papá wouldn't listen to me. He didn't want me to have anything to do with the estancia." Juan Luis picked up his plate and went outside, and Mom didn't say anything else, just sat there staring at her plate as if she'd suddenly lost her voracious appetite for lamb.

I wasn't used to seeing her so subdued, so easily cowed. She looked vulnerable, just a thin wafer of a woman balanced on a broken packing crate. I had an urge to comfort her, to come to her defense, though I had no idea from what, from whom, or how. Juan's remarks seemed benign enough, if slightly patronizing, and their ideas about the estancia didn't seem so impossibly incompatible, at least on the surface of it. They both wanted the land to live up to its potential, that was clear, to produce something more significant than a few cows. I didn't know what was involved in growing rice, but as Juan pointed out there was plenty of land for the sort of thing Mom wanted to do. But though he begged Mom to be reasonable—something of an oxymoron, I must say—he also seemed intent on pulling all her strings. It can be gratifying to pull Mom's strings, but Juan was pulling strings I didn't know about, and I thought I knew them all. It occurred to me then that the two of them weren't really arguing about the estancia at all, but rather, fighting some primordial sibling war that was beyond my comprehension.

3

We didn't, of course, sleep out at the estancia that first time, and it was over a week before we got it together to go back. First, Mom wanted to get her papers in order so she could vote in the upcoming election. This entailed a lot of running around town and waiting in lines at reputedly overstaffed but famously inefficient government offices. Next she wanted to buy a used car, so we could get to the estancia without Juan. And then she insisted that we paint the upstairs bedrooms in Abuela's house, which hadn't been done in anyone's memory but Abuela's. The car turned out to be easy, thanks to Elsa, who put out word to her many friends and turned up a perfectly serviceable 1988 Toyota pickup. Painting the upstairs was another matter.

"Abuela's not going to like the color," I told Elsa. "It's way too cheerful." I was driving our new truck and Elsa was riding shotgun, the cans of sunny yellow paint we'd just bought sliding around in the back.

"She'll like it. She'll just pretend not to. Take a left there." Ostensibly, we were just picking up the paint, but Elsa had talked me into stopping at the shopping mall to buy a present for her granddaughter.

"Mom tried to get her to choose, but she was totally uninterested. She says the whole house was painted a few years ago."

"Thirty years," Elsa said. "At least."

"Oh." I laughed. "That's a long few years."

"Juan had the downstairs painted a few years ago. But no one has done anything upstairs since we got married. Since we met, actually, thirty-five years—" A car with a loudspeaker on its roof pulled out of a side street in front of us, Elsa was interrupted by a blast of campaign music.

I shifted into first and inched along behind the flag-bedecked car—bright red, with "Batlle 15" emblazoned across the middle. "What party is that?"

"Colorado. Jorge Batlle's branch." Elsa rolled down her window and started singing along, swinging her mass of brown hair back and forth in time with the beat. "*Alumbrar el camino, defender la mañana.* . . . ¡juntos! ¡juntos!" The lyrics seemed pointless, but it had a catchy tune and Elsa was clearly enjoying herself—well, Elsa could look like she was enjoying herself when she was cleaning a bathroom. But she wasn't the only one. It was all rather festive. With the election less than a month away, the whole city was geared up—political graffiti covered every untended wall, banners fluttered from apartment balconies, leafleters stood on corners, and campaign cars cruised the neighborhoods blasting party songs and slogans. Cars passing us in the other direction now honked in appreciation, as if we were part of a wedding procession, while a man walking along the sidewalk with two little kids yelled something mildly derogatory about "Jorge," and a woman standing in a shop door gave him a thumbs-up sign.

"It's sort of like Sundays after the soccer games," I said, "when everyone goes parading around waving the team flags."

"That's exactly what Juan says!" Elsa stopped singing, as if I'd caught her indulging some secret childish pleasure. "He complains that people aren't taking the election seriously."

"Do Uruguayans take anything *more* seriously than soccer? At least they're enthusiastic."

Elsa laughed and started singing again, reaching across me to honk out the rhythm on the truck horn.

The only politics I'd known in my lifetime was a passive and somewhat desultory, indoor activity—watching TV, listening to the radio, reading the newspaper, maybe a conversation at the dinner table. There might be a few bumper stickers and suburban lawn signs, the occasional billboard, but I'd never seen politics out on the street like this, accompanied by such panache and passion. "Mom told me Rubén is coming all the way from Venezuela just to vote," I said when Elsa stopped singing.

"He thinks the Frente Amplio has a chance of winning. That's why he's coming. Even your cousin Patricia says she's going to vote Frente. Breaking with family tradition."

"I take it that's Colorado?"

"*¡Colorado como huevo de ciclista!* My father was a Colorado. And my grandfather before him."

I glanced at Elsa, unsure what she meant by "red as a cyclist's balls." Certainly not communist, as the left-wing badge of honor seemed to fall to this Frente Amplio that Rubén and my cousin liked. I supposed it had to do with the history—according to the *Enciclopedia uruguaya*, the Colorado party started out as a band of gauchos who wore red hatbands and fought with the Blancos, who wore white hatbands. In the early twentieth century, they'd all traded their hatbands for party flags, and their horses, guns, and gaucho knives for cars, songs, and slogans. The Colorados had remained aligned with Montevideans' interests, and the Blancos with those of the big estancia owners, but I had no idea what that meant for Elsa's family of small-town shoemakers.

"Jorge Batlle *es un flor de tipo*," she said.

A flower of a guy? "You mean Batlle's gay?"

"Ha! No, *mi querido rubito*, it means he has a good character. Honest, honorable, straightforward. Here, turn right."

She directed me down a side street, past a high-rise Sheraton hotel, and into a sunken parking lot. "El Shopping," as Elsa called the mall, was an imposing stone structure that took up several city blocks and looked more like a fortress than a shopping mall.

"It was built as a prison," she explained as we stashed the paint in the truck cab, "nearly a century ago. The government closed it in the eighties, and it sat empty for years while everyone debated what to do with it. It had a bad reputation during the dictatorship, and some people wanted to tear it down. Finally, they sold it off, and El Shopping opened a few years ago. They did a marvelous job of remodeling, keeping all the old walls, and the gatehouse and entry."

On the inside, the place was a dizzying three-level atrium of shops with a floor-to-ceiling stone arch rising like the Arc de Triomphe in the middle.

"Lili refuses to come here," Elsa said, leading me around the mezzanine. "Says it's a travesty." She giggled. "Remember when I visited you in California? I made her take me to that shopping mall near your house almost every day."

"Valley Fair." I laughed, remembering how Elsa had fallen in love with our San Jose suburb. "The worst of American culture, according to Mom—malls and processed foods. Though I actually think she had a closet love affair with both. One time I caught her munching on Froot Loops, eating them dry, like candy, while she graded papers." I looked around. "This place isn't that bad. Definitely not as ugly as Valley Fair." It was weirdly grandiose, but not entirely unattractive, with the old stone walls and plenty of outside light from the skylights in the roof.

"It revitalized the neighborhood. Lili complains that the chains put the small neighborhood shops out of business, but we didn't have that many small shops here. We certainly never had a baby boutique," she added, steering me into Mi Bebé. My cousin Patricia was coming to visit from Buenos Aires with her two-year-old, who Elsa hadn't seen in nearly six months. "What do you think?" She held up a yellow jumpsuit for me to admire.

"Nice color. It's the same as the paint we just bought."

"It is! Let's see if Celia notices." She handed me the jumpsuit and continued flipping through the tiny hangers.

"Do you think she's glad? I mean, that Mom came back?"

"Celia? Of course she is."

"And Juan Luis? They argue all the time."

"Lili should feel honored. The rest of us just get the silent treatment."

"I guess I thought everyone would be glad to have Mom back."

I must have sounded worried, though I think I was more puzzled than worried. Elsa stopped shuffling through the hangers and laid her hand on my arm. "Of course we're happy to have her home, Gabriel. It's just that no one understands it. Leaving your sweet father. Your lovely house. Her work. It's like going nowhere, like treading a wide circle and ending up back where you started thirty years ago. What does she have here, after all? The estancia?" She turned back to the rack of clothes and extracted a miniature jean jacket with a pink embroidered bear on the pocket. "Oooh . . . isn't it precious? What do you think?"

"Definitely," I said. "She'll love it. At least, I'd like it if I were a baby." Shopping was not exactly my favorite activity, but the combination of Elsa's habitual *joie de vivre* and this miniature icon of American fashion was irresistible. "Come on, I'll buy it," I said, because she was waffling over the price tag. "And you can get her the jumpsuit."

"You can't go spending all your money on presents for Emilia!"

"Why not?" I handed her the jumpsuit and reached for the jacket. "She's the closest thing I'll ever have to a niece. And I'm temporarily rich. Mom even wanted me to subsidize her back-to-the-land enterprise."

Elsa examined my face to make sure I was serious, and then she relinquished the jacket. "I don't know what she's going to do out there," she said as I herded her toward the cash register. "Juan Luis wants to make the estancia lucrative after all these years, but she fights him every step of the way."

I shrugged. "Mom sees the estancia more as a way of living than a business. She thinks it doesn't need to be lucrative, just self-sufficient." Of course, Elsa had already heard this from Mom, just like I had. But Elsa was an innately practical person and none of it sounded at all practical. As far as Elsa was concerned, the estancia wasn't even the issue—not a justification for Mom's actions, but rather, a symptom of some general Mom malaise.

"The money from their father isn't going to last long," she said as we paid for our purchases. "And neither will your savings, if you keep this up. Can you get that job of yours back?"

"Probably." I hadn't even considered it, but I didn't want to get into a long conversation about my future. "Did I see La Cigale down there? I haven't had any ice cream since we got here."

"Yes! Let's go! I don't care if you are rich, I can still buy my favorite *yanqui* his favorite ice cream."

Mom was probably getting impatient for the paint, but I was enjoying myself, and Elsa kept running into friends and stopping to chat. I ducked into a bookstore and bought myself a bound journal and tin of colored pencils. They didn't have anything on the local birds, but I thought I might keep a bird diary and sketch what I saw, something I'd gotten good at when I was a kid—I'd started copying the pictures from the Peterson guide when I was about five, and then it got so I could draw live birds from sight, which had impressed Grandpa to no end. I hadn't done it for years.

We had finally made it to La Cigale and were waiting to order our cones, when Elsa returned to my question about Mom's homecoming. "Don't misunderstand," she said, taking hold of my arm for emphasis. "I missed Lili terribly, probably as much as Celia did. She was only eighteen when she left, and we didn't see her for years. When she started coming for Christmas with you and Keith, Celia was so happy, we all were—but it was always a relief when she left. You never knew who or what was going to set her off—Keith, Celia, Juan . . . and then that horrid, destructive sarcasm. Gabriel, I love having Lili home, and I hope it works out at the estancia, if that's really what she wants. But whoever *knows* what Lili wants?"

"Certainly not her son," I said, savoring my first bite of dulce de leche ice cream—the joyful flavor of childhood, of family vacation, of Uruguayan summer—and thinking, paradoxically, of Dad. If Dad had been with us, we would have gone out to La Cigale ten times by now.

"She was always so full of wild ideas," Elsa said, paying for our cones. "Always stirring things up. It's what I love, what made her so much fun when we were young—but sometimes she stirs the wrong soup. That was in the eighties, the last years of the dictatorship, everything still uncertain, and here comes Lili, flying in with all her bright California ideas, preaching about ecology and trash recycling. As if a bit of trash was the end of the world, as if we didn't have other worries, as if we needed more. You were too young to remember, but one Christmas she got irked about something and left the house for two days, just disappeared. Made us all sick with worry, which is probably what she wanted, but you didn't *do* that in those days, you just didn't."

We walked back to the escalator that ran alongside the Arc de Triomphe, and I listened to my aunt go on about Mom and ate my ice cream as fast as I could, because it was already starting to melt, thick caramelized cream sliding down the sides of the cone and over my fingers, impressing upon me the fluid and unreliable nature of sweet childhood memories. Immigrant, emigrant, *inmigrante, emigrante*—it all sounded the same, especially in English, but I was beginning to realize just how different those inverse views of the same person could be. Mom had been an American citizen all my life, but I had always been conscious of her as an Uruguayan immigrant—of her accent, her outsider's take on American culture, her taste in shoes, her *mate*. It was her identity, a foreignness she cultivated, part of what made her special and exotic, even in California's Latino communities.

Here in Uruguay, however, Lili was an emigrant, someone who had left the country—an identity loaded with so many vectors of remorse, retribution, guilt, and blame, I couldn't possibly sort it out, even if I wanted to. Which I didn't.

Abuela, as predicted, was decidedly underwhelmed by the cheerful shades of yellow paint we'd chosen. What we hadn't predicted was that the house itself would resist our efforts. The walls soaked up the first two coats of paint as if the plaster had turned to sponge, and it took us several days and another trip to the paint store just to do the two bedrooms and the hallway. I began to share Abuela's ambivalence. But Mom wouldn't let go of it. Sure, maybe she felt guilty that Abuela and the house had gotten so old and run-down in her absence, but it was more than that, as if painting those rooms was part of laying claim, reestablishing her right to call Abuela "Mamá," to call the house "home." She complained that everything took too long, that there were too many interruptions, too many old relatives and childhood friends plopping down at the dining room table and expecting her to prepare a *mate* and regale them with her stories and wit. It wasn't really so different in California when I was growing up, despite her complaints that the *yanquis* were too isolated and enclosed in their houses. I pointed out this inconsistency, of course, but she denied it. She claimed that people were doing what they'd always done when she came to Montevideo, trying to cram years of family gossip and friend-ship into weeks—that no one would accept she'd come home to stay. She had divested her immigrant identity of thirty years simply by abandoning her adopted country, but moving back to Uruguay did not change her emigrant status. She might be able to repatriate, but she could not undo the fact of having left.

At the estancia, there were no old childhood friends. No ancient aunts or second cousins. No intractable family home, sucking up her energy like a dried-out sponge. No tangles of remorse and guilt, no unappreciative mother. Just green grass and blue sky and a couple of crumbling buildings that responded to every small attention, where even the most jerry-rigged construction was a splendid improvement. And an accommodating, if not quite complicit, son.

We didn't talk much once we got up there, the truck packed with tools and blankets and food as if for a long camping trip. It was quiet and uneventful, but amiable, the two of us working in parallel, Mom replastering the walls of the house while I dug up a field for planting, a utilitarian line of communication between us that was as uncomplicated as the flat terrain. I'd never worked in Mom's gardens, except for planting seeds and collecting cherry tomatoes when I was little, but I dutifully followed her tedious, labor-intensive recipe for double-digging seedbeds—though I did insist on using a pick to break the sod first. I enjoyed the work in a perverse way, swinging the pick and shoveling out there under the estancia's infinite sky until my arms and mind went numb, ducking attacks from the field's ever-more-outraged-and-brazen resident *tero*, which I quickly reclassified from exotic creature to pest. But mostly, I was just humoring Mom.

It's not that I thought there was anything wrong with Mom's plans for an organic vegetable farm on the estancia. But to hear her talk, the farm wasn't just a midlife hobby or even a second career. It was a creed, a paradigm for the future, something one had to *believe* in, like the back-to-the-land movement Dad told me was so popular in California in the seventies—like the commune in Trinity County where my college roommate was born. I found it impossible, in 1999, to believe that a few organic farms in Uruguay, or anywhere for that matter, could obstruct the insidious, global blights of the oncoming century. Would Mom's rhetoric have made more sense back in the seventies, when she and Dad were young? What if they had moved to the estancia then, when they finished college?

I would have grown up here.

I was in a shoveling daze when this thought occurred to me, and it jerked me to attention the way a dream might jerk you out of sleep in the predawn hours. I leaned on the shovel and looked around at the flat green nowhere place where I might have grown up. Right here.

I tried, briefly, to conjure the versions of myself that might have been, if I'd lived out here with my same eccentric mother and a transplanted not-so-eccentric father. But my daydream immediately encountered problems, not least of which was that the era of flower children and environmentalism in California was an era of dictatorship in Uruguay. Mom had never talked much about it, and I couldn't imagine it making much difference out here—but still, if I thought about Elsa's account of Mom's visits in the eighties and Juan's attitude toward her environmental concerns, it became clear that it wasn't just the wrong decade for Mom's experiment, but, as Juan pointed out, the wrong hemisphere. And Dad—despite his supposedly hippie past and love of our Montevideo vacations, it was hard to imagine him on an estancia in the Uruguayan outback. For that matter, they probably would have sent me to Montevideo for high school, and I would have ended up living with Abuela as a teenager—equally unimaginable. I threw a dirt clod at the *tero* and returned to my shoveling reality.

It was satisfying to see the seedbeds taking form in that expanse of empty pasture, like doodling in the margins of a blank notebook page, watching the sketches grow denser and more detailed, until they transcended doodlehood and encroached on the blank page with real form and substance. By the time our first visitor showed up in the middle of the week, I had decorated the green pasture with three ten-by-twenty rectangles of chocolate-brown soil. I was more than ready for a diversion, when I heard a motor and saw an approaching puff of dust in the distance. At first I thought it must be Juan, though he'd said he couldn't come until the weekend, but as I set out across the field to join Mom in greeting him, a double-bed white pickup truck turned up the track and parked in front of the house as if it belonged there.

A lanky, balding man got out and introduced himself as Manuel Caruso, the neighbor who leased the land for his cattle. He looked to be about Juan's age, and he said he'd known Juan and my grandfather since he was a kid. He'd met Mom as a little girl, but she didn't remember.

"I was glad to hear Juan's finally going to do something with this land," he said when we'd gotten through the introductions.

"Actually, it's his sister who's finally doing something with the land," Mom corrected him, smiling sweetly—a smile that anyone who knew Mom would recognize as sarcastic, but which Caruso apparently took at face value. She resisted remarking on sexist Uruguayan assumptions and maintained a genteel tone as she showed him her work on the house. He recommended a glazier to replace the broken windows, and a skilled *quinchador* for the thatch roof, and he was generally appreciative of her efforts to make the estancia livable—until we walked over to the vegetable beds I'd prepared and she started talking about her agricultural plans.

"If you want," Caruso said when she finished explaining, "I can have my worker bring the tractor over and plow a plot for you. You'd have your whole vegetable garden ready in an hour."

I knew Mom imagined my scrapings in the dirt as something considerably more substantial than a garden, but she just thanked him and told him she preferred to hand dig it. "I don't like what tractors do to the soil," she said. "And I want this place to be as sustainable as possible. Renewable energy," she added, making a show of clasping my growing, but very sore, arm muscle. I rolled my eyes, feeling ridiculous, but it just got worse. She launched into a pedantic explanation of how the tractor mixed the soil layers together, whereas her method of digging left the bacterial life in the sub-layer intact and just broke it up so roots could get through. "You only have to do this once," she said. "And it leaves the topsoil so soft everything else is a breeze." She sank the shovel into the bed I'd just finished preparing and lifted out a spadeful of fluffy topsoil to demonstrate.

Caruso listened politely, but I was embarrassed. The guy was an agronomist, not to mention a second- or third-generation *estanciero*. He ran a huge rice and cattle operation. And here was Mom lecturing him on the benefits of hand cultivation, as if he were going to run home and try it on his thousand hectares. I knew all Mom's theories about soil building and pest control, but I couldn't bring myself to join in, couldn't wax enthusiastic the way one might expect, seeing as how I appeared to be part of her project. I turned aside, gazing back toward the house and our little Toyota pickup, squatting next to Caruso's double-bed white Chevy like a circus pony next to a workhorse. Everything Mom said made perfect scientific sense, of course. But it was ridiculously out of context.

"It's kind of like how the truck farmers around Montevideo used to work," Caruso said, and I turned back to their conversation. "Except they did plow. With horses," he added, and I wondered if he was mocking her.

"And?" Mom said. "Why no longer?"

"They can't farm like that on a large scale. Can't grow enough to compete, especially now, with Mercosur flooding our markets with cheap Brazilian produce. And, of course, some crops are just impossible to cultivate that way. Like rice. Surely your brother knows that."

I could see Mom wasn't satisfied with this answer, but the mention of Juan's yet-to-be-hatched rice plan gave her pause, and Caruso himself showed no inclination to continue the discussion. He declined Mom's invitation to stay for coffee, and as we walked back to the trucks, he invited us to stop by his house, which was not on the estancia next to us, but up the road toward

Lascano. "You'll have to come for dinner next time my wife is here from Montevideo," he said, sliding into the cab of his truck. He grinned. "And if you change your mind about plowing that field, just let me know. Be glad to do it."

"And why," Mom grumbled as he drove off, "do they think they have to grow on a large scale? Uruguay isn't exactly India." But she liked the advice Caruso had given her about the house, and the next morning we drove into Lascano to look for the glazier he'd mentioned.

Lascano reminded me of the forgotten places Dad and I used to pass through in Nevada, on our long summer camping expeditions to Wyoming or Colorado, except now it was our actual destination. I had the sensation that half the town was sitting around in the plaza and café watching us, as if we were the featured entertainment of the week, but Mom didn't care. She was in her high-energy star mode, talking up the baker and the butcher and the cashier in the market, telling them her plans and making her inquiries, as if she were a bona fide member of the community. We finally found the window guy on a dirt track at the edge of town. Mom told him all about the house, admired his collection of old windows, and talked him into driving out to assess the job the next day. People were certainly friendly, though it was hard to tell if they were charmed by Mom, or curious, or just glad to have the extra business. But by the time we got back to the estancia and had lunch, I myself had tired of humoring her and decided to leave my field to the *tero* and Mom to her frenetic wall-plastering and go exploring. Alone.

I wanted to climb a hill or a tree and get the lay of the land, but there were no real hills and no trees other than the eucalyptus, which were home to a noisy congregation of lime-green parakeets but completely inaccessible for an unwinged beast like me. I'd never seen parakeets in the wild. They were building a massive nest up there, some sort of collective housing arrangement or bird apartment complex—also something I'd never seen. I watched for a few minutes and then continued on my way, turning at the end of the track to follow a narrow canal, which traversed the fields with no apparent beginning or end. A few curious cows kept pace with me on the other side of the canal, but there were no cars or buildings anywhere in sight, no electric or phone lines.

The grass was literally popping with little yellow finches, and there were two surprisingly intrepid brown partridges pecking at insects in the dirt track along the canal—I'd brought my binoculars and new journal, and I started taking notes and sketching the birds I saw, all of which were unknown to me. I'd left my tin of colored pencils at the house, but I included pointers with the colors labeled, so I could fill them in later. I even added some random descriptive notes, as if I were making my own eccentric field guide. After a while, I veered away from the canal and headed off across the pasture, ducking through a barbed-wire fence and skirting the edge of a field with a bull in it. I spotted one of the brown thrasher-like birds that were so common even Mom knew the name, now perched like a sentinel on top of a mud nest, which itself looked like a basketball perched on a fencepost. *Hornero*, Mom had called it, an "oven-builder," and the nest was indeed a little like a clay oven—as I was doing a quick sketch, the bird suddenly slipped around the side and disappeared into a small hole. I added some notes: *Thrasher-like behavior, but bill is thrush-like, rufous tail wags up and down. Calls: rapid jackhammer, and a ratcheting sound, like a broken bike derailleur trying to change gears.* I moved closer and peeked into the hole, but the nest had a trick entrance, a tunnel with a sharp bend, so I couldn't see anything.

The topography surprised me again as I came to the top of a billow and had a wide view to the north and east, the landscape simultaneously mundane and exotic, the black glint of what I assumed must be Caruso's rice fields in the near distance, the old palm trees peppered about, looking even more incongruous than they had by the lagoon where I first saw them. I had no idea where I was going or what I would see, and I felt like a kid again, pretending to be an explorer of the wild. No matter that these grasslands had been grazed by cattle for centuries and the water ran in straight canals and the rice fields probably embodied Mom's worst nightmares of industrial agriculture—for the moment, everything was, for me, a momentous revelation.

The grass here was well above my calves, and there were no more cows in sight, but scanning with the binoculars, I spied what seemed to be a flock of large ostrich-like birds. There must have been two dozen of them out there, long necks looping down to the ground, heads hidden in the grass. I snuck closer until I could see them with bare eyes, and then I plopped myself down in the grass and sketched one. They looked like cartoon characters—a big blimp of a body on long stick legs, nothing much in the way of tail feathers, and then the long sinewy neck and tiny squashed triangle of a head, all beak and dark eyes, over five feet tall from head to toe. *Hangs out in herds like cattle*, I noted. At first it looked like they were grazing on the grass, but they were actually picking bugs out of the sod. When I stood up, they all raised their necks in unison, but as I moved closer they started trotting about in random directions, looking so absurd and confused I laughed out loud. I clapped my hands and ran at them, which only caused more chaos—until, as if by magic, they aligned themselves and galloped off like a herd of two-legged deer, the flock completely synchronized as it ran an evasive zigzag. They opened their wings like sails to check momentum and change direction, but they obviously couldn't fly. I added more details to my sketch and a few more notes: *Legs extremely muscular. Incredible wing feathers, but doesn't fly—*

"Are you trying to catch a Ñandú?"

I spun around and blinked up at a man on a horse who, at first glance, might have stepped out of one of the gaucho paintings in the book I'd been reading. Sheepskin saddle, worn brown poncho, leather hat . . . but he was wearing jeans and balancing a case of Coca-Cola on one knee. His expression was friendly, but quizzical, and I realized I must have looked pretty foolish, running around clapping and laughing, scribbling in a notebook.

"Is that what they're called?" I said, the color rising in my face. I closed the journal and tucked it under the waistband of my jeans, against my back. "I'm Gabriel Haynes Quiroga," I added, realizing I'd probably crossed some boundary and was trespassing on his land. "I'm visiting at the Quiroga estancia, helping my mother."

His name was Santiago Martinez, and he worked for Manuel Caruso and already seemed to know who I was. His face was so weather-beaten I couldn't tell if he was forty-five or seventy-five. He didn't seem to be in any hurry, though I imagined the case of Coke must be heavy.

"My daughter lives in Toronto," he told me.

I guess he thought we would have something in common then, but I knew even less about Toronto than I did about Ñandús. "I think it's pretty cold there," I said.

"Oh yes. She hates it! But her husband is an engineer and has a good job there." He gestured at my binoculars. "Did you see the *Carpinchos*?"

"The what?"

"*Carpinchos*. By the canal."

I shook my head, and he shifted the case of Coke farther up his thigh and indicated that I should follow him.

So much for my lone explorer fantasies, I thought as I hurried along beside my mounted tour guide. I could ignore a cow or two, but humans weren't supposed to be part of the game. He led me across the fields until we came upon another canal, where he pointed out three oversized rodent-like creatures lazing in the tall grass along the bank. They looked for all the world like guinea pigs—except they were as big as farm pigs.

"Those are wild?" I asked incredulously. We were some twenty yards away, but they looked so tame, I thought they must be someone's pets.

"Sure. We used to hunt them, but the meat isn't very good unless you're really hungry."

I wanted to move closer, but he was still on his horse and I was afraid he would follow me and scare them away.

"They're not as slow as they look," he said. "You get them mad, and they'll come at you fast, biting like a rabid dog. Guy I know got too close in his canoe once, and they charged and capsized him, tore him up pretty bad."

"They swim?" They looked too chunky to be good swimmers.

"They like the canals almost as much as the *nutria* do. You might see one of those along here also, if you keep an eye out, mostly in the water."

I asked what a *nutria* was, and he described something that sounded like a giant, aquatic rat but acted like a river otter. He said their pelts were worth a fortune and they'd almost disappeared before regulations were placed on hunting—but they bred like vermin and had made a quick comeback. He then told me a shortcut back to the house and bid goodbye.

I watched him lope off down the canal track, the case of Coke dangling from one hand as if it weighed nothing, and when he was out of sight, I turned my attention back to the *Carpinchos*. Despite Santiago's warning, I had the feeling I could walk up and pet them, but as soon as I tried to creep closer, they skittered into the water and paddled away down the canal. Docile-looking, maybe, but definitely not tame. I looked around me at the featureless, green, not-so-empty landscape Mom had chosen for her midlife crisis. It wasn't the sort of place I'd expect to find large wild animals, but here they were, along with all sorts of exotic wild birds. They adapted, of course, we all adapted. Coyotes on cattle ranches, raccoons in cities, ducks on reservoirs, gulls at dumps. Overgrown guinea pigs in canals, flightless birds in cow pastures . . . immigrants in foreign lands . . . And emigrants returning home?

When Juan showed up on Friday night, I began to suspect that the reasons Mom had spent the week plastering walls as if her life, if not the fate of civilization, depended on it were, like everything in the Quiroga family, more complicated than they seemed. She obviously wanted Juan to be impressed by the improvements to the house, but he hardly commented on the new walls, and he pooh-poohed her plan to rethatch the roof, saying only that it was more expensive than tiles and the thatch had to be replaced every five years. He did come prepared to spend the whole weekend, however, and thanked her for cleaning out a bedroom for him. And he was clearly enthusiastic about his own plan to make a map of the estancia—one of the few things he and Mom agreed they needed—and delighted to learn that his nephew was adept with the old surveying rod and theodolite he'd brought along.

There was no way we were going to do a topographic survey of the whole estancia, but Juan did have aerial photos and old survey data, and he figured we could at least do the parts he wanted to develop in the coming year. We worked from dawn to dusk on Saturday, and I began to get a better sense of the place, which still seemed monotonously featureless, the creek and occasional billows notwithstanding.

We were on our way back to the house, resting at the crest of an unusually high billow, when Juan told me that most of the area we'd just covered had been underwater for several months of the year when he was a kid. It was almost dusk, and I was starving, but he laid his equipment down in the grass and lit up a cigarette, in no hurry to get back. We had a panoramic view of the sort that kept surprising me, where I'd suddenly realize I was above everything, even though it all seemed so flat. The grassland tipped slightly toward the northeast, and though we couldn't have been very high, the horizon looked almost curved. Standing there made me feel like the Little Prince in the illustration where he's standing on his tiny home planet looking out over its side. Except this planet wasn't so tiny.

"All this," Juan said, with a sweep of his arm that took in the horizon and included miles and miles of dry pastureland. "You needed a boat to cross the estancia. The cows were in water up to their hips, horses had a hard time. Some places were so boggy and overgrown you couldn't get in there any time of year. There's still a patch like that on our land, down at the end of the creek where you've been getting wood. The *nutria* hunters used to go in there with their canoes, but we never did."

I thought of the remaining marshes around th San Francisco Bay and Delta, marshes that Grandpa had told me were much more extensive when he was a little boy. But that was at the convergence of two grand rivers. Here, Juan said, the land had been like a giant rain-soaked sponge with water oozing out of every runnel and pore, leaking away in a maze of tiny meandering streams, flowing, if it flowed at all, into the huge lagoon that divided Uruguay from Brazil to the north. I sat down in the grass, watching a pair of ducks winging toward us, wishing I had brought the binoculars.

"The ducks used to be so thick in here the air buzzed when they flew," Juan said, sitting down next to me. "Your grandfather took me hunting a few times, but I didn't have much taste for it."

"What kind of ducks?" I asked as the pair passed out of sight, unidentified.

"I don't know. All kinds. Fifteen, twenty years ago, there were so many the rice farmers considered them a pest. They'd fly in low over the fields and sheer off all the seed heads like a giant combine, destroy a whole crop in one pass. At least, that's what people said. I never saw it. The farmers used to put out poison, you'd see piles and piles of dead ducks. It was one of the things your grandfather couldn't abide, turned him against the rice growers."

I turned to look at Juan. "Are you going to do that? Poison ducks?"

"Of course not. There aren't enough left to do any damage anyway. If they ever did."

I turned back to the tipping horizon and tried to imagine the Little Prince's planet as a dripping sponge. I asked Juan why it had all dried up.

He told me the ranchers had been building small dams and canals for decades, but that things had speeded up when the government got involved in the seventies and eighties. "It was one of the dictatorship's screwed-up projects. They built the big dam at India Muerta, and the two main canals. It cost a fortune. And some people lost land to flooding in places where it had never been a problem. But others fared well. Papá was against it, thought the whole plan was stupid, based on something from the last century. But we gained over a hundred hectares of good pastureland. Caruso gained even more—*and* he was smart. He started with the rice right away, irrigating with water from the canal." Juan paused. He blew a chain of smoke rings, and we watched them parade off on the wind like little ghost families. "We should have done the same thing," he said then. "But your grandfather had his head up his ass." He glanced at me, as if he expected some sort of reaction, but I'd hardly known my grandfather.

"And Mom?" I asked. "What did she think about all this?"

"Professor Quiroga? She was in sunny California raising you. Your mother's infatuation with the estancia is a recent event," he added dryly.

A large phalanx of dark-colored wading birds passed above us in a perfect wedge formation, long legs trailing behind them, sickle-shaped bills stretched out in front. Some sort of ibis, I realized as they floated past. They looked sort of prehistoric, the way I imagined pterodactyls must have looked. I'd seen a couple of White-faced Ibis in the Central Valley once, with Grandpa. But this was hundreds. Thousands. The phalanx merged with another, and more rose from the distant fields to join them, each new wedge of birds flowing seamlessly into line to produce a phalanx of birds that must have been tens of thousands strong by the time it faded from view in the northeast. "Incredible," I breathed, and looked over at Juan, but I couldn't tell if he'd been watching the impeccably choreographed flight maneuvers playing out in the distance, or if he was staring at the smoke in front of his face.

Grandpa had told me that most of the great California marshes were converted to agricultural land before he was even born, and the rest disappeared with the big government dam projects in the thirties and forties. He'd done his best to save those last remnants for the birds. He said the water projects had been driven by greed and speculation and government corruption. But he'd also conceded that neither San Francisco and Los Angeles nor California's huge agricultural industry would exist without them.

"So, was it worth it?" I asked Juan.

"What?"

"The drainage project. You said it was screwed up. That it cost a fortune. Did it pay off?"

"The investment? In the larger scheme? Who knows? Who knows where the money came from and where it went. Or even how much they spent. It was the middle of the dictatorship. A few people lost land. And they ran one of the big canals out to the coast, instead of the lagoon, which was idiotic. Ruined the beaches and the fishing, put a couple of hotels out of business. But hell, no one could do anything with all this land before."

It didn't look to me like anyone was doing much out there even now, but Juan said I was looking at first-rate pasture and, in the distance, thousands of hectares of good rice cropland.

"Twenty years ago, most of this was a no-man's-land. Lascano was one of the most pitifully backwards towns in the country. No infrastructure whatsoever, no high school, no paved roads . . . Now it's thriving."

I'd be hard put to call Lascano thriving, but Juan was serious.

"Rice did that," he said. "The highway we drove up on? Wouldn't be there if people weren't growing rice up here. And they couldn't grow rice without the drainage projects."

The so-called highway wasn't even paved, but Juan pointed out that it was oiled and solid, wide enough for two trucks to pass. "That road used to be worse than the one to the estancia," he said, letting out a last blast of smoke rings and grinding his cigarette butt out in the grass. "Used to take half a day to get up here from Rocha."

"Are you really going to plant rice?"

"Sure. It's the only sector of the economy that's growing. A major export. Maybe not a gold mine, but the closest thing we have on offer." He pushed himself to his feet. "Lili isn't going to last out here, Gabe. You know that as well as I do."

I wasn't so sure. She seemed pretty determined. My volatile and mercurial mother suddenly seemed resolute and steadfast, even content with what she was doing. On Sunday afternoon, I headed back to Montevideo with Juan Luis, leaving her all alone out there. And I wondered: If the whole world were encompassed within this empty sweep of grassland, if a person never had to think about what happened beyond that deceptively tilted horizon—would she, in fact, be happy?

4

When everyone was around, Abuela tended to get overwhelmed and disappear into her room with the radio. But with just the two of us in the house, she was downright gregarious. I offered to clean up her backyard, and she spent most of a morning out there with me. She snipped at the grape arbor—which I was forbidden to prune, though it needed a lot more than snipping—while I raked and mowed the lawn and hacked back the overgrown bushes. She even made attempts to be grandmotherly, preparing lunch for me and regaling me with her special brand of wisdom, trying to educate me. "Do you believe in God?" she asked one afternoon, watching me closely, like I might be tempted to lie to her.

"Not really," I said, and she nodded approvingly. Then, having deemed me worthy, she took me by the arm and led me around the house, telling me its secrets.

She claimed that my grandfather had designed the beached ship according to symbolic numeric and geometric relationships. The windows in my room weren't just portholes, they were also, according to Abuela, circles with points in the center. I couldn't really see the points, physical or figurative, but Abuela shrugged off my objections.

"It was his office," she reminded me, as if this explained everything.

The granite stairs turned at a certain angle, and the landing at the turn was an equilateral triangle, the stone subtly engraved with a pattern I'd never noticed before, a star inside a circle. Abuela explained something about energy centers and Pythagoras and the Greeks, but the precise nature of the symbolism still eluded me. It was a way of transmitting knowledge, she told me, of passing it on to the selected few who were receptive to it.

"What sort of knowledge?"

"*Esotérico*. It takes years of study to understand."

Numbers were significant. There were nine stairs above the landing, then two groups of three making up the stretch down to the living room. "As in the three sides of a triangle," Abuela said. "The three stages of human life." I could never tell when Abuela was being cryptic on purpose, to test me, or if she spoke like this—unlinked clauses, nouns without verbs, narrative whittled down to its essence—because she thought my Spanish was so limited it would be easier to understand, or if, in fact, she assumed we shared an empathetic connection that made complete sentences unnecessary, in which case I should be honored. "Youth, manhood, and old age," she went on. "The three senses. The three kingdoms of nature. The holy trinity."

"I thought you didn't believe in that."

"The Bible contains the greatest allegories in the history of mankind. The Christians just don't know how to read it." She peered up at me through her thick glasses. "You have read the Bible, haven't you?"

"No," I admitted. "I always figured it was for religious people." The truth of the matter was, I'd never given it much thought. "Mom and Dad weren't into that sort of thing."

"Lili? Lili read the Bible in school. It was part of the literature curriculum. Of course, reading and understanding are not the same."

We walked through the downstairs rooms, counting windows. "Seven," Abuela pronounced, as if the number had great portent and weight, an essence beyond the mathematical. "Like the seven planets. The seven vital centers. Seven colors in the rainbow. Seven notes in a musical scale."

I nodded agreeably, though her number litanies seemed as meaningless to me as a random list of bird species with white wing stripes or yellow heads. But as she heated up the trays of frozen ravioli she'd bought us as a special treat for lunch, Abuela explained that what sounded to me like New Age nonsense—not what I'd expect from my eighty-six-year-old grandmother—was actually based on the ancient teachings of the Masons.

"A lot of important Uruguayans were Masons," she said. "Your grandfather was widely sought after for his skill with these designs."

"The Masons? Like Masonic Lodge? Isn't that some sort of secret male religious society?"

"It's a *philosophical* society. Beyond religion." She extracted the aluminum trays of raviolis from the oven and emptied them onto the plates I'd set out. Somehow the kitchen hadn't been a priority when my grandfather designed the house. It was a cramped room with an ancient stove and refrigerator, a small sink, a narrow Formica counter and a single rickety stool, everything now yellowed with age. It fit Abuela's lone eccentric existence like an old pair of jeans, but it was hard to imagine it producing meals for a family of five, in the days before prefab frozen dinners became popular. I rounded up glasses and the grapefruit soda Abuela had bought me, and we carried everything into the dining room.

"It is the duty of the Mason to exercise secrecy and caution in all things," Abuela told me, once we were seated. "Some kinds of knowledge are too powerful and can be harmful, if we're not careful. And yes," she said, smiling slyly, "women were usually excluded. But I found a master who agreed to teach me. I achieved the third grade, and then he stopped and refused to take me higher." She was clearly proud of this achievement and didn't seem at all bothered by the fact that her "studies" had been curtailed and she'd been excluded from joining the society. "If I had been properly initiated, I probably wouldn't tell you all this." But she seemed to relish telling me, and so I pretended that it all made perfect sense, just like I pretended to prefer the horrid frozen raviolis with cream sauce she got at the supermarket over the fresh ones that were sold for half the price at the little shop down the street. I rather liked the idea of my cool, aloof Abuela telling me secrets.

"Masons have been behind all the world's liberating revolutions," Abuela said. "Your George Washington was a Mason. So was Thomas Paine. And Benjamin Franklin. Robespierre. The nation of Uruguay was created by Masons."

"Artigas?" I asked, thinking of the gaucho founding father I'd been reading about. "Was he a Mason?"

"Artigas," she said dismissively. "Artigas was a loser. Not to mention a barbarian. It was the Thirty-Three Orientales who fought off the Brazilians, while Artigas was shacked up with some *india* in Paraguay. Do you know about the Thirty-Three Orientales?"

"The guys who snuck across the river from Buenos Aires and drove the Brazilians out of Montevideo. In 1825," I added, glad to show off the random bits of knowledge I'd acquired from my book-grazing activities. Artigas's revolution had gotten rid of the Spaniards and then been hijacked by the Brazilians a few years later, supposedly with the tacit complicity of the Montevidean upper classes. Artigas escaped to Paraguay and faded out of the story, but some of his former captains joined forces with like-minded rural landowners—the Thirty-Three Orientales—and reignited his revolution, winning independence from both Brazil and Argentina. I even remembered a couple of the names, probably because they were also the names of Montevideo's streets. "Lavalleja," I said. "Manuel Oribe."

"They were all Masons," Abuela said, watching my face, as if she were trying to decide if I was worthy of this information. "All thirty-three of them."

Abuela was not the most emotive person in the world. She didn't talk with her hands, like Mom, or with her whole body, like Elsa. But she was a master of the dramatic pause, the lowered voice. "Double three," she whispered. "Like the thirty-three levels of Masonic learning." She pushed her plate away—amazingly, she'd finished off her raviolis, while I was still picking at mine—folded her tiny hands on the edge of the table, and went on to tell me that Masons were also behind the Enlightenment, that Voltaire, Diderot, Goethe, and Mozart were Masons. The way Abuela told it, they'd all been following a secret plan for the improvement of society that went back to the beginning of history—a not entirely unattractive concept, though I was a little surprised that she didn't consider Uruguay's own Artigas worthy of inclusion. According to the *Enciclopedia uruguaya,* he'd been a great champion of democracy and equality, appropriating land from the huge colonial estancias and redistributing it as medium-sized tracts to anyone who agreed to fence in their livestock and build a house. It was something like our Homestead Act, though the *Enciclopedia* didn't say anything about how it affected the gauchos and the few indigenous groups that hadn't already been massacred, absorbed, or disenfranchised by the Spaniards.

It was only later that week, when I went out in search of a bird book, that I realized my *Enciclopedia uruguaya* version of José Gervasio Artigas was just one of many. I went to six bookstores, and the patient proprietor of a dimly lit, labyrinthine used bookstore finally dredged up a single copy of a 1987 edition of *Guía para la identificacion de aves de Argentina y Uruguay*—but books about Artigas were on every display table. There were dozens of them, just from the past few years, all with a different story. According to the back covers and introductions, Artigas was alternately an ignorant gaucho and *paisano*, the son of a rich colonial governor, a juvenile delinquent, a bloodthirsty criminal, an inspired social reformer, an Indian lover or an Indian killer, a closet homosexual, a womanizer, a coward, a loser . . . Abuela's version was not entirely original—though I suspected she'd modified it to suit her, just like I suspected she'd revised the tenets of numerology and Masonic philosophy.

I could happily have spent another few days hanging out with Abuela, but Mom came for a visit and put an end to our peaceful tête-à-têtes. She just couldn't seem to hang out with Abuela on Abuela's terms. The most trivial of rebukes sent her over the edge. When she saw I'd cleaned up the backyard, she immediately started pruning back the grape arbor, and though I told her Abuela had forbidden me to prune it, she went into a funk when Abuela watched over and criticized every cut she made. Mom at the estancia was a much more congenial experience than Mom at Abuela's house, and I was relieved when she decided to go back out there. She wanted me to help her build a chicken coop, and I was also keen to try out my new field guide, so I went with her. I hadn't birded seriously since the last Christmas Count I'd done with Grandpa my senior year of high school, and that was in Point Reyes, where I hardly needed a field guide.

We weren't entirely without experience when it came to chickens. In the third grade, I'd smuggled home two Easter chicks, and they'd grown into the first of a long line of suburban laying hens—and one rooster, which the neighbors, fond of Mom and bribed with gifts of fresh eggs and vegetables, were amazingly tolerant about. Dad had always helped build the chicken coop and its add-ons, but we more or less knew what we were doing—though using the hodgepodge of old posts and planks Mom had collected was a challenge. We spent the better part of a day preparing the site and building the frame, and then I left her working on the walls and set off in search of the boggy patch of land Juan had mentioned.

It was satisfying to be able to name the birds I saw. At the same time, it was something of a letdown to find my personal discoveries had already been described and catalogued. The field guide's illustrations weren't very good—my own sketches, I noted with satisfaction, were more lifelike—and Uruguay seemed to have been tacked on as an afterthought, but the descriptions were clear, and the common names were given in both English and Spanish. The parakeets in the eucalyptus were *Cotorras*, and the stocky flycatcher whose calls woke me up every morning in Montevideo was a *Benteveo Común* or Great Kiskadee—both names somehow onomatopoeic. It had never occurred to me that the way we hear birdcalls depends on the language in our heads, but I was now filled with bilingual ambiguity whenever I heard the call—*kis-ka-deee,* one moment, *ben-te-veeeo,* the next, and, just to complicate things, Juan described it as "*bi-cho-feo,*" which translated to "ugly creature." What had looked to me like yellow-bellied starlings were actually Brown-and-Yellow Marshbirds. The handsome red-crested songbird with the neat white collar that I'd spotted in the brush along the creek was called *Cardenal Común*, though it was completely unrelated to the iconic red cardinals of the eastern United States.

With the field guide in hand, I was torn between wanting to find Juan's bog before the sun dropped and an urge to stop and identify everything I heard or glimpsed along the way. There were no litanies of species in my head here, no familiar silhouettes or calls or flight patterns to draw on: I had to wait for a clear view and really truly look, then search the field guide, and then look again, back and forth between guide and bird any number of times before I could put a name to what I saw. The finches bouncing about in the grass like little yellow ping-pong balls must be *Mistos*—though I wasn't entirely sure they weren't *Jilguero Dorados*. The gregarious cuckoo-like birds in the first clump of bushes I came to were clearly *Pirinchos*, eight of them crowded together on a branch but facing opposite directions, buffoon-like and disheveled, as if bedhead were a genetic attribute. "Abundant and easy to observe" according to the field guide indicator, though I hadn't seen them before.

The brush and trees along the creek were alive with unknown songbirds and flycatchers, but I determined to only stop for the ones that showed themselves off, the more obvious ones—some of which I'd already seen and drawn in my notebook. The impressive sparrow with the bandit face and rusty collar was obviously a *Chingolo*, so ubiquitous it quickly ceased to impress. I saw the blue tanager again, and in the same tree, a lollipop-orange, yellow, and blue one. *Celestón. Naranjero.* I paused to watch a flycatcher fishing insects from the air, not brown or pale yellow like the flycatchers I knew but a brilliant white. *Monjita Blanca.* Little white nun? There was nothing nun-like about it. I did a quick sketch, trying to capture the bird's elegant flirtatiousness, which the field guide didn't mention. *Blinding white*, I scribbled beneath it, *like bleached granite, fresh snow. Black-eyed, tail dragged in tar.*

The creek divided and became more meandering, the brush and trees giving way to clumps of reeds and cattails as it gradually spread into nonexistence. I stopped at the edge of an expanse of swampy, calf-high grass. Above, a group of ibis peeled away from its phalanx and floated down to earth, their plumage flashing iridescent green and purple as they landed in front of me, where I could now identify two species, *Cuervillo de Cañada* and *Cuervillo Cara Pelada*. Beyond, just before the reeds seemed to take over entirely, I located the source of a loud, persistent counterpoint of wheezing calls that sounded like a French horn trying to harmonize with a donkey: a pair of huge, corpulent, gray-plumed, vaguely goose-like birds with chicken bills and hatchet-shaped heads. Bright red around the eye and beak, white collar with a black ruff, and an upright, regal demeanor. They were as easy to find in the field guide as in the field, tucked between the flamingos and the ducks, in a family of their own: *Chajá*, or Southern Screamer. The Spanish ono-matopoeic this time, the English descriptive. They looked so heavy and poorly proportioned, it seemed unlikely they could fly, but as I approached, they ran a few loping steps and pushed off. Once airborne, they were transformed, like a fat couple dancing, spiraling upwards as gracefully as the most skillful of raptors, their hoarse screams rising with them, *chajá, chajá, hee-haw, chajáaaaa* . . . I waited for them to tumble like Icarus back to earth, but they just kept climbing toward the hot sphere of the sun, until they had shrunk to two tiny specks and finally disappeared, their calls fading after them as if they had indeed escaped the earthly pull of gravity.

Earthbound, my own progress was now impeded by a dense, six-foot-high wall of reeds, which was pulsing with sound. There was a chorus of Bay-winged Cowbirds scattered across the top, perched on the tips of the reeds and singing in an assortment of bass, tenor, and soprano voices—their Spanish name was *Tordo Músico*—but beneath their chorus, in the depths of the reed bed, I could hear a whole symphony of screeching, quacking, and whistling. I tried to enter the forest of reeds, easing myself between the sharp blades and letting my feet sink slowly into the muddy water with each step. As my eyes adjusted to the shadowed light, I spied a flurry of tiny, colorful flycatchers flitting around in the upper reaches, and I wanted to delve farther—but the sun was sinking and the reed bed was so dense and uniform my sense of direction would be nil. Not to mention the swarms of mosquitoes and the fact that my sneakers were flooded with muddy water that was probably full of leeches.

I retreated from the reeds and flipped through the field guide to identify the little flycatchers. They were unmistakable kaleidoscopes of color—yellow breasts, blue faces, flashes of green, red, and black—*Tachurí Sietecolores*. I hadn't noted all seven colors, but as I retraced my steps and planned my return, I found myself thinking of Abuela's number superstitions, wondering if being besieged by *Sietecolores* was a good portent—and only then remembering that she hadn't told me exactly what the sevens built into her house by the husband who left her were supposed to signify.

Mom and I finished the chicken coop the next afternoon, and though Juan would probably call it *chapucería*, I thought it looked pretty deluxe. We drove into Lascano to pick up its occupants, and when we stopped at the Agrocentro I bought myself a pair of rubber boots and a bottle of citronella mosquito repellent. Mom wanted me to buy a hat for the sun, but I hated hats and bought a giant tube of sunblock instead. I spent the next few afternoons exploring the marsh, mapping a route into the reeds one careful step at a time, marking it with bits of Juan's flagging tape. Juan had told me *nutria* hunters used to go around the marshes in canoes, but it was hard to imagine navigating even the slimmest of kayaks in there. As it was, I didn't see a single human until I lost my way on the third day—and found myself, again, thinking of Abuela's superstitions and premeditated histories.

The reed bed turned out to be just the entrée to a marsh that was more varied and three dimensional—more magical and unfathomable—than any marsh I'd ever known. It was hard to spot the birds among the reeds, but some hundred yards in, I came upon a small open glade that was so crowded with ducks and strange wading birds I felt as if I'd stepped into a natural history museum diorama: A golden-brown bittern standing in the flooded grass, staring up at the heavens as if waiting for a meteor to land in a ball of fire on the point of its bill. A chicken-like bird with the most intense purple-blue plumage I'd ever seen, walking like Jesus across the surface of a water-lily-covered pond. Two huge pink wading birds feeding in the shallows, stirring the water with bills like large wooden spoons. A pair of little reddish-brown ducks floating low in the water near the opposite shore, which was ringed by an impenetrable, half-submerged tangle of brush and trees. *Mirasol Grande, Espátula Rosada, Pollona Azul, Pato Fierro*. . . . They paid me no heed, and I stayed there watching and drawing the scene for as long as I could bear the mosquitoes, which were unfazed by the citronella.

When I was a kid, I kept a "life list" of birds I'd seen for the first time, placing little checkmarks next to their names in the list at the back of my Peterson guide. By high school, the only new additions were accidentals—migrating birds who'd gotten lost, or inexplicable strays who'd wandered away from their normal ranges. If I still kept that list, I could have added more than twenty life birds in just three days. I was following one of them through the reeds—or, rather, trying to get a look at one I had yet to identify—when I got lost. I'd noticed one lonely, insistent voice in the marsh's evening symphony, a low, hollow-sounding trill, like a bassoon running down a scale and sliding off the end, and then I'd caught a brief glimpse of a fist-sized bird running across the mud. I assumed it was some sort of rail, but it disappeared before I got a good look. I tried to follow its calls, but it led me snaking through the reeds without revealing itself, until I lost both the route I'd marked and my sense of direction. When I finally found my way out, I was on Caruso's property and the flooded rice fields were aglow with the first colors of the setting sun, the neon-green tips of the seedlings floating in orange flames.

I climbed an embankment, trying to get my bearings, and was surprised to see some familiar Californian characters among the ibis and shorebirds feeding in the fields below—Black-necked Stilt, American Golden Plover, Lesser Yellowlegs . . . and in the next paddy over, two Hudsonian Godwits and, standing like a lone heron between two tired-looking palm trees, a single representative of *Homo sapiens*. Young adult female. Slight build. Thin arms, knobby knees. Black hair, pulled into a thick ponytail. Her face was turned away, so I couldn't see much more, even with the binoculars. She had a canvas bag and a bunch of strange contraptions hanging around her neck. What was she doing out there? She set something into the bag and started making her way toward the levee on the other side of the field, where, I noticed, there was a car parked. Even wading through the mud, picking her way between the plants with all that awkward equipment, she moved with such an arresting mix of competence and sensuality that I wanted to stand there watching her all day. I forced myself to lower the binoculars. This was, after all, a woman I was looking at, not some exotic species of heron.

There wasn't much daylight left, but I knew where I was now. I could walk along this levee all the way to the canal road or cut across the fields to the house. Instead, I leapt across the irrigation ditch and proceeded down the levee to the next field.

A heron would have been following my every move, watching me through one eye as I neared, preparing its escape. But the woman approached the car and started disentangling herself from her equipment, seemingly oblivious to my presence. When I was about twenty feet away, still trying to decide how to announce myself without startling her, a *tero* rose from the grass screaming, and she finally looked my way. *"Hola,"* I called, waving and trying to appear unthreatening, though I felt ridiculous with the hysterical *tero* threatening to dive-bomb me.

We introduced ourselves politely—*Gabriel Haynes, Alejandra Silva, encantada, encantado,* pleased to meet you—and I thought how absurd it seemed out there in the middle of the empty countryside. And yet, it was truer to form than I'd ever imagined such a greeting could be, as I was not only pleased, but quite literally *encantado,* enchanted, under a spell. The sensation was so real, so visceral, it was hard to dismiss, for all that I really wasn't superstitious: standing there among those rice fields, glorified as they were by the pyrotechnics of a setting sun, I felt an electric jolt of exalted fate.

She stepped back and looked at my binoculars and my muddy rubber boots, and I looked at her bare legs and equally muddy boots and gestured at the canvas bag she was cradling and the pile of equipment she'd deposited on the ground next to the car.

"What are you doing?" we asked as our gazes met, speaking simultaneously and then waiting, simultaneously, for each other to reply, and, finally, laughing.

She tossed back her head and chortled with obvious delight, then fished a small jar out of the bag and held it up. "I'm collecting samples," she said.

"Of?"

"Mud and water." She opened the ice chest in the back of the car and set the jar down inside. "It's a potent brew of microbes," she added theatrically, "with earthshaking consequences for the future of rice farming."

I'd assumed she must be a daughter from the Caruso family, and that she would have heard about our reoccupation of the Quiroga estancia. But no, she told me as she transferred jars from the canvas bag to the ice chest, she was a graduate student from the university. They were looking for bacteria that might be helpful in cultivating rice, and Caruso had given permission to do the study on his land. "At the moment, we're just trying to characterize the interesting microbial communities in these rice fields," she said, closing the ice chest. She had a raspy Castilian voice that sounded like it came from someone larger and older. Dark green-brown eyes. A dazzling, full-toothed smile. "And you? You don't sound Uruguayan."

"I'm from California. My mother is Uruguayan, and she just moved back—"

"You moved *here* from California?"

"No, no. My mother did. Liliana Quiroga. She and my uncles own the neighboring estancia, and she's trying to fix it up. I'm just here for the summer. Between jobs."

"This isn't exactly Uruguay's most popular beach resort," she said, swatting at a mosquito.

"No," I said. "But it's pretty good for watching birds."

"Is that what you're doing?" She reached up to adjust the elastic band in her hair, her slight figure briefly open to view—small-waisted, small-breasted, round-hipped, and entirely self-assured—as she released and recaptured the mass of black curls. My exalted sense of fate was fast giving way to the more prosaic vertigo of yearning, and I looked away and started telling her about the rail I'd been chasing.

"I didn't get a good look at it," I said, "but it was acting like a rail. Lurking around under the reeds, very secretive, never flying. It has this weird call." I cupped my hands over my mouth and tried to imitate the hollow trill, and then I got self-conscious and fell silent. Usually people glaze over and look for the first escape route when you start talking about birdwatching. I knew this, and yet here I was describing a bird I'd hardly even seen, trying to imitate a call that would have been impossible for even the most adept birdcall impersonator, which I wasn't.

But Alejandra appeared to be listening attentively. When I broke off, she looked around curiously, as if in search of my elusive rail.

The crazy *tero* was the only avian representative in easy view, so I offered her the binoculars and pointed out the shorebirds in the next field. She was inexperienced, and I had to tell her how to find the birds and focus, but once she got the band of ibis in view, she took her time, watching them feed.

"They're eating little crabs," she said.

"I think they just move their bills around in the water until they bump into something edible, whatever it is. If you look a little to the right and behind them, you'll see some shorebirds." I flipped through the field guide for the Spanish names. "The one with the really long legs and black neck is a *Tero Real*," I said, though it seemed unfair that the serene and graceful Black-necked Stilt should share a name with the maniacal *Tero Común*. "The squat little ones with the white eyebrows are *Chorlo*

Pampas. And off to the side there, is a *Pitotoy Chico.* Those two are migrants," I added, skimming the field guide entries. "They breed in North America and come all the way down here for the winter. Unbelievable, isn't it?"

"Yes," she said, lowering the binoculars and turning to look at me, waiting a beat, and smiling.

I could feel a blush rising in my face, and I reached for the binoculars and turned to watch a small group of ducks fly in and land on the irrigation canal by the road. There was never anything subtle about my blush—my entire face, throat, and ears turned a bright tacky shade of pink. Nicole once told me my blush was endearing, that it made girls trust me, which I didn't really believe, but it was completely out of my control and I'd long since given up fretting about it. I moved slowly down the levee to get a better look at the ducks. Alejandra had followed me, so I handed her the binoculars again and pointed out some of the field marks, the black cap and pale cheeks and blue bill of the male *Pato Capuchino,* the extended neck of the *Maicero,* its cinnamon-colored crown and speckled sides.

"I think I may have seen them out here before," she said. "But never up close like this. They're beautiful."

They were beautiful, but it's not everyone who would notice it. The Maicero, at first glance, was just a plain brown duck, but its feathers were edged with an ochre color that caught the last bright rays of sun and produced a fine shimmering mosaic of tiny feather shapes in the otherwise dull plumage. There was a lone female Cinnamon Teal, another bird I knew from home, though according to the guide, it was a full-time resident here. *Pato Colorado,* in Spanish, but there was nothing very *colorado* about the female, and Alejandra wanted to know how to distinguish it from the other brown ducks. "The form," I said. "The shape and color of the bill. And when they fly— Keep looking. Watch the wings." I took a few steps toward the canal and clapped my hands, startling the ducks into flight.

She lost track of them and lowered the binoculars as they rose from the water, but she'd caught the unmistakable sky-blue wing patches as the teal opened her wings.

"So you're an ornithologist?" she said, turning to look at me. "A student?"

"No, no, it's just a hobby. I learned as a kid, from my dad's father. In California I can identify almost anything on sight, sometimes even by call. But my degree was in geography." I didn't want her to think I'd spent my life wandering around aimlessly looking at birds. "I work with computer software, doing geographic information systems analysis and mapping for an environmental firm." Even though I'd quit the job, I figured it sounded respectable. But it was the birds that had caught her fancy.

"You know more than I do," she said. "And I'm a biologist." She scanned the fields around us, as if seeing them in a new light. "We're too specialized. Microbiologists, for example. We never pay attention to what's going on up there in the higher echelons of the food chain."

"You should see the birds in the marsh." I gestured toward the reed bed I'd come out of. "It's not easy to get into it, but it's absolutely incredible. If you want, I could take you birding there."

"I'd like that," she said, and then she thanked me and made to leave, as if the offer were hypothetical, a mere courtesy.

"When?" I said quickly. "When do you want to go? It should be early morning or late afternoon." Fate, I realized, was only going to take me so far.

She turned back to look at me, considering, and then she suggested that I meet her the next time she came up to sample. She really did want to go birding, I could see that, but the date she suggested was two weeks away. I wanted to protest that it was too long, suggest we meet in Montevideo on Sunday, when Mom and I went to visit Abuela—but that was too much like

SUSAN M. GAINES

asking her on a date and I didn't want to risk it. Because if she said no, if she disdained the idea of a date with me, what then? So I agreed to the date she suggested, and we left it that I'd meet her there in Caruso's field at five that afternoon.

I had a friend in college who had a beautiful, well-trained dog, a fluffy white Samoyed that always looked like it was smiling. He claimed that girls who never would have looked twice at him fell in love with his dog at first sight. They'd stop him on the street to ask about it, and if he was lucky, they'd like him by association and go out with him. I'd never imagined using birds to flirt with a woman, didn't even think of myself as the flirting type. But it occurred to me as I was turning up the track to the house and Alejandra's car drove past on the canal road, that it was the birds that had captured this woman's attention. That, and my foreignness, perhaps, the hints of a *yanqui* accent as I described the distinguishing characteristics of Uruguayan ducks.

5

The chickens meant Mom was now fully committed to life at the estancia—but this was a commitment that was even harder for Abuela to comprehend than her daughter's abandonment of California. Mom's latest filial guilt project didn't help. She could only leave the chickens alone for a few days, and she was determined to spend "quality time" with Abuela and get her out of the house more—a project I suspected was even more doomed to failure than the yellow paint. When I suggested we go to a play at a theater I'd seen advertised in *El Pais*, Abuela swatted the idea aside as if I'd suggested we watch a mud-wrestling championship. But I myself had an urge to get out and see something of the city, and it had nothing to do with Mom's misguided schemes.

I'd awoken to the *Benteveo*'s call outside my window, and now it sounded like *ven, te veo*, or *ven-te-y-veo, ven-te-y-veo*, as if the bird could see into my heart and were calling me to come out and see its city—a city I'd visited often enough, but never really seen. To tell the truth, I don't know that I'd ever really *seen* any city as such. I'd grown up in a California suburb, a bland, amorphous amoeba of tract houses, malls, and freeways. And though I'd lived in Oakland and spent time in San Francisco, I'd never experienced them as living entities, with personality and character and history, the way I began to experience Montevideo that week.

I wasn't exactly thinking about the biologist I'd met wading around in Caruso's rice paddy, certainly not expecting to run into her in a city of over a million humans. But as I meandered through the middle-class neighborhoods from Abuela's house in Pocitos to Ciudad Vieja, taking in the hole-in-the-wall *boliches*—the pubs and cafés I'd never stepped foot in—the furniture builder and the hardware store, the row of shuttered houses, the concrete wall overgrown with political graffiti, the schoolyard kids in identical white smocks with big blue bows . . . I'd catch myself thinking about her. Wondering who she was, what she did in her free time. Where she lived. With whom. Of course it was absurd. I had no idea if our brief encounter had impressed Alejandra the way it had impressed me. But the mere possibility of her presence somewhere in Montevideo—breathing the same sea air, negotiating the same trash- and dogshit-strewn sidewalks, blasted by the same relentlessly catchy election jingles—the simple fact that Montevideo was Alejandra's home, added a new dimension to a city that had been, for me, circumscribed by Mom's childhood memories and Abuela's hermetic house.

The bits of history I'd been reading jumped out from street names, buildings, plazas, and monuments: the colonial Cabildo and the Iglesia Matriz, the stone portico to the Spanish port—abandoned like a lone movie-set piece at the entrance to the Ciudad Vieja—and the giant bronze statues of Artigas reining in his restless horse in the Plaza Independencia and Lavalleja wielding his sword in the Plaza de los Treinta y Tres Orientales . . . Never mind that the city had seen better days, as Mom was always ready to point out. The art deco Palacio Salvo's extravagant domed turrets and tower, designed as a luxury hotel with a lighthouse beaming across the river to Buenos Aires, still dominated the skyline of Centro and Ciudad Vieja—no matter that the light was never installed and the twenty-four floors now housed a maze of run-down apartments. The Teatro Solís had hosted some of the finest opera singers of the nineteenth century, not to mention the national theater and philharmonic orchestra, and its graceful columns and porticos still evoked a level of high culture beyond any I'd known in my suburban upbringing. Never mind that it was closed for renovation and the philharmonic was reduced to playing in the foyer of the Palacio Municipal. Never mind that, in 1999, all of Montevideo seemed to be in some transitory state of construction, recon-struction, decay, or abandonment—stone facades crumbling, paint faded or nonexistent, high-rises lined with scaffolding, sidewalks torn up for repair—as if the city had left the present unattended in its leap from past to future. Never mind that the handsome music hall named after Elsa's favorite tango singer had shut down for unknown reasons, or that the Parque Rodó's iconic lake was a stagnant morass of algae and trash, its antique amusement park's charming *juegos mecánicos* long motionless and abandoned. It was still spring in Montevideo, and for this repatriated emigrant's naive *yanqui* son, the city was brilliantly alive, if not quite the beautiful city extolled by the tourist bro-chure I'd picked up at the kiosk in front of city hall.

The old plane trees were decked out in new-green buds, the river-sea blinked out from between the high-rises, the plazas blossomed with spring flowers and thermos-toting old men, the *garrapiñada* vendors filled the air with the sweet smell of roasting sugar and peanuts, and the broken sidewalks teemed with citizens—mothers with shopping bags and toddlers in tow, laborers waiting at bus stops, besuited businessmen, glamorous office girls in high heels, old ladies walking their dogs, students in jeans and sweatshirts . . .

Surely, I wasn't looking for her. But I did find myself climb-ing the steps of a turn-of-the-century structure whose stone lintel proclaimed "Universidad de la República," loitering in the empty foyer—which was devoid of information signs, obviously intended for people who knew where they were going—and venturing into a dank inner courtyard that looked more like a family's private garden than the quad of the national university—and then retreating, quietly, feeling like a trespasser. Later, I learned that I'd been in the law school, and the sciences were all housed in different buildings around the city. What was I thinking? That I would run into Alejandra Silva in a hallway, stumble into her office and request help studying for my microbiology exam? That I would spy the lone heron of the rice fields passing out leaflets on the corner, or undulating with the gregarious flock of whistling, drumming, party-flag-waving citizens I stumbled into on Saturday afternoon?

Curious—and not, certainly not, looking for Alejandra—I joined what appeared to be a campaign rally for the Frente Amplio, the party my uncle Rubén and cousin Patricia were coming from Venezuela and Buenos Aires to vote for. A couple thousand people were crammed into a narrow downtown street, and there was a stage at the end of the block where someone was giving a speech—I couldn't see, and between the microphone's distortions and the crowd's interruptions, it was hard to follow, but I got bits of it. He was comparing Uruguay to New Zealand, "an ideal example of a small agricultural economy for the twenty-first century."

"We too," he proclaimed, "have the talent and knowledge to develop a home-style technology, tailored to our needs. We need to focus on the dairyman who maintains profitability using his pastureland, *without* big loans or a huge influx of foreign technology . . . If we allow the market and its fashions to dictate technological growth and make our decisions for us, we are headed for disaster." There was a round of drumming, whistling, and flag-waving, and the speaker's contemplative philosophical tone turned to impassioned rhetoric. "We need to *divorce* our economy from North America, not remake ourselves in its image!" I started inching along the edge of the crowd, jockeying for a view of the stage. "Do we leave the earnings from our resources to jangle in a few select pockets? Or does the whole society reap the harvest? We can't integrate with Mercosur if we don't first integrate with ourselves, incorporate our poor."

The crowd erupted again, and I stepped up on the threshold of a shoe repair shop and finally got a clear view. The man commanding all this adulation was short and stout, his gray hair disheveled, the cuffs of his brown sweater turned up as if it were a hand-me-down that was a size too big. To me, he looked more like a plumber than a politician, no resemblance to the well-coiffed politicians I knew from American campaign commercials. "Progress," he shouted, quieting the crowd, "does not mean abandoning the founding paradigm of our society! As José Gervasio Artigas said over a hundred and fifty years ago: 'To each his just without exclusion, and the neediest should be the most privileged. Because together with social justice comes solidarity.'"

This time he let the crowd go, raising his arms as if to embrace them, while they chanted, "Pepe! Pepe! Pepe . . ." It was a nickname for José, but José what? I examined the flier that an earnest leafleter had pressed on me, answering my protests that I couldn't vote with a cheerful "*no importa*," as if he were peddling a creed rather than soliciting votes. But the flier didn't profess a creed or, for that matter, say much of anything. It was like all the others I'd been stuffing into my pockets—too much the well-trained *yanqui* to let them flutter off on the wind like everyone else—just a book-sized slip of paper with the name of a party, a couple of small mug shots, and a long list of names. This one had "Encuentro Progresista-Frente Amplio" and the number "609" emblazoned in red across the top. I recognized Tabaré Vázquez, the candidate for president, in one of the mug shots, and the other was the guy I'd just seen, who, I deduced, must be José Mujica, the first name on the list under Vázquez. He'd sounded more thoughtful, and his rhetoric seemed more meaningful, than anything I'd heard at home. But then, who knew what might be meaningful here. It wasn't just that I couldn't vote—quite possibly, if I jumped through all the bureaucratic hurdles with Mom, I could get a *credencial* and register—but that I didn't know enough to vote.

I could now distinguish the main parties, but that was about it. The Colorados were something like our Democrats, though Elsa's Jorge Batlle seemed more liberal than Bill Clinton. The Blancos seemed most like our Republicans, attending to the interests of the rich property owners, though they dealt in cows instead of oil. But my analogies broke down when it came to this Frente Amplio, which seemed to be an up-and-coming third party that had grown out of a coalition of old left-wing parties. And the current president, Julio Sanguinetti, was a Colorado who everyone seemed to hate and consider a right-wing fascist. I didn't really understand the ideologies or context for any of it—and Mom, I suspected, was in the same boat. Intent as she was on voting, she seemed less interested in politics and current affairs than she'd ever been at home.

"Do you even know who you're going to vote for?" I asked her that evening. We were at Juan and Elsa's, clearing up after a wild dinner with my cousin's two-year-old, and Juan had switched on the TV to watch an interview with one of the candidates.

"Of course I know who I'm voting for," Mom said firmly.

"Who?" I was surprised she sounded so adamant. I'd had the impression she was more concerned with reclaiming her citizenship than with the actual outcome of the election.

She gestured toward Juan and the TV at the other end of the room.

"She's going to vote Frente," Juan said flatly. "She's enamored of Tabaré Vázquez."

"And you?" I ventured, plopping myself down on the sofa next to him.

"Colorado."

"But he's obviously wavering," Patricia said, lifting the baby out of her high chair and following me over to the TV. It was weird seeing my cousin as a mother. She was only three years older than me, and last time I was in Uruguay, she'd been finishing *liceo* and talking about going to university to study law. Instead, she'd gotten married and moved to Buenos Aires, dyed her hair blond, gained about ten pounds, and produced this little person.

"I'm not really wavering," Juan said.

"*Vamos, Papá*, that's why you're watching the interview." Patricia handed the baby into his lap. "Emilia, you tell him. Tabaré is the voice of the future."

Emilia immediately stuck her hand in Juan's face and squealed with laughter. She was a little clown, cute, but goofy looking, with big ears and a wisp of hair tied up in a bow on top of her head. Patricia had decked her out in the yellow jumpsuit and jean jacket we'd bought.

Juan moved Emilia's hand aside. "I'm not wild about Jorge Batlle."

"Oh come," Elsa called, still gathering up the dishes we'd left on the table. "You know Jorgito is dependable."

"If the Frente could get its agenda together," Juan said as Patricia dashed out to answer the phone, "I might consider voting for them. But they've never been able to do that. And Tabaré isn't doing it for them."

Unlike the guy at the rally earlier, Tabaré Vázquez was suavely dressed, dapper, and blandly handsome—my stereotype of a politician. I was curious to hear what he had to say, but between all the bantering and Emilia's shrieks of delight every time she shoved her hand in Juan's face, it was impossible to follow anything. Juan didn't seem bothered by this, but then he probably didn't have to hear every word to know what they were saying.

Elsa came over, a pile of dirty plates in her hands. "Do you really think you'd have a job in a Frente ministry, Juan? And then what?"

"I'd go back to consulting," Juan said as Emilia grabbed his nose. "And farming the estancia." I'd never seen Juan acting silly before, but he was playing along with Emilia and he started honking like a goose when she pushed on his nose.

Mom had joined us in front of the TV, but she was clearly more interested in this bit of family gossip than in the interview. "Is that why you're suddenly so eager to farm the estancia? Because you're afraid the Frente will reshuffle the ministry and you'll lose your job?"

"I've been wanting to plant rice up there for years," Juan said. "Job or no job. But the Frente isn't going to win."

Patricia came back into the room with the phone receiver and handed it to Juan. "It's your brother. Why don't you introduce him to his grandniece?" But Emilia was on a roll with her hand-in-Abuelo's-face game, and Patricia had to spirit her out of the room before Juan could talk to Rubén.

I'd never met Rubén either, though he and Mom had kept up a regular mail correspondence and talked on the phone occasionally. Everyone was expecting him to come for the election and spend a few days, but now it seemed that his wife, who was also his business partner, had left him, and he was talking about coming to stay. Mom had apparently known all this for some time, but it was news to Juan.

"Of all the idiotic ideas," Juan said, once the phone had made the rounds and Rubén had signed off. "What's he going to do here? He's got a good business going there. And the kids?"

"A good business?" Mom said. "Are you deaf, Juan? Mariela doesn't want to see his face, and you know as well as I do that Rubén couldn't run that business by himself. Luz Maria has been on her own for years, and Teresa has a scholarship in New York—why shouldn't he come back?"

"Leave it to our brother to screw all that up—"

"Oh get off your horse, Juan. The only reason you're not as messed up as the rest of us is Elsa, and don't you forget it. If you hadn't had the luck, the inexplicable good luck, of marrying a saint and a martyr—"

"Didn't do you much good," I said, the comment popping out like a loud, uncontainable hiccup. "Sorry," I added, "but that's what everyone used to say about Dad." Patricia, who was sitting on the floor with the baby, spun around and raised her eyebrows at me. Mom gave me a pained, defeated smile and went off to join Elsa in the kitchen. And Juan, who couldn't agree with me without conceding Mom's point about his own marriage, shifted in the easy chair and kept his gaze fixed on the TV.

I got up and turned the sound up, but by then the interview was over and it was just the evening news. All I'd really learned about the Frente Amplio's presidential candidate was that he'd been a doctor in his past life and the mayor of Montevideo for nearly a decade.

"A disaster," Abuela said as I shuffled into the kitchen to make coffee the next morning. She was sitting on her stool at the counter, sipping *mate* through a tarnished silver straw and chewing on a piece of toast. "It would be a disaster." The radio was on, and it was unclear if she was addressing me or the commentator.

"Good morning." I maneuvered around her to put the kettle on, still half asleep. She was wearing a blue dress instead of her usual gray gnome one, and she looked wide awake and unusually perky. Had there been some crisis in the middle of the night? Something that hadn't made the evening news? "What would be a disaster?"

"If the Frente wins." They were apparently discussing the election on the morning talk show she liked to listen to. "The communists will move in and consolidate. They're just waiting in the wings."

This sounded strange to me, at this particular juncture in history—all I'd ever heard about communists in my lifetime had to do with their failure, collapse, or defeat—but it was seven o'clock in the morning, and I wasn't about to ask Abuela for clarification. I counted spoons of coffee into the sock-like affair we used as a filter and held my peace.

"People don't realize," she went on, gesturing for the kettle. "You can't have a coalition with communists in it. They don't believe in sharing power. They live and breathe ideology. It's as simple-minded as religion, idols and all. Worse." She poured water into the *mate* gourd and offered it to me absently, forgetting that I didn't drink the vile stuff. "The same people that caused all the trouble are in the Frente," she said, lowering her voice to a whisper. "Terrorists, common murderers."

I thought of the bland-faced doctor-politician I'd seen on TV and the disheveled plumber I'd heard speak, and almost laughed.

"Rubén is caught up with them," Abuela said.

"With the Frente? Mom and Patricia are voting for them too." I took the kettle back and dribbled water into the coffee sock. "Rubén called Juan last night," I said. "I guess he's coming soon."

Abuela nodded. "He's gone and messed up his marriage. Always running around with women—Mariela has had enough."

I smiled, thinking how worried everyone had been about breaking the news of Rubén's divorce to Abuela. She already knew everything.

"You'll have a good time with Rubén," she said slyly, "but you watch out with the women, don't follow his example."

The way she was looking at me made me blush, as if she was privy to my current fixation on the woman I'd met in the rice fields—though any good times were all in my own head. "So who are you going to vote for?"

"Jorge Batlle."

"Like Elsa and Juan."

"Like anyone with any intelligence. He's from Uruguay's oldest, most distinguished political family—you have read about Batllismo, haven't you?"

I hadn't, but I nodded, trying to put a lid on the history lesson. It was too early.

Abuela was not to be discouraged, however. "It's the political doctrine that turned Uruguay into a modern, middle-class country," she said, as if she knew I was bluffing or had read the wrong things. "The brainchild of José Batlle y Ordóñez. Now *that* was a statesman worth his salt. When I was growing up, everyone called him Don Pepe. He defied the church, which was no easy task in those days. Introduced the vote for women, free schooling through university, no religion in the schools . . ."

I heated milk for my coffee and scrambled myself some eggs on the ancient stove while Abuela recited the brilliant statesman's deeds. In the first two decades of the twentieth century—and the first twenty minutes of my day—he abolished the death penalty, introduced the eight-hour work day and a leave of absence for pregnant women, prohibited child labor, supported workers' rights to form unions and strike, and started the state-owned banks and utilities companies, the national gas and oil company, and the railway that no longer existed. At home, I thought, we probably would have labeled him a communist. But then, we labeled anything that interfered with free markets communist. And Abuela had her own definitions. In this morning's version, it was the communists who had destroyed Batllismo and ruined the country.

Mom appeared just as I was finishing breakfast, putting an end to Abuela's morning monologue, and revealing the reason for the blue dress. They had planned an afternoon walk on the Rambla—the grand culmination of Mom's get-Abuela-out-of-the-house campaign—where they were going to stop at the La Cigale shop for ice cream with some of Mom's old school friends. Before I could make my escape, I'd been implicated.

It put a kink in my plan to watch the soccer game at one of the *boliches* I'd discovered, but Abuela actually seemed enthusiastic about the outing, at least for the first fifteen minutes of our walk. She placed a pair of large cat-eyed sunglasses over her normal glasses and joined the Sunday afternoon promenade on the Rambla, parading alongside us like an incognito movie star. She admired the new landscaping, and Mom, who thought it was an ecological debacle because it extended into the dunes, managed to keep her views to herself and mumble something accommodating. We were almost to the ice cream shop and were about to cross over the boulevard when Abuela stopped and announced that she wanted to turn back.

"But we're almost there," Mom pleaded. "We're meeting Lucía and Claudia at La Cigale."

"Why go to La Cigale without Keith?" Abuela said, mispronouncing Dad's name with a wistful tenderness that immediately silenced Mom. "Keith is the big La Cigale fan. And I have a freezer full of Conaprole at home—all Gabriel's favorite flavors," she added, turning to me for support.

I argued in favor of La Cigale, but it didn't help, and I ended up walking back to the house with Abuela while Mom went on to meet her friends. Abuela was right, the outings to La Cigale had been part of Dad's Christmas vacation decadence—Mom preferred the much cheaper Conaprole she'd eaten as a kid. And, it turned out, Abuela had stocked up on Mom's favorite flavors, *triple* and *vainilla,* not mine, but that small gesture of love was lost on Mom. She went back to the estancia, and I spent the rest of the week eating her favorite ice cream and enjoying the city of her childhood in a conscious, deliberate manner that, it occurred to me, Mom herself had never experienced. I scrutinized shop window displays, browsed at used book stores and newsstands, treated myself to meals of steak and veal and fresh gnocchi—all for less than the cost of a hamburger at home—and spent hours in a CD store listening to Uruguayan music I'd never known existed, *candombe* and *murga* and a style of rock that seemed to combine elements of both with the tango and *canto popular* Elsa and Mom liked.

I'd tried to tell Mom about the city I was seeing, but Montevideo was not really part of her repatriation plan. Indeed, she seemed incapable of appreciating the city for what it was, rather than raging at what it had lost. Now that I thought about it, this had been the background music to all of our visits when I was a kid—a litany of outrage about the *bichicomes* with their skeletal horses, the derelict neighborhoods, the proliferation of street stands and vendors, the desperate young men competing to wash windshields at every intersection, the men selling gum and pen sets on the buses, the slums springing up on the outskirts of the city, the ugly high-rises taking over the Rambla . . . all the woes of the third world in the idyllic middle-class city of her childhood.

I had my doubts whether the city of Mom's childhood had been as idyllic as she thought. But it did seem to me there were fewer beggars—and certainly fewer homeless people—on the streets of Montevideo in 1999 than in the first-world cities I knew. I saw a scattering of unfortunate individuals but they quickly became familiar, unlike the faceless plague of neglect I knew from downtown San Francisco and Oakland. Of course, there were slums I hadn't seen, just like there were slums in San Francisco and Oakland I had never seen—the *bichicomes* and their horses didn't live in Punta Carretas or Cordón, or even in Palermo or Barrio Sur or Centro. I did take a long walk around El Cerro, which Elsa claimed was a rat's nest of unemployment and crime.

The El Cerro I saw was a hodgepodge of old brick and not-so-old cinder-block houses, improvised shacks, and small shops clustered around the base and winding up the flanks of Montevideo's only hill. It looked poor, more decrepit than the other neighborhoods I'd seen, but not destitute, and certainly not, on a weekday afternoon, overtly criminal—kids playing on the streets, a few adults walking home from work or shopping, but otherwise quiet. According to my tourist brochure, it was a working-class neighborhood that had once housed laborers in the now-defunct meat refrigeration plants. There was a park at the top, with an old Spanish fort and a lighthouse, which was now a museum—closed for repairs—and a panoramic view of the city and the small Bay of Montevideo. I sat on the grass and gazed out over the little strip of beach at the base of the hill, to the bay full of turbid river water and the bluer ocean on the horizon. I tried to imagine the Portuguese spying El Cerro for the first time, a green bump on a featureless green horizon. The city had purportedly been named for that sighting, but I figured it was for lack of any other impressive feature. I thought about San Francisco, a beautiful city by all accounts. I'd always figured it was the place that made San Francisco beautiful—the spectacular hidden bay with its mystical fog and windswept headlands, its hills—a place that would have been even more beautiful without its city. I wasn't so sure about Montevideo. If it had ever been as beautiful as everyone claimed, I suspected it was a place that had been glorified by its buildings and streets and culture, rather than the other way around.

6

Though I knew Alejandra Silva probably hadn't given me a second thought since our meeting in Caruso's rice field, she had insinuated herself into the most banal of my thoughts for two weeks. Did she like Conaprole or La Cigale, *chivitos* at La Pasiva or hamburgers at the McDonald's, tango or Uruguayan rock, the new play at El Galpón, or the Star Wars movie at the multiplex cinema? Was she infected by election fever like the rest of the city, did she care whether Peñarol or Nacional won the soccer match on Sunday? Would she even remember that she had agreed to meet me and go birdwatching on this Thursday afternoon—had she even been serious about it to begin with?

She was out in the flooded field collecting samples when I approached. I leaned against the back of her car, watching her work and waiting for her to notice me, as nervous as if I were about to take the most important exam of my life. I'd counted down the past few days with all the superstitious import of Abuela reciting magic numbers, even warned Mom that I might catch a ride to Montevideo with a biologist who was working over at Caruso's—though, of course, I failed to mention that the biologist was a gorgeous twenty-something woman I had talked to for ten minutes and been obsessing about for two weeks. And I had no idea if she would give me a ride. This wasn't just another of the cute girls I'd gone kayaking or camping with in college. Not even the slick, thirty-year-old accountant I'd had an affair with at work. This was an accomplished, self-assured, scientist—though at the moment, standing up to her knees in muddy water and juggling her equipment and notebook, she looked like she could use some help. Just as I was about to call out an offer, she finished and started back to the car.

"You need one of those belts that carpenters use," I said by way of greeting.

"Not a bad idea." She set down her bag of sample jars and started untangling herself from the other equipment. "The first time I came out here, there were three of us. But I'm the only one left on the project now, and I haven't come up with a good system."

She had, at least, remembered our birding date, though whether or not she'd given the guide a second thought was unclear. For all I knew, she was married, maybe even had a kid, like Patricia. She'd borrowed a pair of binoculars from a colleague, and when I warned her about the sharp-edged reeds, she extracted a pair of long pants and a blouse from a knapsack and pulled them on over her shorts and tank top. I offered her my mosquito repellent—I'd finally given up on the citronella and resorted to the nasty chemical stuff in the environmentally unfriendly spray can—but she had brought her own. We left the car parked on the levee and set out across the fields.

It was the sort of October day that made me think of Indian summers back home, except this was spring kicking into early summer, not summer revisited. I'd driven out with Juan on Sunday and had been helping Mom run an irrigation line from the creek, birding in the marsh every afternoon, so I could identify most of what we saw now without checking the field guide. I pointed out the little yellow *Mistos* in the grass, and when we came to the creek, I stopped walking and motioned for her to listen to the burbling melodies coming from the brush.

"*Juan Chiviro*," I whispered, trying to track it down among the branches without making it fly. I'd seen it along here before, a frumpish little bird that acted like a vireo, but was bigger and cruder than the vireos I knew, its bill too thick, neck too fat. "There," I said, and raised the binoculars to look. It was perched at the top of a bush like a plump diva, bill parted and emitting these heavenly sounds. It reminded me of the soprano in the one opera I'd seen, an unattractive, overweight woman who opened her mouth to sing and turned into a glamourous, sensuous creature.

"Where?" Alejandra gave an impatient little stomp of her foot in the grass, and I bit back a laugh, surprised. I reminded her that she had to find it with her eyes first, and then I guided her to it from a dead snag in the tree.

"It's not as beautiful as it sounds," I said, worried that she'd be disappointed by its drab appearance. But once she found it, she watched in satisfied silence. When she lowered the binoculars, I showed her the entry in the field guide. She examined the picture and read the description, then looked at the bird again. All without comment.

We continued up the creek in silence, spotting the usual sparrows and one of the pretty blue tanagers. There was a *Monjita Blanca* flitting about the pasture, along with another species of *monjita* that looked like its dark sister, with black wings and tail—*Monjita Dominicana*, according to the field guide. Alejandra caught on right away that first you had to classify the bird, and that the bill and the size and shape and habits were all more important than the color of the plumage, which is the only thing most people notice. She paid more attention to the field guide than I, looked at the classifications and memorized the scientific names, which I never bothered with. But despite her scientist's training and my own unmethodical approach to ornithology—despite the fact that I was in foreign territory and had only just learned the names of most of the birds we saw— she followed my lead without question and was quite obviously impressed by my knowledge.

By the time we got to the marsh, we had stopped talking and were synchronized, as if we'd been birding together for years. She followed without seeming to follow, knew when to start walking, when to stop, when to talk or be quiet. We were nearing the reed bed, making our way through the tall grasses, when, with no more warning than the gasp of air beneath its wings, a small heron lifted into the air three feet in front of us. An elegant bird I'd never seen before, with hues of creamy yellow and pastel blue that gave an almost visceral pleasure as it winged off across the marsh. "Ohh," Alejandra breathed softly next to my shoulder, "oh what beauty," and I felt triumphant, as if the heron were a gift I'd bought her, a box of expensive chocolates or a bouquet of roses—though I had to look in the field guide before I could name it for her. *Chiflón.* Whistling Heron in English. Pretty common, it turns out, though I never did hear the call responsible for its name.

I tried to skirt the pair of *Chajás* so they wouldn't raise a ruckus and scare everyone off, but they started heehawing the way they always did when I approached, and Alejandra was as thrilled as I'd been the first time I saw them. The blackbirds that liked to perch on the tops of the reeds ignored the alarm anyway, and I pointed out the *Tordo Músico* and the bright yellow *Tordo Amarillo* and the dark Chestnut-capped Blackbird and three species of marshbird.

She didn't balk at the mud or reeds or mosquitoes as I led her through the reed bed, following the route I'd flagged. When we stepped out into the glade, no one startled or gave an alarm call. I didn't say anything, just scanned the pond and waited for her to take it in. The pair of *Espátula Rosada* was posed like a primeval pink monument in the water near the bank of the pond. Three species of ibis were feeding in the grass, including one I hadn't seen before—bigger and even more primitive-looking than the others, not as sleek, the feathers along its neck permanently ruffled like a lion's mane. And a couple of *Yabirú*, these huge storks that stood as tall as a fencepost and had bills almost the size of my forearm. A *Jacana* was striding across the water lilies on its giant spider feet, boldly decked out in rust-and-black plumage, pausing theatrically in mid-step like a pianist gathering momentum for the next chord. The pair of *Pollona Azul* and some coots were tucked into the murky vegetation on the far side of the pond. In the water, I spotted the red-faced *Pato Picaso* and a couple of the big, homely black ducks that were called *Pato Real* though the only thing conceivably "royal" about them was their size. They were all just going about their business, feeding in the water, floating or wading about, completely uninhibited by our presence. The male *Pato Fierro* was swimming around like a fat man doing the breast stroke, just barely staying afloat, its black face held aloft and its tail end dragging beneath the surface as if it weren't really designed for swimming. I pointed him out to Alejandra, who was breathlessly trying to look at everything at once.

"*Increíble*," she whispered. "I didn't even know this was here."

"It's like a place outside of time," I said. "Look at the *Yabirú*, that's gotta be another epoch." They were even stranger-looking than the spoonbills, with a long, black, goiteresque neck that was ringed at the shoulders by a bright red collar. "It's like dinosaur scenery," I said. "Everything growing out of water, and all these extravagant birds." She didn't respond, and when I glanced over she had such a pensive look on her face that I thought maybe she was with me in my prehistoric diorama, imagining a time when pterodactyls were winging across the sky and dinosaurs loomed above marshy entanglements to nibble at a canopy of tree-sized brush . . .

But Alejandra was in another dimension of space, not time. She bent over and reached through the grass to bring up a handful of muck. "I wonder what sorts of critters live in here," she said, watching the mud slither away through her fingers. "If they're different than what's in the rice." She looked up at me without really looking at me, considering her own question.

Bichos was what she called them, "bugs" or "critters," some sort of generic pet name for her microbes, but before I could ask her about it, she'd cleaned her hand on the grass and turned her attention back to the birds.

We stayed in the glade for another half hour, identifying all the birds and moving just enough to give the mosquitoes chase. When we started back through the reeds the light was beginning to fade, and I moved more quickly—until I heard the call of the elusive rail I'd been following the day we'd met. I'd heard it twice since then, always at this time in the evening. I stopped so abruptly that Alejandra bumped into me from behind. It called again, and I squatted down to peer through the reeds, but it was too far away and I couldn't see anything.

"You hear that?" I whispered. "Doesn't that sound like the most lost and lonely creature in the whole universe?" I took out my bird journal and made a note. I'd devoted two pages to it already, noting where and when I'd heard it, the call pattern, what it seemed to be doing—the saga of the mysterious rail. "I don't know what it is," I said apologetically. "I think it's some species of rail or crake, but I can't get a good look at the damn thing and I can't figure anything out from the call." I started to put the journal back into my knapsack, but Alejandra held out her hand.

"Can I see?" she said.

"Oh." I paused and glanced down at the notebook. I could feel myself blushing, but I let her slip it out of my hand. "It's just silly notes and a few sketches," I said. "Nothing scientific." I'd been writing down whatever came into my head—whimsical, anthropomorphic bird descriptions that I imagined a real scientist would find abhorrent.

She smiled and started paging through it.

"You're an artist," she said, looking up at me. "And a naturalist! What did you say you studied?"

"Geography."

"And the drawing?"

"I started doing it when I was a little kid, when my grandpa took me birding. He encouraged it, but he couldn't do it himself." I shrugged. "In school they said I should become an artist, and I took a couple of drawing classes in college. But I wasn't into it. I mean, art for art's sake, the whole creative scene. I just like drawing birds."

She waved a cloud of mosquitoes out of her face and examined my drawing of the *Yabirú*. "You're like those guys in the nineteenth century," she said. "Wandering around describing things, painting those beautiful pictures. Like that English guy who lived in Argentina. Guillermo Hudson."

"Not really." I didn't want to admit to my explorer fantasies, though my face was still burning, no doubt giving me away. "Those guys were describing everything for the first time, writing for posterity. They were trying to be accurate, complete. Whereas I'm just quacking away, writing whatever comes into my head. It's not natural history."

"Maybe not. But there's that same mix of careful observation and personal sensitivity. It's like doing science without scientific method—you don't even try to take the self out of your observations."

I retrieved my journal and continued through the reeds. The rail hadn't called again and with all our talking, we had surely scared it deeper into hiding.

"It's a kind of spirituality," Alejandra said, still musing as we came into the open. "They believed in God, you know, those first naturalists. Even Darwin."

"Well, I'm not at all 'spiritual.'" Whatever exactly that means, I thought, recalling Abuela's *esoterismo*.

"Maybe that's not the right word," she said. "It's a sort of reverence or . . . empathy. That's it. Like some sort of special connection to nature." She looked at me inquisitively, as if I were some curious foreign object she'd found washed up on the beach, and I felt my cheeks firing up again.

I shrugged. If she wanted to think that, it was fine with me, especially since she seemed to value it. Where I came from it didn't seem so special, but I guess that was just because I'd grown up with Grandpa Gordon and gone to college in Northern California where all the nature lovers congregated. For the moment, I wasn't particularly thrilled about my special connection to nature, as the sun had just dropped to some magical level that put the mosquitoes into high gear and even DEET wasn't enough to keep them at bay. I picked up the pace and didn't stop to look at anything until we were on dry and somewhat less mosquito-infested ground. I was trying to find a way to ask her for a ride back to Montevideo that didn't seem like an obvious come-on, but finally I just asked outright. She seemed a little surprised, but she readily agreed and drove me by the estancia house so I could pick up my things. Mom was busy planting her vegetable beds, so I just waved at her and stuffed my clothes into my duffle bag, glad that I didn't have to introduce her to Alejandra.

Sitting side by side in her car, the rapport that had emerged so easily while we were walking and birding suddenly evaporated. I became overly conscious of our silence and my knee next to her hand on the gear shift, of keeping it still, not moving closer, or away. At first, I told myself that the silence was special, that it was warm and intimate, filled with the afternoon's experience, charged with anticipation—but by the time we turned onto the highway, I was fretting that what we had was just your everyday garden variety of silence, the empty, indifferent space between two people who had nothing to do with each other. I worried that if I didn't fill it, if I couldn't keep her engaged and challenged, then she'd flit away, disinterested, like a bird attracted by an imitation mating call when it realizes it's been fooled. So I barged into that ambiguous space with a remark about the election and how enthusiastic everyone seemed compared to at home, where only half the population voted.

"Don't you *have* to vote? Here it's obligatory."

"I guess that's one way to get people engaged."

"You don't have to be engaged. You just have to go to the polls. You can put a blank slip in the box, if you want. Or vote Colorado because that's what your great-grandfather did, or whatever." She downshifted as we came onto a rough stretch of road. "What about you? Do you vote, then, if you don't have to?"

"Sure. We don't have to, but we're trained to, or at least I was. It's a knee-jerk civic responsibility. Like picking up your trash at the beach."

Alejandra laughed. "That's not a very good analogy in Uruguay—it means something like 2 percent of the population would vote!"

"Probably doesn't work at home either. I bet more people are conscientious about littering than about voting."

"I guess I'd still vote even if I didn't have to." The road had smoothed out, and she sped up and returned both hands to the steering wheel. "And I'm not even very political," she added. "Though everyone expects me to be."

"Really? Why's that?" I examined her profile openly now, a little brazenly, masking my insecurity. Her face, in the dim evening light, was momentarily stripped of poise, her bottom lip caught between her teeth in an unselfconscious expression of juvenile peevishness. "Why should a microbiologist be political?"

She released her lip and her expression shifted as she looked my way, defensive, almost suspicious. Our eyes met briefly, and I couldn't tell if she liked what she saw or if she was trying to decide whether to stop the car right there in the middle of nowhere and tell me to get out. Then she smiled, brilliantly, perfectly, and turned back to the road.

"My parents were Tupas," she said. "They were famous. Or infamous, depending."

I wanted to ask why again, why they were famous, and what Tupa meant, but I was completely disarmed by the smile. She seemed to delight in my foreigner's ignorance.

She asked me about California then, about San Francisco and the university I'd attended in the northern redwoods, and we filled the rest of the drive with chitchat. I learned that she lived with her aging grandfather in Pocitos, just a couple kilometers from Abuela, and that she spent long hours in her lab at the university—which was, as it turned out, near the Palacio Legislativo, nowhere near the law school—and that as a university employee she was required to spend the whole of next Sunday working at a polling place.

We were on the outskirts of the city before I got up the nerve to suggest that we get together over the weekend. This timidity was new to me, as foreign as the shops and signs we drove past, the landscape we'd traversed. I suppose it was because I'd never felt as invested before, never wanted a woman as much as I wanted this one—and because she seemed so intense and self-contained. I still wasn't sure if she was interested in me beyond my capacity as bird guide, and I figured there was probably a boyfriend in the picture somewhere. But though she was noncommittal about the weekend, when she dropped me off in front of Abuela's house, she did give me both her lab and her home phone numbers.

7

Despite Juan's grumbling about Rubén coming home, Abuela's portrait of her middle son as a worthless womanizer and *travieso*, and Elsa's conviction that he and Mom were tumbling backwards in their lives, their joy at seeing him was obvious and irrefutable. Abuela's dark house seemed to brighten in his presence, as if Rubén had instantly achieved what all Mom's repairs and yellow paint had failed to produce. Mom picked him up at the airport on the Saturday evening before election day, and he ushered us through a late dinner on pure good cheer and the euphoria of reunion. Abuela went up to bed and Juan and Elsa headed home without anyone arguing about politics, or the estancia, or, for that matter, asking about his plans. We'd never met, but he treated me as if I were a favorite nephew he'd known all his life.

"Nothing's changed," he said, laying a hand on my shoulder as we left Mom to finish clearing up and went into the foyer to retrieve his luggage. "Nothing and everything."

"When's the last time you were here?"

"Five years ago. But only for a few days. To vote."

"We painted the upstairs," I offered as we started up the stairs with our first load.

He laughed when he saw his old bedroom. We'd gone all out with the yellow in there and it was really bright. "What did Mamá say?"

"She wasn't exactly thrilled with the color."

"No doubt. But it's nice. You did a good job." He deposited the suitcase he was carrying in the middle of the room, and I followed suit.

"We used to spend Christmases here when I was little," I said. "Dad loves Montevideo."

"I came back when I could." He sounded irritated, and I realized he thought I was accusing him of neglect, which hadn't even occurred to me. "Brought the kids in '86. It wasn't safe before that."

"Safe?"

"I was a Tupa," he said. "Enemy of the state, such as it was. Persona non grata." He examined my face. "Didn't your mother tell you anything?"

I didn't want to say that she'd hardly ever talked about him.

"I should have brought the girls more to see Mamá." Rubén sighed. He glanced around the bright room as if he'd suddenly forgotten what he was doing there. "Your cousins. But then they were teenagers, with their own agendas. And I had a business up there, expenses, high-maintenance wife . . ." He shrugged, then, the good humor returning. "Had," he added with a grin, and we headed downstairs for another load.

Three huge suitcases and a small worn leather one, an equally worn guitar case, and a large cardboard carton: no one had mentioned it at dinner, but Rubén obviously had no plans of returning to Venezuela in the near future.

We piled the suitcases in the middle of the bedroom, except for the little leather one, which Rubén deposited carefully in the corner. I watched him give it an absentminded little pat, as if reassuring himself that it had arrived intact. Indeed, the leather was so worn and ancient it looked like it was ready to disintegrate.

"Mom had a suitcase just like that," I said. "It must have been in the attic for twenty years."

"Really. Papá gave us these suitcases. What does she keep in it?"

"No idea. She dug it out of the attic when she left Dad, but I thought she just wanted him to feel guilty that she was going off with this falling apart suitcase. I don't know that she kept anything in it. What's in yours?"

"Treasures. Books, old letters . . . bunch of junk." He left the suitcase unopened in the corner and started circling the bedroom like a dog marking territory. "A symptom of pathological nostalgia," he said, laughing. He opened the dusty wooden wardrobe, which seemed to be full of old coats and dresses. "I always thought it was an exile's obsession. Didn't expect Lili to have it." He left the wardrobe open and went to the window, pulled up the wooden blind, and pushed aside the lace curtain. The window faced the back garden and neighbor's house, but it was too dark to see much.

I didn't know Rubén had been in exile, which he seemed to consider a different status altogether than immigrant. "Mom was only eighteen when she left," I said, but, of course, Rubén knew this better than I did.

"She left for college in '68. I didn't leave until 1972—until I had to. A big difference, those four years." He had circled back to the cluster of suitcases. It was almost one in the morning and I thought he might want to sleep, or at least start unpacking, but he didn't seem inclined to do either. He was still in reconnoiter mode, and when we went down for the last box he stepped into the ship's prow room and looked around.

"You're sleeping in here? This was Papá's old office."

"We cleaned it out. Abuela didn't want us to throw anything away, but we got rid of the really obvious trash when she was asleep."

"There used to be a desk. And this bed was in Lili's room." He picked up a handful of the election fliers I'd accumulated in my city perambulations and started flipping through them.

"Blanco, Blanco, Colorado . . ." Rubén read off the party names. "You could have been a little more discriminating." He sat down and started laying the fliers out on the bed like a game of solitaire.

"I don't even know what's what," I said. "They're just lists of names."

"These are voting slips. Here we go, Frente Amplio—Partido Socialista. Asamblea Uruguay.

"Ahh . . . you actually put these in the ballot box?"

"Sure." Rubén explained that within the main parties there were a number of factions—what he called *lemas*—each with a different agenda and list of candidates. You voted for your party's presidential candidates, and within your party, for your *lema's* congressional candidates. In his version of solitaire, the four suits were the parties, including one small one I hadn't heard of, and the *lemas* were ranked according to some system of private preference.

"I take it you're voting Frente," I said.

"Of course."

"Abuela says they're terrorists and murderers. And communists and crooks. She seems like she's afraid of them."

Rubén grunted. "You wouldn't believe it, but she was an anarchist in her youth."

"No way. *Abuela*?" All I knew about anarchists was that they were off the political map on the left.

"Sure. Ask her about it sometime. But I'm afraid twenty years of propaganda have taken their toll on Mamá's powers of discrimination. Here you go, the worst of her fears." He handed me the list from the top of his Frente lineup. "Your fearsome revolutionaries gone soft and middle-aged. The Tupas joining the Frente was one thing. But backing Tabaré for president—*that's* hard to stomach."

"What's a Tupa?" I ventured. Clearly, I was supposed to know this. It was what Alejandra had called her parents. I looked at the flier. It was the one I'd been given at the rally, with a head-shot of the rotund philosopher plumber.

"*Nena,*" Rubén said, and I looked up to see Mom standing in the doorway. It was the family's pet name for her, which I always found startling, *la nena,* as if my middle-aged mother were forever and always the one and only little girl in their lives. "You should have educated your son."

She handed us each a glass of beer and tossed a fresh towel on Rubén's lap.

"I was wondering what 'Tupa' means," I said.

"Short for Tupamaro. An Uruguayan revolutionary group in the sixties and seventies. Now they're an official political entity, one of the *lemas* in the Frente Amplio coalition." She told me this in English, her tone uninflected, as if she were reciting from an outdated textbook.

"Really, Lili, you'd think—"

"Why should he know all that, Rubén? He's American."

Rubén sniggered. "Precisely. Precisely for that." He fished another slip out of his Frente lineup on the bed and handed it to her. "Gabriel has been collecting voting slips for us. Check this one out. Number twenty, third substitute."

Mom held the voting slip at arm's length to read it. "Yiyo Perez?" she said, laughing. "That weird guy Juan Luis hung out with in school?"

"Amazing, eh? He'll never be appointed, but still." He set the slip back in his Frente lineup and reached for the one in my hand. "Here, Lili. This one's for you."

Mom stared at the slip he was holding out and shook her head. "I'm voting Lista 90," she said quietly. "Tabaré's list."

"Tabaré is a jerk," Rubén said, sounding petulant. He tucked the Tupamaro slip back in its place on the bed.

"He's okay. A charming compromiser. More or less what we need, at this point."

It was the first time I'd heard Mom offer anything resembling an opinion on the election.

"What do you get," Rubén said, "if you take a teaspoon of

the best South American *yerba mate* and brew it in a liter of water like *yanqui* tea? Tabaré's Frente."

"They like him in the poor neighborhoods."

"For all the wrong reasons."

"You sound like Juan," Mom said, as if this were the worst insult she could hurl at him. "Tabaré grew up in La Teja. His father was a union activist in the oil refinery. He worked his way through school."

"Where was he in '71, eh, Lili? While the rest of us were on the street?"

"I don't know, Rubén. Probably working."

I looked from Rubén to Mom. "What happened in '71?"

"Ask your uncle. I'm going to bed."

"She wasn't here in '71," Rubén said, once she'd headed upstairs. "That was the Frente's first election. The Colorados had sold out to the *yanquis* and were infiltrated by fascists. Most of the powerful Blancos were even worse. For the first time, all the quibbling leftist factions joined forces, trying to keep the country from self-destructing. Communists, socialists, intellectuals from the university, labor unions, anarchists—they all came together to form a new, united party that could compete with the corrupted Colorados and Blancos. That was the Frente Amplio. And the Tupas called a truce and joined them."

"And?"

"In '71? Hell, we didn't have a chance." He downed the rest of his beer and set the empty glass on the bed stand. "Tomorrow, though, is another matter. I don't like Tabaré. But Lili's right. He woke up the working class, consolidated the Frente . . ." Rubén swept his solitaire game into a pile on the bed. "And now, kiddo, this old man's got to get some sleep or he'll miss all the excitement."

I'd just finished brushing my teeth and was getting ready to turn in myself, when Mom came padding down the stairs in her slippers and nightgown, as if she'd just remembered something and hopped out of bed to tell me. "I've got something you might want to read," she said, stopping me outside my room and handing me a large, thick paperback. "What Rubén thinks you should know."

The book looked brand new, but apparently it was something she'd bought years ago. *URUGUAY* was printed across the cover in big blue letters, and then the words *Nunca más* scrawled in red, like lipstick on a mirror. Never again.

"Thanks," I said, glancing up at Mom, who was watching me examine the book. She had a strange look on her face, almost as if she were afraid of me, or afraid of what I would say about the book.

"Rubén is right," she said. "There are things you should know." She looked worn and fragile, standing there in her nightgown, and I thought about how hard it seemed to be, this coming home. "I bought that when it first came out," she added. "But I could never bear to read it." She said goodnight again and went back upstairs, and I sat down on the edge of her childhood bed and started paging through the book. It was a thick tome, and I wondered if she'd brought it in her luggage from California. Or if it had been sitting around at Abuela's house the whole time.

Report on the violation of human rights (1972–1985). Published in 1989 by Servicio Paz y Justicia, Uruguay. When I was thirteen. I flipped through the pages, looking at the pictures, mostly grainy old black-and-white photos. Military trucks blocking the narrow streets of the Ciudad Vieja. The face of a nerdy-looking guy with glasses who the caption identified as a North American advisor to the Uruguayan police. A door covered with chicken wire, a machine gun looped over the handle, a photo of Che Guevara hanging in one corner. According to the captions, the North American advisor had been executed by the Tupamaros, and the door was the entrance to "The People's Prison," though it looked too provisional to be a prison.

There was a photo of the Uruguayan president walking out of the military base after making a pact with commanders of the armed forces in 1971. The front facade of the central university building festooned with banners denouncing imperialism and dictatorship in 1972. A panorama of a large forbidding-looking prison outside the city, a flat, empty landscape in the background. Police photos of three dumpy-looking middle-aged men identified as Communist party leaders. Interior view of a prison cell. The front of the central military hospital in Montevideo. A demonstration by Uruguayan exiles on the streets of Paris. Tanks blocking a street near the port in 1984.

The chapter titles glared at me in bold capitals. *EL PROCESO HISTORICO . . . LA PRÁCTICA DEL TERRORISMO DE ESTADO . . . DETENCIONES. TORTURAS. LA JUSTICIA MILITAR. LA PRISIÓN PROLONGADA. MUERTES.* Arrests, tortures, military justice, long-term prison, deaths. A photo of two women in their underwear standing with their hands bound behind them and black sacks over their heads. The one on the left is plump. The other is thin, but pregnant. A naked woman strapped face-down on a plank, next to what the caption said was a tank of water. A man with a black hood over his head, hung by his wrists from a wooden frame, sun in his face, grass under his dangling feet, a brick wall in the background. Another man is straddling a metal bar with his hands bound behind him. He is naked and all his weight is balanced on his balls. *El plantón, el submarino, la bandera, el caballete.* The photo captions gave the names of the torture, but not of the people. I started reading an italicized section that was an excerpt from an ex-prisoner's statement, and suddenly there were tears sliding down my cheeks and dripping onto the page, little round lenses of water and salt, sinking slowly into the thick paper. I flipped the page. I felt like a voyeur, crying someone else's tears, foreign tears. BEYOND THE PRISON. BREAKDOWN OF CIVILIAN

LIFE, EXILE AND INTERNATIONAL SOLIDARITY. I pressed the book closed and set it on the bedside table.

I knew, of course, that there'd been a dictatorship in Uruguay when I was born. People referred to it, but didn't talk about it. At least, not in my family. To me, it was just some vague phase of Uruguayan political history, not this . . . perversity. Not Hitleresque. Not Pinochet's Chile. Argentina's Dirty War. Not in little old Uruguay, which was so adamantly *not* Argentina. The bloody red lipstick scrawl glared up at me from the nightstand, promising bad dreams. Had Rubén read it? Elsa, Juan Luis? Abuela? If Mom hadn't even read it, I thought, then why should I? I got up and carried the book into the living room, where I squeezed it onto the bookshelf in the back corner, between the wall and something called *De Miedo en Miedo* by Armonía Somers, which seemed an appropriate place to stash it. *From Fear to Fear.*

It was past two in the morning, and there was no glimmer of light upstairs. I pulled open the front window blind and peered out at the deserted street. There was a twenty-four-hour moratorium on the sale of alcohol before the election, and the night was preternaturally quiet. Too quiet, too dark. Too late for TV, which produced only static. But I was wide awake.

I made my way to the kitchen, switching on all the lights as I went, brushing my hand along the wall, running a finger along the edge of the marble window ledge, palm across the polished wood of the dining room table, leaving my fingerprints on the glass of the antique cabinet with the good china no one ever used—soaking in the familiarity of Abuela's house. Her favorite *mate* gourd was sitting reassuringly on the kitchen counter next to her radio and two crinkled apples that had been there since we first arrived in Montevideo. I switched the radio on— more static. Mom had the refrigerator well-stocked with fresh vegetables and yogurt, sausages and cheese, a plastic envelope of

Conaprole milk in the pitcher. I poured myself a glass of milk, finding comfort in the pure white stream flowing into one of Abuela's ancient, slightly discolored glasses—but I didn't really want to drink it. I set the full glass and the pitcher back in the refrigerator, and, finally, went to bed, leaving all the lights on.

8

Mom's name wasn't on the voter list.

"You didn't have to make such a drama about it," Abuela said.

They had just come back from the polls, and I was still sitting at the table with my coffee and a bag of bakery *bizcochos*, trying to shake the hangover left by my nocturnal encounter with Mom's book.

"I didn't make a drama," Mom said, eyeing my breakfast setup disapprovingly.

"Mamá," Rubén said, joining me at the table. "All Lili did was make them accept her voter slip. That's what you're supposed to do. They put it aside to check later."

"I thought you took care of all that when we first got here," I said. I pushed the bag of pastries in Rubén's direction and instructed him to save the *margarita con membrillo* for Abuela.

"Of course I took care of it, I was *supposed* to be on the list. Haven't you two piggies ever heard of plates?" She left us at the table and went around the corner into the kitchen.

"Were *you* on the list?" I asked Rubén.

"Sure. But I voted in '89 and '94, and they only drop you if you miss two national elections in a row. It doesn't matter. She did the paperwork and she had her *credencial*—they'll count it."

But I knew it mattered to Mom, who'd see it as a harbinger of failure for her repatriation plan, even if her vote was, eventually, counted.

106

Abuela sat down with us and fished her *margarita* out of the bag. "Lili has never voted."

"Huh?" I said, startled. "Mom always voted." She and Dad voted in every primary and local election, even when there was no one good to vote for. It would have been sacrilege not to vote in our house. "At home," I added. That was, after all, the point. Home.

Mom set three small plates down in front of us. "I was too young to vote in '67."

"And gone in '71 and '89," Rubén murmured.

Mom glared at him. "You can't vote absentee in Uruguay," she told me. "I couldn't just fly down here for two days."

"She was always gone," Abuela said.

"Right, Mamá. And now I'm back, in case you haven't noticed. But at the moment I am heading to the estancia." She turned to me. "You want to come?"

"Not really. But if you wait until I finish breakfast, I'll help you pack the truck." What I wanted to do was call Alejandra. I had her phone numbers engraved in my memory, but I didn't want to seem too eager and had resolved to call her after the election, on Monday.

"And you, Rubén? You want to drive out to the estancia, check out your inheritance?"

"Now? No way. Don't you want to stay and see the election results? Who knows, we might win."

"I can see the election results in Lascano."

"Lascano?" Rubén chortled, and Mom turned and walked out of the room. "*Nena*—" he called after her, "*espera*. When are you coming back? I'll drive out there with you next time."

But she was headed to the back of the house, where she'd been storing the stuff she wanted for the estancia.

"Juan Luis says she's been working wonders out there," Rubén said.

"No way. He didn't say that."

"Sure he did. Why so surprised? You don't think your mother capable of working wonders?"

"I thought Juan didn't approve. All they ever do is argue."

"They always argued," Abuela said.

"It's how they talk to each other," Rubén said, winking at me. "Juan wouldn't be caught dead telling Lili he thought she was doing something admirable. *Ché*, Mamá, what do you say we drive out to Papá's estancia with Juan next week?"

"We'll see." Abuela pushed herself up from the table with her usual smug smile—though I was never sure what, exactly, she was being smug about—and left Rubén and I sitting there alone.

Rubén gave his potbelly a pat and shoved the rest of the *bizcochos* in my direction. "What about your father?" he said. "She left him in California?"

"They got divorced over a year ago. Did you ever meet him?"

He shook his head. "She got someone else?"

"Mom? No . . . I don't think so." A boyfriend? It sounded ludicrous to me, which wasn't fair—but it didn't seem to be part of Mom's agenda, having someone else.

"Me neither. Yet." Rubén clearly didn't think of this as a permanent state.

"Are you really going to stay here?"

He leaned back in his chair and opened his hands. "Here I am."

"But what are you going to *do*?" I was genuinely curious. The economy was supposedly dead, there were no jobs, businesses closed but didn't open—Uruguay was, according to its citizens, a sinking ship, and no one in his right mind would move there from anywhere, not even from Venezuela. But it was hard to get a serious answer out of Rubén.

"Find myself a rich woman?" he said, with a big grin.

That evening he took me to watch the election results at a little pizzeria north of downtown, in a part of the city I hadn't yet explored. Why we had to go to this particular pizzeria, I didn't know, but that was what he wanted to do. They were already serving beer, even though they were supposed to wait for the polls to close, and the TV in the corner was tuned to the election coverage—mostly scenes of poll workers taking voting slips out of ballot boxes and counting them, with interludes of talk and speculation. I was half expecting Alejandra to appear, but they seemed to like showing the outlying neighborhoods and small towns. Vázquez—5. Batlle—4. Lacalle—2. Michelini—1. It was sort of funny and quaint until nine o'clock, when they got serious and announced the first nationwide totals. The whole pizzeria fell silent, and Rubén, who had been paying more attention to the four women at the next table than the election coverage, suddenly had his eyes glued to the pie graph on the screen: Vázquez 39%, Batlle 31%, Lacalle 21%, and Michelini, for some party I hadn't heard about, with 8%.

"*TA-BA-RÉ! TA-BA-RÉ! TA-BA-RÉ!*" The chant erupted and spread briefly around the restaurant before subsiding into the buzz of a dozen individual conversations, assessments, and speculations.

"*Mirá vos*," Rubén said repeatedly, the words slipping softly between his half-parted lips as he stared at the TV, where the newscasters were babbling on about the significance of the numbers.

"So that means he's going to win?"

"Eh?" Rubén snapped out of his reverie and turned to look at me. "No, no, they just started counting. He needs over 50 percent. Which he won't get—but then, neither will anyone else!" And then he was rising from his chair, tossing money onto the table, and leading me onto the street.

It was a quiet, mostly residential side street, but people were spilling out of doors, all moving in the same direction. "There'll be a *balotaje*," Rubén explained as we joined the stream. "A run-off election between Tabaré and Batlle."

A horse-drawn cart came clattering up alongside us, and I looked up to see the driver with a huge grin on his face, a small boy between his knees and his skinny horse with a Frente flag tied around its neck. We turned onto the upper end of Bulevar Artigas, which was now transformed into a boisterous river of humanity. There was an occasional car or motorcycle floating along in its midst, but mostly it was just people, walking or dancing, singing, drumming, celebrating, and speculating.

"Forty percent," Rubén said as we moved with the current. "That's what Tabaré needs tonight if he's going to have a chance in the *balotaje*. There's a rumor he's going to speak," he added, gesturing up the street.

"I thought you didn't like him."

"I don't. But it's not really about Tabaré. This is about the Frente!" He started clapping out a *candombe* rhythm for a stout middle-aged lady who was dancing her way down the street, wrapped in a Frente flag. The woman smiled, and Rubén danced alongside her for a few steps, murmuring something in her ear that made her laugh, before he fell back in step with me.

The river was gathering mass and energy, growing broader and slower as more people streamed in from the side streets— grandfathers with children perched on their shoulders, frumpy housewives and well-heeled ladies, teenagers and university students . . . and my slightly inebriated uncle, who was like a leaf blown this way and that by gusts of euphoria, one minute hopeful, the next resigned to defeat.

"We won't stand a chance," he said.

"You think? But it looks like half the city is out here celebrating."

"The Blancos will gang up with the Colorados," he said. "They'll salvage their two-party monopoly, even if the Frente wins the popular vote. That's why they passed this *balotaje* amendment with the 50 percent requirement a few years ago."

"I thought the Blancos and Colorados hated each other."

"They do," Rubén said, slapping me on the shoulder. "And that's our best hope. But they probably hate the Frente more."

"Abuela certainly does. She's always complaining about how they destroyed Batllismo."

"Ah, Mamá." Rubén sighed. "The Colorados have revived all the old rhetoric against the left, and she believes it all. They blame the Tupas—and by association, the Frente—for the dictatorship, drumming up fears of a communist takeover and feeding off people's terror of the dictatorship at the same time. Totally twisted."

I thought of Mom's book, unread and out of sight, but stalking me like a nightmare threatening to surface in daylight hours. "But the dictatorship's been over for a decade," I said.

"It's never over. It hovers over us like an uncertain weather forecast. Changed the way people think. Or don't think. Look at Mamá. Her beloved Batllismo was rotten and stinking long before anyone dreamed up the Frente. It was doomed from the beginning."

"Really? It sounds pretty enlightened. I mean, from what I've read—not just Abuela's version."

"So does your American Revolution. But you still ended up with slavery and a civil war." The river of humanity was closing in around us, thickening into a crowd and beginning to impede its own flow, the Frente's campaign song blasting from loudspeakers somewhere in the near distance. A man whose face was painted in swaths of red, blue, and white pushed past us, weaving his way through the crowd, and Rubén called after him to ask where Tabaré was going to speak.

"Bulevar Artigas!" the man shouted over his shoulder—not particularly helpful, since we were already on Bulevar Artigas. But we figured the crowd must know where it was going, so we stayed in the stream.

"The problem with Batlle," Rubén said, "was that he never managed to redistribute the land. And Uruguay is all about land." He grinned. "In that, at least, Lili and Juan are both on the mark."

"I thought that was Artigas's founding paradigm—'A ranch for every family.'"

"That paradigm went into exile with him in the backwoods of Paraguay. What have you been reading anyway?"

"Those old journals in Abuelo's office. *Cuadernos de Marcha*, *Enciclopedia uruguaya* . . ."

"That thing we used to get in installments with the newspaper? There's an education! And *Marcha*! I'm surprised Mamá saved them." Rubén laughed, keeping a grip on my shoulder and talking alongside my ear as the crowd pressed us into each other and the noise level escalated. "Her Batllismo may sound enlightened, but Batlle sold his soul to the *estancieros* to get it to work. As long as they agreed to pay high taxes on their exports, he promised to leave their huge land holdings alone and let them exploit their workers however they wanted. It brought in enough to build up the state and provide everyone with free education and health care. But the whole thing was dependent on the international market for beef and wool. As long as Europe and the US conducted their wars in cold places, it worked. But that all broke down when the Americans gave up on Korea. Lili, Juan, and I grew up in a deflating balloon of prosperity. The Colorados limited imports and modernized the national industries, trying to make us self-sufficient, keep the imperialists at bay. But the state just got more bloated, bankrupt, and corrupt, and by the time we were teenagers, even a supposedly middle-class salary was hardly enough to buy meat and bread—We're not getting anywhere here, are we? Can you see anything up ahead?"

We'd come to a near halt, and though I was slightly taller than average, the crowd was too dense to see more than a few feet in front of us. I pointed out a scrawny tree in the strip of neglected industrial landscaping along the street, and we managed to cut through the crowd to it. With a boost from Rubén, I could shimmy up and pull myself into the lower branches. I wedged a foot into the tree fork, wrapped an arm around the narrow trunk, and leaned out over the street. A truck was marooned in the crowd just ahead of us, children spilling out the windows of its cab and adults in lawn chairs on the flatbed. They appeared to be having a tailgate party, roasting sausages on a small barbecue and passing a bottle of wine and loaf of bread. Two blocks up, I could see an intersection where our human river converged with another and spilled out into a block-long vacant lot.

"You see any moving cars?" Rubén called up. "A stage?"

"No. Just the crowd." *La muchedumbre*. The word rolled out, weighted with import, a bigger, better word than "crowd," one of those words that sounds like what it is.

"How many?"

"No idea. More than I've ever seen in one place." I clung to the tree and hung out over the crowd, unsure what it was I was really seeing. The river was become a sea, churning with fluttering Frente flags and flickering with its own elusive light, like surf full of phosphorescent algae. I thought about Mom, when she'd announced she was moving back here, talking about Uruguay like it was some neat little self-contained toy that you could take apart and reassemble at will. And about the speech I'd heard at the Frente rally, all the nice rhetoric about social equality and an economy for the people, productive and sustainable. Heading into the twenty-first century, it all sounded too nice and deeply improbable. And yet . . . and yet . . . here below me was a sea of ecstatic humanity that included my own ambivalently ecstatic uncle.

I eased myself down through the branches and dropped to the ground, stumbling in the dust next to Rubén.

"I'll bet there are a half-million *Frente Amplistas* on the street tonight!" he said, catching my arm to steady me. "Someone said there's a big crowd out on El Cerro, too. But if you think this is a lot of people, you should have seen it in '71. The plaza in front of the Palacio Legislativo and all the surrounding streets for kilometers were so packed with people you couldn't move."

We could hardly move now as we squeezed back into the crowd, which was crawling toward the intersection an inch at a time.

"People took things more seriously back then, Juan's right about that much. There was a sense of do or die. We had this lethargic old cow of a country, the fascists closing in, selling it off limb by limb to the North American slaughterhouses. We didn't stand a chance, but that night, for a few hours, we thought we could see the light, *la pucha*, all the leaders of the left, and it seemed like half the city was out on the streets with us!" He laughed. "Problem was, that was all of us. *Everyone* who voted Frente was on the streets then, everyone was an activist."

"*TA-BA-RÉ! TA-BA-RÉ!*" The crowd around us took up the chant, and the kids in the front of the truck started pounding out the rhythm on the horn. "*Y ya lo ve, y ya lo ve, el presidente es Tabaré . . .*"

"What the hell," Rubén said, clapping along. "People are just happy. By god, we've got the largest share of the popular vote, a major stake in the legislature! We breached the two-party stranglehold, what we tried to do thirty years ago. People died for this. Rotted in prison. They've got a right to celebrate."

The chapter titles from the lipstick book came parading through my mind—*LA PRÁCTICA DEL TERRORISMO DE ESTADO, LA PRISIÓN PROLONGADA, MUERTES. . . .* But Rubén was smiling and cheerful, waving at the people on the flatbed.

"Come on," he said, tugging on my arm. "Who cares about Tabaré. I know better places to celebrate."

We made our way slowly out of the thick of the crowd, and Rubén led me zigzagging back through the side streets. I'd gotten disoriented and wasn't quite sure where we were, but we ended up on a street where the buses were still running and caught one that headed back to Punta Carretas. Rubén's story about the '71 election seemed to have bumped him back into the Montevideo of his youth, and he kept leaning past me to peer out the window and pass commentary on various obscure city landmarks, as if he had a personal relationship with every corner. We got off the bus in front of El Shopping and crossed the street to a dark little *boliche* that was obviously closed.

Rubén knocked on the door anyway. "I guess they decided to go out," he said, sounding forlorn. He turned away and stared across the street. El Shopping was lit up like a Disneyland castle, though it was also closed. "You been in there?"

"Yeah. With Elsa. It's a bit over the top, but she likes it. She said it used to be a prison."

"Right." We crossed the street and walked past the main entrance in the front wall to the corner. "When I was a little kid, this was just your typical middle-class neighborhood. No one thought much about the prison in the middle. It was part of Uruguay's vanguard penal system, a place to educate and reform criminals. But in the sixties they started throwing Tupas in there with the criminals, and educate turned into *re*educate. By the early seventies, the penal system had gone to hell and they were throwing all sorts of upstanding citizens in there."

The images from the lipstick book had finally cut loose and were now reeling through my head, *el plantón, el submarino, la bandera* . . .

"There were riots in '86," Rubén went on as we rounded the corner, "and then they emptied the place out. Set all the Tupas, citizens, and misfits free." He emitted a derisive snort. "A few years ago, just to make sure no one gets the wrong idea with all those old leftists on the loose, they turned it into a monument to consumerism. Obvious solution. The ultimate neoliberal victory."

TORTURAS, MUERTES, DESAPARICIONES . . .

I eyed Rubén. "Have *you* ever been in there?"

"Nope. Always managed to avoid the place. Then and now."

We were walking along the side wall now, heading down toward the Rambla. "Mom gave me this book," I said. "*Nunca más.*"

Rubén stopped walking and turned to face me. "Lili gave you that? When?"

"Last night. After you went to bed." I was already sorry I'd mentioned it. I didn't want to talk about the lipstick book. But neither, it seemed, did Rubén.

"See that house?" He indicated a modest one-story house across the street. "It's the site of one of the greatest prison escapes ever. In 1971, a hundred Tupas dug a tunnel under the street with spoons and exited though a hole in the living room floor." I looked at the house, but there was nothing to see. It looked like your typical 1920s Montevideo house, like all the others on the block—lived-in, but momentarily dark, as if everyone were either asleep or out partying somewhere else. "The Tupas held the couple who lives there hostage while over a hundred prisoners got through the hole, changed clothes and scattered around the city. Started in the middle of the afternoon and took until the next morning—and when the couple called the prison to report it, the *milicos* said it was impossible because the prisoners were still asleep in their cells. They didn't have a clue, until they found out that the sleeping prisoners were wads of old clothes stuffed under the blankets. Hard to say if the Tupas were brilliant or the *milicos* were just stupid, but it made the Guinness World Records."

"Yeah, right." I thought for sure he was exaggerating.

"It did! Biggest prison escape of all time! Uruguay's one claim to fame, next to winning the World Cup in 1950."

La bandera, el caballete, el planton—I forced the book out of my head. I hadn't even read the damn thing, but it made me feel like I had some sort of undiagnosed astigmatism, a dissonance of perception that was only compounded by Rubén's gleefully ironic nostalgia.

We ended up on the Rambla, taking the scenic route back to Abuela's, as if that had been our intention all along. There were still a lot of people out on the Rambla, celebrants from both Colorado and Frente camps cruising the boulevard and strolling along the promenade in small groups, all apparently convinced they would win the *balotaje*. It was pleasant, walking along with the city on one side, the sea on the other, the rumble of waves obscuring the noise from the boulevard.

"*En la noche fría . . .*," Rubén sang, opening his arms to the wind. "*Se ha perdido aquello, se extravió su alma, por el vendaval . . .*" The words were melancholy and wistful, something about a soul getting lost in a cold night gale. But there was no hint of irony or bitterness in Rubén's voice now, just an unadulterated tenor longing that turned heads as we passed and reminded me of the stories Mom used to tell of her Montevideo childhood. "*Tanta hermosura, que alegró las tardes, que encendió las luces, de nuestra ciudad . . .*"

It was, in fact, a pleasantly mild spring night, and the wind was uncharacteristically gentle. As we rounded the point and followed the long pale curve of the Pocitos beach, Rubén kept up a running medley of old songs, interrupting himself now and then to lament the loss of some eccentric old house, or point out a lonely survivor wedged between the high-rises on the other side of the Rambla. The most eccentric of the survivors had the prow of a ship sticking out from its facade and a winged goddess as galleon figure. She'd lost her head, but at least they hadn't torn the building down yet.

"*Naciste en Montevideo, junto a un río como mar, no busques lugar más bello, porque no lo encontrará . . .*" You were born in Montevideo, by a river like a sea, don't look for a prettier place, because you'll never find it.

Prettier places I knew in plenty, but strolling along the Rambla in the dreamy light of a half moon, with the beach trash invisible in the penumbra and the wall of high-rise apartments blending into the night sky, it wasn't hard to envision this glorious city of the past—which, from the smiles my singing uncle drew, seemed to live on in the mind's eye of some good measure of the population. I thought of Alejandra, wondered if she was also outside with this same breeze in her face, this same moon overhead, this mythical city in her mind's eye.

"*Casuales casualidades, me llevaron a nacer, en un lugar escondido, tan chatito y tan perdido, que en el mapa no se ve—* What do you think, kiddo," Rubén said, breaking off his song, which was about being born in a place that was so flat and lost that it couldn't be seen on the map. "You like Montevideo, you want to stay?"

"Too flat."

He laughed and sang another snatch of the song. "*No tengo rumbo o destino, no tengo mucho que hacer . . .*" I have no direction and no destiny, I haven't much to do . . .

"So what *are* you going to do here?" I asked him, the song bringing me back to the question he'd sidestepped that morning.

"I don't know. Maybe I'll go help your mother grow potatoes. Or whatever it is she's growing. What is she growing?"

"Everything. She's trying things out. Tomatoes, peppers, herbs . . ."

"Maybe I'll plant some potatoes. Or squash. Something practical. Maybe I'll get me a milk cow, make cheese."

"Juan Luis wants to plant rice."

"So I hear. I'll help him too. Juan likes to think big. And modern. No little gardens for our brother." Rubén shifted his posture and pronounced, in a perfect imitation of Juan, "Farming is serious business."

I smiled, but I couldn't imagine Rubén living out at the estancia, and I felt vaguely frustrated that he didn't have a real answer for me.

9

On Monday afternoon, I sat with the phone in the living room, punching the dial button and starting through the numbers, then cutting it off before I finished, planning what I would say if she answered, what I would say if her grandfather answered, what message I would leave if an answering machine answered, my heart thumping away as though I was about to leap out of an airplane, and it was only Abuela walking past and me feeling ridiculous sitting there playing with the phone that made me complete the act of dialing Alejandra's number. And then we had the briefest and most mundane of conversations. No, thank you, she was too busy to go to dinner tonight or tomorrow or Wednesday, but she was going out to Caruso's on Thursday, and yes she'd give me a ride, she could use some help collecting samples and she'd love to go birding again, *muy bien y chau*. I hung up the phone wondering if the no meant no or the yes meant yes, over-interpreting every nuance of our brief conversation, but whatever the case, she was at Abuela's door at eleven o'clock on Thursday morning, as promised.

She'd told me there was plenty of room in her car, so I'd packed up a couple cartons with stuff Mom had requested from Abuela's garage and stacked them at the ready in the foyer. I hadn't planned to tarry or invite her in, but I noticed Rubén standing in the entryway to the dining room watching us, and it would have been rude not to introduce them.

He repeated her name softly and stepped into the foyer, staring as if he were about to shower her with *piropos*, lingering too long in his greeting, all of which annoyed me more than it should have. And then he wanted to chat. "So, what are you doing out at the estancia?" he asked, somehow making the simple question sound intimate, as if he really cared, his voice simultaneously paternal and seductive, his gaze taking her in.

I watched her respond—a subtle shift in posture to reveal the tiny waist and curve of breast beneath her sweater, a hand flitting up to brush back a lock of hair, a hint of a smile—and felt a wave, a rising tsunami, of jealousy. It wasn't something I had much experience of, jealousy, but I recognized it immediately, a turbulent flood of anger, resentment, and humiliation—and felt immediately foolish.

Alejandra answered Rubén's questions, briefly and matter-of-factly, and then he helped me carry the cartons out to the car and saw me off with an amiable wink that brought another blush to my face. I decided I'd made a tsunami out of a ripple—jealous of my compulsively flirtatious uncle who was almost fifty, for Christ's sake. And with a woman I had yet to touch.

We drove through the city and I tried to make conversation, recounting my foray through the post-election festivities with Rubén.

"I went home after my poll closed," she said. "Watched it all on TV with my grandfather."

"And who did you vote for?" I ventured.

"Frente. Tabaré's list."

"That's who my mother voted for," I said. "But Rubén voted for the Tupamaro one."

"*Puf.* They're so stuck in the past they can't see their own noses. Does he live abroad too? He's got a weird accent."

"Venezuela," I said, glad, despite myself, that she disdained his voting choice—though I did remember her saying that her parents were also Tupamaros.

"And he came back to vote?"

"That's the official line. But it looks like he's going to stay."

"Really?" she said, glancing at me. "Like your mother? At the estancia?"

"I don't think so. He just lost his business in Venezuela. And his wife. Doesn't know what he's going to do."

"Ah." That was all she said, putting an end to the conversation and leaving me searching for new themes. There was a leather satchel with her *mate* and thermos on the floor next to my seat, and I offered to serve it for her.

"You drink *mate*?"

"No. But I can prepare it for you."

I did it all wrong of course, pouring the water in too fast and moving the straw when I shouldn't have, but she didn't seem to mind, just laughed at me, a low-pitched sort of giggle that I didn't at all mind having directed my way as I passed her the gourd.

If I was going to help her collect samples, I figured I should know something about her research, so I asked about her project in the rice paddies. That got her talking again.

"We're looking for nitrogen-fixers," she said. "Bugs that can convert the nitrogen gas in air into one of the two forms of nitrogen plants can use. Basically, we're looking to build a microbial fertilizer factory right there in the mud, in situ. That's the short version, anyway. The one we told Caruso."

"So you can add these 'bugs' to the rice paddy instead of chemical fertilizer? Is that the idea?" I'd figured out that *bicho* was her pet name for any sort of microbe. And that when she switched to English, which she did now and then in her explanation, she called them bugs.

"Not exactly. A factory is a complex thing. And in this case, it's a living factory. A microbial community, to be more precise, not just one bug. But that gets you into the long version." She held the *mate* out for me to refill, and I slipped it out of her hand

and added more water—taking care, this time, not to flood the *yerba*—and handed it back. I watched her face, delighting in the intimacy of this small domestic operation, waiting for a complicit glance as our hands touched. But she kept her eyes on the road and left me to admire the long curve of her dark lashes in profile, the sweet pucker of her lips on the *mate* straw—I turned away and looked out the window.

We were out of the city now, on the uneventful stretch of highway between Montevideo and Rocha. "So let's have the long version," I said.

She shot me a look, her face a caricature of skepticism.

"It's a long drive," I said.

She laughed then, and as she started into what promised to be an extended monologue, I knew I'd found the right theme.

"Say we find a nitrate-producing microbe that thrives in the rice paddies—that's the form of nitrogen most plants need, nitrate. It might seem straightforward enough to grow this bug in cultures in the lab and then dump the cultures back into the fields, instead of adding a bunch of expensive, useless, polluting fertilizer. But the chances are, we won't be able to grow our microbe in culture. And even if we can, and we dump it back into the fields, it's questionable that it will thrive in greater numbers or produce more nitrate than it would have if we hadn't done anything. And even if it does thrive and starts producing nitrate like crazy, chances are there are other bugs that will snatch up the nitrate and convert it back to nitrite, and still others that will turn the nitrite into nitrogen—neither of which do the rice any good. That's actually what happens when the growers use nitrate fertilizer. Very little of that nitrate gets to the plants. That's been proven, but the growers still waste their money on nitrate fertilizers. They think they're feeding their crop, but they're just feeding the microbes. It's the bugs who have the last word. If you want to regulate nutrients in a rice paddy, you've got to pay attention to them, and not just one species or even one group—you have to manage the whole community, regulate the ecology."

"How do you do that?" She'd paused, and I wanted her to know I was listening, that I was interested.

"With great difficulty. You can try to regulate the amount of oxygen in the water, or the acidity, or the dry periods between crops, or the decay of organic matter, the rice straw after harvest. It depends on the microbes you want to encourage. Timing is crucial. You want certain communities to take over at certain times of year, and others to recede."

"And these jars of mud you're collecting?"

"Oh, they're full of little surprises! I'm trying to culture some of them in the lab. And I've got colleagues in Germany analyzing my extracts with the new genetic methods. There aren't many studies on the microbial makeup of rice paddies— none of them in this part of the world, and none with the new methods. There could be hundreds of species in there that we know nothing about, with as many different tasks and niches!"

The only bacteria I'd ever seen were a bunch of little splotches on a microscope slide in my high school biology class. But to hear Alejandra talk, they were as beautiful as a flock of Roseate Spoonbills on the wing in the setting sun, as varied as the entire plant and animal kingdoms. She told me about bugs that consumed oxygen and needed light, and others who ate carbohydrates from rotting plants and turned out sulfur, and still others who lived off the sulfur. About bugs that lived deep in the mud where there was no oxygen and released methane, and others nearer the surface who imbibed the methane as it bubbled upward. . . .

"In the microbial world," Alejandra said, "your waste is someone else's food, and your food is someone else's waste. You have these cycles like cogged wheels in the layers of mud and water—the cycles in the mud geared with ones in the muddy water, and then those with the clear water, and those with the air—like the way a city is linked to a state which is linked to a country which is linked to a world."

We rolled through mile after mile of Uruguayan grassland while Alejandra described how microbes could derive energy from the chemical bonds in so many different minerals and gases, her hands dancing up from the wheel to punctuate a sentence, her eyes flashing my way to make sure I was following her. As she went on about her wondrous microbial worlds, I became acutely aware of my own hands lying on my thighs, of the conscious effort it took to keep them from floating up of their own accord and losing themselves in her hair and slipping down the side of her bare neck. . . . It was almost a relief when we stopped to pick up sandwiches at the *fiambrería* in Rocha, and I had the mundane task of eating a sandwich and drinking Coke to keep my hands busy.

We stopped by the estancia just long enough for me to dash in and get my boots and birding gear, and then drove straight out to Caruso's fields, leaving Mom's stuff in the car to unload later. Collecting samples turned out to be more complicated than just filling the jars, and I wondered how she'd managed it with just two hands. She had to measure the oxygen and pH level at each depth in the water and mud where she took her samples because, she explained, different types of bacteria liked different levels of oxygen and different acidities. She handed me a clipboard with a chart on it and showed me where to write down the numbers as she called them out. Other than that, my job was to hold things.

"You wouldn't believe," she said as we stepped into the water, "but there are at least four different ecosystems in these twenty centimeters of water and mud."

Oxygen sensor, pH meter, sample jars . . . pH: 7.6, 6.7 . . . O_2: 10.2 . . . 5.5 . . . Surface, mid-depth, bottom . . . It was hard to imagine that all the fascinating stories Alejandra had been regaling me with came from such repetitious and tedious work. We fell into a companionable exchange of numbers and simple directions, starting a few feet from the edge of the field and moving out into its middle, sampling every fifteen yards or so, wading back to the levy to leave off the full sample jars and retrieve the empty ones. It was a gorgeous day, not yet windy, warm but not hot, and I found myself in a state of absolute contentment, following her directions and watching her capable, limber movements as she operated the oxygen probe or folded at the waist and submerged her arm in the water to retrieve a sample.

We had just finished the first set of measurements, and I was scanning the rice fields for shorebirds while Alejandra stashed the jars in the ice chest, when Manuel Caruso's truck pulled up.

"Señorita Alejandra!" he called as he climbed down. "And the Quiroga boy. Gabriel." He had Santiago with him, the guy who'd shown me the *Carpinchos*, though he seemed almost like a different person without his horse. Caruso introduced him, and then turned to Alejandra. "Are you going to tell me what's brewing in my rice?"

"Not yet." She smiled at him. "Science is slow. We won't have results to speak of for months yet." She turned the conversation around and started asking him for details about the fields we were working in—when they were treated with fertilizer, what kind, if he would be adding more. . . .

Santiago was standing a little apart sucking on *mate*, and I joined him, raising the binoculars to watch a little band of ducks fly in and splash down in the canal. I'd seen them before, dabbling for bugs in the canals, one of the first ducks I'd identified—a plain brown species of teal that was stunningly beautiful in flight, the wings a shimmering blue-green, set off by a bright white patch on the inner feathers.

"Those are *Patos Brasileros*," Santiago said next to me.

I turned to him. "They seem to be very common around here. You want to look?" I held out the binoculars.

He handed me his *mate* and thermos and slipped the binocular strap over his head. He didn't really know how to use them, so I explained how to locate the birds and focus.

Caruso finished answering Alejandra's questions and stepped over to say goodbye. "You like to hunt ducks?" he asked me. "Like your grandfather?"

"No . . ." I said, though I'd never tried it. "I just like to study them. All kinds of birds, not just ducks." I don't know why I said that, *que me gusta estudiarlos*, but somehow saying I just liked to watch them felt funny in Spanish, like claiming I *only* liked to "observe" women. I gestured in the direction of the reed bed. "Over in the bog. There are a lot of species I've never seen."

"That's right," he said, nodding. "You've still got a big chunk of bad land over there. That could make a fine paddy if you drained it, virgin soil. I told Juan that eons ago—but it would take a big investment. This is where the most birds are though, right here in the rice. We had a hunting tour group come here all the way from France. They paid big money to visit the estancia, said they'd never seen anything like it. Those guys knew what they were doing, knew the names of all the ducks. They were big conservationists too, careful not to shoot too many. Last year, we let a British journalist up here to film a documentary—but she made it look like the birds were disappearing and it was all the rice growers' fault. That's just an outright lie. The truth is there are *more* birds since we started planting rice than ever before. Isn't that right, Santiago?"

Santiago appeared to be touring the estancia through the binoculars, scanning all the fields. "There are a lot of birds," he said. He returned the binoculars and I handed back his *mate* and thermos.

"You want to study birds," Caruso told me, "this is the place. The rice is full of them. Come over any time."

He'd taken me seriously, and I didn't set him straight, that I looked at birds for the sheer joy of looking at birds. Nor did I let on that my presence in his rice field at that moment had less to do with the explicit pursuit of scientific knowledge than it did with my inexplicit pursuit of the scientist.

"Is that right?" I asked Alejandra as the truck backed away down the levee. "That there are more birds in the rice than in the marsh?"

"Is that what he meant? More than in the marsh? Or more than in the pastures, before he started growing rice?"

"Oh. Well that's a big difference." I couldn't believe there were more birds in the rice than in the marsh. Unless you just counted ibis. There were definitely a lot of those. As we sampled the other field and the sun got lower, huge flocks flew overhead, hundreds and hundreds of them, landing in the paddies to feed.

"Maybe," Alejandra said as we waded back with the last set of samples, "I should be comparing them."

"Comparing what?"

"Microbial communities. In the rice and marsh. They can change so swiftly . . ." She paused in the middle of the field and stared at me, or through me, her eyes unfocused, as if she was thinking about something that had nothing to do with what she was looking at. "I wonder if I could get samples out there. From the marsh."

My parents had both studied sciences, and I thought of them as scientists. They knew a lot of clean, unambiguous facts about chemistry and biology, and Mom liked to teach her students to think the way she did, in logical chains of ifs, ands, buts, and maybes. But neither of them had ever done research like this, where they tried to find out something that you couldn't look up in a book or on the Internet—something you couldn't even deduce from what was already known. Neither of them was a scientist like this, trying to answer questions that no one else had asked.

"We'd need more jars," I said. We climbed out of the field and placed our full sample jars in the ice chest.

"There are extras in the trunk. But do you think it would be okay? Shouldn't I get permission? From your mother, or your uncle?"

"What, to take a couple jars of mud from the marsh?" I laughed. "I guarantee you they won't care."

So we ended up going microbe hunting instead of birding. I loaded up my knapsack with the equipment and empty jars, and we left the car where it was and cut across the fields to the creek, so we could hike in on my marked route. She chose one spot in the reeds and one in the glade, in the densest part of the bog, on the other side of the little pond. It was easy enough to sample in the reeds, but we couldn't get through the brush around the pond, so we had to wade around its edge. This time, Alejandra led the way. The water was less than a foot deep, but the mud at the bottom was soft and uncertain, and we hadn't gone more than a few yards when she let out a panicked cry.

"I can't get my foot out! Some kind of suck hole, keeps pulling me down."

I was just a few feet behind her, but I couldn't move quickly—I had to hold on to the branches and feel for purchase with each step—and she had sunk up to her thigh by the time I got close enough to give her a hand. It felt like pulling someone out of a vat of wet rubber cement, but finally she inched upward enough to grab a tree branch with her free hand, and with me still pulling on the other one, yank herself out, without, miraculously, losing her boot.

I couldn't tell which of us was more shaken. I kept thinking of those old movies where people got stuck and sank in over their heads. *Arena movediza*, she told me, still clinging to my arm, that was the Spanish term for quicksand, "shifting sand."

"The bottom dropped out from under my foot, and then the mud closed in and I couldn't move it." She let go of my arm and we made our way carefully back to solid ground, where she balanced on one foot and dumped the water and mud out of her boots. Her scream had startled all the imperturbable waterbirds and the glade was as quiet as I'd ever seen it.

I suggested she choose another spot to sample, but she was determined to get something from the brushy area, so we walked all the way around the open side of the pond and tried wading in from the other direction. This time we went more slowly, testing each step and clinging to branches until she found a little gap in the brush where the mud was stable and she could go through her routine—pH, oxygen, surface jar, bottom jar. . . . It took us the rest of the afternoon. We marked the spot with a bit of the flagging tape I'd taken from my reed bed markers, and I drew a crude map of both site locations on the back of one of her charts.

By the time we made it out of the reeds, the first evening stars were blinking to life in the graying sky, and we cut across the pastures and walked back as fast as we could, hardly stopping to look at anything. The wind had come up by then, and though our pants dried quickly, we were both shivering when we got to the car.

Alejandra was eager to get back to Montevideo, but she drove me by the house, where she helped me carry Mom's cartons in and used the bathroom. Mom had already lit the oil lamps and was out chasing the chickens into the coop when we arrived, but she came through the door just as Alejandra was leaving.

"Go look what Santiago gave me," she said. "In the chicken coop, bottom left corner."

"Santiago gave you a chicken?" I didn't even know she'd met him, but I was glad to hear he'd been checking in on her.

"Go look." She turned to greet Alejandra, brushing cheeks and inviting her to dinner before I'd even had a chance to introduce them.

"Alejandra Silva," I said quickly. "My mother, Lili Quiroga."

"Alejandra?" Mom stepped back to examine Alejandra in the dim light, and for a moment I feared she was going to shine the flashlight she was holding in her face. "Silva Paden? Eva Paden's daughter?" She nodded, not waiting for Alejandra to respond. "I grew up with your mother. . . ."

We were standing by the open door, and Alejandra seemed nonplussed. It must have been unnerving, the way Mom was staring at her.

"You don't remember me, do you?"

"No," Alejandra said stiffly. "Gabriel says you lived in California. That you just came back."

"Yes. A little over a month ago. So you're the biologist who's working at Caruso's. Something to do with birds?"

"Microbes," I interjected, and Mom's gaze jerked from Alejandra to me, her expression flickering like the sky after a storm, fragments of black cloud blowing past an overly bright sun.

"I'm finishing a PhD project in microbial ecology," Alejandra said politely.

She had declined the dinner invitation, and we hadn't moved from the doorway, but Mom started plying her with detailed questions about her research.

Alejandra gave Mom, the biology teacher, a somewhat more technical explanation than the one she'd given me in the car. I had the sensation that Mom was trying to ingratiate herself— nothing unusual about that, just Mom being Mom, too bright and too charming, and it shouldn't have bothered me but it did, almost as much as Rubén's flirtatiousness had.

"Your son took me into the marsh on your land," Alejandra said. "I thought I might sample there, compare its microbial ecology with the cultivated fields. If you don't mind . . ."

"Of course not," Mom said. "Sample to your heart's content, any time."

"Every two weeks, when I sample Caruso's fields—or whenever Gabriel is willing to help." Alejandra turned to me. "I don't think I can manage it alone."

"My pleasure," I said. "Though maybe we can do some birding next time." I could see she was ready to leave. She still had a four-hour drive ahead of her, then morning classes to teach and her samples to process—but Mom seemed loathe to let her go.

"What does Manuel Caruso make of your study?"

"Caruso? I think he's mostly interested in keeping good relations with the university, doing his bit for science—as long as it doesn't interfere with his farming. But of course he's also eager to reduce fertilizer expenditures, which is our excuse for the study."

"He's uninterested in my experiments with compost and cover crops—not manipulating microbial populations like you're trying to do, but leaving the soil structure and biota undisturbed—"

"Mom," I interjected, "if Alejandra is going to make it to Montevideo before midnight, we should probably let her go."

Alejandra immediately took the cue and said goodnight, and I ushered her across the dark yard with Mom's flashlight. The wind had quieted, as if lulled by the twinkling stars, which were now on full display in a moonless night sky. I flicked off the light for a moment to get the full effect. Now that I'd extricated Alejandra from Mom, I didn't want to let her go either.

"You want to see Santiago's mystery chicken before you go back?" I asked, only half joking. "A consolation prize. Since I didn't get to show you any new marsh birds."

She laughed. "Is it close? I really should get going."

"Right there," I shined the flashlight on the chicken coop.

"It's kind of interesting," Alejandra said as we crossed the yard. "What your mother is doing here. Uruguay may have the latest agricultural science, but when it comes to environmental issues, we're still in the dark ages."

"So is my mother, if you ask me. In the big scheme anyway. Small and sustainable doesn't cut it, when everything around you is global. Economy, resources, climate . . . the only thing you can do small is live your life. That's all Liliana Quiroga is really doing. But she has this grandiose illusion that it's a model for the whole planet, that it makes a difference."

"There are worse illusions . . ."

"True," I said, handing her the flashlight to hold so I could see the latch on the chicken-house door. "It's funny that our mothers knew each other. Does yours still live in Montevideo?"

"My mother? My mother died when I was four."

"Oh." I stopped fiddling with the latch. "I'm sorry. I didn't know."

"No . . . you wouldn't." She laughed, as if she were both surprised and pleased by this revelation.

"I'm sorry," I said again, caught off guard by the clear note of delight in her laugh.

"No need. I hardly remember her. Or my father. Though everyone else in the world does . . . everyone, that is, in the Uruguayan world. Which really isn't saying much, is it?"

I didn't know how to respond, so I just unlatched the door and ducked into the chicken house. We squeezed into the narrow space in front of the nesting boxes, and I shined the flashlight at the left corner as Mom had directed.

"What in the world?" Alejandra whispered.

The nest was occupied by one of the original hens, the little black one that never wanted to go in at night. She was sitting on an egg that was twice her size, and she looked like a ship gone aground, her breast tilted awkwardly upward and her wings askew as she tried to cover both it and the four normal eggs nestled around it.

"Is that real?" I whispered back. It looked like something from a fairytale or a comic strip.

Alejandra leaned forward to get a better look, and I laid my hand carefully on the small of her back, found the narrow strip of bare flesh between sweater and jeans, my fingers curling around her tiny waist. "It's a Ñandú egg!" she said. "Santiago gave your mother a Ñandú egg!" She straightened up and my hand fell away. "People eat them around here."

"She was supposed to eat it?" I asked as I followed her out of the coop.

"Who knows? Maybe Santiago told her to put it there." Alejandra giggled. "That poor hen doesn't know what to make of it. You think it will hatch?"

"It'll think it's a chicken," I said, and then we were both giggling, making our way across the yard like stoned teenagers.

"Thanks for helping," she said as we neared the car. "And for pulling me out of the quicksand."

"Are you sure you want to drive back in the dark?" I asked, hoping she would change her mind. "You could stay here. There's plenty of space," I added, not wanting her to get the wrong idea. Yet.

"Thanks, it'll be okay. There isn't much traffic. But let's start earlier, next time. I do want to see more birds."

"Maybe we'll find some nests. Some baby ducks." But I didn't want to wait another two weeks to see her. "I'm going back to Montevideo on Friday . . . maybe we could do something in the city."

"Maybe," she said, her hand on the car door handle. "I'll call you."

"*Chau—*" I bent to kiss her cheek and the kiss slid around to brush her lips, even as the momentum of saying goodbye moved us apart. But she lingered for just an instant, and our eyes met in the way that eyes meet in the dark, hers glistening, darker than the starlit night—not exactly an invitation but surely not a reproach—before she got into her car, closed the door, and started the engine.

I watched her drive off, and then I turned and walked slowly, very slowly, back to the house, cooling my blood in the night air before I went in to join Mom for dinner.

She was at the stove in the corner, and the room was already filling with the aroma of frying meat. I made a beeline for the loaf of fresh bread on the table and broke off a chunk. "Are you sure you weren't supposed to eat that Ñandú egg?"

"Of course not. Santiago said it was still alive and if I put it in the chickens' nest it would hatch. He said they make good pets."

"Too bad he didn't bring you a puppy." The only pets I'd ever had were the chickens and a white rat she'd brought home from the college lab. "Where'd you get that stove?"

"It was here, just needed a tank of propane."

"Not exactly sustainable," I said. Pointing out Mom's inconsistencies was a childhood habit I hadn't bothered to break. Somehow, we both expected it. "But this bread is delicious."

"Stop inhaling it and go clean up, will you? You look as if Alejandra's mud was sampling you, rather than the other way around. There's even running water," she added as I started down the hall to the bathroom.

I stopped. "You broke down and bought a generator?" The bathroom had, so far, operated on the bucket principle.

"I found someone to fix the windmill!" She was smiling triumphantly. "They still make these things. We even have warm water."

"How'd you do that?"

"Black paint and a raised holding tank. Very high tech."

It worked beautifully. I took a warm shower in a fully functional bathroom, and by the time I reemerged, Mom had finished preparing dinner and set the table. She'd replaced her board-and-crate affair with a pinewood table from an estate sale, replete with six matching chairs. Tonight it was set for two. With candles. I rummaged through the boxes of supplies we'd left by the door and extracted the only things I'd bought that weren't on her list—a corkscrew and two bottles of Uruguayan Tannat. The wine shop owner had told me that Tannat was doing well on the international market, one of the latest hopes for the economy—anything that sold outside of Uruguay was considered hopeful—

but what clinched the deal was when he found me one made from organically grown grapes.

I poured wine into a couple of small water glasses, and Mom served up the *milanesas*, set out a bowl of salad, and sat down across from me. The candles and the big empty table made the simple dinner seem elegant, and for a moment I felt bad that Mom didn't have someone besides her desperately hungry son to share it with. I sliced the loaf of bread I'd mutilated and loaded up my plate with salad. Dad would have loved this. He probably would have taken his vacation time and flown down to join us for dinner, if she'd invited him. But, of course, Dad was out of Mom's picture. I wondered what she'd do when I left for good, if she'd stay out here eating candlelit dinners by herself for weeks on end.

"Aren't you even going to *look* at what you're eating?" Mom said. She was just sitting there watching me eat, hardly touching her own food. "At least register its general form and function, if not the more subtle attributes of taste and freshness?"

I paused my fork in midair and examined the food on my plate. I was so hungry, I'd simply loaded up and started shoveling it in. There was the homemade bread, which I'd already praised. Her standard beef cutlet shouldn't need remarking. And salad—"Ah," I said. "The salad. It's from the garden."

"Yes, *mi hijo sonámbulo*, the first thinnings. Where in Uruguay have you seen salad like that? Huh? Arugula? Four kinds of open-pollinated lettuce? Baby leaves? Where?"

"Nowhere." I crammed as many of those baby leaves onto my fork as I could and shoved it into my mouth, feigning a culinary orgasm.

"Who raised such a monster? Eh?"

I swallowed and raised a toast. "To your first harvest. To running water."

She clinked glasses with me. "And," she added softly as I tasted the wine, "to reuniting with Eva's daughter. All grown up."

I took another sip of the wine, already beginning to regret having introduced Mom to Alejandra, envious of her prior claim to my discovery.

"The grandfather seems to have done right by her. It's ironic that she became a biologist."

I wondered why it was ironic, but I didn't want to ask, didn't want to reveal that I was interested in Alejandra as anything more than a casual birdwatching companion. I was afraid that whatever was budding between us would wither under Mom's bright gaze, and I wanted to keep her at bay—at least until I knew what sort of plant we had. "What do you think of this wine?" I asked, though she hadn't even tasted it. "It's organic, from a little winery north of Montevideo, near Florida." It was even darker than the Zinfandels Dad liked, and rawer tasting, an impenetrable mix of tannins so astringent my tongue felt like a piece of leather after the first sip. Definitely a macho wine, I thought, or an acquired taste, like drinking espresso or eating raw jalapeño peppers.

She took a sip, and I waited for her to grimace, but she was still lost in her memories. "I always wanted to look her up," she said. "But, really, it's like seeing a ghost. Like falling into a time warp, Eva in her twenties. She's the spitting image."

"I don't know if it needs to age," I said, examining the bottle label. "Or if it's supposed to be that way."

"It's okay." She took another sip and went back to picking at her food. "We were best friends," she said after a moment. "In those days, the Quiroga house was the neighborhood hangout for all our friends, especially mine and Rubén's. Eva was there all the time. She was an only child, and she liked the constant commotion. Mamá, believe it or not, cooked and baked for whoever was around, but even then she was something of a misanthrope. That's part of what attracted our friends—she left us alone, didn't hover about like the other mothers. And if she did talk to you, it

136

was a big deal. You felt honored, like you were someone special, cleverer than the rest."

"That much hasn't changed," I said, relieved that Mom had shifted her attention from Alejandra to Abuela.

"I suppose not," Mom said, smiling. "Eva was Mamá's chosen one, at least for a while. She really worked at it, posing as an eleven-year-old intellectual, trying to impress Mamá, which was no easy task since Mamá was predisposed to the boys. She thought girls made inferior intellectuals—but she made an exception for Eva, and Eva played right along with her. I never understood that about Mamá. She was permanently bitter that she didn't get to go to university—not many women did back then—but she bought right into the prevailing myths that had kept her from it. Her involvement with the Masons was the ultimate irony. She was looking for some identity besides being the ex-wife of the architect Quiroga, but then she turned for confirmation to an all-male society that revered him and locked her out."

"What do you think Abuela would have studied? If she could have gone to college."

"Probably history or philosophy. She considered philosophy the highest form of knowledge. That's what Eva told her she wanted to study. It was a complete fabrication, of course, vintage Eva—she wanted to be an architect, like my father. And I wanted to be a doctor, like hers."

Mom sipped at the wine and slipped half of her *milanesa* onto my plate. "I was never one of Mamá's chosen ones," she said after a moment. "No matter what I studied, no matter that my grades were always better than Juan's and Rubén's. Even when I got the scholarship to Madison, I wasn't exceptional enough for her. No matter what I did."

"I guess that hasn't changed either," I said, and she laughed morosely. I'd heard the story about getting a scholarship to Madison, going to graduate school in Berkeley, falling in love with Dad, having me. But I didn't know she'd wanted to be a doctor. And though her school friends had always come by when we were in Montevideo for vacations, Abuela had certainly never cooked or baked, and I'd never heard any mention of an Eva.

"Of course, I was a little jealous," Mom went on while I polished off her *milanesa* and the last of the salad. "Eva spent so much time with us, we were like sisters, in competition for Mamá's approval, and Rubén's. Juan Luis was too much older, but we worshipped Rubén, thought he was the god of worldliness. He was benevolently indifferent, until he fell for Eva. We were only fourteen then, and Rubén was seventeen, but Eva was the one who called all the shots. She kept him on a string for years. She wanted excitement and adventure, which Rubén couldn't provide, once the first-lover novelty wore off—she'd known him when she was growing up, he was practically like a brother. But she used him as a sort of homing mechanism, even after she dropped him for Natalio. And Rubén just couldn't let go. I suppose I should tell him we met their daughter out here."

"He met her today," I said. "When she picked me up at Abuela's."

Mom looked up from her salad. "Rubén met Alejandra?"

I nodded.

"And? How was he?"

"I don't know. I introduced them, and then we left." I shrugged and reached for the wine bottle, omitting the fact that I had such a crush on her friend's daughter I'd been jealous of my uncle.

"She must be twenty-six, now," Mom said, holding out her empty glass for a refill. "So accomplished and self-composed."

I filled both of our glasses. I'd decided I liked the wine better, that it had just needed to breathe, but Mom rarely drank more than a half glass and I was surprised that she wanted more. "Rubén said he wants to help you out here," I said.

"Really? That's news to me."

"I don't know if he was serious."

"Oh well, I can answer that. Rubén is never serious."

"I think he was a little drunk. It was the night of the election—do you even know what happened?"

"There's going to be a *balotaje*. Santiago told me. When is Rubén coming?"

"I don't know, he didn't seem to have a plan. Beyond flirting with every unattached woman in sight."

"Typical. Women always liked him. Girls." She looked at me and smiled. "He was a little like you when he was young, Gabe. Handsome. Sweet, a little funny . . ."

"Come on, Mom. Eyebrows are the only thing Rubén and I have in common. And I don't flirt like that."

"No," she said, chuckling, "you don't. But then neither did Rubén when he was young. He was just immensely amiable. He charmed them without trying."

She was studying my face, as if she hadn't been looking at it all my life. I wondered if she was getting a little drunk. The stuff was strong, and we'd gone through most of the bottle. By the time I'd finished her *milanesa* and the last of the salad, done the dishes, and helped her unpack her supplies, I was on my third glass and feeling the effects myself.

Mom had always bragged about how close we were when I was growing up, and I'd never found reason to contradict her. But as I said goodnight and made my way down the hall to the room I'd claimed as my bedroom, I pondered how it could be that after twenty-three years of close relationship with my mother, I'd just spent an entire evening hearing stories I'd never heard before. Maybe she had told them before and I just hadn't been listening. Or maybe the close relationship was one-sided. After all, I thought, how deeply did we really *want* to know our parents?

The pallet of blankets I'd slept on last time I'd stayed at the estancia had been replaced by a narrow pine bed, which was made up with fresh sheets. There was a little table next to it with an oil lamp and matches at the ready, a real vase with sprigs of herbs, the smells of lavender and sage. I dropped my knapsack on the floor and went back to the living room, where Mom was squatting in the corner, examining the contents of the old toolbox I'd found for her in Abuela's jam-packed, mouse-infested garage. She had a pipe wrench cradled in her hands as if it were an heirloom piece of jewelry. "Thanks Mom," I said, the simple English words sounding sweet and childish, as if my languages had done a flip-flop and my baby language was now my real language, my real language relegated to childhood. She looked up and smiled, but I retreated before she could say anything.

10

Juan revealed his plans for the estancia with such pedantry that I almost felt sorry for him. He deserved a better audience than the one he convened in Abuela's dining room that Saturday afternoon: Rubén perched on a stool in the corner, picking at his guitar, Elsa putting away the groceries she'd brought Abuela, Mom sipping *mate* with studied indifference, his nephew paging through the newspaper and munching on cookies. Abuela'd had a sudden fit of hospitality and set the table with a festive tablecloth and cookies and grapefruit soda, all of which seemed to belie Juan's businesslike seriousness. But she, at least, was properly seated, hands folded in front of her, attention on her oldest son.

Juan moved the soda and glasses and plates of cookies to the sideboard, swept aside the tablecloth, and made a show of wiping down the table with sponge and dish towel before he would lay out his map. He unfurled it carefully, as if he were unveiling some great masterpiece, running his palms lovingly across the surface to smooth it out, then stepping back from the table so everyone could admire it.

It was, in fact, a carefully hand-drafted map of the sort we'd learned to make in my first cartography class—but a hundred times more precise, informative, and beautiful than anything we did as students. No one drafted maps like that anymore.

"Here's the house," Juan said, stepping back up to the table and pointing with the eraser end of a pencil. "And here's the canal

141

and the border with Caruso's land." He looked at Abuela, who nodded appreciatively, which I could see was irritating Mom. Abuela hadn't taken any of *her* plans for the estancia seriously.

"Here's your orchard, Lili," Juan said then. The little icons he'd drawn for the trees were decorated with tiny red apples, golden peaches, and purple plums. "You can expand it into this area here if you want, five hectares. Nice, well-drained land, pretty good soil. And here are your vegetables. There's another five hectares. The rest of this green area we'll keep pasture. We can lease it to Caruso for the next year or two, then maybe try some of our own cattle. This year, I want to get the rice fields ready. We'll start with fifty hectares, here." He indicated an area of the map he'd colored in tan. "And add another fifty next year. We plant rice for three years, then we seed it back to pasture for five years and run some cattle. By then the soil is almost as good as new, and we replant with rice."

He told us he'd joined the Rice Growers' Association and had been doing some market research, talking to other growers. Their main problem, he told us, was that there were no controls on the prices in Brazil, which was the main market for Uruguayan rice. "Caruso says he had his best-ever production this year, but prices were so low it wasn't worth anything. The international rice market is flooded with impossibly cheap rice from the US, where the producers are so heavily subsidized they could give it away and still make money. With a hundred hectares and no subsidies, we don't stand a chance. Unless we do something different."

Juan paused, and Rubén started strumming a crescendo of trills to add suspense. Mom started laughing, and I couldn't help joining in—Juan looked so ridiculous standing there in Abuela's dining room lecturing to the four of us, his belly straining at his button-down shirt. Abuela peered myopically at the map, mumbled something appreciative, and then announced that she was tired and went upstairs.

Juan, absorbed in his presentation, ignored us. He set out a hand-drawn spreadsheet where he'd worked out the budget, replete with tractor, labor, seed, and water costs. Then he showed us income projections from the first five years of crops, based first on a range of sale price predictions from Brazil, and second, from Europe.

"In Europe," Juan said, "there's a totally underexploited niche market for organically grown rice." He looked up from his charts and focused on Mom. "Those big *yanqui* producers can't be bothered, but we've got the perfect situation. Virgin soil, so the first two crops should be easy. Even if production drops in the third year of the rotation, with these sorts of prices we'll be okay. There's a guy in Treinta y Tres who started growing organic a couple years ago. He says there's a processor all set for it, and if we can get certified they'll buy whatever we produce. Caruso claims it's impossible to grow rice without herbicide here. But I think we can do it if we cut the rotation with pasture down to three years instead of five." Juan paused expectantly, but Mom was furiously working the *bombilla* in her *mate*, not looking at him. "As for your produce," he went on, "I talked to a distributor in Holland. They want off-season organic apples and tomatoes. You could fill this upper five hectares with apple trees and you'd have a market, Lili, no problem. And if you do tomatoes on the other plot, they'll take those too. Of course, you'd have to plow, you can't dig all that by hand the way you've been doing."

Juan clearly assumed she would be pleased by his plan. Even I thought she might be pleased—after all, Juan had taken her farming seriously and come up with what seemed like a good compromise. But compromise was never Mom's forte.

"So glad you've decided there's something to my '*tontería ecológica*,'" she said finally looking up. "But you miss the point entirely."

"The point is the market, Lili. Period. The point is to grow something we can sell at a good price, grow it well, sell it well—"

"The point is I don't want to do just apples and tomatoes," Mom said. "And I don't want to sell to Europe. How are we supposed to ship this stuff, may I ask?"

"Oh yes, you may," Juan said. "We send the rice and apples by ship, the tomatoes by cargo plane—"

"By plane? Juan, don't be ridiculous. I want to sell locally. Small amounts of multiple products for a small market. In Montevideo, or better yet in Rocha—"

Juan let out a sputtering laugh. "*Rocha*? Get real, Lili."

"Yes, why not Rocha? Have you seen what's on offer there? One kind of lettuce, one kind of squash, one kind of bean, one kind of melon, tomatoes with no taste—and it all looks like it's been in a sauna for a week."

"It's the distribution system," Juan said. "The intermediaries. You can't just take your harvest to the *feria* in Montevideo, you have to sell it to one of these mafiosos and then they cart it around from *feria* to *feria*. And they won't guarantee you a market, forget it. If it comes cheaper from Brazil, they buy from Brazil. There's no such thing as 'local,' Lili. Half of the *zapallitos uruguayos* in the *feria* last year were from Brazil—"

Rubén interrupted him with a round of loud ominous chords. "Welcome to Uruguay, Mercosur! Regional bargaining power and solidarity? *Andá a cantarle a Gardel.* Our tiny market gets flooded with Brazilian produce while the Brazilians buy their rice tariff-free from the omnipresent cousin to the north? Twenty-first-century imperialism, welcome!"

"The growers are trying to get Brazil to impose tariffs on rice from outside Mercosur."

"You'd better hope the Frente wins the *balotaje*," Rubén said. "Because your Colorados aren't going to do anything to help that cause." He started strumming and singing, "*Que los países hermanos, de Centro América y Sur, borren las sombras del norte . . .*"

"Tell you what, Juan," Mom said, talking over Rubén's song, which seemed to be about the South American struggle against northern interference. "You worry about your rice. I'll take care of my produce."

"*Por toda América soplan, vientos que no han de parar; hasta que entierren las sombras*—Victor Lima," Rubén announced, interrupting himself. "Mid-sixties. And nothing has changed."

"Maybe I'll just trade," Mom said. "What do you think, Rubén, product for product?"

Rubén shrugged noncommittally and started strumming another song, now competing with the phone ringing in the kitchen.

"I traded lettuce for some cheese the other day," Mom went on. "There's a guy near Lascano—"

"Great, Lili, that's very efficient. You drive all the way to Lascano to trade a few leaves of lettuce—"

"Gabrielito," Elsa said, coming in with the phone in one hand, laying the other on Juan's shoulder, as if to still the rising gusts of sarcasm. "It's for you."

I abandoned them to their sniping and took the phone into the living room. Someone had raised the blind, and I stood there gazing out at the quiet street in the gathering dusk, elated by the sound of her voice pronouncing my name in proper liquid Spanish, the way no girl had ever pronounced it. "Gabriel," she said, "it's Alejandra," and it was as if she were stepping forward to realize the phantom kiss I'd brushed past her lips in parting the other night. I hadn't been sure she'd really call, and I felt triumphant. She had her first results from the rice samples, and she was excited, and I was the one she wanted to tell.

"Two new species," she told me.

"New? You mean, as in no one has seen them before? Ever?"

"Yes. That's not so uncommon with microbes. But still . . ."

"What do they look like?"

"Those two? We don't know. We don't have them isolated—we identified them from the genetic makeup. The ones we have isolated in culture are just the usual spheres and rods. But it's what they're doing that's interesting."

"Did you find your fertilizer factory?"

She laughed. "Not yet. We've got some nitrogen-fixers, but we don't have them isolated."

"*Che,*" I said, suddenly realizing I was missing my chance. "Why don't you let me take you to dinner tonight? Where are you, I could meet you." But she suggested I meet her at her lab after work the next day.

"I'll show you my rods and spheres," she said. "And you don't even have to put on insect repellent or hike five kilometers through treacherous mud to see them."

I insisted she let me take her to dinner afterwards and told her to choose the restaurant because I didn't know the nicest ones, and she agreed easily, suggesting a new place in the Ciudad Vieja that everyone was raving about. Then she gave me directions to her lab and said goodbye.

I could feel the telltale blush burning its way from my throat up to my forehead as I walked through the dining room, but Juan was holding forth again and no one noticed me. Elsa was still in the kitchen puttering around. She watched me set the phone back in its cradle, and I could tell she was just dying to tease me, but I wasn't yet ready to be teased, even by Elsa. "You might have to make a peace intervention in there," I mumbled to distract her, and headed back into the dining room.

Juan had resumed his presentation and was now explaining the system of dikes and canals on his map. Any other family might have found his almost childlike enthusiasm touching, but ours was just irritated and amused—specifically, Mom was irritated, or, rather, furious, and Rubén was cynically amused, still offering bits of musical mockery from the sidelines. And I, well,

I was bemused. I went to the table and took a closer look at the map. He'd used colored pencils like I used for my bird drawings and turned our mundane survey data into a work of art. It was meticulously detailed and color coded. Blue lines for the canals and irrigation ditches, darker blue for the creek. Dark brown for the contours of the levees. Rice was tan, pasture bright green, and the area with the marsh, where we hadn't surveyed, was a muddy olive-green color.

"Juan—"I pointed to a black line across the creek, about a half kilometer above the house. "This is a dike, here?"

"Yes. That's the main dike. And we excavate a pond here— I'm hoping you'll help me do the survey for that next week."

I pointed to the olive-green patch. "And here?"

"That's the bad land," Juan said. "It's probably too expensive to do anything with it. Though Caruso thinks we should."

"I was just wondering about the dike," I said.

"That's the key to the whole plan. Free water. We dike there and build our own little pond. Then we can do everything with gravity flow and a few small pumps. Otherwise we'd have to take water from one of the canals and pay a fortune for it."

"If you dike there, won't it dry out the bog?"

"Probably. That would make it easier to clean out, if we want to plant there later."

"This bad land," I said, tracing around the green patch with my finger. It was bigger than I'd realized. "It's bird utopia."

Juan looked at me blankly, as if I were speaking some unexpectedly incomprehensible language.

"Gabe's been birdwatching out there," Mom said.

"I know that," Juan snapped. He moved closer to the table and set his hand flat along its edge, leaning on his arm. "The swamp," he said slowly, looking at his map, the pencil still dangling in his free hand. "You don't want me to clean up the swamp." The sigh he emitted was so involuntary, so unconscious, it was almost embarrassing to hear.

"Well," I said apologetically. I hadn't meant to rain on Juan's parade, especially since Mom was so unappreciative of his attempts to accommodate her vision of the farm. And I certainly didn't want to get in the middle of their feud. "It's just that there are thousands of birds living in there."

"A nature reserve!" Rubén exclaimed. "*Find me in my field of grass,*" he sang, strumming the old Beatles song. "*Mother Nature's son . . . swaying daisies sing a lazy song beneath the sun—* Papá would have loved it! He could have taken his duck-hunting cronies there. Shown it off to his women."

"Rubén," Elsa said, in a tone that silenced him, if not his guitar. She had come in from the kitchen and taken a seat at the table with Mom. "You're in Celia's house, have some respect. And speaking of which, her birthday is coming up."

"Ninety? Is she ninety?"

"Eighty-seven."

"We're planning a party," Mom said. "With all her old friends."

"She never wants a big fuss," Juan Luis mumbled, rolling up his map.

"For your information, sir," Elsa said, glaring at him, "it was her idea to have a party. She says eighty-seven is an important birthday."

"Does she have any friends?" Rubén said.

"Gonzalo," Mom said. Gonzalo lived across the street. Apparently, he'd been keeping an eye out for Abuela for decades. "And the people next door, who used to rent the garage—what's their name?"

"Señora Urrutia," Elsa said. "The husband is long dead. Celia doesn't think much of her, but no matter." They started running through the list of possible guests then, Rubén strumming the tune to "Happy Birthday" in the background while Elsa elaborated the guest suggestions with gossip, telling stories the way only Elsa can tell them—her arms waving and her whole body in motion, her pretty face screwed up in the oddest expressions, so even I was laughing, though I didn't know any of these characters.

"It's a whole three weeks away," Juan said, but he stood by quietly as Elsa told her stories and made party plans.

It was almost eight by the time they left, and Mom announced to Rubén and me that she was going to drive to the estancia. I was sure she was trying to make me feel guilty for not going with her, since I'd already told her I wasn't going back until the weekend. But if she was going to play the filial guilt card, so could I.

"I thought you wanted to spend time with Abuela," I said.

"If you wait 'til tomorrow," Rubén told her, "I'll go with you. Right now, I suggest we go to Salú, get some *chivitos* and beer, listen to some tango—as an antidote for listening to two hours of our pompous old fart of a brother."

Mom and I both declined the *chivitos* and tango, but she did calm down and wait until the next day to drive up to the estancia. And Rubén did go with her.

11

I took the bus as far as Centro and then walked up a street lined with shops dedicated to building and fixing things— wood, hardware, paint, auto parts—toward the Palacio Legislativo. Like much of Montevideo, the parliament building was a testament to glorious times that hadn't been quite as glorious or long-lasting as anticipated, a grand neoclassic structure of marble columns and carved facades. I skirted an austere plaza that was designed, I suppose, to show off the building's grandeur, though, to me, it just looked abandoned, with a couple of lonely statues and no trees or benches. The whole neighborhood seemed oddly forlorn for seven in the evening—until I got to the university building, which was an oasis of activity.

The building itself was a dilapidated concrete affair, the common areas torn up for renovation, but Alejandra's laboratory on the second floor looked brand new and, to my untrained eye, ultra-modern. The door was open, and she was standing at a lab bench with a stout, gray-haired woman, deep in conversation. I stopped in the doorway, waiting for them to finish, but as soon as Alejandra saw me, she interrupted herself and waved me in. The sight of her—the smile of welcome, the delicacy of her neck in the white lab coat, the wild hair confined to its ponytail— filled me with such visceral joy, I feared my own smile would erupt into irrational laughter. But she was introducing me to her colleague, and I made an effort to play it cool. The woman's name was Serrana Contreras and she was apparently the head of the department and Alejandra's boss.

"A *yanqui* from California," Alejandra told her, "who knows all the birds of our Bañados del Este."

I started to deny it, but she was clearly enjoying the irony of her own pronouncement, so I held my tongue.

"The one who inspired you to look at the marsh bugs," Serrana said.

I felt myself blushing, unable to think of anything clever to say, just trying to keep my joy from burbling inappropriately to the surface—an unnerving but not entirely unpleasant sensation. "We can go out there anytime," I said lamely.

"Next week," Alejandra said, "when I sample in the rice again. Look here, this is what was in the mud." She indicated the petri dishes on the lab bench, and as Serrana took her leave, I examined the seemingly random arrays of spots and splotches growing in the agar. Alejandra explained how she diluted her mud samples and spotted them onto agar plates containing different kinds of microbe food. The splotches I was seeing were mixed "colonies" of bacteria. If she scraped an individual colony off and put it on a new agar plate, it would again differentiate into colonies, and if she kept doing that, she could, with luck, isolate a single species or strain of microbe. She indicated a plate where the splotches looked more uniform, and then she took me over to a microscope and set it up with a slide of one of her isolates.

"How can you distinguish different species?" I asked as I peered through the eyepiece. "Or strains, or whatever you call them." All I could see were a bunch of rod-shaped things with no visible internal or external structure.

"It's not really so different from what you do when you see a bird—except we can't do it just from looking at morphological characteristics. When you look at a bird, you don't just notice

151

its color or size, but also the way it behaves, the way it moves and flies, if it's catching bugs, if it's solitary or gregarious. But we have to do that chemically, in the lab." She removed the slide and covered the microscope, and then she moved around the lab, putting things away and shuttling dirty glassware into a sink as she talked. She pointed out the culture incubation cabinets where they could regulate the temperature and atmospheric gases, and explained how she characterized the microbes based on what they consumed and released. It was a sophisticated form of trial and error in which she added different chemical "foods" to the culture flasks and agar plates, to encourage different kinds of microbe. Heterotrophic bacteria, which got their energy from decaying plant matter in the soil and water, grew when she added sugars. Sulfate-reducing bacteria liked a mix of sugars and sulfate compounds, couldn't tolerate oxygen, and released hydrogen sulfide, which was easy to detect because if you added iron it reacted and produced a black residue. "But many microbes," Alejandra said as she ushered me into the hall and locked the door, "won't grow in the lab. Most, actually. The only way to distinguish them—the only way to *detect* them—is to look for their genes, something we've really only understood in the past decade. The two new species we found in the rice didn't grow in any of our cultures."

She led me down the hall to her office, a small crowded room with two desks, a computer, bookshelves, and piles of notebooks and papers in every available space. She sat down at the desk with the computer and told me to wheel her absentee roommate's chair around next to her.

"This is a phylogenetic tree," she said, indicating the diagram she'd brought up on the computer screen. "A sort of family tree for these microbes. Those two little red branches are our new species. We only know they exist because we found genes in the mud samples that don't match those of any known microbes."

I peered at the diagram, which she said was based on comparing the sequences of known microbe genes with those found in the mud—though how you could "find" genes in a bunch of mud was beyond me. When I said as much, she took it as a question and immediately started explaining.

The gist of it was that they froze and heated the samples to bust up the cells and then extracted the nucleic acids into a solvent, so they ended up with a soup of nucleic acids from hundreds, even thousands of organisms. "The DNA from an entire ecosystem," Alejandra said, "all mixed together." The amount of any particular DNA molecule in the soup was too infinitesimal to isolate and analyze, even if they had the wherewithal to sequence it. But in recent years, a technique called polymerase chain reaction had changed that, revolutionizing the way they studied microbial ecology. It worked like a molecular photocopying machine: you could now add an enzyme to your soup and start a chain reaction that made billions of copies of the gene that coded for ribosomal RNA—a gene that was present in all prokaryotes and would have a species-specific sequence of nucleotides.

I lost her again in all of this, and she patiently backed up and explained what a gene was and what DNA and RNA and ribosomes were, all things I thought I knew, but had never actually visualized in the hands-on way she was describing them. Somehow, you put your amplified mixture of genes on a "sequencing gel" and applied an electric current, which made the different genes travel up the gel at different rates and collect in bands at different heights. You could then cut a band out of the gel, determine the sequence of nucleotides in it, and try to match it to a sequence in the large databank of known microbe gene sequences. If your nucleotide sequence didn't match any of them, it belonged to a new species, and you had to try to figure out who its closest relatives were and estimate where it fit on the tree. For the time being, Alejandra told me as she shut down the computer, they sent everything to a lab in Germany for sequencing. But Serrana was applying for a grant to purchase the equipment for their own lab.

"Does this happen often?" I asked. "That you find a new species? A rice paddy seems like a strange place . . ."

"We find new species almost everywhere we look!" She stood up, and I followed suit, wheeling the chair back to the other desk and trying to get out of the way as she slipped out of her lab coat and got ready to go. "It's like when the first microscopes were invented, and people realized there was a whole universe of living things they didn't even know existed. Now we find out that this microscopic universe is exponentially larger, more varied, and more complex than anyone ever imagined. People estimate that we've identified less than *one percent* of the microbe species on earth! After four hundred years of study! Those bugs I just showed you in the cultures? Those are just the most tractable ones, the ones that do well in captivity, usually not even the most abundant or important ones in the ecosystem they come from." She pulled the elastic band out of her hair, took her purse out of a drawer in the desk, and extracted a brush.

"It's hard to imagine," I said, trying not to stare as she brushed out her hair. "You have this gene, but you can't see what the organisms look like, can't even see their bodies. . . ." I could feel myself starting to blush, overly conscious of my word choice, since it was precisely her body I was trying not to look at, but she didn't seem to notice.

"Sometimes you can see the cells, with fluorescent labeling and an electron microscope. But you just nailed the problem. We discover a new bug, but we don't know what it *does* in the ecosystem, how it lives, what it eats and excretes. If its closest relatives in the phylogenetic tree are all nitrogen-fixers, we might surmise that it's capable of fixing nitrogen. But *is* it fixing nitrogen in the rice paddy mud? In the floodwater? Is it making nitrate, or ammonia, and is some other bug just sucking that up and turning it into nitrogen gas? That's why we measure the gases in situ, to give a general idea of what's produced and consumed, where and when."

She was wearing a silky white blouse and tight black jeans, and as we left her office, she tossed a red blazer over her shoulder. I didn't know if she'd dressed that way for our dinner, or for work, but whatever the case, I was glad I'd at least thought to wear a button-down shirt with my jeans. She stopped off in one of the teaching labs, where she consulted briefly with a colleague—she'd told me she was still working on her doctorate, but she also seemed to be a full-blown member of the teaching staff—and as I stood in the doorway waiting for her, I noticed that the students, like her colleague and everyone else I'd seen, were all women.

"Alejandra," I said as we headed down the hall toward the stairs, "why aren't there any men in your department?"

"Oh, that. You should ask Serrana." Before I could protest, she'd veered off course and was tapping on Serrana Contreras's open office door, not waiting for an invitation to enter. "Serrana, Gabriel wants to know why we have so many women in the department."

I cringed, because to my over-sensitized ear, conditioned by years of Mom's feminist complaints, the question sounded sexist or patronizing—though, given the blushing bewilderment that this bastion of female intelligence seemed to inspire in me, I couldn't think of anything further from the truth. But Serrana just turned away from her computer screen and started telling me about the history of the department.

"Chemistry and microbiology were originally part of the medical school," she said, "taught as part of the pharmacology degree. And in the sixties, when more women started wanting careers, pharmacology was considered an appropriate choice because pharmacists worked indoors and had to measure small quantities, like cooking. By the time we established separate academic departments in the eighties, we were all women. There was no money for research then, so for years we just taught young women to measure things and everyone ignored us. But in the early nineties, I went on the offensive and started collaborating with foreign universities and writing grants for international funding. Now," she said, smiling, "the boys are beginning to get interested. Not that we mind being unisex."

"We have one male professor," Alejandra said. "From Holland."

"And three male graduate students." Serrana went on to tell me about the department's research and teaching program, which she was obviously proud of. I nodded and tried to sound appreciative, but I was relieved when she finished and shooed us out of her office. She was friendly and interesting, but I was beginning to fear Alejandra would invite her to dinner with us—and I had other ideas about the evening.

The restaurant Alejandra had chosen was on a pedestrian street in the Ciudad Vieja, a few blocks from the Plaza Independencia. The street had been beautifully renovated—one of the few projects the city had actually managed to finish—and was lined with hopeful new shops and *boliches*. This one had just opened the week before, and people were still checking it out, which, Alejandra told me, was why it was so crowded, even on a Monday night. When we stepped inside, I realized that it was nicer than anything I'd stumbled across in my daytime perambulations around the city. It was in a refurbished nineteenth-century warehouse, all red brick and pine, with a graceful sweep of mezzanine around the perimeter and a hand-crafted wrought-iron spiral staircase in the middle. The only lights were parchment-covered lamps and candles, so that even busy as it was, the place had a warm, intimate feel.

"Is it too expensive?" Alejandra asked as we studied the menu.

"By California standards it's downright cheap," I said, and we ordered generously, salads and miniature cannelloni, veal and steak, and a half-liter of Merlot.

I told her about my wanderings around Montevideo, and when the wine came, I sat forward in my wooden chair and raised my glass in a silent toast to her city, and to her, and to us. Later, I would worry that she hadn't clinked glasses, that it was a one-sided toast, but it didn't seem that way in the moment. She took a sip of wine, and I wanted to tell her how beautiful she looked in the candlelight, but I didn't dare. I wondered what she would think of the narrow bed in my ship's prow room, and it occurred to me that I could afford to take her to a hotel, though I knew even less about hotels in Montevideo than I did about nice restaurants.

"When do you think you'll go back?" she asked, eyeing me over the top of her glass.

"Go back?" I said, still distracted. A hotel room seemed a little crass. Also, it was unsustainable, without eating through all my savings. I was sure I was going to want more than a night or two with her.

"To California."

"Oh. I don't know." She looked amused, as if she'd noticed my distraction. "I'm not sure what I want to do," I said, returning to reality.

The waiter set the plate of cannelloni down between us then, five delicate little wraps filled with ground sausage that we immediately consumed, politely jostling the fifth one back and forth until Alejandra gave up and ate it. I didn't say that I had a return ticket at the beginning of January—or that I could change it for $150, a sum I could still easily afford. Instead, I found myself telling her about my job with Envirorep, trying to explain the concept of an environmental consulting firm that made a lot of money keeping multinational corporations in line with US government regulations. "Basically," I said, "I sat at a computer all day playing with data in a GIS program."

"Seems totally out of character."

"It paid well." I was thrilled to hear that she'd been paying attention to my "character." I remembered what she'd said about my bird diary. I'd dismissed her comment about nineteenth-century naturalists, but it had hit a nerve, memories of a childhood aspiration. I told her as much. I told her how I'd started university as a wildlife major, but only lasted a year. The classes were boring, especially ornithology, and the whole premise of wildlife management had depressed me—I'd done a summer internship at Yellowstone and felt more like a zookeeper than a naturalist, more custodian than observer. "What would a twenty-first-century naturalist even do?" I said. "There's nothing left to discover—not even much *real* nature left to observe."

"In the microbial world there's lots left to discover. Yellowstone! I would love to go there. The first studies of microbial ecology were done in those hot springs."

"Do *you* think of yourself as a naturalist?"

"No. I lack the empathetic connection." She was grinning and watching my face, her expression curious, half-teasing, flirtatious. "The spiritual dimension."

"Ha! You sound downright evangelical when you talk about your bugs!"

"That's just scientific enthusiasm. It's hard to get spiritual about microbes—though I would if I could. They really are the essence of life."

We bantered back and forth a bit and I refilled our wine glasses, and then I asked her a question I'd been thinking about since we'd left her lab. "Are there endangered species of microbes? Like there are birds and animals?"

"Probably. But when it comes to microbes, species aren't really the point. Their definition and significance is murky. More important are the communities, the functions. In the fossil record, paleontologists can detect five global-scale mass extinctions in the last billion years—times when the extinction rate was exponentially higher than the low rate of evolution and over

75 percent of extant species disappeared over relatively short periods. The most severe was about a quarter-billion years ago, before the dinosaurs took over. More than 90 percent of the detectable, fossil-forming species on earth disappeared, and the entire marine environment, maybe even the atmosphere, was transformed. It was a total apocalypse, though it did take millions of years. The mass extinction that did away with the dinosaurs appears to have been more sudden, apparently triggered by an asteroid slamming into the earth and filling the sky with dusts and noxious gases. That one wiped out some 75 percent of the earth's fossil-forming species. It's unclear what happened to microbial life during these extinctions because microbes don't leave much of a fossil trail. We can infer changes in the dominant metabolic and energy-generating processes from molecular biomarkers we find left in the rocks, but we have no idea if and how microbial diversity was affected, or if that even mattered—" She broke off abruptly. "Sorry," she said. "Am I boring you?"

"No!" I said, startled. Bored? I had been listening with every sense engaged, subsumed in all levels of aesthetic, intellectual, and sensual pleasure, watching her talk, watching her eat. Our meat had arrived, and she was explaining all this between bites, eating with as much abandon as she was talking—none of the small thin girl picking daintily at her food that one might expect from looking at her.

"What we're doing now," Alejandra went on, taking me at my word, "will probably show up in the future fossil record as a very sudden mass extinction, like the one that did the dinosaurs in. Except instead of finding iridium from an asteroid in the sediments, they'll find all the paraphernalia of industrial civilization."

"Who's going to be around to look?" I said.

She laughed. "Right. Though *Homo sapiens* should have some advantages over dinosaurs, like consciousness and foresight."

"Hasn't done much good so far."

"I guess not. The current rate of species decline is estimated to be thousands of times higher than the natural background rate. In past centuries, higher rates were mostly due to over-predation by humans, but now habitat destruction and climate change are taking an even greater toll. I saw one estimate that 10 percent of all *known* species had disappeared in the twentieth century, and who knows how many tropical species of insect or amphibian might have gone under that we never even knew about. And the microbes?" she said, coming back to my question, her fork halting in midair and etching a little circle above her plate. "We only know a tiny percentage of the extant species. And they adapt so quickly. . . . If you lose a very specific, isolated ecosystem, you will probably lose species. Take the thermal springs in Yellowstone. If they disappear, you might lose some species of microbes. Or say, a lichen goes extinct—it has a specific symbiotic relationship with a certain bacteria, and that bacteria might disappear with it. Or maybe even if some mammal goes extinct, there might be a particular set of intestinal microbes that go with it."

"What about your mud? What if you dry it up, or dig it up, or burn all the vegetation and plant something else?"

"That's a huge environmental disruption, from a microbial point of view. Any sort of agriculture is. You lose an ecosystem, a microbial community. But does it matter in terms of species diversity? How specific are these soil communities? That's why I wanted to sample in your marsh. On the one hand, the rice and the marsh offer similar environments for the bugs—water, mud, an oxic zone, an anoxic zone, et cetera. But unlike the rice fields, the marsh doesn't completely dry out every year. And the chemistry and physical structure of the mud should be different. In that sense, I expect the marsh to be more complex—maybe not in the reed bed, but certainly in the pond, where there's more variety in the vegetation."

"My uncle is planning to dam the creek that feeds into the marsh," I said.

"The uncle I met at your house? From Venezuela?"

"No, no, not Rubén. His older brother, Juan Luis. He works in the agriculture ministry. Lives in Montevideo."

"And why is he damming the creek?"

"He wants to build an irrigation pond and plant rice."

"Ah. It's hard to argue with rice. Everyone is growing rice up there. It's probably the only thriving part of the Uruguayan economy."

"That's what Juan says. Even Caruso, who has been leasing it for his cows, says it's crazy that no one ever planted rice on that land."

I'd finished my dinner, and I figured I should stop asking questions and give her a chance to eat. I tried to refill her wine glass, but she covered it with her hand, noting that she had to drive, so I emptied the carafe into my own glass, and we nestled into a comfortable silence as she finished eating, the hum of the busy restaurant and other peoples' conversations wrapped around us like a cocoon, breached finally by the busboy clearing our plates and the waiter offering dessert, which we both declined.

When we ventured back outside, the spring breeze had become a strong wind, blowing off the water and tunneling between the buildings in chilly gusts. The shops had closed and the only people about were going to and from the restaurants, like us. Alejandra remarked on the cold, and I used it as an excuse to put my arm around her shoulders and pull her close as we strolled back to her car.

It would be easy enough to slip into my room unnoticed. Abuela would be upstairs, either watching TV or sound asleep. Rubén might still be downstairs, and I didn't relish the idea of running into him just then, but when we pulled up in front of the house, the only light was coming from the porch light and the lamp in my room, which Abuela must have left on for me in one of her occasional random acts of grandmotherly love. Alejandra left the motor running. She turned to me and told me how much she'd enjoyed the evening. She said she was looking forward to going birding next week and sat there waiting for me to kiss her goodbye and get out.

I reached past her and turned the key to shut the motor off. Then I asked her quietly to come in with me. She shook her head one small time, not very convincingly, so I got out of the car and went around to her side and opened the door. I reached down and took her hand from the steering wheel, tugging at it gently, until she flowed softly out of the car and into my arms. We stood in the street next to the open car door and kissed until the clip-clop of a horse and a clattering cart disturbed us, and Alejandra slipped out of my arms. The cart stopped in front of the overflowing dumpster across the street, and as the driver started pulling stuff out and piling it up in his cart, Alejandra retreated into her car.

"*Ven*," I said, "it's okay." I leaned over to get a better look at her face, not sure if it was me or the idea of Abuela's house that she was balking at. "That's my room in front, where the light is." It looked warm and inviting, a soft yellow light glowing through the aged glass of the porthole window, but she shook her head again, and I had to step back as she reached to pull the door closed.

"I'll see you next week," she said, and left me to dream of next week.

12

The estancia was beginning to seem like an actual place, if not the center of the universe that Mom made it out to be. The ruin where I'd pulled weeds out of the floor could now be called a house, if a slightly ramshackle one. It had three functioning bedrooms, there was a growing assortment of used furniture, and the whitewashed walls of the living room even sported a few old etchings that Mom had liberated from Abuela's garage. Rubén had convinced Mom to buy a small gas generator and a refrigerator, so we didn't have to drive to Lascano for ice, and he'd strung up an electric light in the kitchen. It turned out that he had a knack for making things out of abandoned objects—not jerry-rigged utilitarian solutions like Mom's, but attractive, well-crafted things that just happened to be made out of recycled junk. Juan and I drove out on Friday and found the turnoff from the main road marked by a whitewashed wooden arrow with "Quiroga" painted in fanciful black lettering, and the dirt track to the house adorned with an arched portico made of old horseshoes and fencing wire. The chicken coop had been whitewashed and Rubén had painted its door bright red. In front of the house, he'd somehow turned a pile of large rocks and a few old planks into a sturdy bench—also painted red—replete with stone armrests.

Mom seemed surprisingly content out there. We'd set up a simple gravity-fed drip irrigation system from the creek, and her vegetable beds now covered a full acre. She said it made more sense to plant the trees for the orchard in the winter when they were dormant, but she'd planted two young apple trees to mark the space. I'd lived with her suburban gardens most of my life, but this was something else altogether, and not just because I had so many gallons of sweat invested. In that vast, monotonous expanse of pasture, each sprout of lettuce and chard and spinach seemed to burst through the ground with individual resolution and optimism. Mom was experimenting, planting everything she could get her hands on, looking for open-pollinated varieties so she could reproduce her own seed, supplementing local sources with seeds she'd smuggled from home, which included all sorts of open-pollinated heirloom varieties. There was every kind of lettuce and squash imaginable, corn, tomatoes, sweet peppers, beets . . . I knew she had struggled with snails and beetles and funguses, and some things had failed completely or been demolished as soon as they emerged from the ground. But the overall effect was one of success, of plenty.

Juan Luis would never admit that he was impressed by what Mom had accomplished, but on that particular weekend the two of them pursued their separate visions for the estancia in peaceful parallel, as if they had reached some sort of truce. They even seemed to enjoy each other's company. The good weather and the new chicken family helped. The little black hen was now trailing four fuzzy yellow chicks and one long-legged brown bundle of down. The Ñandú had a propensity for running in confused circles and it was impossible not to laugh every time it dashed past. Rubén's failed attempts to train it and his creative puttering only added to the general hilarity. For my part, I was happy enough to play resident gaucho for all parallel versions of the estancia. I helped Mom with the weeding and, despite my worries about what it might do to the marsh, I helped Juan stake out his irrigation pond.

I found a *Chajá* nest full of yellow chicks on the creek shore near where Juan and I were working, and when we finished on

Sunday afternoon, I went looking for nests, thinking about what I would show Alejandra. The breeding season was in full swing, and I discovered an artfully woven sack of grass dangling from a branch in the *monte*, though no one flew in or out and I had no idea who the artist was. Perched at the top of a clump of reeds in the swampy field before the reed bed, an eye-catching red-headed blackbird was whistling so loudly and cheerfully you would think it didn't have a care in the world—but suspended in the middle of the clump just below its perch was a nest of mud-plastered reeds. It was yet another life bird, easily identified as a *Federal*, its head and shoulders looking as if they'd been dipped in melted red-orange crayon.

Usually, I was so focused on getting through the reed bed without cuts, that I didn't see much except the lively horde of psychedelic *Sietecolores*. Now, however, I stopped every few yards and moved off my marked route, squatting down to search the ground and understory all around me. That's how I spotted the *Pato Capuchino* nest less than a yard from my feet, its occupant holding her ground with duckish determination, brown-eyed, hooded, and implacable.

My prehistoric glade was unusually empty. The *Pollona Azul* had built a floating nest and was reigning over the pool in royal blue glory, but no one else was in sight. The tangle of brush on the far side was as noisy as ever, however, so I figured everyone must be hidden in there with their nests. It looked so forbidding, I hadn't attempted to go farther than the sampling site at the edge, but now I made my way around the pond and tried to find a way in.

It was rough going. I had to break through the brush and watch out for the quicksand mud, finding strong branches to hold onto with every step. I got about five yards in without seeing anything, and I was resting on a little oasis of solid ground and ready to give up, when I heard the trilling call I'd been chasing for the past few weeks. It sounded as forlorn and lonely as ever—except this time, its call got an immediate answer, and the answer sounded very close by. I knelt down and stared into the undergrowth. As my eyes adjusted to the dim light, a bundle of order emerged from the tangled chaos and I made out the nest tucked into the brush some ten yards from me. It was about two feet above the mud and seemed to have a sort of entrance ramp leading up to it. I raised my binoculars, and in that same moment I heard the call again and a small rail-like bird strode up the ramp and posed like a model on a runway—as if it knew I was watching and would want to sketch it. It had the short neck and body of a crake, a stubby tail cocked up at a sassy right angle, a black-speckled brown breast, and rust-colored ladders running up its sides. Red legs. Red eye and two brown stripes on the head. The bill was long and olive green, more like a rail's bill than a crake's. It had something in its mouth. As I watched, it darted the rest of the way up the ramp, did a little hopping turn, and then ran back down and disappeared in the reeds. The second bird was on the nest, but all I could see was her red eye and the top of her head, which looked exactly like the male's.

I took out my field guide and paged through all the rail family entries, but I still couldn't identify it. It wasn't to be found among the crakes or rails—*burritos* or *gallinetas*—or, for that matter, anywhere else in my field guide to Argentinian and Uruguayan birds. In my journal, I noted the pair as accidentals, outside their normal range, though I'd never seen a nesting pair of accidentals before. I did a quick sketch of the bird the way it had posed on the ramp, and as soon as I got back to the house, I set myself up with my colored pencils and tried to render it more carefully and vividly.

I sat outside on Rubén's bench and used the broad stone armrest as a table. I drew quickly in the fading light and tried to include the whole nest. It was quite the estate for such a little bird, a half-dome of woven twigs and grasses, with that incredible entrance ramp constructed of small branches.

Juan came out of the house and sat down next to me. "How can you see out here?" he said, lighting a cigarette.

"I can't." Dusk had fallen, and though there was a half moon and a bit of a glow coming through the window from Mom's oil lamps, it wasn't really enough to draw by. "I just saw this little guy in the marsh and wanted to get it down before I forgot. The nest is really cool."

Juan leaned around me to look at the sketch. "You're pretty good at that," he said. "You just see it, and then you can draw it like that, like you took a photo? Like Rubén with a song?"

"Sort of. I sketched it while I was out there, and took some notes." I glanced up at him. "Didn't you want to get back to Montevideo tonight?"

"On my way," he said, but he made no move to leave.

I closed the journal, snapped shut the pencil tin, and shifted around so we were both facing the yard.

"I'll be back on Wednesday," he said. "The tractor operator's coming to look at the pond site. He says if this weather holds we can start digging next week." He leaned back and let a stream of smoke jet up into the sky, and we sat there in silence for a moment, watching the first stars appear, contemplating the empty yard, the dark shapes of Juan's car and Mom's truck lurking at its edge, the base of the *parrillero* Rubén had started building out of old bricks. It was after seven and he had a four-hour drive ahead of him and work the next day, but he seemed unworried. "I'm going to leave that land alone," he said, as if he'd just decided this. "It's too expensive to clean up anyway." He blew smoke out the side of his mouth and glanced at me. "You can have your nature reserve."

"If you dam the creek, it'll probably dry up anyway."

"That area is low, the rains will keep it wet. I don't think your birdies will notice if we divert a bit of their water."

I wasn't so sure that my birdies wouldn't notice, or for that matter, that the vegetation wouldn't notice. But at least he wasn't going to bulldoze it.

"Anyway, they'll have water all over the place when we flood the fields."

I toyed with the thin leather cover of my bird journal, thinking of the *Jacana* and the *Pollona Azul*, my nameless little rail. The ones that didn't like to fly, that needed cover. If the marsh dried out, they would have to go somewhere else—if they could find the right "somewhere." A few would manage it, simply scatter. But the more fastidious ones? The shiest, the ones who needed cover, the most demanding, the rarest? They would probably die. "Can't you just use water from the canal?" I said. "Instead of damming the creek?"

"Way too expensive. Caruso buys that water from the India Muerta reservoir and we'd have to pay him. And put in a pump system that's even more expensive than our pond. The only reason I could get a loan for this project is because I convinced the bank I can do it with water from the creek. But don't worry, Gabriel, the ducks will love our pond. You'll see."

"Won't they eat your rice?" I asked.

"What?" Juan turned and looked at me.

"The ducks. You said the farmers used to poison them because they ate the crops."

"*Pues . . .*" Juan flicked his cigarette ash into the yard. "There aren't as many as there were in the old days. Caruso says they're only a problem if you don't drain the field properly after planting. Then they eat the seed from the places where the water pools, so you get patches with no germination. But we should be able to manage that without murdering any ducks."

Mom emerged from the house and sat down next to Juan. I waited for her to cough or make some comment about his smoking, but she just leaned back against the side of the house and praised Rubén's bench, and the *parrillero* that would replace the open firepit we'd been using for *asado*.

"Who would have thought our brother could be useful," Juan said, stubbing out his cigarette and tossing the butt into the yard.

"He already fell asleep." Mom giggled. "With the Ñandú."

"He's *sleeping* with the Ñandú?" I leaned around Juan to look at Mom.

"He put it in a basket next to his bed, like a baby. It was getting all henpecked in the coop. Poor thing has ugly duckling syndrome. It tries so *earnestly* to fit in with the chickens, but all they do is peck at it and pull its feathers out. Even the mother and the other chicks."

"It is kind of cute," Juan said.

"Won't stay that way," I said. "I don't think he's going to want to sleep with it for long."

"It's adorable," Mom said. "Rubén named it Ángel. He thinks it looks like an angel, the way it sticks out its wings when it runs around. *Un angelito.*"

The Ñandú was undeniably cute, but whether it looked angelic or diabolic zigzagging about the yard like some wacked-out cartoon character on amphetamines was a matter for debate. That's what it was doing when Alejandra arrived on Wednesday afternoon. It was frenetically searching for Rubén, who'd gone into Lascano to buy supplies, or its foster mother, who was hiding in the coop with her chicks. At least, that's what I assumed it was doing, since when one of them was in sight it was relatively calm, and when both were in the yard, it ran in circles. It was still uncertain where to place its mother trust, though the choice seemed obvious enough—the chicken snubbed and pecked at it, whereas Rubén fed it crackers and apples, and tickled it under its wings.

It was late afternoon by the time Alejandra arrived, and no one was around but me and Angelito—Mom gone with Rubén, and Juan off somewhere with his backhoe operator—but she greeted me with such cool reserve, I wondered if I'd just imagined the easy intimacy and warm goodnight kiss of our dinner date the week before. She'd already collected her rice field samples by herself, and she was still in work mode, better prepared this time, with a knapsack and a small cooler bag for her instruments and sample jars, but no sign of binoculars. I began to doubt I'd even get a chance to show her the rails. Let alone lure her into bed with me that night. But then Angelito ran by her feet, and I realized that the coolness was just focus.

She let loose a delighted squeal and stopped what she was doing to watch the baby bird race about the yard. "When did it hatch?"

"Last week."

Angelito came to a sudden stop in the middle of the yard and stood motionless, watching us out of one eye.

"Did you name it?" Alejandra asked, laughing.

"Rubén named it," I said. "Ángel. He thinks it's male, but you can't really tell."

"Angelito," she called softly, crouching down to baby Ñandú level and holding out a hand. Even in rubber boots and baggy pants, she moved with such delicious fluidity I could have stood there all day watching her. Like a dancer, but more organic, unselfconscious.

"It will only go to Rubén," I said, turning to watch Angelito instead. "Rubén bribes it with El Trigal crackers, claims those are the only ones it likes, that it refuses all the imported gringo brands."

"A truly Uruguayan bird!" She laughed and stood up, taking a few careful steps toward the motionless chick—but it started running circles again, and she gave up and turned back to her preparations. She had saved the little map I'd made of the marsh sampling sites, but I told her we didn't need it, that I knew where they were.

"Did you bring your binoculars? I've got something better than a baby Ñandú to show you."

"What could be better than a baby Ñandú?" She retrieved her binoculars from the car and looped them over her neck.

"A nest full of baby *Chajás*?"

She wasn't disappointed. I'd been birding the same area for the past three days, working my way up the creek and picking painstakingly through the reeds and around the pond to the rails' nest. I always saw something new, but sharing my discoveries with Alejandra was a pleasure in and of itself. I hadn't known the *Chajás* could swim, but we found the whole family out on the creek, six fat yellow chicks paddling around in the murky water while the adults looked on with the relaxed vigilance of parents minding their toddlers at the neighborhood playground. Alejandra would have squatted there in the grass watching them all afternoon if I hadn't coaxed her on with promises of more and better surprises.

She spotted a *Monjita Blanca* lording it over an elaborate mud construction it had expropriated from an *Hornero*, and the crayon-headed *Federal* perched upside down on his reed and dropping grubs from his slick black beak into four open mouths. I heard her whispered exclamations of delight as I showed her the three cream-colored eggs in a *Sietecolores* nest and silently pointed out the brown *Pato Capuchino*, who didn't seem to have moved for three days—and I felt triumphant, like a playwright or director sitting in the audience on opening night. Except, of course, I hadn't staged any of it. It just was.

Now that the sites were chosen and we knew where and where not to step, collecting samples went quickly, even in the pond. The *Pollona Azul* eggs had hatched, and when Alejandra saw the blue queen and her three black babies lined up on their floating empire she thought surely that was the big surprise of the day—but no, I told her, it was just the warm-up act. The main act, I said, was less flamboyant but more interesting.

We left her knapsack with the samples in the glade. She looked skeptical when I told her we were going into the brush, but she followed me, uncomplaining, and when we got to my island of solid ground and I knelt down to wait for the rails, she followed suit. I didn't tell her what we were waiting for, but I did point out the nest. We could just barely see the top of the sitting bird's head, and I was tempted to clap and try to flush her out so Alejandra could get a look—but the rails were so reclusive I worried they might abandon the nest if we disturbed them. I was hoping the male would appear on the ramp if we waited long enough, but they weren't even calling. It was like watching a movie that was stuck on its most boring frame, and it wasn't exactly comfortable, kneeling there in the wet grass, with the mosquitoes whining about our heads and drilling into any spot we'd missed with the repellent. "Maybe we should go," I whispered, glancing over at Alejandra, who had her binoculars trained on the nest. But we waited another five minutes, and finally, we heard the trilling vibrato of a rail calling from somewhere in the thick of the marsh. A pause, a few beats, and there was an answer from the nest, another pause, and then there he was at the bottom of the ramp. He hopped left, hopped right, dashed up and crammed something into the female's beak, and ran back into the reeds.

"¡Pa!" Alejandra lowered the binoculars and turned toward me, her face radiant. "It's the bird you were chasing! I guess he isn't as lonely as you thought."

"Right," I said, pleased that she remembered. "Probably what I thought was one bird leading me around in circles was actually two." I pushed myself to my feet. "Let's get out of here. It's getting late and I'm being eaten alive."

"What are they called?"

"I don't know, they're not in the field guide. I think they must be in the rail family, but that's about all I can see."

She wanted to see for herself, but I made her wait until we got past the pond and through the reed bed, before I would stop and extract the field guide from my knapsack.

She studied the illustrations of rails and crakes, reading the short descriptive texts, paging forward into the coots and shorebirds, and backward into the guans and birds of prey.

"None of these are it," she said finally.

"I told you. It's not in there. But this only covers Argentina and Uruguay. They probably wandered down from Brazil—though it's hard to imagine rails going very far from home. You hardly ever see them fly, and when you do, it's just short little dashes down close to the ground, as if they're afraid to go too high. Maybe we can find a field guide that covers Brazil."

"There's a biologist at the university who studies birds, Eduardo Schwartz. We can ask him."

"I've got a drawing you can show him. And a description."

"You drew it? Let's see—"

I handed her my journal and waited for her to examine the sketch and read the notes.

"It's better than the pictures in the field guide," she said, and watched me blush as I returned the books to my knapsack.

The sun was starting down, and we cut back through the pastures without stopping until we got to the rise above the house, where I caught the scent of woodsmoke and sausages, and a faint hint of cigarette smoke. They'd all be down there, I realized, Mom and Juan Luis and Rubén, inaugurating the new *parrillero*. What was I thinking? Idiotically, I'd straightened up my room, made the narrow bed, folded my clothes, and set my few books out on the little table Mom had set up. As if I was going to invite Alejandra to an *asado* with my mother and uncles, and then convince her, in this state of pre-seduction where every move was transparent and loaded with meaning, to spend the night with me there. I slowed my pace and then stopped, turning to gaze back over the tilting grassland toward the seemingly impenetrable mass of reeds and brush we'd exited. The sky was spectacular, wisps of cloud moving on the wind, orange and pink clashing with the endless green of pasture and marsh.

"Do you think they ever come out of there?" Alejandra had stopped next to me and was following my gaze.

"The rails? They like to stay hidden—but they must have come from somewhere." I was gratified to see that, even after all the afternoon's spectacular surprises, she was as obsessed as I was by the timid little birds.

"Maybe they're not lost!" She reached out to grip my forearm where it lay resting across my binoculars. "Maybe the species has always lived in these marshes. Before the rice, before the drainage projects. It could just be that no one ever noticed them."

She was looking up at me intently, but I was too distracted by her tiny hand gripping my arm to answer. I laid my free hand over it and pressed it hard against my arm—so I could feel it, so it couldn't escape. Then I leaned down to kiss her. Slowly, now, on the lips, and beyond the lips—a kiss so perfectly tuned and timed it seemed we had been practicing it our entire lives. When it ended, we were both shivering—though whether from cold, or elation, or anticipation was unclear. She was just wearing a thin sweater, and I pulled her up against me, hiding her from the biting wind, her arms folded up between us and mine crossed awkwardly above her knapsack. I rested my chin in her lush hair and watched the sun settle over the horizon, and we stood like that for I don't know how long, before she wiggled free and we continued across the pasture toward the house.

"Someone would have seen them," I said, finally coming back to her suggestion that the rails had always been here. "People live out here—Juan says the *nutria* hunters used to go all over these marshes in canoes."

"You think a *nutria* hunter would have noticed these little birds? They're not exactly easy to spot, even when you're looking for them."

Despite my skepticism, the idea thrilled me. I felt lightheaded, blessed, walking across the grassland with Alejandra springing along by my side and this shared knowledge between us, these two little birds that only she and I knew were there. We stopped at the car, and as Alejandra put the samples in her ice chest and exchanged her muddy boots for a pair of loafers, I told her I wanted to drive back to Montevideo with her. This hadn't been the plan at all, but she nodded as if she'd assumed as much. I plucked the last lone sausage off the *parrillero* and we went in to wash up and see if there was anything else to eat.

Mom and Juan and Rubén were still having dinner, a plate piled high with *asado* in the middle of the table. Mom had set a place for me, and before I'd even toed off my boots or finished chewing my sausage, she jumped up to set one for Alejandra. I was starving, and I assumed Alejandra was also, but as Mom introduced her to Juan, I immediately began to have second thoughts about sitting down to dinner with them.

Juan mumbled, "*Mucho gusto*," and stood up to brush cheeks, but he looked as cold and stiff as an English butler.

"She's doing a PhD in biology," Mom told him. "Eva's daughter!"

I knew Mom was remorseful that she hadn't gone on to get a PhD herself, but she sounded so weirdly proud of Alejandra that I wondered if she was making a jab at me for not going to grad school. Dad had been the one who'd always pushed me on that front, not Mom.

"Maybe we'll just grab some sandwiches," I said as Alejandra excused herself and headed down the hall to the bathroom. "Alejandra needs to get her samples to the lab, and I'm going to drive back to the city with her." I broke off a chunk of bread and reached over to extract a steak from the platter of *asado*, but Mom swatted my hand away.

"Be civilized and make some proper sandwiches, if you must." But she took the platter over to the counter and started making them herself.

"Why don't you drive back with me tomorrow," Juan said. "What's she doing here, anyway? *La señorita* Silva Paden." He sounded peevish, pronouncing Alejandra's family names as if they were tainted.

"Something wrong?" I said, looking at him. "She's been collecting mud samples in the marsh."

"Of course not," Mom said, dribbling chimichurri on a sausage sandwich. "Juan, I told her she could sample out there whenever she wants. And I guess she needs Gabe's help."

"She's interested in the birds," I said.

But Juan had picked up his plate and was headed out the door. "She just reminds everyone of her mother."

Rubén rolled his eyes. "God forbid, we should be reminded of our dear friend Eva the terrorist."

I glanced nervously toward the hall, worried that Alejandra would walk in on this conversation, annoyed that my family thought she was here to fuel their arguments, that the sibling peace treaty could collapse so easily.

"I think I like being reminded of Eva." Mom set the *asado* platter back on the table in front of Rubén. "It doesn't bother you?"

"She's lovely." He grinned. "Like her mother. Maybe I'll drive back with them."

"Don't you want to stay with your precious Ñandú?" I said, making a show of filching a sausage behind Mom's back, trying to dissemble the fact that I did not want his company. "It thinks you're its mother."

"It's a him," Rubén said. "Santiago confirmed that Ángel is a male."

"Just what we need around here," Mom said, just as Alejandra came back into the room. "Another spoiled male."

"Santiago says the Ñandú really is a male," I explained.

"How does he know?"

"Gaucho intuition," Rubén said. "*Ché*, Alejandra, do you mind if I drive back with you and Gabriel?"

"Of course not—"

I wanted to snatch her smile out of the air before it reached my uncle, wanted to reserve it for my own consumption—but Rubén returned it in kind. And then he chatted her up the whole way back to Montevideo, sitting in the middle of the back seat eating a steak sandwich and leaning forward to talk into her ear while I fretted about how and when I would be able to recapture the mood of our shared sunset. But Rubén was not as oblivious as he seemed. When we pulled up in front of Abuela's house, he quickly said goodnight and jumped out of the car, as if it were understood that I wouldn't be accompanying him in.

We drove by the lab, and I carried the ice chest upstairs and waited while Alejandra deposited her new samples in the refrigerator. Then, without discussion, she took me to her grandfather's house, a tidy two-story affair in the older part of Pocitos. It was after midnight when we arrived, the grandfather asleep somewhere upstairs, and we were in her bedroom, already half undressed and all over each other when Alejandra realized we were still caked in dry mud from the marsh and put the brakes on the whole operation. I had never, ever wanted to make love as desperately, as uncontrollably as at that moment, and it was as if she wanted to hold me, hold us, in that state, where each look, each touch, each movement or word generated a current of yearning and pleasure so acute it almost hurt—as if to ensure we would remember making love this time, this First Time, for the rest of our lives. She handed me a big white towel and pointed me to a bathroom, and then she disappeared upstairs for what seemed an excruciatingly long time.

I took a quick shower, wrapped myself in the towel, and went back into the bedroom to wait for her, pacing around and examining the paraphernalia of her life. A bookshelf still full of children's books, some of which I recognized—*El cuento del Fernando, Aventuras de Alicia, El maravilloso mago de Oz*, ten volumes of Mafalda cartoons, *La balada de Johnny Sosa*. . . . A couple of worn-looking board games, Monopoly and Scrabble.

An antique-looking Nintendo. A small desk in the corner was piled high with scientific journals and papers, but tidier than her office desk. The dresser top was home to a not-quite-haphazard arrangement of old dolls and stuffed animals—a black cat sitting on the back of a threadbare green tortoise with an extended neck, like the animal friends in a fairytale; a large brown teddy bear leaning against the wall with an old baby doll cradled in its lap, a Barbie-like fashion doll leaning against a toy horse . . . I sat down on the bed, which was covered with a soft pink comforter and matching pillows. The pillows had ruffles.

"Have you lived here all your life?" I asked when she finally reappeared. "With your grandfather?" She was wrapped in a thick white robe, her hair hanging in damp ringlets around her face.

"And my grandmother, but she died when I was a teenager. I moved out for a couple years. Came back a year ago." She paused, and I guessed that she'd been living with a boyfriend, but all I could think about at the moment was untying the bathrobe.

Looking at Alejandra, listening to the low, sandy cadence of her voice, experiencing the cool analytical edge of her intellect . . . it was hard to imagine her melting into my arms the way she did then, the unexpected cries of release that carried her voice into another register, hard to imagine that I could take her to this place out of control, that I could wield such power. That I could make her love me.

13

I spent the week in Montevideo dipping into and out of euphoria and anguish. I would have seen her every day, slept with her every night . . . but she was too busy. She had friends I'd yet to meet, classes to teach, her bugs to attend. And, apparently, her grandfather was getting seriously senile and there was no one to stay with him after the maid left in the evenings. A whole day would go by when I wouldn't hear from her, and then I'd worry that I'd dreamt the whole thing, that I was deluding myself. Maybe she was too old for me. Too smart, too self-assured, too mature. She knew what she was doing on this earth, had a real career, a calling. And me? I was at loose ends, as directionless as Angelito zigzagging around the yard. Okay, I'd had a lucrative job in California, and I still had a good bank account. Maybe that counted as a grown-up accomplishment, some form of male authority, if I wanted to play that card, but I didn't think it interested Alejandra any more than it interested me. I was just a cute, amusing foreigner with a knack for drawing birds. I was a fling, I thought, and for the first time in my life, I did not want to be a fling.

When we were together, however, doubt disappeared in a shimmering sea of shared joy and fascination, leaving as little trace as a cormorant diving for fish. I had never been so aware of the details of a woman, not just when we were making love, but when we were sitting across from each other drinking a beer or walking down the street, as if every move, every look, every word were a sort of long drawn-out foreplay, as if I hadn't really known how to make love before. We went to dinner, we went to a movie, we strolled hand in hand along the Rambla in the evening, and we stole unnoticed into her grandfather's house and screwed each other into oblivion in her pink ruffled bed. We spent Sunday at the big Tristán Narvaja market, buying groceries and presents for our respective grandparents, wandering happily through the festive jumble of vegetables and pastas, antique junk and used books, handmade *mate* gourds and shoes, cheap Brazilian clothes and contraband watches. Rubén tried to get us to go with him to a Frente rally on the Friday before the *balotaje*, but Alejandra didn't want to go and we went to a movie instead. Her aunt had come from Buenos Aires for a few days, so she didn't have to worry about her grandfather, and we stole into the ship's prow afterwards and spent the night fused together in my narrow bed. I wasn't quite ready to subject Alejandra to Abuela, but when I went to the kitchen to fetch us coffee in the morning, Abuela and Rubén were sitting at the dining room table, waiting in ambush.

"If the girl is worth sleeping with," Abuela announced without preamble, "you can surely invite her to breakfast." Discretion was clearly not on the agenda.

Rubén was grinning. "We bought extra rolls. And both newspapers."

There was a platter of *bizcochos* and rolls in the middle of the table, a jar of dulce de leche, butter, slices of ham, and marmalade—a much more elaborate breakfast than anyone was accustomed to at Abuela's house. Even the window blind was open, the room bathed in the gray light of an overcast morning. They seemed an unlikely pair of conspirators, but there they were, sitting next to each other with their dueling newspapers, savoring the mutual but amiable disapproval that marked their relationship.

"You forgot the coffee," I said, ambling past the table into the kitchen.

We sat down across from them, and Abuela bypassed the introductions and said good morning as if Alejandra were part of the family and there was nothing new or unusual about her joining us for breakfast. Rubén proffered his *mate*, which Alejandra declined in favor of the coffee I'd prepared, Abuela pushed the platter of rolls toward us, and then they both went back to reading their newspapers. Alejandra and I fixed our rolls and sipped our coffee, and I thought we might be in for a nice quiet breakfast. But then Rubén finished reading *La República* and slid it across the table toward us, and Abuela folded the front section of *El País* and did the same.

"*¡Ajá!*" Abuela said, looking triumphant as Alejandra picked up *El País* to look at the headlines. "I take it you're not going to vote Frente. Like my misguided son." She had taken to sparring with Rubén about the *balotaje*, now that the Blancos and Colorados had joined forces and she thought the Frente didn't stand a chance.

"Excuse me?" Alejandra said.

"She's wondering about your choice of newspapers," Rubén said helpfully. He also had the weekly *Brecha* in front of him, which Abuela hated even more.

Alejandra looked from the paper in her hand to the one on the table. "Ah. Sorry to disappoint you." She smiled at Abuela as though she really were sorry. "I am going to vote for Tabaré."

"Mamá, no young person in their right mind would vote for Jorge Batlle."

"I remember when his uncle died. The whole country went into mourning, young, old, you have it. There were grand parades—"

"That was his *great* uncle, Mamá. And Jorge doesn't even deserve the family name. Speaking of voting," Rubén said, looking at me. "Where's Lili?"

"Lili can't vote here," Abuela said.

"Yes she can. They just screwed up her papers."

"She's at the estancia," I said, reaching for the plate of ham. "Says she doesn't want to waste more time with the idiotic Uruguayan bureaucracy."

"Juan Luis is finally fixing things up out there," Abuela said. "Making it profitable."

"Right," I said, glad Mom wasn't around to hear her. "He's going to plant rice. But Mom is the one doing the fixing up. And growing vegetables."

"The bureaucracy is idiotic," Rubén said. "But she should have been more persistent. If you force the issue it goes through. Lots of people have recouped their voting rights."

"It is kind of dumb," I said. "After all the noise she made about wanting to vote. But that's Mom." I turned to Alejandra. "Do you have to work the polls again tomorrow?"

She nodded, but her attention was still on Abuela. "Did you really know Batlle y Ordóñez?"

"Of course. Everyone knew Don Pepe. He was such a presence. An intellectual, a philosopher. Not just an empty-headed politician, like the idiots we have now."

"Precisely," Rubén said, and opened his *Brecha*.

Abuela folded her hands on the edge of the table, gazed into her myopic distance, and began to recite:

"*Mi verdad revelada, más fecunda*
que la verdad mentida
de la leyenda bíblica, está escrita
en el libro sagrado de la ciencia—"

She broke off her recitation and turned to Alejandra. "You're not Catholic are you?"

Alejandra laughed. "I'm a student of the 'revealed truth,'" she said, quoting Abuela's lines back to her, "in the 'sacred book of science.'"

"Good. Don Pepe offended all the Catholics with that poem."

I laid my hand on Alejandra's thigh under the table. I was glad she was humoring Abuela. It implied that she took our fling seriously. "Alejandra's a scientist, Abuela. She meant that literally."

Abuela took in this information, her eyes still on Alejandra. "My daughter is a biology teacher," she said. "Gabriel's mother."

"Yes, we met—"

"She wanted to be a doctor, but that's as far as she got. How old are you?"

"Twenty-seven."

"Twenty-seven," Abuela repeated, lowering her voice and filling the number with portent. "Three to the third." She glanced at me, as if I, personally, was the beneficiary of the portent and should understand its significance.

"There's something special about threes," I explained, though the only significance I could see was that Alejandra was four years older and wiser than me.

Abuela had turned her attention back to Alejandra. "You're Eva and Natalio's daughter, aren't you?" she said suddenly, and before Alejandra could answer, Abuela's gaze shifted to Rubén, and she added, "Rubén was almost as hot for your mother as Gabriel is for you."

Rubén looked up from his newspaper and burst out laughing, and Alejandra and I looked at each other and blushed. Watching the rare burgundy-red smolder rise in her cheeks, I almost laughed myself, knowing how it must clash with the gaudy pink that covered my own face.

"Unfortunately for Rubén, lots of boys were hot for Eva," Abuela went on. "But they were just teenagers. Eva was two years dead by the time she was your age. She was a wild one."

"So I hear," Alejandra said, the smolder fading from her cheeks, even as mine burned on.

"She wasn't wild when they killed her," Rubén said quietly.

"I suppose you would have to vote Frente," Abuela said.

"Of course she does," Rubén said. "Though there's nothing wild about today's Frente, either. If there ever was. Tabaré is as docile as an overfed cow."

"We all have to vote," Alejandra said carefully. "And I do plan to vote for the Frente. Nothing to do with my mother." She turned to Rubén, her tone simultaneously coquettish and sarcastic, her face an impassive facade of cool bronze. "I also read *El Pais,*" she said, rustling the paper. "Better news coverage."

Rubén raised his eyebrows and lifted a hand in reluctant acknowledgment of the newspaper's superior quality. But Abuela plowed on.

"Don't get me wrong," she said. "I liked Eva. She was the cleverest of Lili's band of friends, the most intelligent. She was twelve or thirteen when I realized she also had The Gift." She lowered her voice, her eyes still on Alejandra. "Extrasensory perception. Most of the great Masons had it."

Rubén closed his *Brecha* and stood up. "If Celia is going to start telling Masonic secrets, I'd better get out of here. I'm not worthy."

"I'm not telling secrets," Abuela said, shooing him out of the room. "Just history. The Masons who made the highest orders," she told us, "were almost always gifted. In ancient times, they were scattered around the world and it was the only way they could communicate and keep track of what was going on. Of course, it's one thing to have The Gift and another to master it. That takes training and a disciplined nature, which Eva definitely did not have."

I tried to catch Alejandra's eye, but she was concentrating on her breakfast, spreading butter and jam on a roll.

"What kind of scientist are you?" Abuela asked, leaning back in her chair as if she planned to spend all day sitting at the breakfast table chatting with Alejandra. I couldn't believe how sociable she was being, for all her lack of tact.

"Microbiologist."

"You want some more coffee?" I offered, trying to relieve her of Abuela's interrogation.

She held out her cup for more coffee, but she didn't seem to mind the interrogation. "I study bacteria and other tiny critters. You might say it requires extrasensory perception—microscopes, chemical analysis, inference."

By the time I'd heated the milk and returned from the kitchen with our coffee, Alejandra had given Abuela a *Reader's Digest* version of her research. And Abuela, in return, seemed to have invited her to the birthday party on Tuesday evening. I was relieved and grateful, and when Alejandra and I parted that afternoon, I tried to tell her as much and apologize for Abuela's rude comments about her mother. But Alejandra brushed off both thanks and apologies with a dismissive flutter of her hand, which also quelled any inclination I might have had to inquire about her mother's fate. She had heard it all before, she told me, except the parts about Rubén and "The Gift." And she hadn't been humoring Abuela for my sake at all. Abuela interested her. Sure, she was pedantic and tactless. But she was also direct and playful and, somehow, charismatic. "She's sour and opinionated," Alejandra said, "but also sweet."

"*Sweet*? You think Celia is *sweet*?"

"Sure." She laughed and gave a little shrug. "Don't you?"

"Yes . . ." I said slowly. "But why? Why do we think that? I mean, all this stuff about *esoterismo*, all the intrigue." I laughed. "A bunch of nonsense. But with Abuela . . . I don't know, you almost start to believe it. And what's the deal with the Masons?"

"They played a big role in Uruguayan politics and intelligentsia. In your grandmother's time, being a Mason symbolized intellect and power."

"She says they excluded women, but that just seems to have made it more attractive. My mother says she's a misogynist."

"Who knows? She's a would-be intellectual."

"Rubén thinks she is getting senile. She used to be really sharp."

"I heard a rumor that Tabaré is a Mason." Alejandra laughed. "I wonder what she'd say to that. Actually, I wonder what your uncle would say. The left doesn't much like the Masons."

"It would just confirm all his suspicions about Tabaré. But Alejandra, you don't really have to come to her party. It's going to be a bunch of old relatives."

"Oh, I wouldn't miss it." She planted a fleeting kiss on my lips, and was off.

On the evening of her eighty-seventh birthday, my sweet-and-sour Abuela paraded down the stairs like a little girl playing dress-up, enveloped in a belted, full-skirted cotton dress from some previous decade and some larger, plumper version of herself. It had a bold pattern of large blue and yellow checks that I would never in my wildest imagination have associated with Abuela, but Rubén said he remembered the dress from when he was a kid. The neckline rested on her shoulders like a tent on its poles, but her bare throat and arms were as tender white and innocent as a baby's. Not even Rubén had the heart to tease her, and we feared she would see through our compliments, so we all acted as if it were perfectly normal to see Abuela in such a dress.

We had spent two days preparing. I'd already bought a present, a magnifying glass I'd seen laid across the page of an antique book in the window display of a used bookstore. Mom hunted down an Umberto Eco novel she thought Abuela would like and was shocked when I told her Abuela was having trouble reading anything smaller than a newspaper headline. But she liked the idea of the magnifying glass, so we decided to wrap our presents together in one package. Elsa baked a giant cake. Mom made piles of little sandwiches and quiches. And Rubén and I set up tables and decorated the backyard.

Rubén had been in a funk since the *balotaje* on Sunday. He'd returned from voting and ensconced himself in front of the TV, downing beer after beer and becoming more and more morose as the afternoon wore on. By the time Tabaré conceded the election—with three fatuous sentences delivered from the lobby of a swanky Carrasco hotel while his supporters waited in vain at the Frente headquarters—Rubén was totally drunk and talking at the TV, telling the Frente supporters to go home, calling Tabaré a son of a bitch . . . *un imbécil, un cretino, un nabo.* . . . Abuela came downstairs to gloat and I feared he would turn his expletives on her—a turnip?—but instead he raised a long rambling toast: to Abuela who could stop worrying about the communists taking over, to Juan Luis who could keep his job, to Elsa and all the misguided Uruguayans who voted Colorado because they'd built the country—no matter that they'd also destroyed it—to Jorge Batlle who didn't deserve his great uncle's name . . . The hangover seemed to last for days, but on the morning of Abuela's party Rubén was back in form. He hadn't bought her a birthday present because he said she was impossible to please and would disdain the gesture, which was probably true—but he'd thrown himself into decorating the backyard with me, dredging folding tables and chairs and a long strand of red Christmas lights out of the garage. We'd hung the red lights on the grape arbor, which we managed to prune without Abuela noticing, and set up the two tables beneath it. Then we'd gone wild with the balloons I bought, fashioning a trail of them that led from a bush in the front yard, through the house, to the plane tree in the backyard, where we filled the lower branches with rainbow-colored balloon bouquets.

It was all overkill, given that Abuela wasn't likely to last long with so many people around, but she did seem pleased by the attention. In fact, she was quite sociable, at least for that first hour. She had decided that Mom and I were worth showing off, with a bit of creative embellishment—Mom was transubstantiated into the University of California biology professor she never became and I, for reasons that eluded me, into an aspiring computer geek. This annoyed Mom, who went around setting the record straight and telling people she was farming on an estancia near Lascano, but I played along with Abuela. I ferried the arriving guests through the house to the red-light-lit backyard, patiently answering the same inane questions about how old I was and what I thought of Montevideo at least five times within the space of a half hour. I was dying to see Alejandra, but as the yard filled with old aunts and neighbors and second cousins, I started hoping she would get waylaid at work and arrive after they all went home.

When the door traffic slowed down, I retired to the garden to consume the surfeit of sandwiches and chat with a particularly ancient specimen, who introduced herself as my *tía abuela política*. She was my grandfather's deceased older brother's wife—I didn't even know he'd had a brother—and I was listening to her go on about how loyal she'd stayed to Abuela after the divorce forty years ago, when I saw Alejandra emerge from the house with Mom. She was wearing a thin cotton dress that casually divulged every sweet curve, and I wanted to wrap my arm around her waist, cup my hand over her breast, and whisk her off to the anonymous shadows of the beach below the Rambla or a corner table in some hole-in-the-wall *boliche*, or better yet, jump in the car and drive east to the estancia, now, while everyone was gathered here and only Angelito and the chickens would note our arrival. All this, along with the tacit understanding that we would, in present company, maintain some reserve, flashed between us as she caught my eye and soared past me to greet Abuela. Juan had just stepped over to the food table, and I quickly offloaded the *tía* on him and casually made my way over to the plane tree, where Abuela was holding court.

"It's about time," Abuela was saying as Alejandra leaned down to brush cheeks with her. "I'd almost given up on you."

"You're looking chic," Alejandra said easily, and then she wished her happy birthday and presented her with a tiny potted plant.

Abuela held the gift up to her face to get a better look. It was a small cactus, a gray-green globe covered with delicate inch-long spines. "The girl has a sense for these things," she said, a smile tugging at the corners of her mouth.

"At least it won't ever wilt," said Gonzalo, her old friend from across the street.

"That too," Abuela said genially. She thanked Alejandra, but I could see she was already beginning to tire of being gracious. "Let's serve the cake," she said, leading her entourage off toward the table.

"She's not offended, is she?" Alejandra asked as we lingered by the plane tree. "I was really just looking to buy flowers. But then I saw the cactus . . ."

"It's perfect. No one else knew what to get her. Look—" I gestured after Abuela, who was setting the diminutive cactus down in the middle of the table, like an understated centerpiece. She pushed all the other gifts into a pile and sat down next to it, waiting for the rest of us to join her. But Elsa hadn't brought the cake out yet, and people were still standing around, so I stayed where I was, talking to Alejandra, who I hadn't seen since Saturday. Having decided to maintain some distance, the urge to touch her became almost irrepressible, like the urge to cough at the crucial moment in the theater. I busied myself peeling puzzle pieces of bark off the plane tree trunk, handing them to her one by one as I recounted watching the election results with Rubén. "Were you disappointed?" I asked. "It seemed sort of anticlimactic."

"It was already in the cards." She looked down at the bark I'd handed her and started trying to reassemble the puzzle.

The truth of the matter was that I'd felt vaguely disappointed myself. I hadn't been rooting for Tabaré and the Frente, per se, any more than I'd been rooting for Batlle and the Colorados. But I'd been moved by that sea of humanity I'd seen on the first election day, moved by *la muchedumbre*. "Somehow it seems like it should mean something," I said, trying to explain the sensation to Alejandra.

"They were just celebrating the rise of the underdog, the Frente garnering so much support." She crumpled her bark pieces and tossed them away into the grass. "It was all about the past. Of importance for people like your Rubén, even if they didn't win."

"I know, Rubén told me all that. And you could hear it in the speeches and rhetoric. But there weren't just Rubén types out there. There were people our age. Lots of them." I peeled another piece of bark off the tree, unsure how to explain that reading snippets from Uruguayan history and hanging out in a prehistoric diorama and watching all those hopeful citizens on the street had me thinking about history and the future as one continuum that stretched backwards and forwards into the new millennium. I'd been imagining generations of enigmatic Artigases and Don Pepes leaping down off their horses to pen new paradigms for society in a land ruled by buzzing ducks and giant guinea pigs and wild cattle—but the feeling flickered out of reach the moment I tried to put words to it. The scale was at once too small and too big, and the horses and buzzing ducks and new paradigms were a history without future. I let it go, suddenly unsure why I'd felt that way. And Alejandra was much more interested in deciphering the puzzle of our nesting rails, than she was in understanding my vague gringo ideas about politics.

"Eduardo says your drawings are fantastic," she said. "But he can't identify the bird!" She'd given photocopies of my journal entries to her colleague—reputably the country's leading ornithologist, for whatever that was worth. "From your description," she went on, "he thinks it might be an undersized member of the *Rallus* genus. But he isn't sure. He said he's never seen anything like it, has no idea of the species. Just think, Gabriel, maybe you've found a species new to science!"

"Did he say that?"

"No, of course not. He's much too careful. But he wants to see them."

"Alejandra, it's not like with your bacteria. You don't discover a new species of bird, just like that, in some backyard marsh in Uruguay. People have been watching birds for centuries. All the early explorers and natural historians were cataloging them. Banks. Humboldt. Darwin. Wallace. That guy you said lived in Uruguay, W. H. Hudson. Amateurs, scientists, everyone looked at birds. I don't even know when the last new species was discovered. Maybe there are some tropical species that escaped detection, hidden deep in the jungles of Africa or Brazil, but they're probably on their way to extinction now anyway."

"And why not here? Who in their right mind goes crawling around in that marsh? Did your grandfather ever go in there? Liliana? Your uncles?" She gestured toward Juan Luis, who was standing near the end of the table nursing a glass of red wine, and Rubén, who'd just emerged from the house with his guitar. "Eduardo said he could drive up there this weekend. What do you think? I could sample then also."

I suddenly felt protective. Did I want to show *our* rails to a stranger? Did I even want them to be identified? I rather liked it that they were incognito out there in the marsh, that no one but Alejandra and I knew they existed. But Alejandra's curiosity was contagious. She wanted to *know* those birds—who they were and why they were there in that particular little patch of marsh, how they got there and when. For a start. To her, I realized, understanding was the highest tribute, the only way to appreciate nature's mysteries, and I didn't want to argue with that.

"Saturday's fine," I said. "And now I think we'd better join the party."

Most of the old folks were already seated at the table, and Rubén had started strumming some kind of birthday song medley on his guitar. But Elsa was nowhere to be seen, Mom was still flitting around with the serving plate of quiches, Juan hadn't budged from his observation post, and as we approached, Elsa stepped out of the kitchen and called the guest of honor away to answer a phone call.

"Surprised to see you here," Juan said to Alejandra.

She smiled politely. "I was honored to be invited."

I poured us both wine and handed her a glass. "Abuela invited her," I explained, refilling Juan's glass.

"Celia?"

"Your mother has me under her spell," Alejandra quipped.

"Or vice versa," Juan grumbled, in another tone altogether— one I hoped would be lost in the general hilarity as Abuela stepped back outside and Rubén's quiet instrumental medley suddenly morphed into full-fledged rock 'n' roll with vocals.

"*They say it's your birthday . . . We're gonna have a good time . . . I'm glad it's your birthday, happy birthday to you . . .*" Rubén was hamming it up like a rock star with a groupie, and indeed Abuela almost looked the part, encased in her over-sized retro party dress like a prepubescent teen in her mother's gown. Mom and her friend were in stitches. Even Juan cracked a smile.

"*Take a cha-cha-cha chance, I would like you to dance . . . Dance, yeah . . . Whooo . . . Come on . . .C'mon . . . Baby . . .*"

Abuela swatted Rubén out of her path, as close to laughing as she ever got. "That was my son-in-law," she announced, "calling to congratulate me from California. Gabriel, he wants to talk to you."

"Oh. Dad," I said, stupidly surprised.

"*Yes, we're goin' to a party, party . . . Yes, we're goin' to a party, party . . .*"

I left Alejandra with Juan and hurried into the kitchen, where Abuela had left the receiver lying on the counter.

"Hi, Dad."

"Gabe. How's it going down there?"

"Okay. Rubén's rocking out, singing the Beatles birthday song for Abuela." I felt a wash of guilt. I'd almost forgotten Dad was part of this family. We'd exchanged a couple of brief emails, but I hadn't talked to him since before I left California.

"Rubén is there? I never met him."

"He came from Venezuela to vote, but it looks like he is going to stay."

"So what have you been up to? Any girls down there?"

"Yeah Dad, millions. They're knocking down the door, you know, can't wait to meet the surfer from California."

"Well. And your mother?"

"Planting vegetables at the estancia. And getting on Abuela's nerves. Fighting with Juan Luis."

"Same old, same old," Dad said, as if he even missed fighting with Mom. It was odd to hear his voice, his unaccented American English, mine. He was lonely, I realized, and just wanted to chat. "Have you seen the news, Gabe? The demonstrations at the World Trade Organization meeting in Seattle?"

"No. They've been pretty obsessed with the national election here."

"Thousands of people on the street. We haven't seen anything like it since the Vietnam War. They're sending in the National Guard."

"Really. There were a hundred thousand on the street here," I said. "Just for the election. And no violence to speak of." He made me tell him about the election and explain the *balotaje*, none of which had made a blip on the national news in the US. I was impatient, thinking of Alejandra outside with my unfriendly uncle, and I gave him the bare-bones summary. "Dad, I should go. Abuela's opening her presents out there."

"Of course. It's good to talk to you, Gabe. When are you coming home?"

"I don't know."

"What about your job?"

"Dad, I told you I quit. I hated that job. And I've still got plenty of money."

"Maybe you should consider applying to grad school. Doing something you really like."

"I've been birding a lot. At the estancia. Dad, I gotta go."

When I walked back outside, Alejandra was sitting at the table, wedged between Mom, who was chattering in her ear, and Rubén, who was charming the neighbor lady on the other side of him. Elsa was ferrying slices of cake around on little dessert plates, Juan was standing where I'd left him, his arms folded across his chest like a silent overseer, and Abuela was opening her gifts with all the attentiveness of someone sorting through the daily junk mail. I stood near the opposite end of the table, waiting for an opportunity to spirit Alejandra away. Why hadn't I told Dad about her? Dad would approve. He would find her smart, likeable, beautiful—what was not to approve?

Elsa handed me a slice of cake, and Mom broke off her conversation and called across the table at me, getting everyone's attention. "What did your father have to say?"

"Nothing much. He was riled up about some big anti-WTO demonstration in Seattle. He sounded sort of lonely," I added, and immediately regretted it.

"Of course he's lonely." Abuela looked up from her unwrapping operation and trained her gaze on Mom. "He should have come with you."

Then everyone started talking about Dad, Abuela's nice American son-in-law. Lili and her *dos rubios,* that's how they remembered us from our Christmas visits, though Dad was really more brown than blond. Mom kept quiet, but I could see she was incensed, flickering like a fluorescent light about to pop. Why the hell did she ask me about Dad, if she didn't want to set them off? The doorbell rang and she got up to answer it, Elsa hurrying after her.

I ate my cake and watched Abuela open presents, wondering how long it would be before Alejandra and I could escape without being noticed. Abuela seemed to place more value in the wrapping paper than what it contained, smoothing and folding it into neat squares and stacking them up on the table, while the chocolates and rose vases, even the box of hand-painted note cards Gonzalo gave her, were set aside with barely a second glance. She frowned at the recycled newspaper Mom had wrapped our gift in, but the magnifying glass briefly caught her attention. "It's to help you read," I called out, and she turned the disapproving frown my way before adding magnifying glass and book to the pile on the chair. Rubén shot me an I-told-you-so grin, and I was glad Mom wasn't around.

I thought Mom might have decided to abandon the party altogether, but then she and Elsa reappeared with my cousin and her baby in tow. Patricia's surprise visit from Buenos Aires got a better reception than the presents did, and in the general excitement and baby goggling that ensued, Alejandra extricated herself from her seat.

"I should go," she said, moving past me into the house.

I followed her in, and as we came into the empty dining room, I succumbed to the need to touch her, bending to brush her lips with a kiss, letting my palm ride down the neat curve of her hip.

"You should stay and help out," she said. "And I should get home."

She didn't say anything about the party except that Abuela seemed to be enjoying herself, but she was clearly anxious to leave, impervious to my protests that she should stay, or we should go together. We made a plan to take Eduardo Schwartz to see the rails over the weekend, and then she left me standing in the foyer feeling bewildered. This was not how I had imagined the evening.

I was not at all eager to rejoin the festivities in the backyard, and I turned slowly away from the door, trying to decide what to do—only to find Abuela coming toward me from the dining room, apparently making her own escape.

"You can't really expect her to like this sort of thing," she said, peering up at my face and making a cursory gesture toward her party in the backyard.

"You're the one who invited her."

"Of course I did." Abuela pressed her lips into a satisfied little smile. "She's an interesting young woman." She continued toward the stairs and the haven of her bedroom, and I changed my own course and switched on the TV in the living room. If Abuela could abandon her own party, so could I.

"Gabriel." She had stopped on the triangular landing and was standing there watching me. "Don't worry, she's crazy about you. And more disciplined than the mother."

Blushing and vaguely annoyed, I turned back to the TV and flipped through the channels until I found the international news and a report on the Seattle protests, with video clips and brief interviews with protesters and the police chief. Now that I thought about it, I had received a couple of emails from one of my college friends about some kind of anti-globalization demonstration, but I hadn't paid much attention. I watched with a mixture of amazement and skepticism. A group of young people chained together across an intersection, swaying back and forth, singing songs. A mass of protestors marching down a boulevard toward a line of police in full battle garb. A bunch of people walking around in sea turtle costumes. . . .

Rubén wandered in, looking for Celia. "People are starting to go home," he said, "wanting to say goodbye."

"She already went upstairs."

"Ah, well. She lasted longer than we thought she would." He looked at me sitting alone on the couch. "What happened to Alejandra?"

"She had to go." I gestured at the TV, eager to change the subject. "Did you hear about this? There's a big demonstration in Seattle." I didn't know the Spanish name for the WTO, but Rubén knew the English one. "Dad says it's the biggest protest since the Vietnam War."

"Who are they?"

"A hodgepodge of groups. Anarchists, I think. Environmentalists. I don't know what else. Maybe like your Frente, the way you described it in the seventies?"

"What are they doing protesting the WTO in the country that benefits the most?"

"Not everyone benefits," I said. "It's a big country. And—well, we do have our altruists." I paused, thinking again about the Frente demonstration, the feeling I'd been trying to describe to Alejandra. These were my compatriots, marching arm in arm toward a line of Darth-Vader-cloned riot police, singing and chanting anti-globalization rhetoric. Should I be out there with them, instead of mooning around watching birds and reading about the irrelevant history of little Uruguay?

"What's with the turtles?"

"I think they're trying to call attention to the ways the WTO weakens environmental laws and trade bans. We have laws banning shrimp imports from countries that allow fishing nets that kill turtles, and the WTO has challenged those laws, even though the turtles are endangered."

"Bunch of eccentric *yanquis*," Rubén muttered.

I glanced at him, surprised. "Are they so different from your Tupamaros?" I gestured at the TV. "It's about who gets to co-opt the world's natural resources—or whatever's left of them. These guys are fighting imperialism, just like you did."

"*Bah*! Living in the belly of the beast."

"And you guys? You were protesting your own government—"

"We weren't protesting it, we were trying to change it."

"So are they. But it's not countries anymore that are the imperialists, it's multinational corporations—even more insidious because they don't answer to anyone, you can't vote them out of office or stage a revolution, can't even find them. And they don't care if the resources they co-opt are precariously limited, if their deals are one-shot."

"We demonstrated for endangered *people*," he said contemptuously. "And," he added with a sly grin, "we had guns."

"Who would you point a gun at, Rubén? President of the WTO? The CEOs of the world? Bank presidents? Oil-platform workers? Japanese fishermen? Jetliner passengers? How do you find the bad guys? We're all fucked."

The TV reportage focused on the violence and disruption, with little analysis of the reasons for the protest. "I guess that's supposed to be symbolic too," I said as we watched video footage of black-clad figures in face masks bashing in windows with baseball bats. "Bashing in capitalism. Though I doubt the people who work in the stores get it." I was in a generally foul mood, irritated with Abuela, with Rubén, with the whole family. "What about your guns, Rubén? Did they get you anywhere?"

He stared at me for a moment, and then he sort of laughed and deflated at the same time. "The Tupas killed a few *milicos* and monsters. The infamous chief of police. The CIA agent who taught the *milicos*' torture techniques. That was the worst mistake, killing the *yanqui*, but all the brains were in prison by then. People say the Tupas caused all the trouble, but that's bullshit. Corrupt Colorados caused the trouble, and it had been getting worse for decades. The Tupas tried to take action, do something about it—and failed miserably. People died, people suffered . . . But if the Tupas hadn't acted, there'd be no Frente running Montevideo, no Frente in parliament. Uruguay would be just another complacent neoliberal pawn, a US protectorate with no hope at all." He gestured at the TV. "What the hell. Maybe this is what we need, eccentric *yanquis*. An uprising in the belly of the beast." He turned back to the foyer to see off Abuela's guests, who were now exiting en masse.

I switched off the TV and followed him, brushing cheeks with Gonzalo and my *tía abuela política*, and then stepping into the dining room to talk to Patricia and admire Emilia. Patricia told me that she and Daniel wanted to move back to Montevideo, but it was almost impossible to find jobs. She set Emilia down on the floor to demonstrate her new ability to crawl, but Emilia just lay there on her belly demonstrating her old ability to scream. She was tired and cranky, Patricia said, and I promised to visit in Buenos Aires and sent her off with the crying baby. I felt pretty tired and cranky myself, but I saw off two straggling old ladies whose names I couldn't remember and went to help clean up, my general feeling of irritation tempered by guilt. It was, after all, Abuela's birthday, even if Abuela herself had retired to her quarters.

Rubén and Juan were putting away the chairs, so I gathered up a load of dirty dishes and crowded into the kitchen, where Mom was rearranging Abuela's refrigerator to accommodate the leftovers. "Oh good," she said as I set my pile on the counter. "We've got a dishwasher."

"Haven't you guys ever heard of paper plates?"

Mom frowned at me. "Who raised you?"

"I didn't even know Abuela had this many dishes," I said, but I obediently started filling the sink.

"She keeps it all in the dining room cabinet," Elsa said, squeezing in behind me with the last plates of food. "Never uses anything."

I scrubbed and rinsed and stacked Abuela's china while Elsa and Mom bustled about behind me, dealing with the leftover food and gossiping about Patricia and Daniel and the baby and the old aunts and neighbors. Elsa was packing up some of the quiche and cake to take home, and the clean dishes were starting to overwhelm Abuela's minimalist version of a dish drainer, when Rubén and Juan Luis came in from the garage.

"Leave some cake here!" Rubén said, ensconcing himself on Abuela's stool at the end of the counter.

"Rubén," Elsa said, "you're getting fatter than a castrated cat."

"Can someone dry these plates?" My pile was getting precarious.

"It's too crowded in there for a fat guy."

"You can go with me to the estancia tomorrow and work it off," Mom said, taking up the dishtowel.

"Love to," Rubén said. "But I'm helping out in Carlos's print shop for the rest of the week. Remember old Carlos?"

"What's he paying you?" Juan Luis asked.

"We have a deal."

"You can at least put these away," Mom said, stacking the dry plates on the counter in front of the two of them. "And you, Gabe? You coming with me tomorrow?"

"I'm going on Saturday, with Alejandra. We're bringing an ornithologist to see the birds in the marsh."

"I didn't even say goodbye to her," Mom said. "She was telling me about an unusual bird you found out there."

"Yeah, a rail. Really shy. That's why the ornithologist—"

"We're going to start excavating the pond on Saturday," Juan interrupted. "I don't want a bunch of strangers tromping around."

"Don't be such a scrooge," Rubén said. "Elsa, pour your husband a glass of beer. He needs to relax."

"We'll be out in the marsh," I said. "Nowhere near the pond site." I looked over my shoulder at Juan Luis. He had picked up Mom's pile of plates and was holding them rigidly in both hands, like a soldier awaiting orders.

"Dining room cabinet," Elsa said, but Juan made no move to put them away.

I turned back to the dishes. "It's just the three of us. Me and Alejandra, and this professor she knows at the university." I gathered up a handful of forks, running the soapy sponge over their tines.

"You're sleeping with her." Juan made it sound like an accusation, like he'd just discovered I was a drug addict or worse, a scourge on the family.

"Of course he's sleeping with her," Rubén said. "Wouldn't you?"

This all seemed so completely off-the-wall, so out of place in the Quiroga family kitchen banter, that it took me a moment to respond. The forks slid back to rest on the bottom of the sink, the sponge floated free, and I lifted my hands out of the sink, water and suds sliding up my wrists and dripping onto the floor as I turned around. "*Her*?" I looked from Rubén to Juan. "I take it you are talking about Alejandra. That's the woman's name. Alejandra Silva Paden."

"Precisely. She's trouble, Gabriel, just like her mother. A beautiful girl, but she screwed Rubén around like a toy rabbit when he was your age."

"Juan," Elsa said quietly.

"They're just friends." Mom's voice was so falsely bright and strained it sounded like she'd given up breathing. She set her hand lightly on my shoulder. "She's almost five years older than Gabe."

I shrugged Mom's hand away and wiped my hands on my jeans. "What's it to any of you, who I sleep with." I pushed past them, out of the kitchen.

"Gabriel," Rubén called after me. "Don't take it personally. Juan always has to worry about someone. He just thinks you're going to get your heart broken, like his little brother."

I was moving away from them, across the dining room, but they weren't really talking to me anyway.

"She did more than break your heart, Rubén."

"What do you know, Juan."

"It's different times," Elsa said.

I closed the door to the bedroom and deposited myself on the bed, stunned and confused. No wonder Alejandra had left. Who knew what Juan had said to her. Or Abuela, for that matter, with her abstruse comments. Or Mom, with her cloying friendliness. I contemplated calling to apologize, whatever it was, but my limbs were filled with inertia and I just lay there staring at the cracked ceiling. I felt like a swallow flying into a glass window, stunned senseless by an invisible wall that had suddenly, inexplicably, materialized in my path. I was supposed to be the outsider here. The wry observer. The innocent bystander in Mom's family dramas. Lili versus Juan Luis, Lili versus Abuela. Mom versus Dad. That's how it had always been. But now I seemed to have moved center stage in some festering family war over an ancient love affair of Rubén's—simply because I'd fallen in love with the daughter of one of his million women.

There was a light tap on the door and I swung my feet over the side of the bed and sat up. "What?" I thought it was Mom, but it was Elsa who opened the door.

"Gabriel," she said. "*Amor*, I'm sorry."

I didn't say anything, and she came into the room and sat down on the bed next to me.

"This bed must be way too small for you."

"It's okay."

"Lili said you cleaned out all the old junk Juan stashed in here after Mario died." She looked around the room. "Funny, about Celia and your grandfather. He lived with another woman the last forty years of his life, but Celia left all his stuff in here. And Mario told me once not long after he'd finally moved out—

at our wedding, actually, he'd had too much to drink and was getting sentimental, took me aside and told me Celia was the love of his life. He wanted me to know that."

I fidgeted with the book I'd left on the bedside table, a biography of José Batlle y Ordóñez that Abuela had pulled off her shelves for me. I'd had enough family history for the day, but Elsa talked on.

"Juan Luis and I lived in this house, you know. With Celia and Rubén, the first few years we were married. That's when we moved Lili's bed down here and put the double bed in Lili's old room. We didn't have much money. Juan was just piecing things together as a private consultant, working for a couple of big landholders up in the northern provinces. He'd wanted to develop the estancia, but your grandfather wouldn't have anything to do with it, wouldn't even talk to him about it. He'd never really forgiven Juan for studying agronomy. Patricia was just a baby, and Juan was gone most of the time."

I glanced at Elsa. Her hands were uncharacteristically still, lying folded in her lap, and she was staring at the bookshelves in front of us. I was surprised to see tears pooling in her brown eyes. She blinked once and continued her story, reciting it to her dead father-in-law's dusty architecture books.

"Eva showed up one rainy afternoon when Juan Luis was gone, just a few months after the coup. We hadn't seen her in months. Rubén wasn't here, but Celia invited her in for tea. Celia always had a weak spot for Eva, even at her wildest. We made *tortas fritas*, and Eva hung around all afternoon. She seemed agitated, half-heartedly playing with Patricia and chatting with us, going into the living room to look out the side window every few minutes. I thought she was waiting for Rubén to come home, though the last I'd heard she'd broken it off with him and taken up with that Natalio, who we all knew was in deep with the Tupas. Rubén had been moping around and heartsick for the past year, so I was sort of hoping he wouldn't show up. Then about four o'clock, Eva suddenly said she had to go and left out the back door into the garden. A few minutes later the *milicos* were ringing at the door. Celia let them in, you didn't have any choice. They asked if there was anyone else in the house, and she said no. They were polite, but they walked through the whole house, looking in all the closets and cabinets, under the beds. Celia was very calm, very dignified. But then they took her in with them, said they wanted to ask her some questions.

"When they left, I looked out the window and saw that the street was crawling with soldiers. There was a tank parked at the corner and they were going door to door, searching every house. I don't know how Eva got out of the garden—if she climbed the fence or got out through the garage, but she was gone. I was terrified, I didn't know what to do. Juan Luis was up north, out in the boonies somewhere, and I couldn't get hold of him. So I called your grandfather Mario and told him they'd taken Celia in for questioning. Of course I didn't say anything about Eva, that wasn't the sort of thing you could say on the phone, and he didn't ask for details. But he was well-connected. He got Celia out, brought her home about eleven o'clock that night. She was trembling, but she said they hadn't done anything to her, just left her sitting in a room by herself at the police station. I don't know to this day if that was true.

"The next morning, we heard that a gang of Tupamaros had escaped from the women's prison, and I realized Eva had been one of them, that she was on the run. Juan Luis went into a rage when he found out. I think if he'd known where Eva was at that moment he would have turned her in. As it was, she got away, went to Buenos Aires. And Rubén. Rubén had gotten involved also. Because of Eva. Celia and Juan made him leave, gave him what money they could and put him on a bus headed north. That's when we found out they'd been using this house all along, Eva and Natalio and their gang, hiding their homemade bombs in Rubén's mattress upstairs. Rubén told Juan about the bomb in his mattress when they were on the way to the station. Juan had to slice open the mattress and get the bomb out of the house in the middle of the night. He dumped it in the river, I don't even know where.

"They didn't think about what would happen to the rest of us if they were caught, didn't care about anything but their slogans and propaganda. If the police had found Eva here that day or checked the mattress, they would have taken all of us. And Mario wouldn't have been able to do a thing about it."

"What about Mom?"

"Lili?" Elsa turned slowly to look at me, as if she were surprised to see me sitting there next to her. Then she sighed, long and slow, settling back into the moment, talking to her lovelorn *yanqui* nephew in 1999. "Liliana was already in the US, studying. She never really understood what was going on here."

"Elsa," I said, because I didn't know what else to say. "I'm sorry. Mom never told me any of this. It's awful. But it has nothing to do with us. With Alejandra and me. She hardly even remembers her mother. And even if she did . . ." I let the sentence flutter away, it was just such a ridiculous cliché to think that the mother's sins should be visited on the daughter.

"I know, sweetheart. But it's hard. She looks like a clone of Eva. The same smile, same sexy charm. She even has the same *voice*. And you as infatuated as Rubén ever was. '*They're just friends.*' Ha. I love your mother, but she is oblivious. As self-absorbed at fifty as she was at fifteen." Elsa paused, laying her hand on my arm. "Of course it's unfair," she said gently. "It can't have been easy for Alejandra. But you have to understand Juan Luis. He was responsible for this family, or he thought he was. And Eva wreaked havoc with it. Celia treated her like another daughter, protected her long after she should have banned her from this house. Rubén was madly, idiotically under her spell. That's the only reason he got sucked into the Tupas. And Lili. Everyone worried about *la nena*. She was so impulsive, everything she did was so . . . *exaggerated*. We thought she was safely out of the way, settling down with your father in the US. But she clung to that childhood friendship like her life depended on it. She was crazy to be flying down here when she was pregnant, putting you at risk. To help Eva. As if there was anything anyone could do to help Eva."

"Is that why she was down here?" I said, looking up as Elsa pushed herself off the bed and moved toward the door. I knew I'd been born in Montevideo a few weeks too early, but I'd assumed Mom had come to visit Abuela.

"We didn't even know she was here. Apparently, she'd been looking for Eva in Buenos Aires and the police picked her up and shipped her over here to the military hospital. Keith told us later. He said they wanted to send her back to California, but she went into labor early, so they kept her until you were born and big enough to travel. He was crazy with worry, angry that she'd undertaken the trip to begin with. Thank god she had a *yanqui* passport. No one ever did tell Celia. She thinks you were born in a nice hospital in Berkeley, California."

I reached up and pushed the porthole window above the bed open. For all my grandfather's Masonic symbols, the house seemed more haunted than transcendent, so steeped in the stale odors and stink of my family's lives that one could hardly breathe. My own birth wasn't something I'd thought much about, certainly not something I'd ever talked about with Abuela. I felt a surge of nostalgia for the insignificant windows and simple rectangular forms of the suburban tract house I'd grown up in, for my taciturn but straightforward father.

Elsa was standing with her hand on the doorknob, watching me. "Gabrielito," she said. "You're really smitten, aren't you?"

I looked away, looked down at my hand on the edge of the bed next to me, the soft brown wool of the blanket it rested on. "It isn't just an infatuation."

She stayed where she was, waiting.

"There are lots of things I don't know," I said, still not looking at her. "Things I never even thought about until now. What I want to do. Where I want to live. If I want kids. But I know this: whatever I do, wherever I end up, I want it to be with Alejandra." I laughed self-consciously.

"And Alejandra? Does she feel the same way?"

As if I could possibly know. As if we'd talked about our future. As if we'd had time to even sort out our present. "It must sound ridiculous," I said. "We only met two months ago."

"Ay, Gabrielito, you can never know. But I'll tell you a secret—" She broke into one of her goofy gap-toothed grins and reached out to mess with my hair as if I were five. "Juan Luis proposed after two weeks!"

I fell asleep thinking about secrets that ceased to be secrets. The hidden marsh with its lonely rails. Abuela's Masonic formulas. The images in Mom's lipstick book. . . . I dreamt I was standing next to the stone arch in the Punta Carretas Shopping. It was late and the place was dark and devoid of shoppers, but a bright, peppy version of "Feliz Navidad" was playing through hidden loudspeakers, and strands of red Christmas lights were twinkling on the indoor palms. The music sounded like glass shattering, and after a moment I noticed that there were small groups of people running around breaking things. They were all dressed in black tunics. A woman with a crowbar slammed it into the stone of the arch next to me, chipping off a jagged piece of granite. She handed me the rock, and I started running too, leaping up the steps of the stalled escalator, dashing around the mezzanine. The tawdry signs of the multinational chain stores glowed in the dark as I ran past displays of clothing and shoes, lingerie and computers and toys, looking for a window to throw my rock at. But there weren't any windows. The shops opened directly onto the mezzanine like a series of jail cells, their entrances blocked by metal bars. I stopped in front of the baby shop and peered in, but it had been emptied of merchandise. The white sales table in the middle was now occupied by a lone sea turtle. It was lying on its back with its flippers stretched out and pinned down to the table with spikes, its beak open in a silent scream. It appeared to be alive.

I ran away. I couldn't leave, but I was free to run in circles around the prison, and that's what I did, until I circled back to the ground floor and found Abuela. The Christmas decorations had disappeared and she was sitting on a wooden chair in the middle of a gray cement courtyard. She was naked and skeletally thin. Her mouth was set in a thin line and she wouldn't talk to me, but somehow I learned that she was on a hunger strike and refusing to let the doctors near her. I walked in circles around her, trying to pretend she wasn't naked, pulling things to eat out of my pockets and offering them to her, *plantillas*, her favorite *bizcochos*, dulce de leche ice cream, birthday cake. But she refused it all, growing smaller with each circle I walked, shrinking before my eyes until she was no larger than a baby balanced on the chair, and I woke myself up, my scream as silent as the sea turtle's.

I switched on the light, trying to exorcise the nightmare. I got up and went to the bathroom, and then I followed the wilting balloon bouquets into the kitchen, where I found Abuela sitting on her stool, fully dressed in her usual shapeless gray dress. She was listening to the radio and eating a large chunk of bread with jam. It was four thirty in the morning.

"They're talking about the millennium," she said in answer to my sleepy *buen día*. "These people think it means something. But it's all superstition. They've got the numbers wrong."

The only thing I'd heard about the millennium was that the world's computers were supposed to go haywire and raise havoc with everything from banking systems to air travel. I was pretty sure that wasn't what Abuela was talking about, but I wasn't up for an explanation and didn't inquire. I went to the refrigerator and poured myself a glass of milk. Alejandra's cactus had moved to the windowsill above the sink, and the Umberto Eco novel was lying out on the counter, but all the other presents had disappeared. I stood next to Abuela and drank my milk, letting the radio babble spill incomprehensibly into my sleep-addled brain. Then I mumbled goodnight and went back to bed and a dreamless sleep, comforted to know that Abuela was eating and listening to her radio in some semblance of abnormal Quiroga normalcy.

14

Only the chickens and Angelito were around to greet Alejandra, Eduardo, and me at the estancia on Saturday, though Mom's truck and Juan's car were both parked in the field. I hadn't talked to Mom since Abuela's party, but I had seen Juan. Elsa must have worked her magic on him, because he'd seemed contrite. I'd gone to their apartment to use the computer, and Elsa had insisted that I stay for dinner. Juan hadn't explicitly apologized, but he did offer me a ride to the estancia, and he seemed amiable enough when I reiterated my plan with Alejandra and the ornithologist. He'd even suggested that Alejandra and I stay the night. But the idea of spending the night at the estancia with Mom and Juan Luis, contrite or otherwise, was considerably less attractive than the room with a *cama de matrimonio* I'd reserved for us in Rocha's quaint turn-of-the-century hotel. Eduardo was staying there as well and had promised to take us to his favorite birding spot at the Laguna de Rocha on Sunday morning. So we'd stuck to our plan, Alejandra and I rendezvousing with Eduardo in Rocha and driving up to the estancia together in his car.

We parked next to the truck and started pulling on boots and gathering up binoculars and knapsacks. The chickens ignored us, but Angelito stood at attention and watched, his long neck and pinhead rising above theirs like a periscope, his right leg forward, poised to run. He must have grown a foot in the past two weeks. I squatted down and held out my hand, wiggling my fingers and calling his name, trying to sound like Rubén—but he immediately took off in his dash-around-in-circles-at-top-speed routine. He made five rounds before coming to a halt by my side.

Eduardo had stepped around the car to watch. He was a stocky man, with thinning brown hair and glasses, probably in his early forties, though he was one of those guys who seems to have been born middle-aged and might well have been younger. On the drive up, I'd taken him for humorless, but now he was smiling, watching Angelito. "I've heard of gauchos keeping them as pets," he said as Angelito pushed his beak into my out-stretched hand in search of crackers. "But I've never met a tame one."

"That's my uncle's doing. This is actually the first time he's come to me." I tickled Ángel under his wings, the way I'd seen Rubén do, and he suddenly folded his legs under him and sat down.

Alejandra sank to the ground next to us. "He's got Bambi eyes," she said.

"Oh, he's got much better eyesight than Bambi," Eduardo said. He retrieved a khaki hat from the car and started dousing it in mosquito repellent.

"Do they have predators?" I asked, joining him by the car and digging out my own can of repellent. "We're mostly keeping him inside or locking him up with the chickens at night."

"Foxes and hawks, even large rats, can pick off the chicks. But once they're grown, humans and dogs are probably *Rhea americana*'s worst enemies. The cougars and jaguars that used to hunt them are mostly history around here."

Angelito didn't look at all worried. He stretched his neck out flat in the grass and pushed his legs out straight behind him. "It feels like a feathered snake," Alejandra said, running a finger along the sinewy neck, which Angelito proceeded to lift off the ground and lay in her lap.

"Oh, that's a new trick!" I said. "He seems to like you more than Rubén. El Trigal notwithstanding."

"They're strange birds, even in the wild," Eduardo said. He had a large knapsack full of camera and recording equipment, and he was strapping a tripod to the outside of it. "The male builds the nest and has a harem of females to lay eggs in it—but the females wander from male to male whenever it suits them."

"Your basic bird orgy," Alejandra said. "Who takes care of the chicks?"

"The male incubates the eggs and takes care of whatever hatches in his nest, whether he's the actual father or not."

"Very progressive," I offered, ever my mother's son.

"But just about a week before the eggs hatch, he pushes one out of the nest and cracks it open. The chick dies, of course, and when it starts rotting it attracts flies and maggots, so its brothers and sisters have a ready food supply right outside the nest when they hatch."

"It's like they're farming," Alejandra said.

"Right," I said, laughing. "With a sacrificial twist."

"There's usually a couple dozen eggs in each nest," Eduardo said, "so they can afford to lose a few."

"You see?" Alejandra said to Ángel, gently pushing him off her lap. "Having a chicken for a mother wasn't such a bad thing."

My own mother seemed to be keeping to herself, which was fine with me. She was out hoeing weeds on the other side of her field, and she waved and called a greeting as we set out across the pasture, but she didn't pause in her work or try to detour us for a chat.

Summer had set in and the air was warm and stagnant, the sky shimmering with a blanket of humid white haze that instantly raised a glistening film of sweat on the skin. The mosquitoes, and the birds, loved it. The resident *tero*, which usually alerted the whole neighborhood to any human invasion, had either taken a vacation or gotten fed-up and emigrated, and the flycatchers and songbirds along the creek were unwarned of our arrival and out in full force.

Eduardo knew them all. Any vague misgivings I'd had about taking this university professor to see the rails quickly evaporated. He was a bit of a dry character, the quintessential nerd—nothing like Grandpa or the amateur birders I'd known—but he could identify everything that was flitting and hiding and singing in the brush along the creek, usually without even seeing it. He knew all the calls and songs, something I'd never been very good at, even in California. We moved along at a good clip, Alejandra like a quiz-show host, asking Eduardo to name the source of each song and call we heard, lagging behind as she tried to page through my bird book and walk at the same time. Eduardo was clearly impatient to get to the marsh and see the rails, but we did stop to look at a *Capuchino Corona Gris*—a tiny finch-like bird he said was almost endangered—and he obligingly narrated the biological symphony as we walked. Long monotone rattle—*Misto*. Upbeat, downbeat, trill—*Chingolo*. A rhythmic tri-tone tweet—*Verdón*. The decidedly unmusical squawk of a *Garza Mora*, the lovely octave leaps of the whistling *Federal* . . . and the cold mechanical hum of a backhoe.

"Looks like your uncle means business," Alejandra said as we neared Juan's pond site and the backhoe drowned out the rest of the symphony.

Juan was on the other side of the creek, standing next to a raw gash in the pasture and directing the backhoe operator, too intent on his task to notice us.

"Rice?" Eduardo asked.

"He wants to plant a crop next summer." I was searching for the *Chajás*, as we weren't far from their nest—but we didn't see or hear them until we got to the field in front of the reed bed, where they'd hung out before they started nesting. The chicks had grown as much in girth as Ángel had in height and were as placid as he was frenetic, waddling about with their parents in the muddy grass. Eduardo was surprised to see them there. He said they usually nested near deeper water and stayed there until the chicks could fly. They didn't breed in the dozens like the Ñandús and they couldn't run very well, but they were good swimmers, so as long as they stayed near the water, the chicks were relatively safe from foxes and rodents. It occurred to me that the *Chajá* family was already missing a chick, and that they might have been driven away from their creekside nest by the commotion from Juan's backhoe. But Alejandra hadn't noticed and I decided not to point it out.

Before we entered the reedbed, Eduardo stopped to assemble his recording apparatus, which consisted of a small tape recorder that hooked over his belt and a collapsible satellite dish affair with a microphone in the middle that he mounted on a telescoping rod and could extend up over his head or out in front of him. Just getting through the reeds with it was hard work, and I suggested he wait until we heard the rails call to set it up, but he insisted on carrying it.

We were just a few feet from the glade when the first trill penetrated the marsh's auditory pandemonium. Eduardo didn't need us to tell him it was the bird we were after—he stopped walking and had the recorder on before that first trill was even halfway down its scale—and Alejandra and I waited expectantly for him to name it, like he had everything else we'd heard. But he just shook his head and swiveled slowly, following the calls of the rail as it moved through the reeds. It was nearby, but I knew we'd never get a look at it in there. And, unlike the first few times I'd heard it myself, I now knew where its circuits would eventually end up.

We continued into the glade, where Eduardo made a quick inventory of the impressive birdlife and repacked his equipment. He knew about the quicksand and clung carefully to the tree branches as I led the way into the tangled heart of the marsh. When we got to my little island, he reassembled the microphone, set up his tripod, and trained his camera on the rails' nest. He had a huge telephoto lens, stronger than my binoculars by far, but only the top of the expectant mother's head was visible, and there was no sign that any eggs had hatched. When the male called again, she became restless and shifted so that we could see her whole head, and Eduardo snapped a couple of photos. He'd done something to silence the camera shutter, so that it just made a soft, barely audible ticking sound one.

"The male should come up that ramp in a minute," I whispered.

He glanced at me. "How do you know it's the male?"

"I don't." I had no grounds whatsoever for thinking the sitting bird was a female, except that it was sitting on eggs. Inexcusably sexist of me. It could be like the Ñandú. Or the democratic *Chajás*, where the male and female took turns on the nest. Male or female, the mate was taking its time, and my minute turned into ten, and then twenty and thirty. It was as if the circling bird knew we were watching its nest and was trying to divert us, calling from one direction one moment and, a few minutes later, from another. We didn't talk, didn't even fidget much, just knelt there like Catholic penitents sweating and praying at nature's altar, occasionally making a sweep at the mosquitoes or lowering the binoculars when our arms got tired.

Finally, without announcement, the mate appeared at the bottom of the ramp. It stayed there for a moment, looking about, and then it made its dash up to the nest—but this time, instead of cramming food into its partner's mouth and dashing back down, there was an abrupt changing of the guard, and the two birds seemed to meld into one as the sitting bird exited and the other entered the nest. The new arrival settled immediately into place, and the bird I'd thought of as the mother dashed down the ramp and disappeared into the marsh. Briefly, we saw them side by side, and I had the impression that the incoming partner was slightly larger than the outgoing one, but I couldn't make out any other distinguishing features between the two. It seemed sort of incestuous, like being married to your identical twin, but then the birds could probably make out differences that we couldn't.

Alejandra and I lowered our binoculars, and Eduardo moved his eye from the lens and sat back on his heels, letting go of the shutter release cable for the first time since he'd set up.

"I do not know this bird," he said softly, but unequivocally. "Have you seen the eggs?"

I shook my head. "It's hard to get over there. You'd have to cut your way into the thicket—I don't think you could do it without wrecking the nest, or at the very least scaring them into abandoning it."

He packed up his camera and recording equipment without another word, and we made our way out of the marsh as quickly and silently as we'd entered it, without stopping. Only when we moved out into the open and started talking again, did I fully comprehend what Eduardo was saying.

"I know the Rallidae," he said. "This bird is distinctive in both morphology and voice. I would place it in the *Pardirallus*, but there are none so small. And the bill is the wrong color, should be green. It's more like *Laterallus*. . . . The bill is too long for that, but then it's really too small to make it a *Rallus*. And the call—the call is like nothing I've ever heard. Some of the *Laterallus* trill like that, but more scratchy, not so musical." He glanced at me, and I realized that he was, in his nerd way, excited.

"It's like a bassoon playing scales," I said. "With trills."

"A scale of half notes, with all the sharps and flats. You've only seen the two?"

I nodded. "But I haven't explored the entire marsh. And they don't call that often. Until I found the nest, I thought there was only one. There must be others somewhere, right? Someone must have seen them."

"Maybe. Maybe they're right under our noses. With a shy little bird like this, you can't tell if it's rare, or just hard to detect—

both crakes and rails are notoriously quiet, when they're not mating. But I've never heard any stories about them, here or anywhere else, and they've certainly never been described in the literature. That much is clear."

We were walking in a skewed row across the pastures, with me in the middle and Alejandra skipping a little in front. The tractor was silent and a couple of songbirds were singing solos in the trees along the creek, but we were too distracted by Eduardo's recitations on the elusive rails of South America to pay much heed.

Apparently, more than a dozen species of Rallidae had been described in South America, but very little was known about the habits and movements of most of them. I'd never seen a rail of any sort venture into the open or fly more than a few yards at a time, but Eduardo said a couple of species were known to migrate across the Gulf of Mexico from North America and up and down the long coast of Chile every year. They also tended to move around when the weather rendered their wetland habitats too dry or too wet from one year to the next, and there were frequent reports of individual rails getting lost in transit, appearing in strange places, far from their documented homes. He said it was quite possible that a rail had wandered down from Brazil or northern Argentina, though he thought it less likely that a pair would have wandered off together. And he found it just as plausible that the species had been resident in the eastern Uruguayan wetlands for longer than Uruguay was Uruguay, and no one had noticed them before, like Alejandra had suggested.

"There used to be a lot of this sort of habitat up here," Eduardo said. "But by the time anyone thought to do any systematic surveys of the birdlife, the drainage projects had done away with all but a few patches. There's a big one just up the road and another down at Laguna de Castillos—but I've spent quite a bit of time in both and never seen or heard the bird you have here."

"Have you ever documented a new species?" Alejandra asked him.

"New to the region? An accidental, outside its range? Sure. Newly endangered? Yes. But new to science? No." He patted my shoulder in an understated version of Uruguayan gregariousness. "Your drawings are spot-on," he said. "Maybe as useful as my photos."

"*Laterallus gabrieli,*" Alejandra said softly, leaning into me from the other side.

I was supposed to be thrilled. But somehow the scientific revelation of a species new to science seemed less exciting than the private game of discovery I'd shared with Alejandra. For all my end-of-millennium exploration fantasies, I hadn't actually expected to discover anything that was new to anyone but myself.

As we made our way back to the house and Alejandra peppered Eduardo with questions, I learned, to my astonishment, that new species of birds were discovered every year, that some fifty had been described in the past decade. More amazing still was that the numbers were *increasing.* Eduardo said this was because concerns about decreasing biodiversity had awakened an exploratory flurry not seen since the nineteenth century. Biologists were mounting expeditions to the most obscure corners of the globe, he said, racing to inventory the full range of life before more species succumbed to habitat destruction and climate change. A lot of the new species had actually been observed long ago but were only now being verified and described by scientists. Some were merely the result of reclassification when closer scrutiny and new DNA studies revealed that two races or regional subspecies did not, in fact, interbreed and were actually separate species. But at least half of the fifty were really new discoveries, birds that even the local people were sometimes unaware of, found on steep mountainsides and in dense tropical rainforests and inaccessible valleys. They were mostly songbirds but there were also a few owls. And just in the past two years, Eduardo told us, three entirely new species of rail—all on the verge of extinction—had been discovered on a couple of small, isolated Pacific islands.

There were no unexplored valleys in Uruguay, certainly no mountains, and though the countryside was sparsely populated, it had been overrun with cows and humans for centuries. Who would have thought such a place would harbor a species of bird no one had ever seen? How could anything have remained hidden from view in such a two-dimensional landscape? I looked at the little cluster of cows loitering on the other side of the creek, Juan's tractor looming over the fresh gash in the stream bank, the undulating green expanse that unfolded before us as we neared the top of the pasture behind the estancia house. . . . How deceptively guileless it all was!

By the time we'd driven all the way back to Rocha and sat through dinner with Eduardo, I had learned everything I ever wanted to know and more about bird classification, which was by no means the done deed that my old Peterson field guide made it seem. Apparently, the same genetic methods that opened Alejandra's hidden microbial worlds to exploration had thrown the well-studied world of birds into disarray. Eduardo said that long-established taxonomic and evolutionary relationships—beyond species and genus, at the level of family and order—were turning out to be inconsistent with the genetic relationships revealed by analyzing and comparing segments of DNA. Classical taxonomy was based in large part on the structure and appearance of birds, which, presumably, reflected evolutionary relationships. But appearances, it turned out, could be deceiving: species that lived in similar habitats often evolved similar forms and colorations that made them look as if they sprang from a common ancestor, when in fact they were completely unrelated. In the Rallidae family, which included over 150 species scattered across the entire globe, the morphological distinctions between species were particularly vague. And, Eduardo said, genetic studies were no silver bullet. Analyzing different segments of the DNA sometimes yielded conflicting results. You still had to consider a bird's actual physical presence in the world—plumage and skeletal structures, mating calls and behavior, distribution and habitat—or the whole system became biologically meaningless.

"Now you know," I said, pushing my empty plate aside and turning to Alejandra, "what it's like to bird with a *real* ornithologist."

"The real ornithologist," she said, "is too much like everyone else I hang out with." She reached over and gave Eduardo's arm a friendly squeeze. "Detached. Properly scientific. Your version, Gabriel, is more personal. Connected. It's like you're out there playing hide-and-seek with your best friends."

She was beautiful in her summer dress, her hair still damp from the shower, a freefall of ringlets around her shoulders. I was looking forward to our night together, our nice hotel room—but I was also enjoying Eduardo, whose dry nerdiness had been tempered by the wine and the excitement of discovery.

"Field ornithology was always an amateur's science," he said. "There are probably a million amateur bird experts in the US and England—though in Uruguay, they're rare. Unfortunately. We could use them in our surveys."

I poured the last of the wine into his glass. "I guess I don't even think of birding as a science. . . . You should have known my grandpa Gordon. He could identify any bird you might find in western North America. Tell you its habits, its moods, what it had for breakfast every day. He could hold a conversation with a screech owl. But he wasn't a scientist."

"There's nothing amateur about those drawings of yours," Eduardo said. "Makes me wonder if we should be using illustrations instead of photographs in the book I'm working on. But with the new cameras, a good photograph is easier to come by than a good illustration—certainly better than what's in Narosky's field guide." He went on to tell us about his book, a collection of in-depth Uruguayan bird biographies based on his and his colleagues' research.

"Gabriel wanted to study natural history," Alejandra said. "But he thinks there's nothing left to discover—no real nature left to describe. Maybe you want to change your mind, Gabriel. Now that you've discovered a new species."

"Right," I said. "One that's on the verge of extinction, for all we know."

"There's plenty to discover," Eduardo said. "But not exactly a lot of jobs. I take it you were more practical."

"Not much. My degree is in geography. But I did get a job, doing GIS for a corporate environmental consulting firm." I didn't mention that I wasn't sure I wanted to go back to it, even if Envirorep would have me, which I suspected they would.

"GIS would be useful for ecologists—not that ecologists are likely to have any money to hire anyone."

I was ready to go—we'd agreed to leave at dawn for our morning birding excursion, so the night would be short—but Alejandra was in no hurry. She ordered an espresso and started quizzing Eduardo about the rails.

"So what's next for *Laterallus gabrieli*?" she asked him. "If it was a microbe, the first clue I'd have to its presence would be a culture or a molecular analysis of a mud sample. But you've seen the rails now. You can describe them in detail. You have photos, and Gabriel's drawings."

"And the recordings." Eduardo looked at me. "Do you know how old the eggs are?"

"She—they—were already sitting on eggs when I found the nest about three weeks ago. No idea how long they'd been there."

"They must be ready to hatch any day now. Maybe you can take some more notes for us, keep track of the dates. See what time they become active, what they're up to in the morning."

"I'll try," I said noncommittally and gestured for the bill. I wasn't sure I wanted to stay at the estancia all week, though staying in Montevideo was seeming less attractive since Alejandra had told me she would be gone. She'd convinced her aunt to stay with her increasingly needy grandfather so she could go to a scientific conference in São Paulo.

Eduardo insisted on paying the dinner bill, and we finally started back to the hotel, still talking about the rails as we crossed the street and made our way slowly through the plaza, which was now bustling with small-town Saturday evening energy. The benches were occupied by smooching couples of all ages, teenaged boys were circling the plaza on revved-up mopeds, and coveys of girls were standing about on the corners waiting for the boys to stop gunning their engines and sprinkle them with *piropos*. I dropped my arm over Alejandra's shoulders, staking my claim, while she continued bombarding Eduardo with questions.

"What if those are really the only *Laterallus gabrieli* around?" she asked. "How will the chicks find mates? Do they mate with each other?"

"They might," Eduardo said.

"Seems like it would mess up the gene pool," Alejandra said. "I mean, microbes don't care, they just keep cloning themselves. But one of the advantages of sexual reproduction is that it diversifies the gene pool, and if you mate with your siblings . . ."

"There's not a whole lot of research on this," Eduardo said. "But so far, no one has found evidence that birds systematically *avoid* inbreeding, except in the sense of maximizing the probability that a random choice will be unrelated. Rails, for example, often disperse after fledging, which allows them to stake out new territories and broaden their selection of mates, maintaining a diverse gene pool. But there is nothing that stops birds from inbreeding, especially species with limited habitats or in isolated or immobile populations—it has certainly been observed."

"But what about the parents?" I asked. "What happens to our pair next year? Do they disperse also, to find new mates? Or do they stay together, for lack of any better options? I mean, I know condors and eagles mate for life, but I've never heard of rails doing that—at least, not if they have a choice."

"Good question. My guess is that the mating pair will stay put. They've staked out their territory and as long as no better options wander into it they'll keep mating there, year after year. Probably with each other, if the young disperse—but I don't know that for sure. Maybe some of the chicks will stay around."

We came to a stop in front of the hotel, but no one moved to go in. Alejandra ducked out from under my arm and stepped around so that we formed a little circle there on the sidewalk across from the plaza.

"We'll need a type specimen," Eduardo said. "A species reference. We should try to take one of the chicks, if they hang around long enough after they molt, leave the successful mating pair. I'm not a very good shot, but I've got a colleague who—"

"I didn't think modern ornithologists did that," I interrupted as I realized he was talking about killing a rail. "Shot birds to identify them."

"We don't, on a regular basis. But it's still the standard procedure for establishing a new species. The descriptions and drawings in all the field guides rely on well-preserved museum specimens. That Narosky guide you're using. Your Peterson's for North America."

I'd never thought of that before. That for every drawing in my field guide there was a stuffed bird in a museum somewhere. "I don't need a dead bird to describe it," I said. "Or draw it."

"That's apparent," Eduardo conceded. "But you don't know what details you might have missed. Coloration under the rump, for example. Plumage that is only shown during mating. And you can't see the inside of the bird. The skeletal morphology and musculature, the arrangements of wing feathers—all the gross morphology that was used to classify bird groups."

"Our rails don't even look like anything else. You said that already. Either someone has described them before, or they haven't, but there's no mistaking them."

"There's more to it than that. We have to place them taxonomically, systematically. We need a fixed point of reference, something others can examine. There's a lot of debate about the taxonomy of the Rallidae family and this is likely to stir things up."

"You see," I said to Alejandra. "*That's* the difference between me and a *real* ornithologist. I could care less about being systematic."

"Not true—" Alejandra said.

"The museum collections are invaluable," Eduardo said. "Especially now, with such a high extinction rate, because they allow us to document lost species for future generations. Some ornithologists think we should start collecting *more*, updating the nineteenth-century collections—"

"No," I said flatly, interrupting him.

They both stared at me.

"You're not going to shoot a rail," I said. "It's ridiculous."

Alejandra tossed her head back and started laughing. "It *is* ridiculous! For all we know the birds are endangered, and we're going to shoot one in the name of science?"

"Even if they're not endangered," I said. "Even if there are millions of them hiding out in the Brazilian marshes. You're not going to shoot one of the Quiroga estancia rails."

"It's not just 'in the name of science,'" Eduardo said. "If they *are* endangered, we need to establish them as a species before we can take measures to protect them."

"What good is that," I said, "if they don't have any habitat left? So you can put them in a zoo and breed them?" That's what they'd done with the California Condor when I was a kid. I'd seen one of the last wild ones with Grandpa when I was nine, perched on top of a telephone pole by a road in the hills outside Palo Alto, more magnificent than I'd ever imagined a vulture being. They'd all been captured a couple years later and put in jail, as Grandpa called it, submitted to a program of assisted reproduction. The idea was to breed them, then release them back into the wild—except, they weren't wild. They were bred in aviaries and zoos, and they had to be trained to avoid people and power lines. And they were still numbered, literally, with big colored tags tacked to their wings.

"He's right, Eduardo," Alejandra said. "Since when has Uruguay enforced conservation measures? Didn't we sign some kind of international agreement to preserve all these wetlands? And then everyone ignored it?"

"The Ramsar Convention. The dictatorship signed it with one hand while building India Muerta Dam with the other—turned 99 percent of the wetlands they'd promised to conserve into pasture or rice fields." Eduardo paused, waiting for an inordinately loud motorcycle to pass. "You know," he said then, fixing his gaze on me, "that growing rice on your estancia is likely to do more damage to these rails' existence than collecting one specimen bird."

"It's not my estancia." But I found myself defending Juan's plan despite my misgivings, thinking about what Elsa had told me. "My uncle has wanted to farm it all his life," I said, "and rice is the best cash crop. He isn't going to clear out the marsh. And he said he'll let as much water through the dike as he can." I shrugged and broke up our circle to pull open the hotel door, not at all convinced this would preserve the marsh for more than a year or two.

"Has anyone ever used phylogenetic analysis to confirm a bird species?" Alejandra asked Eduardo as we filed into the lobby. "Can you extract the nucleic acids from feathers?"

The lobby was empty except for the bored concierge, who set aside his magazine as we entered.

"I only know of one such attempt," Eduardo said, waving at the concierge, who was clearly hoping we would stop and chat. "But it's controversial. A researcher in Somalia discovered a new shrike and was worried it might be on the brink of extinction because he could only find the one bird. He and his colleague decided to capture it live, instead of collecting it. They photographed and measured it, collected feathers with diagnostic markings, and took a blood sample for molecular analysis. They named it *Laniarius liberatus* and planned to release it to the wild after a couple of weeks, when they finished describing and documenting it."

We made our way slowly toward the stairs, too engrossed in Eduardo's account of the African shrike to make small talk with the concierge.

"Their plan was thwarted by the civil war in Somalia," Eduardo said. "The researchers were evacuated, and they took the captive bird with them. It lived in an aviary in Germany for almost a year before they could return it to Somalia. The blood sample they'd taken was lost in the post, so they ended up extracting the DNA from the feathers—but that destroyed their only feather specimens, so people didn't have anything to refer to later. In the end, their species report was flawed, not definitive. They failed to include all of the similar species in their comparison of gene segments in the phylogenetic assessment. And the morphologic differences with other species of African shrike were confined to the plumage coloring, so they couldn't eliminate the possibility that the bird was just a hybrid or a color morph of other African shrike species.

"It caused a big controversy in the ornithological community. Some people said they wasted the bird, that they should have collected it for museum safekeeping—if it was really the last one, then the species was doomed anyway, but at least there would have been a clear record of it for other scientists to study. Others say they should have just published a report on their field observations without trying to name the new species, especially since there was no chance of conservation efforts in the region."

We had come to a stop again and were standing at the bottom of the marble staircase. Eduardo sighed and rubbed his hand across his balding head. "So yes," he said, "it is possible to do a DNA analysis from a few feathers. And, in principle, to name a new species based on it. Whether or not it will be accepted, however, is another matter. It's definitely not standard practice, Alejandra, like with your microbes, but it's not unprecedented. And we do have a couple cases that are arguably more successful than the Somalian shrike."

"What happened to the bird?" I asked. "Was it really the last one?"

"No one knows. They'd discovered it in a little patch of acacia in a hospital yard, but by the time they tried to return it, war and fire had ravaged Somalia, the hospital was gone, and the whole area was devoid of trees and bushes. They released the shrike in a nature preserve far up the river, in a quite different ecosystem. People have looked for it since, but with no luck. Whether it was the last of its kind, or just a color morph or hybrid of one of the many widespread species of African shrike, remains unclear."

"I could get you the nest," I said. "After they abandon it. There should be feathers in there. The broken eggs. You could photograph the inside of it, see what color and size the eggs are. Store it in your museum." I actually had no idea if I could get through the brush to retrieve the nest, but I did not want him to capture a live bird any more than I wanted him to shoot one.

Eduardo took off his glasses and started rubbing the lenses clean on his shirttail, taking his time. "The marsh is dense," he said after a moment. "Be hard to shoot a rail that small. . . . Probably even harder to trap one live." He replaced his glasses and looked at Alejandra. "There's a group studying the phylogenetics of the Rallidae in New Zealand," he said, nodding as the idea took root. "Maybe they could do the analyses." He turned back to me and a huge, big-toothed smile appeared on his face, making him look more like a school kid putting one over on the teacher, than a serious middle-aged professor. "Actually," he confessed, "I hate collecting."

We loitered at the bottom of the staircase for another ten minutes while he and Alejandra discussed the DNA analysis, the concierge eyeing us curiously from across the lobby, imagining, I'm sure, some other sort of conversation altogether. Apparently there were several options for the analysis using different segments of the DNA, similar to what Alejandra did with her microbes. I leaned against the wrought-iron banister, waiting for them to finish, admiring my lover's round face in half profile, the fine nose and full cheeks and heavy-lashed eyes, watched her delicate hands dancing out her words as she and Eduardo worked through the details of analyzing rail blood, and then, finally, we made our way up the stairs to our rooms, and I had her to myself.

We made love. And talked. And made love. Slept. And talked, as if the night were endless, despite our early birding date.

"It's curious," she murmured as the moon rose and shone into our eyes through the gap in the curtains, waking us both at the same time. "Our hierarchies of life. We don't mind killing microbes." She was curled into the open arc of my torso, facing away from me, so that her words floated vectorless into the air in front of us.

"They aren't the last of their kind. And even if they are it probably doesn't matter. So you said."

"You said you wouldn't kill a rail even if there were millions of them."

"Any more than I would hunt ducks. Very unscientific of me."

"And inconsistent. You would eat duck."

"I have never eaten a duck."

I felt her laugh, vibrating against me. "Pheasant, then. Or quail."

"I don't think anyone ever offered me pheasant or quail. Not that I ever really thought about it. I just never wanted to eat a duck."

"Chicken! I know you eat chicken."

"That's different."

"Why?" She wriggled around to face me.

"A chicken isn't wild," I said. "It's born and raised as food."

"My bugs are wild. You're just prejudiced against lower life forms!"

"Oh, I love your wild lower life forms." I played my fingers lightly across the down on the small of her back. "Did you see the news about the WTO protests last week? The guys with the sea turtle costumes?"

"There you go. You'd never see them in single-cell-organism costumes."

I laughed. "Too small to see with the naked eye. Invisible protestors." I wrapped myself around her and shut my eyes, feeling her settle in against my chest, her sigh merging into my own, exhausted and contented, on the front end of sleep. "Little brown rail costumes are probably just as unlikely," I murmured, thinking of the rails out there in the dark, waiting for their chicks to hatch, my mind oscillating between rational thought and the nonsense of dreams, clinging tenaciously to the edge of consciousness. I imagined the two birds huddled together on their nest like Alejandra and I in our hotel bed, the moon leaking through the dense undergrowth the way it leaked through our curtain . . . then corrected the scene, for surely only one rail was on the nest and the other was hunkered down in the mud somewhere outside. What would Grandpa have thought? He had never discovered a new species. I imagined him kneeling in the wet grass and peering through his old spotting scope, running through a litany of field marks, his excitement building as he realized he didn't know what he was looking at.

Laterallus gordoni. That's what we would name the rails.

"Are you asleep?" I whispered.

She mumbled something that could have been yes or could have been no, but I started talking anyway, my mind now littered with images of California landscapes, images from my childhood and from Grandpa's childhood, images of lost landscapes. I told her about the vast maze of tule swamp that had once spread from the San Francisco Bay to the Central Valley, a region I'd known only as asphalt-covered suburbs and dusty cropland. I told her about the magnificent Sierras where I had spent my childhood summers camping and backpacking, about the eerily beautiful salt lake on their eastern flank, with its swarms of migrating shorebirds and nesting California Gulls—about the sweet irony of watching the master scavengers of Los Angeles dumps and beaches circling like white angels above a desert lake. I told her how Grandpa and a bunch of birders had banded together when I was a kid and stopped Los Angeles from drinking that lake dry, saving the entire western population of gulls from oblivion. I told her about Grandpa. How he had tried, unsuccessfully, to keep the last California Condors out of jail. I told her about the one I'd seen, how the face and neck were blushed like mine, how Grandpa said this should make me proud, which I wasn't so sure about, since it was such an ugly face. I told her how Grandpa and his cronies had preserved Point Reyes "in perpetuity" before I was born, about counting Snowy Plover nests with him when I was small and how the dunes now had to be fenced to protect them.

Alejandra was silent and unmoving in my arms, and I had no idea if she was awake or asleep or somewhere in between, but I rambled on. I described a new move to reclaim the tidal marsh that ranchers had diked off in the nineteenth century, make it part of the park. "When we have kids," I said, "that's all they'll know. Wild things in parks. Managed ecosystems. Reverse eugenics for birds of prey." I thought of the Peregrine Falcon and Bald Eagle, which a ban on DDT and a bit of reproductive technology had brought back from the brink of extinction. Unlike the California Condor.

"Better than no wild things at all," Alejandra said clearly, apparently wide awake. "Better than dead ecosystems." She extracted herself from my hold, pushed herself up in the bed, and lay her head on my arm so that we were face to face.

"They'll never see a wild sea turtle."

"Have you ever seen a wild sea turtle?"

"No. But I know they're out there. That's the thing. And I know what wildness looks like. I can imagine it, take comfort in its existence. I've seen eagles. A wild condor. Little brown rails that no one knows exist."

"They're like the Snowy Plovers," she said. "Like the California gulls."

"What, the rails? If there's only the one nesting pair and their chicks, it's much worse. More like the condors."

"No, I mean the way your grandfather must have felt. He wasn't fighting for an abstract concept, for sea turtles he'd never seen. He *knew* those gulls, those condors, they lived next door, in his backyard. It's like the difference between fighting to save faceless babies on another continent from famine, and saving your own son."

"You think? What, it's more instinctive, less altruistic? But what's the use? You save your baby from a car wreck, just so he can get fried in the global cataclysm when he's twenty."

"That's exactly what we do," she said. "What we're hardwired to do. Save the babies. The car wreck is immediate. We know what it looks like—tangled metal, smashed heads. But the global cataclysm is just a concept. Climate change. Mass extinction. Too big to grasp, even if we're in the middle of it. Even if we cause it.

"I love the way you feel nature," she said after a moment. "Like it's all intuitive. What did you say once, that you inherited a 'birder gene' from your dad's father? Those beautiful drawings . . . Eduardo was impressed."

I stayed quiet, considering. I'd never thought of my bird habit in such an exalted light before.

"California must be amazing," she said.

"Was. In Grandpa's time. Now it's half covered with highways and city. But we'll go there, I'll show you the best places. What's left."

When. We. Have kids. The thought meandered after the words, taking its time, ambling between the lines of our conversation, loitering in the open space between our faces, forming itself. An unprecedented impulse, an urge, a longing, an expectation beyond any I had known in my twenty-three years of uneventful life: I had been flying backwards into the future, watching Grandpa's receding world melt into oblivion, and only now, just now, in this moment, did I turn around to look at what lay ahead of me. Of us. I kissed her, softly, on the lips. On her temples, and neck, and breasts, everywhere. "Let's get married," I murmured into the flat plane of her belly. "And save our babies from car wrecks."

She took my head between her hands and pressed my face ever so gently into her belly, putting my kissing orgy on pause. "Your family would not be happy," she said.

I pushed myself up and looked at her face in the dim glow of moonlight that still filtered past the curtain. "Mom likes you," I said. "And Rubén, and Abuela."

"No they don't. They like the idea of me. And your uncle Juan hates me."

In the thrill of our sojourn into the marsh and seeing the rails, I'd almost forgotten what had happened at Abuela's party—Juan's rudeness, what Elsa had told me. I settled onto my back, and for the first time all night our bodies were separate. "It's not you," I said. "It's got something to do with the past, with your mother."

"Of course. It always has something to do with the past. And politics. It's always about politics." She said it casually, with practiced indifference, but I could feel her withdrawing, shrinking away from me into some cold distant place.

"I think it is more personal."

"There's no difference. Not in Uruguay. Not for that generation."

I slid my left hand across the narrow gap between us and let it rest like a bookmark against her hip. Then I told her the story Elsa had told me. I didn't want there to be any secrets between us. I wanted to share everything I knew, even if it hurt. I told her about her mother running from the *milicos*, hiding at Abuela's house, endangering Elsa and Abuela and Patricia. How Juan and Elsa blamed Eva Paden for Rubén getting involved with the Tupamaros and having to flee the country, how terrified they'd been. "Elsa did say it wasn't fair . . . to resent you. I think she even talked to Juan about it."

She had been lying very still and quiet, eyes wide open in the moonlit penumbra, and when she started talking, her voice was faint and disembodied, the joy and irony and self-assurance of the woman I'd been talking and making love to all night completely absent.

"I never knew my father," she said, "but my grandfather used to talk about him. Not the Tupa version, the guy who escaped from prison and was assassinated in his bed six months before my birth. He told stories about him as a kid, about his knack for mathematics and science, how he wanted to be an engineer. He never said much about my mother, and her parents died before I was born. But she's the one who shadows me. The one other people think they recognize when they see me. Eva Paden. The femme fatale of the Tupamaros, brilliant seductress and Marxist fighter. The martyr. The heartless terrorist tearing the country apart. My grandfather says they were just naive, overly idealistic kids, but I think he's the only one in the world who believes that. My aunt never says a word about either of them. It's all other peoples' memories, anyway, mostly from before I was even born. I don't really have any of my own."

I turned on my side and rested my arm between her breasts, caressed her cheek, brushed my hand gently across her open eyes and left it buried in her hair. It was obvious that these weren't things she liked to talk about, that it was an act of trust, and I felt honored, loved.

"People say I look like her."

"So what? People say I look like my father, but I'm nothing like him. Alejandra. You're the most beautiful woman I've ever met, the smartest, the most interesting, and the most fun."

She laughed softly, wryly, a short humorless burst of air that sounded nothing like her usual laugh. "That's the kind of stuff people say about my mother. Some sort of myth. Brilliant and beautiful. Martyr or terrorist, the men worshipped and coveted and longed for her. Look at your uncle Rubén. Longing still. And now here's the girl demon back to haunt him."

"Alejandra. You're not a ghost." The word slipped out and I remembered Mom using it when she first met Alejandra, the look on Rubén's face when he saw her in the dark foyer to Abuela's haunted house—a shiver ran up my spine. "You're *not*. You're just you. Flesh and blood." I was suddenly filled with corporeal craving, a desperate need to make love to her again, frantically, aggressively, as if to make the point—but she resisted my first move, captured my hand and held it still as it slid down her belly, and I knew it would be the wrong thing, that for her it would only repudiate what I so desperately wanted to confirm.

"I loved how innocent you were," she said, moving my captive hand up to a more comfortable position. "So candid and unwitting, so sweetly *yanqui*. You could tell me the names of all the Uruguayan birds I'd never noticed, take me into a wetlands landscape I never imagined, right here in the Departamento de Rocha . . . but you'd never heard the legend of Eva Silva Paden. I don't even think you knew who the Tupas were. I loved the way you looked at me, from that very first day out in Caruso's field, those blue *yanqui* eyes observing me, seeing right into me, the real me, without all the usual Uruguayan baggage and pre-conceptions." She paused, and I felt a sigh roll up and down her body, her ribcage expanding and contracting under my hand. "Then your mother said she had been friends with Eva. . . . And your uncle Rubén—I thought he was just your usual Tupa exile come home to vote for the Frente, a charming old flirt. But of course he had to be one of Eva's lovers. And the other one, Juan Luis—"

"Alejandra. I don't care who your parents were. To me, you're a completely new bird. A life bird," I added in English, with a birder's solemnity, playing the pun out in silence, close to my heart: this bird would be mine for life, not just an entry on a species list. Even as I said it, I understood that I did, in fact, care about her past, that I would *have* to care. If I were to love her, I would have to forego the *yanqui* innocence that had lured her to me and try to comprehend the ghosts that had entrapped her. I also knew there were things I could not ask her without entangling our relationship in precisely the past she yearned to be free of. "I bet your mother never lay in bed with a man talking about hierarchies of life," I said. "She probably never even saw a 'bug' through a microscope."

This time, when she laughed it was her usual, low-pitched giggle. I had inadvertently struck the right chord. I followed my own lead and asked her to tell me about the conference she was going to.

It was a big, four-day international conference on microbial ecology, she told me, and she was going to present some results from her rice paddy study. I felt her relaxing as she described the talk she was planning, her grip on my hand loosening, her body softening under my arm, sinking back into the pillow. She said she had discovered consortia of nitrogen-fixing and methane-eating bugs living in the surface layers of the rice field after flooding. They were quite active, she said, but they went quiet and all but disappeared when Caruso added his nitrogen fertilizer.

She seemed to be wide awake, her speech and thoughts as bright and insistent as the *Benteveos*'s morning song, and I let her ramble on, trying, through the fog of exhaustion and contentment that was creeping in to claim me, to remember what she'd told me about microbial communities and how they both determined and were determined by the amounts of oxygen, sulfur, and methane in the mud and water. I tried to understand the significance of these consortia she'd found, which sounded like some kind of utopian housing cooperative within the larger microbial communities. . . . But my mind kept wandering from her microbial story to our mammalian one, our hands now intertwined in such comfortable cohabitation it was as if they belonged to a single person, to some contented old man relaxing in his rocking chair with his hands folded across his belly.

It was the first intimation I had of what science might be for Alejandra, that her intellectual passion might be more complicated than it seemed. It wasn't just a job or even a vocation, it wasn't a game or an art. It wasn't even an escape, like stepping through the wardrobe into Narnia or falling into a rabbit's hole. It was the core of her being, her survival as a person, what lifted her above mortality and kept her from disappearing completely in the quagmire of other peoples' memories. I thought of her standing in the muddy water with her necklace of odd instruments, calling out numbers for me to write down, reaching down to fill her sample jars—the undeniably real, visible actions that had somehow generated this tale of invisible worlds. Were they real? I had no idea. My concepts of biology and chemistry derived from the standard high school classes—I could not visualize a microbe or a molecule the way Alejandra did, could not see the transformations she described. But if I wanted to truly *know* Alejandra, I needed to appreciate the recondite questions that drove her curiosity. I would have to listen patiently to her tales of invisible worlds and learn to experience them as just as real, material, and irrefutable as the fantastic avian worlds I'd witnessed at Point Reyes or Mono Lake or the unnamed pond in the not-so-wild wilds of the Departamento de Rocha, Uruguay.

If I was to fully love and appreciate this woman, I thought as we finally drifted into sleep together that night, I would need to understand both what entrapped and what freed her. If I could do that, I thought, I would be both liberator and liberated.

15

Laguna de Rocha was cut off from the sea by a narrow sandbar that Eduardo said breeched and let in salt water a couple times a year. The lagoon looked to be some ten miles wide, but he told us you could wade across the whole thing, that it never got much more than a meter deep. It was supposed to be a national park, but this didn't mean much because all the land was in private hands—there was a small fishing village on the shore, a fish-processing plant upstream, and the seawater breech was managed with a canal to accommodate the surrounding ranchers. But the place was teeming with tens of thousands of waterbirds and shorebirds, dozens of species of residents and migrants, which seemed to come from all directions. Sandpipers, Sanderlings, and phalaropes from as far away as Alaska and northern Canada, still in drab winter garb. Plovers from Tierra del Fuego in full courtship finery. Four species of grebe, only one of which I'd ever seen before, flocks of graceful Black-necked Swans and white, goose-like *Coscorobas* and pink Chilean Flamingos. . . . But the most breathtaking spectacle was the hundred-strong flocks of *Rayadores* that swept across the lagoon. They looked like oversized terns with oversized bills—except they flew low and moved together, banking and turning like troupes of airborne synchronized swimmers, red legs trailing, cone bills skimming the water and leaving Escheresque patterns of wake to glimmer in the morning sun. This was the scene I wanted to capture when I sat down on Rubén's bench with my journal and colored pencils that Sunday afternoon.

Alejandra had departed for Montevideo from Rocha, and Eduardo had driven me back to the estancia—it was out of his way, but he wanted to spend the afternoon in the marshes around India Muerta and then head back to the city via Minas, where his parents still lived. Juan had already left, and Mom was out staking tomato plants when I arrived. I opened one of the beers Rubén had left in the refrigerator and spent more than an hour drawing, embellishing and coloring the sketch I'd blocked in while we were at the lagoon. I was inspired by Eduardo's praise of my rail drawings, but this was turning out to be more of a landscape than a precise bird profile, not something I had much practice with. The journal page was really too small for it, and it wasn't one of my better creatioins, but I was content to be sitting out there in the afternoon shade drinking beer and drawing, Angelito ensconced at my feet like a faithful hound.

"Those are *Rayadores*," I told Mom, when she came in from her fields to see what I was doing and make us something to eat. "Black Skimmers. But that doesn't really do them justice." I tried to describe the magical scene that my sketch failed to capture.

"I like it. It's more impressionistic than your usual sketches. Maybe you should get a real sketch pad and some pastels."

"I don't know. I like the pencils." I'd used pastels when I was a kid and in one of the art classes I'd taken in college, but I wasn't sure I wanted to get into all that now.

We tried to eat outside, sitting on the bench with a plate of cold cuts and bread and a bowl of cherry tomatoes between us, but Angelito had developed a liking for anything he saw us eating and Rubén hadn't taught him any table manners. "Be civilized!" I told him, moving the plate to the back of the bench, just out of his reach, and drawing a smile from Mom at my rendition of her maternal remonstrations. We hadn't really talked in a while, and I was feeling loquacious, still high on birds and love and lack of sleep, excited about our discovery. I told her about collecting samples with Alejandra and about our excursion with Eduardo, showed her my drawings of *Laterallus gordoni* and explained that Eduardo thought they were a new species, that we were going to collect feathers so he and Alejandra could analyze the DNA.

Mom admired my sketches and listened intently to all this, but she seemed distracted, less curious about the rails than I'd thought she would be. She closed my journal and set it aside. "Gabriel . . . it's great that you've found people who are interested in the birds here. And the study Alejandra is doing is fascinating, I'm glad you're helping. . . . But I hope—Gabe, I'm glad you met Alejandra, glad you're friends. Her mother and I were so close when we were young. . . . But I just hope you're not getting too wrapped up here."

Wrapped up? What was that supposed to mean? *Envuelto.* Getting, got, gone. Meaning obsessed. Besotted. Infatuated. Involved. I turned to look at her, my euphoric mood beginning to give way to irritation. She was examining me as if I were her prized possession, as if I were twelve years old again, and she wanted to see how much I had grown.

"That's really nice, Mom. I'm glad you're glad. Though to be honest, we didn't become friends for your sake."

"*Bichito.* I don't want you to get hurt. The girl has a complicated past. Her mother—Eva's death cast a long shadow."

I thought about what Elsa had told me and what Alejandra had said about our families' entanglements, and I wanted to fire off a flip rejoinder about not being Romeo in medieval Verona—but there was something strange about Mom's voice, something pained and half strangled, that made me hold my tongue. I picked a cherry tomato out of the bowl and offered it to Angelito. I think it was his first tomato ever, and he looked surprised when he snapped it up and the juice spurted in his face. I laughed, and glanced at Mom, but she wasn't watching.

"You can't imagine, *hijo*, how many times I've reimagined Eva's life. If she had been the one to get the scholarship at Madison instead of me. If she had left, like I did, before we knew what we were leaving." She was gazing out across the yard, her arms folded against her body as if she were cold, though the sun was still on the horizon and the breeze lapping against our bare arms and legs was warm.

Nothing that Mom or anyone else in my family could say was going to deter me from being *envuelto* with Alejandra. But there were things I didn't know, that I needed to know about the past—about the Uruguay that Alejandra had been born in, the Uruguay that wasn't yet in the history books. Why her parents died, why they had been turned into a legend—why her likeness to her mother unleashed such a rash of misplaced memories and feelings in everyone who saw her. My thoroughly *yanquified* Mom—who had lived in the US all those years, who hadn't seen fit to tell her son about the Tupamaros, who hadn't even read the book she gave me—was the last person I expected to enlighten me. I was annoyed with her for subsuming the daughter in the mother's ghost—for any intrusion whatsoever in a relationship that was, to my thinking, mine and mine alone. But she had been close to Alejandra's mother and clearly wanted and needed to talk about her. So I put a lid on my irritation, and piled ham and cheese on a piece of bread, and prepared to learn whatever I could about the long-dead mother of the woman I was in love with.

"When we were in school," Mom said, "I wanted to be a doctor, like Eva's father. And she wanted to be an architect, like mine. Having children wasn't on either of our agendas." She shifted on the bench so that she was facing straight ahead, as tense and self-conscious as a schoolgirl preparing to recite a difficult poem.

Angelito sat himself down on my left foot and laid his neck along my leg, his beak pointed skyward in quiet supplication, as if he too were settling in to listen—though he was, in fact, more interested in my sandwich than anything Mom had to say.

"I hadn't been back to Montevideo since before the coup, but we'd kept in touch, and when I moved to California, we started writing more—it was too expensive to phone back then, and the connection was always bad. Eva was in Buenos Aires by that time, raising Alejandra. We were both a little lonely, I think. She'd found a good father for Alejandra, an Argentinian artist. He had a steady job as an illustrator for one of the national magazines, but Eva wasn't working and they lived more modestly than she had growing up. I used to tease her about giving up her career for the revolution and giving up the revolution for children—I was still studying then, and for once in our lives, I felt superior—but she didn't care. She loved being a mother. It changed her. Slowed her down, made her selfish, more careful. She wanted a just world for her kids, but she wanted to live with them in it, not die for it. She got pregnant again, this time planned, and then a few months later I was pregnant—unplanned, but your father was ecstatic, and I was under the illusion that motherhood could be a hobby, something to do while I got my PhD. We wrote each other practically every day then, comparing notes on first kicks and morning sickness, exchanging lists of names. . . . The letters took weeks to arrive, but one came almost every day. It was almost like when we were teenagers."

Mom paused, and, tired of having Angelito glued to my leg, I tossed my last bit of sandwich across the yard for him. I was thinking about Alejandra, wondering if she'd want to hear about this version of the mother she'd hardly known, a woman who sounded nothing like the ghost that haunted her—wondering, as Mom talked on, if I myself wanted to hear these revelations from the mother I'd known so well.

"Rubén called from Caracas. He'd been living in Buenos Aires, where he'd set up a little news kiosk that was doing pretty well, but he'd left everything. He said the Argentinians were rounding up all the Uruguayan exiles in Buenos Aires. He'd found out early and made it to Venezuela with one of his friends, but he was worried about Eva. I told him she was just raising kids, that she'd quit being political, though of course he knew what Eva was doing, he never lost track of her. He laughed at me, I remember that, he was scared to death, but he laughed.

"I was an American citizen. I thought that would count for something, I thought the ambassador would help me, thought I could get her out of the country. There were some rumors about a rogue CIA agent, but we didn't know then that the Americans were part of the plan, that Kissinger had signed off on all the torture and killing.

"Your father didn't want me to go. Said I was too pregnant to travel and I wouldn't be able to do anything anyway. He'd never met Eva. To him, the dictatorship was a political problem. To me, it was a personal problem, but he never could see that. We had our first big fight."

Mom hadn't looked at me once during this whole monologue, and her face, in profile, was expressionless, weirdly immobile, like a wax mask of itself, her gaze fixed on the eucalyptus trees on the other side of the yard.

She'd gone to Buenos Aires against Dad's will, gone straight to Eva's apartment from the airport because she couldn't reach her on the phone. "I still thought it might be okay, that I'd gotten there in time, that Rubén had exaggerated . . ." She described the apartment building on Avenida Córdoba, the neighbors who didn't want to talk to her, and the shops along the street where she was walking, looking for a *pensión* to stay in, when the *milicos* picked her up. "They were authorities, in uniform, and I thought they just wanted to see my passport. I was too stupid to be scared, until they handcuffed me and put a bag over my head.

"I don't know where they took me. Some big cavernous building that smelled like a garage, an inferno of echoing sound, lots of people but no one could see each other, we all had bags over our heads and handcuffs. Argentinian and Chilean accents. Cuban. Uruguayan. Engines roaring, a train passing, music blasting at random intervals, and the sounds of animal agony— screams, whimpers, sobs . . . gasping and gurgling, someone drowning.

"I had been asking for Eva, and after a while they took me to her, in a small room upstairs, and they took off the hand-cuffs and the bag. I don't know why they took me there. If they planned it, if there was any logic at all to their evil.

"She was lying on a mattress in the corner, wearing only a torn blouse and underwear, all stained with dried brown blood. Shivering. Hugely pregnant. There were two other women in the room. And Alejandra. She was playing with a doll next to the mattress—they'd let her bring her doll—and she was pretending it was a nurse, taking care of Mamá. She had on a pink cotton nightgown with a ruffle around the bottom, and I remember thinking, absurdly, before I realized what I was seeing, that Eva was raising her daughter to be the sort of girl we'd spent our adolescence trying to unbecome. I didn't know yet about children. How they choose their own selves no matter what you do."

She paused, and in the pause a huge shooting star streaked across the horizon, bright enough to send Angelito running circles around the yard, and I let out a small reflexive exclamation—but Mom's gaze was unwavering from the eucalyptus, and she talked on as if nothing had happened.

"Eva's whole body was blue, except the belly. Her hands hung like fallen angels at the ends of her arms, wrists broken. Her breasts were covered with black marks, her lovely face completely destroyed, the bones broken. But she was conscious. She could talk, though you had to get right next to her to understand.

"I told her I'd come looking for her. Told her I was going to get her out." Mom laughed, a dry rustling, joyless sound in her throat. "She told me I was an idiot. But she was happy to see me. Comforted. I should take care of Alejandra, she said, and of the baby when it came.

"She was proud of her big belly. Proud she and the baby had survived. She said they hadn't touched her belly, and I imagined some elemental shred of humanity. But Eva said they were just superstitious.

"The other two women were in better shape. A middle-aged Argentinian, and another Uruguayan girl, couldn't have been more than eighteen. There were three blankets and the one mattress, which they'd given Eva and Alejandra. A bucket for pee. For anything else you had to yell and beg at the door until a guard took you to a bathroom downstairs. Eva couldn't go to the bathroom, so we propped her up on the bucket. They'd done something to the nerves, so her legs couldn't hold her."

I thought of the book Mom had never read. Of Alejandra and what she didn't remember, of her little girl's bedroom with its pink ruffled bedspread and stuffed animals, the old dolls propped up on the dresser. *El plantón, el submarino, la bandera.* I wondered if the Argentinian names were the same as the Uruguayan. *El caballete.* Which of them would leave black marks on the breasts and ruin the nerves? What sort of beating could turn a woman's entire body blue?

"There were no windows. A light bulb hanging from the ceiling was always on. They gave us a pitcher of water. Some bits of bread. A bowl with meat in it, the half-eaten leftovers from a dinner, with toothpicks and cigarette butts thrown in. We fished out the meat for Alejandra. She sat on the floor next to the mattress playing with her doll. Sometimes I lay on the mattress also, trying to keep Eva warm.

"They left Eva alone now, came for the Uruguayan girl

instead. We'd hear her screaming. When they brought her back she couldn't speak.

"Alejandra ran to the door when she heard her stepfather. I don't know how she recognized him. The screams hardly sounded human. I picked her up and covered her ears. We sang to her on a day that we thought was March third. Her fourth birthday.

"I never saw what they did in the other rooms. They gave the others numbers in lieu of names, but I was just *la Norteamericana*. They didn't touch me. I made them nervous, they couldn't decide what to do with me."

She paused again. I didn't know what to say. I had an urge to comfort her now, a familiar childhood urge that brought with it a memory of my own: I was eight years old and terrified that my mother would commit suicide. As far as I knew, it was a memory of a non-event, of a fear that could as well have come from a child's nightmare as reality—though I also knew that Dad had convinced her to go to a psychiatrist for a few months, so maybe there was some foundation for the fear.

"Mom?"

"They took me to Montevideo," she said, and I had the sensation I was watching a video that had been broken and badly spliced together. "To the hospital. I must have been unconscious. Maybe they drugged me. I don't remember being on the ferry, only the hospital room, and the Uruguayan *milicos*, a doctor who wouldn't tell me anything, and you in my arms, nursing. They wouldn't let me call Mamá or Juan Luis. Only Keith. For three minutes, to say we were safe, that you were born, that they'd send me home as soon as you were big enough to fly, that I was not allowed visitors, that he should not come to Montevideo. He tried anyway, but in those days you needed a visa and it took two months. He was frantic. He called Rubén in Venezuela, and Rubén told him not to call Abuela or Juan, that it would endanger them. Told him I'd be okay with an American passport, that the hospital was good, not to worry."

I waited for her to go on, to connect the dots, but it was as if her story had crashed into a wall or stepped off a cliff. I got up and pushed the plate out of the way, sat back down next to her, and put a hand tentatively on her shoulder. She flinched at my touch, and then her face resumed its normal plasticity, melting back into Mom, the tears flowing down her cheeks.

"Keith never understood," she whispered. "He was so relieved when he saw you. . . . And so angry at me. He didn't really want to know anything, he shut me out."

"Did you even talk to him?" I asked as gently as I could. "Or was he supposed to be clairvoyant?" I defended Dad as if by reflex, even as I moved to comfort her and a dozen other questions clamored to be asked.

"Even when they killed Eva. He left me alone with my grief."

I held her awkwardly, a little stiffly, her forehead pressed against my chest, my arms loosely encircling her. At some point growing up, the bilateral act of hugging my mother had become a passive one of being hugged by Mom, and now, as an adult, I didn't quite know how to do it the other way around. We must have sat like that for fifteen or twenty minutes, and when she got up to chase the chickens in for the night, my shirt was so wet from her tears that the warm breeze against it left me chilled. My own eyes were strangely dry, and I marveled at how much easier it was to cry for the strangers who'd told their stories in the lipstick book than it was to cry for my own mother.

I thought about her giving birth to me, alone in Montevideo, neither immigrant nor emigrant, without her husband or a friend. Without her mother. I thought about the fights with Dad, with Juan Luis, with Abuela, never arguing about what she seemed to be arguing about, struggling with a hidden subtext no one wanted to read aloud. I wanted to know how long Mom was in the room with Alejandra and her doll and her ruined mother. How they killed Eva. What Alejandra saw. How her grandfather found her. I found myself caught between the need to know and sympathy and resentment—but Mom didn't broach the subject again that evening or in the coming days, and I didn't dare ask.

She seemed to have shoved all her memories back into whatever closet she'd kept them in all these years and was completely focused on the estancia. If anything, she was even more obsessive than ever, as if this budding sustainable farm in the Uruguayan outback really was the world's beacon of hope for the future, as if it mattered to anyone but a few chickens and a lone Ñandú. I hung around for a few days, laid some more irrigation tape and helped plant a new field, but I was restless and Mom's company was beginning to wear on me. I went birding and checked on the rails, even got up at dawn one day to see what they were up to. But the rails were generally quiet, their chicks hadn't hatched, and I missed Alejandra on my birding forays. I wanted access to news and email, to the books I'd left in Montevideo and the music I'd recently discovered. Mom suggested I drive to the city without her, but I didn't want to leave her out there without the truck, and finally, on Thursday, I talked her into going with me.

Santiago had taken a fancy to Angelito and was happy enough to take care of him and the chickens, but Mom still only lasted one night in Montevideo. She had become as reclusive as her misanthropic mother, cutting herself off from her old friends and even from Elsa. But whereas Abuela's misanthropy was constitutional and never bothered me—perhaps because I was so successful in the family competition for her attention—Mom's withdrawal both worried and irritated me. I was afraid of what she might have unleashed in herself, worried that all her frenetic activity was about to implode into its inverse—that she would cease to act, to speak, that she would freeze out everyone who loved her and self-destruct. It was not an unfamiliar worry, though when I was growing up the searing ice of Mom's unhappiness was always pointed like a weapon at Dad—whereas now it seemed to be aimed at Abuela and at me. I knew there was nothing I could do about it, and when she returned to the estancia, I stayed on in Montevideo with Abuela and Rubén.

Rubén was busy with the wave of pre-Christmas business at Carlos' print shop, and I spent the days until Alejandra's return from Brazil reading and thinking. I went over to Juan and Elsa's apartment and used their computer, wrote emails, and did a bit of haphazard research on international environmental agencies that might care about a previously unheard-of endangered species of rail. Eduardo and I met for lunch and discussed the possibility of featuring the rails in his book, and I spent an afternoon at the Pocitos beach, swimming in the choppy little waves, missing the Pacific. The Rambla was now in all-out summer vacation mode, and I tried to get Abuela out for a walk, but it was hopeless. She seemed frailer, somehow, as if she had aged in the week since her birthday, and we were all worried that she was sick, that she wasn't eating enough. Rubén cooked her steaks, but they were hard for her to chew and he just ended up eating double portions. Elsa turned the *zapallitos* and chard and tomatoes we'd brought from the estancia into fancy casseroles and tarts, and I tried making a big salad, but Abuela would take a few dainty bites and nudge the plate away. She wasn't sick, at least she claimed she felt fine, but she seemed, suddenly, so ephemeral that I found myself wondering if that was the significance of the number eighty-seven, which she'd kept such a mystery, if it was supposed to be a turning point in the grand scheme of mortality.

I thought a lot that week about how people decide what matters, individually and collectively, and what they try, or don't try, to do about it—what they can and can't do. The personal in the altruistic. Rescuing your babies from the car wreck, a species in your backyard. I thought about the scale of things. Saving a marsh, a species, a planet. A friend . . . a country. Saving a shrike in Somalia while the humans around you all killed each other. Tilting at windmills. I thought about Juan Luis and his rice-farming operation. Would a man forgo a lifelong dream just to save a tiny corner of paradise that no one even knew existed—a paradise that he and everyone around him considered badlands?

Despite an ebullient email from a friend who had been at the Seattle protest, the consequences seemed as unremarkable as the ripples from a rock skipped across a fast-moving river. It had, briefly, disrupted the WTO, and a bunch of people had landed in jail and been injured, but nothing changed. When I searched the Internet for news, there was a lot about the screwed-up Seattle administration and police brutality, the sort of stuff Dad had told me about from the Vietnam protests. But there still wasn't much about what the protests actually meant. My friend went on about the "anti-globalization" movement, but I wondered who was supposed to respond to the protests, besides the local police and the National Guard. A nonexistent global government? Multinational corporations, which, by definition, responded only to markets? He said they were planning more protests at the IMF and the World Bank, that the WTO was just the tip of the iceberg. But what was anyone supposed to *do*? No matter how you divvyed things up, the resources were as limited, finite, and off-balance as the atmosphere and climate, as the planet itself. I wrote my friend back and said as much, but encouraged him anyway, asked him to keep me posted. I told him I was in Uruguay and head-over-heels in love, unsure when I would be back. We'd been housemates in college, pretty tight, though he was more of a stoner than I was and a bit starry-eyed when it came to politics.

I thought about the world, the physical world, that Grandpa Gordon had inherited, a world still immense and full of wonder, with untouched spaces full of wild things one might never see or even hear about—wilderness for its own sake, unknown, out-of-bounds, like God. Was it just a lack of imagination on my part that I yearned for that world, that I wanted it, even now, for Alejandra and me and our children? Surely Alejandra was right that managed ecosystems were the best we could aim for in the world she and I had been born to. A domesticated world with nature preserves—if we were lucky, if we worked hard. Plovers on fenced beaches and rare rails in marsh museums. But how could we even think about managing ecosystems when we couldn't even manage ourselves, our consumption and waste? That was what my friends were protesting. The problem was that there was no viable alternative path on offer—no one had penned a new paradigm.

I imagined Alejandra on her scientific perch with her god's-eye view of microbial worlds, changing the scale with the twist of a knob, watching the coming and going of species, ecosystems, atmospheres, climates, mass extinctions . . . How liberating it must be to see us as just one species among many, one catastrophe among many—despite our capacity to observe our wake of destruction. Did human history and politics, individual lives, even Grandpa's wild places "preserved in perpetuity" lose significance on that scale? And yet here we were, the observers trapped in their own dioramas, lacking in significance, but inflated with meaning.

I finally read the biography Abuela had given me of her hero, José Batlle y Ordóñez. It portrayed him as a visionary, a believer in utopias who was also a pragmatic dealmaker and power-monger, which was obviously why he accomplished so much. I wanted to know what made the man tick, but the book was just about his deeds and didn't give much insight into his inner life. "The man *is* his deeds," Abuela said. But when I asked her about page 167, where the hero, then in his sixties, challenged a young journalist to a duel and shot him dead, she brushed it off. Was it political, was it personal? Had the journalist propositioned Don

Pepe's wife? Why wasn't he charged with murder? Abuela, who was eight at the time, said it was just a tragedy, an accident. Duels were common back then, she said, accepted, if not quite legal. But Don Pepe? Was he even remorseful? Where was the progressive humanist I'd been reading about? It wasn't as if the journalist had been killed by an act of nature. Artigas as an enigmatic hero in the eighteenth and nineteenth centuries was one thing, but shouldn't a twentieth-century hero be more accountable?

Mom's story nagged at me. Indeed, the more I thought about it, the more I resented her for dumping it on me at this particular juncture in my life. Four months ago, when she'd been lobbying me to go to Uruguay with her, she'd told me it would do me good. I'd ridiculed her, but in a strange way she'd been right. Watching the political show on the streets of Montevideo and reading about Uruguayan history—the *paisito* breaking free of Spain and Brazil, ever in search of its independent brand of utopia, South America's model of contentment and economic ease, its steamrolled Switzerland—wandering around in our bit of marsh and loving Alejandra, I did have the sensation that my end-of-millennium ambivalence was on the out. Even if nature was ending with the millennium, I could see that the world was moving forward into a future I might, as a member of the one species capable of perceiving a future, actually have a small role in creating. It wasn't lost on me that Mom had been trying to brainwash me to believe this all my life, with her arguments about what people *should* do, how things *ought* to be. So why had she suddenly decided to tell me this horror story that she'd kept to herself for more than two decades? Why now? What did it *mean* that people had inflicted such bizarre suffering, that people I knew were on the receiving end? People I loved.

On Sunday afternoon, I retrieved the lipstick book from the living room bookshelf where I'd stashed it and took it into the dining room. It had rained earlier, and the sunlight that streamed into the room when I pulled the blinds up was bright and optimistic, washed clean. I opened the book carefully to the preface, where there were no photos.

When I'd asked Juan Luis to recommend a book that covered late-twentieth-century Uruguayan history, he'd told me not to bother, that nothing worthy of history had happened in Uruguay since the 1960s—that the past few decades were the negative underside of a bright past and a bright future and deserved to be forgotten. But the group of unnamed lawyers, doctors, and human rights experts who had researched and written *Nunca más* thought otherwise. Here were memories like Mom's and worse, memories that no one wanted to remember, that burned whoever touched them—memories that had been abandoned to smolder and fester in the ever-deepening crevasse between then and now. According to the book's preface, it had taken a great effort—a conscious, civil effort—to drag them to the surface and piece together a coherent history. The book was based on official documents, news reports, surveys, and interviews, modeled after similar efforts in Argentina and Brazil. It was a cautionary tale, I thought, like the gruesome fairytales of old.

I read the preface and the first section, which described the events leading up to the dictatorship: economic decline and deteriorating quality of life, strikes and counterstrikes, the authoritarian measures and constraints on civil rights imposed by the ruling party in the 1960s, the Tupamaros and their armed struggle, the rise of the Frente Amplio, and the handover of power to the military in 1973. More or less what Rubén had told me in bits and pieces.

The rest of the book dealt with the years of repression and fear just before and during the dictatorship. Alejandra's entire childhood. The second part on the "practice of state terrorism" was the longest. It contained the results of surveys and interviews with political prisoners, and the text was interspersed with tables of statistics and photographs. I skimmed the first chapter on "arrests," and then I carefully turned the rest of the pages in the section in one thick clump, avoiding the nightmare photographs and interview excerpts, and skipping forward to the third part. I was reading about the limits to civil rights and the general breakdown of everyday life, when Abuela came trundling in on her way to the kitchen.

She greeted me and paused by the table, wincing at the bright sunlight. It was three in the afternoon, and I hadn't seen her all day.

"What are you reading now?" she said.

I slid the book across the table, and she bent forward to look at the cover.

"Why in the world are you reading that?"

"Part of my education in Uruguayan history."

"That's not history." She pushed it back across the table with one finger, as if the red lipstick of the cover might stain.

I shrugged. "Mom gave it to me. Have you read it?"

"*Bah!*" She flicked the idea away with the back of her hand and continued into the kitchen without answering me.

The government had assigned everyone a letter. A, B, or C, depending on how "*subversivo*" you were. People who were classified C were banned from working as civil servants or teachers and often had trouble finding jobs in the private sector. Anyone who was considered a leftist, broadly defined, was assigned a C. That included everyone who had been associated with any of the parties in the Frente Amplio or been a member of a labor union, or anyone who had traveled to the wrong country or been observed fraternizing with leftists. Abuela's Don Pepe, I thought, would have been a C.

Abuela returned with her *mate* and a plate of *plantillas*, which I always thought of as old-lady cookies, maybe because Abuela was the only one I ever saw eating them. They weren't bad dipped in coffee, but Abuela ate them dry, with *mate*. She seemed to be living on sweets these days, but at least *plantillas* appeared to have a lot of egg in them. She set the plate down in the middle of the table, retrieved a book from the sideboard, and sat down next to me. I noticed she was also reading a gift from Mom, the Umberto Eco novel she'd tossed aside with such indifference on her birthday. She was even using the magnifying glass I'd given her. But I knew better than to comment.

I found my place and tried to read on, but my mind was wandering. Had Abuela been an A, because she was so anti-communist? According to Rubén, she didn't used to be that way. Maybe she'd been a C, because she'd once been an anarchist. Or because her son was a Tupamaro. What about Juan Luis and Elsa? If you were a C you couldn't have a job in the government, so Juan couldn't have been a C. Probably not even a B.

I took a *plantilla* and pushed the plate closer to Abuela, but she was engrossed in the novel and ignored it.

"Abuela."

She looked up, the magnifying glass posed over the page.

"What was it like during the dictatorship?"

"Which one?"

No one ever asked that. The dictatorship was The Dictatorship. Uninflected. "Here," I said. "In Uruguay."

Of course she knew what I meant. She'd seen what I was reading. But she told me about the Terra dictatorship instead. I'd read about it in the *Enciclopedia uruguaya*. One page, after Batlle y Ordóñez died, in the 1930s. Real history.

"We elected Terra as a Batllista and an atheist," Abuela said. "But he got married to a Catholic and went to hell."

"I heard you were an anarchist," I said.

"Who told you that?"

"Rubén."

She chuckled. "That was earlier, when I was a teenager. We liked to hang around in the cafés philosophizing with a couple of charismatic Spanish anarchists. It annoyed my father, who was an ignorant old Catholic *Gallego*, but no one else paid any attention to us."

"And later? In the seventies and eighties?" There was no cogent name to attach, no Hitler or Mussolini or Pinochet, no single power-hungry monster worthy of the honor. Though there must have been monsters. "Weren't you scared, Abuela? When Rubén left? When Alejandra's parents were killed?" I laid my hand on the book, one of its statistics running through my head: more than 50 percent of the adult population in Montevideo had been detained by the military authorities at one time or another. "People went to prison," I said. "They were tortured. Killed."

"Don't believe everything you read," Abuela said. She nudged her book aside and moved her *mate* center stage, cradling the gourd between her hands. "If you weren't involved, they didn't bother you. You just had to remember to carry your papers around when you went out, even to the beach. And be careful who you talked to. Speak softly. You never knew who was listening. Who was going to get the wrong idea." She fussed with her *mate*, pushing gently on the straw to lift the *yerba* exactly the way Mom always did. Same movement, same hands, now that I thought of it—they didn't look much alike, but they had the same solid, chunky hands. "I had a friend who died in 1980," she said. "A lawyer, just turned seventy, been in prison for almost five years. But he was *metido*."

"*Metido*?" I said. "With whom?" Involved. I thought of Elsa's story. Of Mom's. Were you *metido* if the *milicos* searched your house for escaped prisoners? If you were the daughter of a dead Tupamaro-turned-housewife?

"With the *subversivos*." She leaned closer to me and lowered her voice, as if even now she had to be careful who heard what. "Before my friend was arrested, an acquaintance from Buenos Aires brought me a letter and asked me to give it to him. A *sealed* letter."

"And so? Did you open it?"

"Of course not." She leaned back in her chair and brushed the idea away with a flick of her wrist. "We were good friends. I handed it to him and told him it was sealed when I received it. He thanked me as if that were normal and stashed the letter in his pocket without opening it. Very strange behavior." She said that in Uruguay, any letter or package you entrusted to someone to give someone else should be left unsealed, or sealed in that moment. I didn't know if this was true or just another of Abuela's superstitions, but she seemed to think the letter for her friend was a subversive document. "Three days later," she said, "they arrested him."

"It says here they arrested people just for being in a labor union."

"*Puf.* The unions. That's where the Tupamaros started. They were all paid by Russia and Cuba. That's when the real repression started. When the government realized how deeply the foreign communists had infiltrated. The danger."

"Rubén was paid by Cuba?" For once I wanted Abuela to make sense, to focus her aging intellect.

She shook her head. "Rubén. Eva. They got caught up in the student protests, distributing leaflets. Lili and Eva were still in school. There was reason enough to protest, Pacheco was a terrible president. So at first, one indulged them. The whole country indulged them."

She paused just long enough for me to imagine Rubén as a young student passing out leaflets with a girl who looked like Alejandra.

"I had no idea, mind you, that they were involved with the *subversivos*. Not at first. They'd come and go, hang around, just like they'd always done. Luckily, Lili got the scholarship and left for the US, and then Eva started coming around with this older fellow, Natalio Silva. Alejandra's father. He died in a big shootout at one of their hideouts. Probably in your book there."

I glanced down at the book lying open in front of me. I hadn't thought to look for names of people I knew. Or knew of. Could you have a shoot-out from bed? Alejandra had said her father was shot in bed.

"Poor Rubén was just her trial run. She tossed him aside like a used tissue once Natalio came round. Rubén was a fool, wouldn't listen to me or even to Juan Luis. He made friends with Natalio just so he could stay close to Eva. Such was her charm." She sucked on her *mate*, fixing me in her gaze just long enough to make sure I didn't miss her point. "Natalio had been in prison and had all his teeth knocked out, which made him a hero. And he had a gun. He liked to wave it around and expound on revolution, but I told him to put it away when he was here. I wasn't impressed with his phallic fetishes. But Eva had a weakness for that sort of thing." Abuela made a dismissive movement with her hand. "They all fancied themselves Che Guevara," she said, "with their guns and black berets, middle-class kids playing at war. But this wasn't Cuba or Bolivia. What did we want with revolution in Uruguay? All we needed were some better politicians. Instead, we got a bunch of communist infiltrators and the military in power."

Abuela poured more water into her *mate* and picked a single *plantilla* off the plate.

"What happened to her?" I asked carefully. "To Eva."

"She was in prison when Natalio died, pregnant with his daughter. But then the women escaped also," Abuela said, a smile threatening her caved-in mouth, as if she were proud of the escapade, despite disapproving of the *subversivos*. "She got away to Buenos Aires just as the Argentinian communists were laying out the welcome mat. Took up with some radical artist. *Un Porteño*," she added with a flick of her wrist, as if being from Buenos Aires merited an extra measure of her scorn.

I thought of the things Abuela seemed to have left out of her account—Eva hiding in the house, her own trip to the police station, the bomb in Rubén's mattress—and of how Abuela seemed to subscribe to all of the self-contradictory myths about Eva that Alejandra had described.

"The Argentinian military executed her when they took power a few years later," Abuela said. "The body was found in Buenos Aires, riddled with bullets, stuffed in the trunk of an abandoned car. Some people say the Uruguayan government was behind it. But the Argentinians were more experienced with these things, more brutal."

I examined Abuela's face as she told me all this. Impassive. Pausing between sentences to nibble on her cookie.

"They say she was pregnant again when they shot her. And that her little girl was with her."

"Alejandra."

Abuela nodded. "No one knew where she was. Eva's father had died the year before, mercifully. And her mother was in the mental hospital. But Natalio's father went ballistic when he heard that his granddaughter had disappeared. He went to Buenos Aires and visited all the big newspapers, convinced them to run ads with a picture of Alejandra, begging for her return—a dangerous thing to do, but he was a well-known businessman with lots of connections in the US. Two days later, Alejandra showed up at a bakery near Eva's apartment in the wee hours of the morning, and the baker called the number in the paper."

"What about the *Porteño* artist?" I said, remembering Mom's story about Alejandra crying out for him in Buenos Aires. "Her stepfather."

Abuela peered at me through her yellowed glasses. "She remembers him?"

"Not really. But her grandfather told her about him." Alejandra had never mentioned a stepfather. But I couldn't very well tell Abuela what Mom had told me, not if the whole family had corroborated in keeping Mom's visit to Buenos Aires a secret for twenty-three years.

ACCIDENTALS

"I don't know," she said. "He was a communist, and the Argentinians shot a lot of them. Now they're saying they dropped people from airplanes into the river. Where is Alejandra, anyway? You didn't break up, did you?"

"No," I said. "She's at a conference in São Paulo. Comes back tomorrow."

"Good," Abuela said. "Bring her by and tell her I want to see some pictures of microbes." She held up her magnifying glass as if she expected this to help her see the microbes, and I smiled, thinking of the elaborate microscope that Alejandra had shown me in her lab. But Abuela slid her novel back in front of her, putting an end to the conversation before I could disenchant her with the details of modern science.

I turned my attention back to the open book in front of me, trying to read the section on exiles and international solidarity. But I couldn't concentrate. I flipped to the section titled "Medical Attention for Political Prisoners" and studied the photo of the military hospital where I'd been born. Then I turned to *Anexo II, LISTA DE PERSONAS MUERTA.*

The appendix was divided into categories and subcategories, depending on cause of death. *Muertos en operaciones callejeros de las fuerzas armadas. Muertos en prisión.* Died in prison. From torture. Suicide. Illness. Unknown causes. Additional names provided by the Asociación de Madres y Familiares de Uruguayos Detenidos-Desaparecidos. Children who had been kidnapped and disappeared, children born in captivity who disappeared, children who reappeared. There was a long list of Uruguayan detainees who had disappeared, most of them in Argentina. A few in Uruguay, Paraguay, Chile . . . No dates given, just names and the countries where they were last seen. The earliest entries were in 1972, though according to what I'd read in the historic section, the violence was already going strong in the sixties. The last entries were in December of 1984. I was eight years old, in Montevideo for the second time, when two people died in prison. Cause of death: torture.

I found Natalio Silva on the died-as-a-result-of-military-operations-on-the-street list, August 1972. They didn't have a category for military operations in bedrooms.

"You should marry her before I die," Abuela said next to me, and I looked up, startled. She closed her book, leaving the magnifying glass as a marker, and pushed up from the table.

"When are you going to die?"

Abuela answered with a cagey half smile and I grinned back as if we were just playing the Quiroga chess game of who can be the most acerbic. But I wasn't at all sure we were joking. Did she know that I'd just proposed to Alejandra, was it written all over my face? Not that Alejandra had taken my proposal seriously. I didn't even know myself if I'd been in earnest, though I figured I would get earnest fast if she said yes.

"She's as smart as her mother," Abuela said. "But not as foolish." She took her *mate* and thermos into the kitchen, and then paused again by the table on her way out. "Eva had The Gift," she said, fixing me in her myopic, glass-filtered gaze. "Sometimes it skips a generation—but I wouldn't be at all surprised if her daughter has it."

I turned back to the book, thinking of Alejandra, wondering if I could remember anything from when I was three or four years old—but the earliest memory I could summon was from kindergarten, when I was five. Eva Paden's name was on the list headed "Uruguayans who died in Argentina for reasons apparently related to the situation in Uruguay." June 1976. The list didn't have any subcategories and it didn't say how she'd died.

16

It took me a moment to realize that the woman stepping out through the courtyard gate of Alejandra's house on Tuesday evening was, in fact, Alejandra. She was wearing a knee-length black dress in some sort of slinky material that clung to her figure and was slit up to her hip on one side, black net stockings, and black sandals with three-inch heels. She had her hair pulled tightly back and tied up with an iridescent green scarf, and her lips were lined with blood-red lipstick, the only makeup I'd ever noticed her wearing. She looked so elegantly sexy that I froze in my tracks, too intimidated to embrace her.

She'd only been gone a week, but I had missed her so badly I'd wanted to throw down the phone and dash over to her lab to abduct her when she'd called on Monday. Instead, she'd made me wait, told me to put on my best clothes and pick her up at her grandfather's house at nine on Tuesday evening. And now here I was, dutifully dressed in a white shirt and khaki pants, staring at this beautiful stranger who I didn't dare touch.

She laughed, placing a kiss coquettishly on my cheek and asking me about the rails.

I forced myself to stop gaping and told her that the rails hadn't yet hatched when I was last out there on Wednesday. I felt a sudden pang of worry, thinking of the missing *Chajá* chick and the rodents and foxes and wildcats that supposedly frequented the marsh. "We can check on them Thursday," I said, "when you drive out to sample." I told her what Eduardo had told me, that the babies were likely to fledge within a few days of hatching and might be hard to find after that. I was still staring at her as if she were some million-dollar work of art that I was afraid I'd damage by touching. "You look gorgeous," I said. "But why are we so dressed up?"

"We're going to dance tango."

"I don't know how to dance tango."

"I'll teach you." She looked down at my feet. "These are your best shoes?"

I was wearing a pair of brand-new black *alpargatas*, the canvas slip-ons that had been a staple of my childhood summers. I thought they looked pretty good. "They're new," I said, and then I finally came unfrozen and pulled her into my embrace.

We took a taxi downtown to a large, elegant old *boliche*. It had two long narrow rooms joined by French doors, high ceilings and polished wood floors, old photographs of dancers and musicians on the walls, clusters of tables around the edges, and a bar in back. Couples of all ages, shapes, and get-ups were gliding about to the music of some old tango recording like the ones Elsa liked to listen to. Some people were dressed up like Alejandra in sexy dresses, the men in narrow black slacks and white shirts, but others were in T-shirts and jeans and even, I noticed, sneakers. I didn't see anyone in khakis and *alpargatas*, but the crowd was enough of a hodgepodge that I didn't feel out of place—as long as I stayed off the dance floor.

We stood near the door, watching the dancers, and Alejandra told me there had been something of a tango revival in the last few years. She pointed out a slick-looking young couple who she said were friends, and I watched them go through what seemed like a choreographed routine of incredibly complex moves, turning and posing, with the woman's legs swinging and looping enticingly between and around her partner's until he finally swept her off her feet and over his shoulder with her legs split like a ballerina's. I glanced at Alejandra.

"Don't worry," she said. "They're members of Joven Tango, almost professional. I just learned from my grandfather." She gestured at a middle-aged couple that was slithering about less spectacularly, but no less impossibly. "That's more my style there."

I watched as the woman's feet slipped out from under her and her partner held her suspended above the ground between his legs, leaning over her in conquest for a beat before lifting her back to her feet. "Forget it," I said. "I'd drop you on your head."

Alejandra laughed and pointed out a couple of octogenarians who were gliding stiffly but expertly across the floor in what appeared to be a sort of waltz-like move that looked almost manageable—not that I'd ever danced a waltz before. I was relieved, however, when the song ended and we went to sit with her friends at one of the tables near the bar. The women all seemed to be from Alejandra's lab. The department head, Serrana, was there with her husband, and Alejandra's officemate, Julieta, and a few master's students whose names I didn't catch. And one other boyfriend. We ordered beers and snacks, and in this unlikely environment, with the melodramatic sweeps of tango in the background, the conversation turned to microbiology and the conference Serrana and Alejandra had gone to. The other two men in the group seemed uninterested and struck up a conversation with each other, but I was at the opposite end of the table. And I was curious to hear the women's scientific gossip, at least to the extent that I could follow it.

Alejandra's paper about the nitrogen-fixing and methane-consuming bug utopias had made a splash, and they were all congratulating her. Methane had apparently been a big topic at the conference because people were concerned about if and how the methane produced in different kinds of wetland soils might contribute to global warming. Serrana said there were lots of papers about methanogens, which were, I surmised, bugs that pissed methane. But Alejandra's was the only paper about methanotrophs—bugs that consumed methane—and the only one to underscore the complex ecology that ultimately determined how much methane actually leaked out of the mud and water into the atmosphere. She'd told me about this discovery before she left, but only now, listening to them discuss it, did the methane part become clear.

"So your bug consortia can produce nitrogen for the rice *and* get rid of a greenhouse gas?" I asked. "Can't you just tack on something that eats CO_2? Then you've solved the most pressing problem of the next millennium."

They laughed. "Lots of microbes consume CO_2," one of the students said. "And produce methane . . ."

"The consortia produce nitrate," Alejandra explained, "that the rice plants can, in theory, use. And they consume methane that might otherwise leak into the atmosphere. But the extent to which they accomplish that task is dependent on a million other variables."

"Hypothetically, it might be possible," Julieta said. "If we could figure out how to domesticate a whole ecosystem."

"I can't even grow the consortia bugs in culture, let alone isolate them."

I'd already eaten two of the little pizzas, but Serrana saw me eyeing her French fries and pushed the plate toward me. "Someone gave a talk on 'unified soil microbe management' for agriculture," she said. "But it was pretty theoretical."

"No one would use it, theoretical or otherwise—I couldn't even get Caruso to try different water and fertilizer regimes in a small test plot." Alejandra emptied the last bottle of beer into my glass. "The growers want optimum yield with lower expenses—an unlikely combination, unless we tax chemical fertilizers or require them to cut down methane emissions."

"None of which is ever going to happen in Uruguay," Serrana said.

"Or the US," I said. "Despite the organic food movement.

And," I added, for Alejandra's sake, "decades of Liliana Quirogas. We're still the industrial agriculture capital of the world."

"To hypothetical solutions!" One of the students whose name I couldn't remember raised her glass and the whole table drank the toast and then rose en masse for the dance floor, the two extra women debating which of them would make the better man—while Alejandra tugged on my hand, and I held fast to my seat.

"Wrong shoes," I said.

"Take them off. You can dance in your socks."

I shook my head.

"Come on, it's just for fun. I promise we won't laugh at you."

It was a promise she couldn't keep, but I didn't really mind. I left the shoes on, and she stood next to me and walked me through the basic steps, giggling at my big-footed shuffling gait. "Now we do it together," she said when I thought I was getting the hang of it, proudly stepping and sliding alongside her. I groaned. This was the part I was worried about. She arranged me with one arm bent at the elbow and my hand sticking up, fit her own hand into my palm, slid her left arm around my neck, and told me to embrace her with my other arm.

"Now what?" I asked, though I would have been content to just stand there like that, listening to the music with Alejandra leaning lightly into my chest, her nose and forehead brushing my neck, the silk of her dress and the taut muscles of her back beneath my palm. Serrana and her husband glided to a stop next to us to give advice, moving my hand up higher on Alejandra's back, telling me to bend my knees and loosen up. They tried to demonstrate some simple moves, but I was afraid I'd get out of position if I turned to watch.

Alejandra gently prodded me into motion. "Good," she said as I followed her lead. "But backwards. You're supposed to guide us." Step step step-slide step . . . I had no idea where I was supposed to guide us, but once we got moving, the music seemed to take over and we were whooshing around the room almost gracefully. It was exhilarating, riding the slippery crescendos and mood changes of the bandoneons and strings. I was imagining swallows diving and dashing high in a spring sky, with their sudden turns and reversals, and I got carried away and tried to whip around behind her the way I'd seen the others do—but instead I seem to have stuck my foot out and tripped her. She let out a squeal of surprise, catching herself on my arms to keep from falling, and as we were sorting ourselves out I felt a tap on my shoulder and turned to find Rubén grinning at me.

"Let me show you how it's done," he said, stepping smoothly around me to stand in front of Alejandra. She smiled at me and shrugged, stepping just as smoothly into his arms, and I moved out of the way. It was the first time I'd seen Alejandra really dancing, and I was writhing with a mixture of jealousy and admiration at the way my uncle took her twisting, flirting, and gliding around, as if the two of them had been joined at the torso since birth. Despite his jeans and loafers, he danced with smooth, confident, subtle moves, showcasing his beautiful partner and camouflaging the seduction in what seemed a completely different dance than that of Alejandra's showy Joven Tango friends. He caught my eye over her shoulder and then whipped around behind her in something like the move I had dreamed of, their legs slipping out from under them in perfect unison. I went back to our table, and when the song was over, Rubén deposited Alejandra at my side and joined the friends he'd come with at a table across the room.

I'd never been a huge tango fan, but I was enjoying myself immensely. Alejandra danced with me for hours, and by midnight, I felt like I could at least shuffle around the dance floor in my *alpargatas* without maiming anyone. Rubén danced interchangeably, I noticed, with two women in his group of friends, and when they left, he came over and danced with Alejandra's friends, and then when they left and we were wanting to leave, he joined us in the taxi home and talked us into stopping in Punta Carretas for a last drink. "At least we can hear some real music here," he said as we got out at the little *boliche* across from El Shopping.

"I thought you had to go to work tomorrow."

"Carlos can get by without me for a few hours." He pulled open the door and ushered us inside.

Except for the live music, the place seemed like your typical neighborhood joint, with a bartender and one waitress, both of whom greeted Rubén by name. We found a free table in the corner, and Rubén ordered more beer for all of us, even though he was already slightly drunk, I was on the verge, and Alejandra had announced that she didn't want any. The music, it turned out, was not only live but also exceptionally good, a trio of bandoneon, bass, and violin. The place was packed with middle-aged couples and small groups of men, and there was a low murmur of conversation, but people were clearly there for the music, mostly attentive. The musicians seemed to be friends with half the patrons, and they paused to chat between numbers, as if they were practicing in their living room rather than giving a show. During one of the pauses, Alejandra and I got to talking about the rails, and I told her my idea of using them to get some kind of grant or water subsidy so Juan could fill his pond without cutting off the flow from the creek.

"You'd have to wait for Eduardo to verify and publish the species," Alejandra said. "That will take at least a year, maybe more."

"I don't think the marsh will be that affected the first year, do you? As long as it gets the normal summer rain—"

"What's a rail?" Rubén asked. I hadn't even realized he was listening.

"A kind of bird. Gabriel discovered a completely new species at your estancia—hasn't he shown you?"

"He's never even seen the marsh," I interjected. "Rubén, why don't you drive up to the estancia with Juan on Friday. I'll give you both a tour. It's just a few kilometers up the creek behind the house, on the border with Caruso's land."

"Why would I want to go out there? It's all muddy."

"Right. That's what a marsh is."

"Can we borrow horses from Santiago?"

"Horses can't get in there. And anyway, they'd scare all the birds away."

"Birds. You want me to brave the mud to see birds."

"It's worth it," Alejandra said. "Trust me."

"You've been in there?"

"Oh yes, I've been in there all right, up to my knees—almost didn't come out once! I've been taking samples there. And," she added, "birdwatching."

I laid a hand on her thigh under the table. It was hard to imagine her in her silky dress up to her knees in mud.

"Rubén," I said. "Don't you think you should know what's on your own land? Just think, you would be the fourth person in the whole world to see *Laterallus gordoni*."

But Rubén's eyes were on Alejandra, and I couldn't tell if he was still listening to me. The musicians were starting up, and I was a little afraid he was going to ask her to dance in the small space up front—but instead, he leaned back in his chair and started singing, loudly and expressively, the Quiroga eyebrows working overtime.

"*Si pensará alguna vez en lo que fui . . .*"

Alejandra laughed and leaned over to whisper in my ear. "At least he sounds good!"

He did sound pretty good. And sad. *If I were to reflect on what I was, I wouldn't even have the strength to live . . .*

The matronly woman who'd served our beers stepped into the little dance space, and the bartender moved out from behind the bar to join her. She was short and round and he was tall and lanky and must have been pushing seventy.

"*Pero yo sé que hay que olvidar y olvido sin protestar . . .*"

The bandoneon player gestured for Rubén to join the band up front. But Rubén didn't want to perform, he just wanted to sing.

"En la negra caravana de dolor, de los hombres que perdieron el hogar . . ."

The song was all about a guy who'd lost his home and his past, about forgetting and moving on in a "dark caravan of pain." I thought about Rubén with his broken marriage, bankrupt business, and distant daughters, returning from exile after so many years, struggling to reconnect with people he'd known when he was my age, people who'd never left. About Mom after a lifetime of immigrant assimilation in the US, holing up alone at the estancia and shutting out her Montevideo friends.

I thought about home. About Dad and my friends in California. We emailed now and then, but I missed Alejandra more after three days than I missed any of them after three months, including Dad. I moved my hand from her thigh to the back of her bare neck and leaned back in my chair, listening to the sad tango and watching the old couple moving their two, very differently shaped bodies as if they were the interdependent parts of one. I wondered where we'd end up, Alejandra and I, where home would be. Here, or in California, or going back and forth like the migrating shorebirds we'd seen at Laguna de Rocha. Maybe she could get a job at one of the universities in California when she finished her PhD. Given what people said about the Uruguayan economy, it seemed unlikely I'd find a job here. At that moment, however, I hardly cared, so convinced was I that no matter where we went, our wanderings would be bright and filled with joy, that the tango's sad, dark *caravana de dolor* was not for us.

"That's a story with a happy ending," Rubén announced, when the song came to an end.

"Happy?" I turned to look at him, the heartbreaking tango

lyrics and his mournful tenor singing voice running through my head.

He nodded in the direction of the dancing couple, who were frozen in their final pose. "A happy love story," he said, sounding perfectly cheerful, "not a happy life. El Negro there was an infamous bank robber, locked up in the prison across the street nearly half his life. But when the place started filling up with Tupas, they reformed him, gave him an education in economics and politics." Rubén waved at a friend who had just wandered in, and Alejandra signaled me that she was ready to leave, but the friend paused at the bar, and Rubén went on. "He had a cell on the top floor," he said, "with a small window, where he could just see the roof of this house. Solitary confinement, nothing to do. He'd watch this woman hanging her laundry out to dry on the roof, and he thought she was just another spoiled bourgeois Punta Carretas housewife until one day just before the referendum in 1980—when the *milicos* put their constitution up for a sham vote and there was a clandestine campaign to vote no—he saw a Frente Amplio flag hanging on the line with her laundry and took it as a sign— *Bo*! Martín, grab a chair. Just telling my *yanqui* nephew about El Negro."

I wanted to hear the end of the story, but Alejandra was already relinquishing her seat to Martín and calling the waiter over to pay the tab, so we made our escape.

"I've heard that story a million times," she said as we stepped out onto the street.

"So what happened?" I took a welcome breath of smoke-free air and gazed up at the windows of El Shopping, with its eerie halo of white Christmas lights.

"He somehow got a message to her via another prisoner's mother, and she started visiting him. And when the prison closed down and they gave everyone amnesty in '86, he just moved across the street and they opened the *boliche* together and lived happily ever after. Or something like that—it's always a little different. Come on," she said, tugging at my hand. "There aren't any taxis. Your uncle was totally drunk," she added as we started walking up Ellauri.

"That didn't keep you from dancing with him."

"He wasn't drunk then."

"I'm a bit tipsy myself," I said.

"I know. But I don't mind." She snuggled up under my arm, lending ballast to my alcoholic vertigo as we walked through a sleeping Punta Carretas, making plans for the week and picking up bits of the evening's unfinished conversations. She said she wouldn't be able to go to Caruso's until Sunday, but I resolved to drive out with Juan on Friday so I could check on the rails—and on Mom, but I didn't say that.

"Have you told your uncle about your water subsidy scheme?"

"First I have to see if it's even a possibility." I was pleased that she'd taken the idea seriously, but I wasn't yet sure it was worth taking seriously.

"First, you have to get him on your side. Make him see the marsh the way you do." She slipped out from under my arm and took my hand again, picking up the pace.

"I can take him on the tour with Rubén," I said after a moment. "I'll take them birding, show them the magic pond. Hope for a peek at the rails. I'll get Mom to go with us, make it a family outing." We were walking alongside the scrubby park near Elsa's apartment, the site of a lively market on Saturdays but now deserted and so quiet we'd gotten self-conscious and started whispering. "After all," I said, "the estancia belongs to the three of them."

At the rate we were going, we wouldn't have gotten home until after three in the morning, but we spotted a lone taxi pulling away from us on 21 de Septiembre and chased it up the street waving and laughing until it stopped.

"Whose house?" I said as we slid into the back, and she answered by giving the driver her address.

"The bed is bigger," she whispered in my ear. "Better for sleeping with drunk men."

I pulled away and looked at her. "What are you, an expert?"

She smiled noncommittally, and when we entered the pink-and-white space of her little girl's room, being careful not to wake the doting grandfather I had yet to meet, I had to laugh—not that I knew the answer to my question. But we had time, I thought, my hands riding the slinky dress up her hips, my eyes straying over her shoulder to the age-yellowed plastic baby doll on the dresser top. Plenty of time to learn everything there was to know about each other.

17

"You realize," I told Rubén as I stepped through the open door to his room on Friday morning, "that this means Abuela doesn't plan to die for at least another year." We had convinced Abuela to walk over to the neighborhood pizzeria for lunch, and she had eaten a whole portion of pasta. With sauce! But it wasn't so much her increased appetite that dispelled my fears as the theory of the millennium she'd spent the hour regaling us with. I explained to Rubén my theory that eighty-seven was supposed to be a turning point in her mortality, but if the millennium didn't start until 2001, as she claimed, then the turning point wouldn't be until next year. Once I'd explained this, I wasn't sure what it meant, so I was glad Rubén didn't take me seriously.

"*Che*, Gabriel, you don't really believe all that nonsense, do you?"

"Don't worry about it," I said, picking my way through the jungle of clothes, books, pamphlets, music CDs, and half-empty beer glasses that littered his room. Rubén had called me upstairs, saying he wanted to show me something, but he stood there empty-handed, music blasting from the boom box on the nightstand.

"Mamá thinks she is grooming you to become a Mason, you know. Lili must be jealous. She was always jealous of the way Mamá doted on me and Eva, no matter what we did. Or what she did—she was the best at everything, but she could never win Mamá's approval. And now you have both Mamá *and* Eva's beautiful daughter under your spell."

I didn't know how serious he was—one never knew—but if I understood anything at all about Mom—which I wasn't sure I did—it was that she was pleased by my current status as Abuela's favorite grandchild—even though it did fit right in with the male favoritism theory, since I was the only grandson. I pushed aside a nylon duffle bag and a plastic bag full of packs of El Trigal crackers—he was packing for his weekend at the estancia— and sat down on the edge of the bed to listen to the music. It was a wild version of *candombe* rock with jazzy electronic rifts and bizarre rhythmic sound effects. An Uruguayan band called Opa, Rubén told me, recorded in the US in the mid-seventies. I decided this must be why he'd called me upstairs, to listen to the music. But no, he said there was something else and pointed to the old leather suitcase lying open on the end of the bed.

I appraised the contents, which he didn't seem to have un-packed since he arrived. Mostly old papers. A couple of books. A pile of newspaper clippings. A leather *mate* bag and a coin purse of the sort you could still buy at the Tristán Narvaja mar-ket. A flattened old fedora and a black wool scarf. Everything discolored and wilted with age. Rubén removed a thick bundle of letters that was tied up with a red velvet ribbon, like a gift box. He lifted it to his face and inhaled deeply, as if he were smelling a flower, and then he sat down next to me and carefully untied the bow on top.

I was slightly embarrassed, watching this private ritual, but Rubén was unselfconscious. "Eva's letters," he said. "I thought Alejandra might want them. I don't know that she has much from her mother."

I looked at the six-inch-thick pile of envelopes in his lap, the ribbon hanging loose across his knees. Would Alejandra want them? These frayed yellowed envelopes, their flaps slit and torn, letters to an old boyfriend? This limp and faded velvet ribbon, the sort a girl might wear in her hair? Artifacts of the past that haunted her. "I don't know." But Rubén had started looking through the letters and hardly seemed to hear me.

"She used to give them to Lili for hand delivery. For a while, she even got Natalio to deliver them, irked us both. Sometimes she mailed them." He paused and slipped one of the letters out of its envelope, unfolding it partway to peek at the first few lines. "I wrote her love letters," he said. "And she wrote these political soliloquies—sprinkled with perfume, just so I wouldn't forget." He chuckled softly. "She talked about becoming an architect, like our father. But instead of houses for the bourgeoisie in Pocitos, she wanted to design low-cost housing on El Cerro. She was reading everything in those days—Marx, Castro, Lamarca, Che, Artigas . . ."

"I didn't know Artigas wrote anything."

"More was written about him than by him, but he left some letters, some speeches. The Tupas reclaimed him from the fascists. Reinterpreted him. A true revolutionary, a man of action. That's what the Tupas wanted for a hero. Ideology wasn't getting anyone anywhere."

"But they *did* have an ideology. Compared to today. I mean, they believed in something, right?"

"Of course," he said, sounding surprised. He reached over and lowered the volume on Opa. "Of course we believed in something. Jobs. Fair wages. Government without corruption. An end to imperialism, resources to benefit everyone, land for the poor. But lots of people had believed in those things, for over a century. The Tupas were about making it happen. Here, in Uruguay. Getting rid of Pacheco. Unseating the corrupt oligarchs. Revolution. That's what Artigas symbolized. Action."

"Abuela says he was a loser."

"Ha." Rubén grunted. "She's right. An appropriate hero for the Tupas." He was flipping slowly through the envelopes, occasionally pausing and pulling out a letter to look at, as if he were searching for something in particular. I got a glimpse of faded blue ink and cramped lines of a tiny handwriting that somehow seemed too symmetrical and proper for the femme fatale revolutionary, martyr, and terrorist of legend.

"Did you ever kill anyone?" I asked Rubén, suddenly remembering Abuela's story about the bomb hidden in his mattress.

"Me? No. I wasn't in the action wing. Eva was. But I don't know if she ever killed anyone. The Tupas were divided into small cells and no one was supposed to know what the others were doing—she never talked about the *operativos* she was involved in." He slipped the letter he'd been looking at back into its envelope and continued flipping through the pile. "Eva read all the theory," he said. "But she was innately impatient. She was all about action, a perfect little Tupamara." He glanced up and smiled at me. "She wasn't very big, but when she was in a room, you knew she was there. Like Alejandra. Always the star of the show."

"That's nothing like Alejandra—"

"The difference is that Eva knew she was the center of attention. She cultivated it, depended on it. Alejandra just is."

I wasn't sure that was true either, unless you happened to be in love with her—or with the ghost of her mother. But I held my peace. I knew that Rubén had spent nearly two decades raising a daughter and running a business with his Venezuelan wife, Mariela. And yet Eva, it seemed, was the one who had left her mark.

"I don't know why I saved all these. I guess I wanted to remember who we were. Somehow it kept me from getting too cynical, too bitter. Made her death seem less pointless." He pulled another letter out of its envelope, unfolding it all the way this time, three small stationary pages filled on both sides with that tiny blue writing. I waited for him to read it aloud, wondering what it had been like to really think you could change the world you lived in—even a world as small as Uruguay—but Rubén skimmed through the first page in silence and then refolded it, as if he knew the rest by heart. He set the letter carefully in the suitcase. "We got together again in Buenos Aires," he said. "Right after Alejandra was born. It only lasted a few months. Three to be exact, before Eva took up with Willy. Nice enough guy. A bit older. Good to her, good to Alejandra." He paused, staring down at the letters. "They shot her seven times. Through the head, the belly. She was eight months pregnant."

"Mom told me," I said. "About going to Buenos Aires to help Eva. I'd always thought she was visiting Abuela when I was born, but Abuela didn't even know she was down here."

"*Puf. Lili. Más loca que una cabra, tu madre.* I should never have called her, but I was desperate. They were watching Eva, there was no way she could get out of the country. We knew the CIA was pulling the marionette strings for the whole continent, and I thought maybe Lili could do something to protect her." He shrugged and continued flipping slowly through his letters. "Lili was American, and I thought the Americans were in charge of their government. That she could call up Kissinger, that he might call off his thugs if an American asked."

I let out an inadvertent little laugh. In *el paisito* you would probably know someone who knew someone who knew the secretary of state, but the idea that Mom could just pick up the phone and call Henry Kissinger was absurd.

"God knows what I thought. I certainly didn't expect her to come down here. Pregnant. It was insane. Suicidal or self-sacrificial."

"She was totally traumatized," I said. "She could hardly talk about it, now, more than twenty years later. I don't even know how much she told Dad."

"Traumatized? Hell, she was lucky. They didn't usually distinguish the revolutionaries from the revolutionaries' friends." He glanced up at me. "Or their unborn babies."

"Were you there also?" I was taken aback that he could be so dismissive of the horrible experience Mom had described. Even if he did think she was "crazier than a goat."

"Where?"

"Where they took Mom and Eva. In Buenos Aires."

"What are you talking about? She never found Eva. They picked Lili up on the street and shipped her to Montevideo, direct to the Hospital Militar."

I shook my head, confused. I told him Mom's version of her trip to Buenos Aires. The prison or whatever it was they took her to, the room they put her in with Eva and Alejandra, the Argentinian woman and the Uruguayan girl, the brutality, the screams. I omitted the details of Eva's condition.

Rubén kept his eyes on my face the whole time I was talking, his hands resting on his stack of letters, a finger inserted between them as if he'd been interrupted while reading a book. "Why wouldn't she tell me?" He looked perplexed, almost suspicious, as if I might be lying to him, as if I were anything more than a conduit for my mother's story.

"It sounded pretty ugly. What they did to Eva . . ."

"Oh, come. I knew they'd tortured her. They tortured every-one. Except, apparently, the American."

"Maybe that's why," I said gently, thinking of the guilt and recrimination that seemed to stain Mom's every relationship with her family.

"Sometimes I wonder if she's even crazier than we think," Rubén mumbled, and then he went back to his search through the letters. He pulled out a particularly thick one, handling it as if it were some ancient sacred text, though it was just four sheets of lined school notebook paper, folded in half and then in fourths to fit in the envelope. This time, he seemed intent on reading the whole thing. Slowly.

I stood to leave. The Opa CD had finished playing, and Juan was supposed to pick us up soon.

"Wait—" Rubén quickly refolded the letter and placed it with the other one in the suitcase. "I wanted to give you these," he said, tidying up the rest of the pile. "For Alejandra. The later ones are clever, coded with puns and metaphors, just in case they fell into the wrong hands. She was good with language, Eva was." He carefully retied the ribbon and held the bundle out to me. "Maybe she'll like that. Reading her clever mother's thoughts."

I hesitated, unsure if I wanted responsibility for something that clearly meant so much to him. I told him he could give the letters to her himself. But he didn't want to. He said he didn't know her well enough, that he *couldn't* know her, could only ever see Eva when he looked at her. I would be a better judge of whether and when to give Alejandra the letters, he said.

I wasn't sure I understood, but I took the bundle into my care, wrapped it in a plastic bag from the bakery, and set it on top of the architecture books on the upper shelf in my room. Now that I understood how oppressed Alejandra felt by peoples' conceptions of her mother, I was determined to protect her, and our relationship, from the Quiroga family's emerging morass of memory. Someday I would give her Rubén's letters and tell her what I knew about her fourth birthday. But not this weekend. This weekend, the last naturalist and the terrorists' daughter were going to look to the future, not the past. This weekend was about microbes, mud, mosquitoes, *Laterallus gordoni*—about nature's secrets, not my family's. Endangered birds, not people. Species, not individuals—though when I visited the rails' nest that afternoon and found it popping with little black chicks, I had the distinct sense that it was indeed these individual birds I cared about. The babies in my backyard.

There were five or six of them all trying to poke their heads out from under their mother—I was convinced it was the female—who kept rearranging herself to cover them up, nudging them back into the nest when they tried to scramble over the side. It was quite the spectacle, and I crouched there on my little island watching them and grinning ear to ear for at least half an hour. Whether *gordoni* as a species was on the verge of extinction, or just rare and secretive, this particular individual seemed, for the moment, a little less lonely.

I was looking forward to showing the chicks to Mom and Juan and Rubén the next day, but my family bird tour was a total wash. First, Mom, who I had counted on for an ally, backed out at the last minute. Then Angelito tried to follow Rubén and we had to double back and shut him up in the barn. I'd borrowed Alejandra's binoculars for them to share, but Rubén gave up when he couldn't immediately find the birds I pointed out, and though Juan made a show of looking, he never used the focus knob and I had the feeling he was just pretending to see the birds because he didn't want to seem inept. Rubén was briefly charmed by the babies, the four surviving *Chajá* chicks grazing near the reeds and the *Pollona Azul* chicks on the pond, but he spent most of the time fretting about having imprisoned Angelito and complaining about the long walk and the mosquitoes. I got them as far as the pond, but the birds all seemed to be hiding out on their nests or lurking in the vegetation at the edge of the water, and my uncles were too impatient and too clumsy with the binoculars to kneel there in the mud trying to spot them in the shadows. Neither of them wanted to follow me farther into the brush and mud, not even when I told them they'd get to see the nest of a bird that only three people in the whole world had ever seen.

Juan was at his most taciturn, and I couldn't tell how much he noticed or what he thought. I'd been naive to think that he would be able to appreciate the inimitable magic of the marsh on one short visit. This was no national park. There were no majestic trees or tumbling waterfalls, no sculpted peaks or wave-carved coastlines. No exotic sea turtles or large cuddly mammals on display. The giant guinea pigs and playful *nutrias* had their appeal, but one was as likely to see them in the canals as in the marsh. Unless you stood still and listened, unless you looked really closely at the birds—or the frogs or the plants or the microbes—the marsh was just a dull, mosquito-infested mass of reeds, a quicksand-riddled rat's nest of brush. A cacophony of noise, rather than a magnificent natural symphony of unique instruments.

I knew Alejandra was right that any effort to preserve the marsh would be an uphill battle unless Juan appreciated it as something more than the estancia's "bad land." But I had the sensation that the whole exercise had an inverse effect: instead of showing Rubén and Juan how the marsh looked through my eyes, I'd ended up seeing it through theirs. Wasted land.

"Maybe you can invent a microbial water factory to keep Juan's pond full," I quipped to Alejandra as we walked up the creek together on Sunday. "So he won't have to close the dike."

"Hypothetical solution," she said, chuckling. "More than improbable . . . if not exactly impossible."

All the birdlife that had been hiding on Saturday was now on display. It was as if the reed bed were breathing flycatchers and blackbirds, and we stopped and watched as it exhaled and inhaled, swirls of *Sietecolores* and *Federales* and *Tordo Músico* rising into the air to feed and then dropping to their perches. There were hordes of brown-plumed juveniles trying out their wings with little bumbling jumps into the air, somehow monitored by, but out of sync with, the colorful adults. I glanced over at Alejandra, the binoculars pressed to her face, lips parted in wonder and joy, and I wished Rubén and Juan could have seen what she saw, what we saw.

"It wasn't like this yesterday," I whispered. Or was it? Was my uncles' disinterest so contagious that I'd failed to notice? Probably it had just been too early, or Rubén's loud running commentary of complaint had driven everyone into hiding— but I couldn't help but think the birds knew when they had an appreciative audience. We made our way to the first of the marsh sampling sites and hurried through our routine—pH, oxygen, surface jar, bottom jar—then moved on to the pond, which only seemed to underwrite my theory. Six fat little stripe-faced *Pato Fierro* ducklings were showing off their new diving skills, dipping beneath the surface and reappearing every few seconds, their backs covered with glistening green algae. The *Pato Picaso* family was nestled up against the shore, but the shy, oversized *Pato Real* had produced a neat dozen brown duck-lings and lined them all up on a branch that stuck out just above the water. The *Espátula Rosada* and the *Chiflón* were still no-where to be seen, but three *Jacana* chicks were high-stepping across the water lilies on feet twice the size of their bodies. The pond community had literally undergone a population explo-sion.

"Have you found any new species in here?" I asked Alejandra as we were packing the jars into the cooler bag, getting ready to head into the brush to the rails' nest. "Any lonesome endangered pairs of bugs?"

"Microbes don't exactly come in pairs, Gabriel. Lonesome or otherwise. They come in hundreds, thousands, millions. But I've found at least five new species or strains in here, so far." She tapped the lid of the sample jar she'd just set in the cooler bag. "It's a genetic maze in there," she said. "A lot more diversity here than we have in the rice or, for that matter, at the reed site." She paused and looked up at me. "It's a little like what you see with the bird distributions, actually."

"I'm not exactly doing a scientific study—"

"No. But I am. It's surprising. I thought we'd see differences in the depth profiles and relative compositions. But I didn't expect to see so much variation in the actual species makeup at these sites. Of course, it's not like your rails, which might depend on this specific bit of marsh for survival. These new bugs are probably found in wetlands all over the world. It's just that no one has looked before."

We could easily have spent another hour watching the variety show at the pond, but we were eager to get into the thick of the marsh and see what the rail babies were up to, if they had fledged. We'd packed a knapsack with equipment for collecting the nest and feathers, just in case, but I really expected to find them still in or around the nest. I was not prepared for the sudden and absolute abandonment we encountered. The nest was empty, and though we scanned with the binoculars and waited for nearly an hour, we saw no sign of the rail family. Of course, a single rail could be hiding within a few feet without us spotting it. But the whole family? All those popping, unruly chicks? How could they simply vanish? Probably, they had just gone deeper into the marsh, but I worried again about foxes and rodents.

Finally, we gave up and set about trying to get to the nest. The mud was treacherous, but the brush gave us something to hang on to, and we ended up climbing through it like monkeys. I'd brought Mom's clippers and folding pruning saw, and a tool I found in the barn that was something between a hatchet and a machete. Rubén had helped me sharpen this, and it was what I mostly ended up using, hacking my way through the smaller branches, climbing over or around the larger ones. I had imagined going in alone, but Alejandra pointed out that we would need four hands to collect the samples. She followed in the wake of my hacking, but I felt more like I was part of a demolition crew than collecting evidence for science. It took us over two hours to move less than ten yards.

There were no signs of a struggle, just five empty eggshells lying peacefully in the bottom of a small husk of leaves and grasses. Alejandra had brought sterile plastic bags and tweezers and a small camera, and I held on to her waist while she leaned over at a precarious angle and took pictures. The ramp was constructed of crisscrossing twigs and branches, some of them several times the size of the rails, an amazing engineering feat for such tiny birds. We left it intact and nudged the nest off the top of it into a plastic bag. Eduardo had assured us the rails would rebuild their nest, but we hoped the ramp would make things easier and encourage them to use the same site.

It was almost dark by the time we got back to the house. Rubén and Juan had left earlier, and Mom was in the kitchen making empanadas when Alejandra and I walked in. We were muddy, covered with mosquito bites and scratches, and so exhausted that I was worried about Alejandra driving back to Montevideo alone. She had to teach the next morning, and I suggested that I drive back with her, but Mom seemed almost frantic to have me stay, and Alejandra insisted that she would be fine. We'd brought the nest in to show Mom, but she hardly glanced at it. She didn't even question Alejandra about the molecular analysis, just filled her *mate* thermos with hot water, wrapped up a couple of empanadas, and sent her on her way, as if she couldn't wait to have her gone.

She wanted time to talk to me alone, Mom explained, when I had showered and returned to find a plate piled with hot empanadas and an open beer on the table. Tomatoes with cilantro. A bowl of spinach salad.

I had a return ticket to California in early January, and she wanted to know what my plans were. Why this conversation couldn't wait until later in the week—she'd be in Montevideo for Christmas, in any case—was unclear, but I let it be, exhausted as I was. It was the first time since we'd arrived in Uruguay that she'd shown any real interest in what I was or was not going to do. I wasn't sure if she was afraid of my leaving, if it had dawned on her that she'd set herself up to live at the opposite end of the Americas from her son, just as she had from her own mother. Or if she was just concerned about my future. She almost sounded like Dad, quizzing me about how much money I still had, if I planned to go to grad school, or go back to my job, or look for another one.

"What's with you?" I said. "Have you been talking to Dad?"

"No!" she said, with a vehemence that surprised me. "I haven't talked to Keith since we left California," she added more quietly.

I had suspected as much, but I was disappointed to hear her say it. I answered her questions. Told her I still had money. Told her what I was not planning to do—grad school, old job.

"What, then?" she asked impatiently, and I gestured for her to slow down while I savored an empanada, though I could tell I was making her nervous. She had never been one to want the standard answers from me, the usual goals of "successful young man" that Dad always lobbied for, and I thought she would be mostly pleased with what I had to tell her. I took a deep draught of beer.

"Do you remember," I said, "when you were trying to talk me into coming down here? You said Uruguay would do me good. Make me 'less cynical.' And I thought you were completely bonkers. But Mom—" I paused for dramatic effect, like Abuela talking about Masonic secrets. "You were right." I was absolutely serious, but I laughed, trying to make light of my own earnestness. "You had better take note," I said, "because this is probably the first and last time you'll ever hear that." I slid the last of the tomatoes onto my plate and caught her eye. "*You were right,*" I repeated, this time in English.

She didn't laugh or fire back a rejoinder, but rather waited in expectant silence, an uncharacteristically morbid expression on her face, as if she were waiting for me to announce that I had cancer, instead of that I was excited about a new endeavor and making plans to stay in Uruguay—not to mention in love with an amazing woman.

I filled her in on the plan I'd been incubating over the past couple of weeks, though I wasn't at all sure it was ready to hatch. Eduardo wanted to contract me to illustrate his volume on Uruguayan birds, a serious science book that was going to be published by some North American university press. I'd never thought about it before, but he'd decided my drawings were better than photographs because they highlighted a species' character rather than capturing just one moment in an individual bird's life. When I did a drawing, it was usually a composite of many moments, sometimes of different individual birds. I could make all the field marks and characteristics visible at once. It was a fictional creation, Eduardo said, that told a truer story than the limited hard facts of a photograph.

"I'll get to work in the field," I said, "and draw birds. I'll correct his English in the text. It doesn't pay much—a tiny fraction of what I made at Envirorep—but I only need enough to keep me from burning through all of my savings while Alejandra finishes her PhD." As I talked, my embryonic notion of our future took on the form and heft of an actual plan, at least for the next year. Most of Eduardo's field work was in the northeastern wetlands, so I'd be staying at the estancia a lot, which I thought would please Mom. I told her I was serious about finding a way to get water for Juan's rice without drying out the marsh, that it was looking more and more like the rails I'd discovered were an endangered species, maybe even on the brink of extinction. If I needed more money, I figured I could find some small translating jobs or GIS work somewhere. "Alejandra thinks she'll be done with her dissertation by next summer," I said. "She has an open offer for a postdoctoral fellowship in the lab that does her analyses in Germany. But there's also a group at UC Davis she's interested in. Not exactly my favorite part of California, but I can probably get a job around there, and it's only a couple of hours to the Sierras, or, for that matter, to San Jose. It will be good for Alejandra to live abroad for a while. Here she always feels like she's living in the shadow of the past, of her mother's fame and infamy."

Mom was shaking her head. There were tears sliding down her face.

I sighed. I pushed my plate aside and leaned my arms on the table, knotting my hands together in front of me. "Mom, please . . . I know you have horrible memories, and you've just let them out of the bottle for the first time in twenty years. But Alejandra is not a memory. She's the present, the future, *my* future. You have to get to know her for herself. All of you—Juan Luis, Elsa, Abuela. Rubén. She's amazing. You even said so yourself, when you first met her."

I didn't fully understand what I was arguing against, but I knew what I was arguing for. I was beyond posturing indifference: I wanted my mother's approval. She could argue the logistics, be maternal and tell me to slow down, fret about finances, tell me to call Dad for advice—but I wanted her to celebrate my choice. "Mom," I said. "I love this woman. I have never been surer about anything." I spoke slowly, punctuating each word with a full stop, as emphatic as I was shy. I hadn't talked to my mother about my feelings since I was a little kid. "We might end up back in Montevideo," I said. "To raise a family. You'd have your grandkids nearby. You could buy them ponies—"

"*Basta*—stop."

I closed my mouth. Stop what? Living, dreaming, talking? She'd wanted me to talk.

"Buenos Aires," she said. "Nineteen seventy-six."

"Mom, it's okay. Rubén and Abuela told me the rest. What happened to Eva and Alejandra—"

"They don't know anything."

I stared at my mother, waiting for her to tell me what it was her mother and brother did not know. She had turned so that she was sitting at an awkward angle to the table, not looking at me, not looking at anything, her folded arms pressed into her stomach. The tears had stopped and her face was expressionless, blank, frozen.

"I don't know how long we lay there on that mattress. Belly to belly." She spoke slowly, haltingly, picking up the shattered fragments of the story that had walked off a cliff two weeks ago, offering them up now, piece by piece, her voice as uninflected as her face. "Days, nights, we couldn't tell the difference. Alejandra had a birthday.

"Eva's belly was bigger. Hard to believe a baby was alive in that brutalized body, but I could feel it kick. Bliss in the middle of hell.

"When we went into labor, the others made a pallet of blankets for me, next to the mattress. I don't remember the girl's name, but the Argentinian woman was Sara. She'd had three babies, she knew what to do. The guards were having a party. Drunken voices, breaking bottles, blasting music.

"We held hands. We squeezed when the pains came."

Mom sounded like she was underwater, her sentences emerging in cryptic bubbles whose trajectory I struggled to follow.

"I was too early. I knew it was all wrong, but it seemed right. To be hurting together, with Eva.

"They yelled for a doctor, Sara and the girl, and little Alejandra. Sara said we needed boiled water, clean towels, blankets. They pounded on the walls, but the music was too loud.

"Finally, a guard wandered in and looked at us. He said he would bring a doctor and went away. He was drunk. He didn't come back for a long time. We were already nursing you when the doctor came. Passing you back and forth.

"Sara said my baby was too small for this world. She said it wasn't ready, wasn't a baby yet. But you were more than ready. You pushed your way out of that ruined, battered body and gave a loud cry of triumph."

I stared at my mother, but she was hunched over in her chair and didn't look up. She had tightened her hold on her stomach, as if she was trying to forestall spontaneous evisceration, as if she would fall open and her innards would spill out if she let loose. We. It. You. Baby. Who? I stared at my imploded mother, and stayed in my seat with the table between us.

"The doctor cleaned us. They gave us water, some food. A few days? A week? I had some kind of infection. Fever, deliria. They killed the artist. William Gabriel Davies. Left him underwater too long, and then shot him when he came up brain-dead. One of the guards told us all the details.

"She named the baby after him. When they took us away, she begged them to send Alejandra with us. But they refused."

The baby. It. You. Me. Gabriel. Suddenly I was with Alejandra in that room, a protagonist in Mom's nightmare, but I couldn't fathom my role.

"At the hospital, they took care of us. I lived only to nurse you, in a daze of drugs and fever. I asked for Eva. They said they didn't know who I was talking about. They said I was delirious. The doctor said you were mine."

I felt my dinner washing up my throat. Her. My. Baby. Dead. Was my mother really crazy, was she mentally ill? I wanted her to look up and explain, to be sane. I wanted her to stop talking.

"When you were a month old, the *milicos* handed me a birth certificate and an American passport for you. Gabriel Jonathan Haynes Quiroga. That's what Keith and I had planned to call you. Jonathan. I asked again for Eva, and they told me to forget her. They told me she'd died in Buenos Aires. They put us in a van and drove us to the airport. Put us directly on the plane."

My chair scraped against the tiles, and she finally looked up. I stood, dazed and vertiginous, understanding nothing but the need to put more distance between myself and the madwoman sitting across from me.

"Gabriel, *bichito* . . ." As I backed away, her face went taut with fear and her voice resurfaced, suddenly fast and fluent and sane, too sane. "I meant to tell you, I wanted to tell you. I didn't know what had become of Alejandra, only that Natalio's father had raised her in Montevideo. I never dared intrude. I'd planned to look her up and I wanted to tell you both, I thought it was time. . . . But then you found each other, and there she was, standing right here in front of me, looking more like her mother's ghost than any sister to you, and I—Gabe, I couldn't. You liked each other, I thought you were becoming friends, that you'd be so pleased to have a sister like that, I meant to tell you, I just needed more time—"

I ran out to the yard and puked into the dust, coughing up the beer and salad and empanadas I'd just consumed, startling Angelito, who must have been lying next to the door.

"Oh, Gabe—" She had followed me out, and now she reached to hug me, but I took a step back and shook my head, in such an incoherent froth of rage and incomprehension I feared I might slap her. I turned and started walking away, and then I was running, stumbling across the yard in the moonlight, across the *tero*'s field and up the incline toward the creek, her cries following me, a doleful keening, calling my name, the name of a dead man, a phantom. I ran until the reeds loomed up in front of me, and only as I plunged into them did I realize that Angelito was with me.

I stopped and stepped back into the open, giving him a push toward home. He trotted around in a little circle and then lunged at me, twisting his neck around to bite my arm. He was as tall as my hip now, stronger than I would have imagined, and we danced around each other like two wrestlers, until I caught hold of his neck in a sort of headlock. "Go home," I pleaded, tears flooding into a reed cut on my face, the welcome burn of salt in wound, though I hadn't known I was crying. I carefully eased my grip and pushed him away. He stood stock-still. "*Go!*" I felt around on the ground for a pebble and threw it at him. He trotted a few paces, stopped. I found another pebble, and another, and then I showered him with small rocks and mud clods until he finally trotted off the way we'd come and left me to my own self-flagellating path.

It was darker among the reeds, and I moved blindly forward, at the full mercy of contradictory impulses—letting the reeds slice unimpeded into my face, tempting the marsh to swallow me, but moving along the path of least resistance, vaguely aware that my mindless flight had a destination.

The pool was glistening in the moonlight, its occupants asleep in the shadows, indifferent as I made my way past them into the black heart of the marsh, grabbing at branches and yanking myself free with adrenaline-fueled efficiency each time the ground gave way and the macabre otherworldly suck of quicksand threatened to bring me down. I knew the way too well, and it was no accident that I found the little island near the rails' dismantled nest. I collapsed in the grass. And slept.

I dreamed a collage of homesickness. The smell of redwood humus, curled up in the damp, fire-hollowed heart of a giant tree, rain in the woods. Grandpa Gordon, grinning, with a California Condor perched on his head. Dad tossing M&M's over the back of his backpack for me to catch as we climbed on a steep trail. And the froth of Pacific waves rolling back into a receding ocean, washing it all away, leaving me with a self that was as blank as the wet sand, a flock of Sanderlings scurrying across it in random patterns, but leaving no footprints.

I awoke to a feeling of loss and denial so profound it would have driven me back into my confused dream, but for the hollow wail of a certain familiar species of bird, unnervingly close. I lay still, listening to the trills running repeatedly down the scale like a skipping CD, opening my eyes on a dark so intense it rendered the action irrelevant, registering wet clothes and cut face and mosquito bites, physical indifference, mental lethargy. The moon must have set, and the dawn was nowhere apparent. It was too dark to see anything but the tiny patch of stars that blinked through an opening in the brush above where I lay. The rails sounded so close I thought they might run across my outstretched arm. I could even hear the delicate peeping of chicks between the trills, which seemed to encircle me, overlapping and coinciding, syncopated in a way I'd never heard them, to my right, to my left, behind my head—as though I were lying in the middle of a trio of trilling bassoons. . . .

I laughed. There were three rails, not two. They were nocturnal, active when only owls and night herons and nightjars should be up and about. The laugh immediately collapsed into my chest, a soft, joyless bark. "Do you have a name for yourselves?" I whispered, or maybe I just thought it. *Laterallus* or *Rallus* or *Pardirallus* or something else entirely? Do you know who you are? Is that a thing you know in your access-ramp-building bird brains? Who you are? What science has yet to discover? They started moving away from me, fading gradually into the marsh in three directions. Finally, they stopped calling altogether, and for a while, the night was almost as quiet as it was dark.

I waited for the dawn. I didn't think of the lies. I didn't think of the woman who I knew as Mom. Or the one who'd been tortured blue and shot through her no-longer-pregnant belly. I didn't think of the man I'd been named after, or the politics and history that had trapped them all, the imperialists and dictators, the torturers and revolutionaries. Terrorists and martyrs. No. I lay there until the first glimmer of light and the predawn rush of mosquitoes and sound brought me to my feet, thinking of Alejandra, the biologist. The scientist.

I thought of what she did not know, the memory she did not have, which had somehow ended up in the wrong hands, my hands, her lover's hands, whoever he was. Of what I could or could not tell her. I thought about being in love, filled, possessed, ravished by love. Could that be washed away by one bizarre revelation? Did it matter if we shared some genes? Didn't all humans share genes? We didn't *have* to make children, after all.

With the first hint of light, I rose and headed out of the marsh, moving through the brush and reeds almost as blindly as I had the night before, oblivious to the dawn pandemonium of avian activity—not even following my path now, but moving toward Caruso's fields. The only plan in my head was to walk out to the road and hitch a ride back to Montevideo. I stopped at the canal to rinse the blood and mud off my face and shoes, and then I squished along the track that led to the main road. I didn't register Santiago coming up behind me on his horse until he spoke.

"You're out early," he said.

"So are you."

"I'm always out early. Headed over to the other ranch."

"I'm studying a nocturnal bird," I said, hoping he wouldn't notice my lack of binoculars. "A rare bird no one had ever seen before. Maybe on the verge of extinction," I added, wondering if it was, wondering if it mattered, wondering if I cared.

Santiago nodded gravely, and I went on, conscious of my wet, scratched face, my muddy clothes, trying to deflect any questions. "Angelito tried to follow me into the reeds," I said, "and I had to chase him off."

"Really? Ñandús don't usually go into the reeds, unless they're chased and cornered."

"He was chasing *me*!" I protested.

He chuckled. "Well, Angelito is not your normal Ñandú."

"No. They spoil him."

"How's your mother doing?"

"Okay," I said carefully.

"We've been trading her pork for tomatoes. Tell her I'll bring a *lechón* on Thursday. I promised her one for your Christmas Eve *asado*." He didn't wait for a reply, just loped on down the track in front of me, calling a *chau* over his shoulder.

How is your mother, who is not your mother? Who did not give birth to you in a hospital in Montevideo, who nursed you, who relied on you, who lied to you all your life, who might be sane or not sane? Suddenly, after not thinking about her all night, I was thinking of Mom and her tortured animal cries, and instead of walking like a zombie out to the road, I was turning up the track with the horseshoe portico, and running—as if it would make a difference, as if it would matter if I arrived five minutes sooner or later.

The oil lamps were still on in the house. The generator was still running.

I burst through the door, and stopped, the fear like an eagle's talon in my gut.

She was slumped over at the kitchen table, her head lying in her arms.

"Lili?" I doubt my voice was much louder than a hoarse scratch, but she lifted her head and looked at me as if I'd slapped her out of a bad dream, her face twisting with relief and pain.

I breathed. Calmed the thumping heart. Realized how dry my mouth was.

"I'm sorry, Gabe. I'm so, so sorry." Simple English words. Sorry. A mother's sorry for hurting her son. Sane, profound. As deep as sorry could be.

I stood still, like a cardboard man, and let her hug me, my arms dangling at my sides. Then she started going through the motions of preparing breakfast, as if it were a normal morning.

I went to the sink and gulped down two glasses of water.

"Who knows?" I said.

She finished counting spoons of coffee into the sock filter and screwed the top back on the coffee jar. Took a deep breath and said, in a normal voice, "No one. No one who is alive, no one who knew my name, who might remember. A drunk Argentinian *milico* . . . Alejandra, who was too young—"

"Alejandra doesn't remember anything."

"I don't know what the doctor at the Hospital Militar thought. What the Argentinians told him." She turned to look up at me, leaning against the counter next to her. "You're all slashed up," she said.

I shrugged. "Reed cuts." But she was already moving to the aloe vera plant she kept in a pot on the front windowsill. Had always kept. In San Jose, in the rented cottage in Santa Rosa. This one was still small. She sliced the largest leaf from its base and came back to stand in front of me, but when she tried to smear the gel on my face, I pushed her hand away. Gently. Pity was not entirely absent from the maelstrom of emotions I was caught in.

She handed me the leaf. "I never told anyone."

"What about Dad?"

She shook her head. "He never asked, Gabe. I was so lost in grief, and he was so angry and relieved, I could only talk about Eva, couldn't acknowledge, even to myself— You were my baby, Gabe, that's what they'd told me and I decided to believe it. If you'd seen the look on his face, when I placed you in his arms. He loved you instantly, loved his new state of fatherhood. He was outraged by what happened to Eva, but he couldn't cope with my grief, couldn't fathom the depth of it. He wanted to move on to the business of raising you, the way we'd planned."

I ran a fingernail down the length of the aloe leaf, simultaneously reassured and horrified—that Dad was not complicit, that she hadn't told him. And what should he have asked, who would think to ask? "If no one knows," I said, "maybe it never happened. Maybe you just imagined it." We were still speaking English, and the words felt as cool and pragmatic as the aloe gel I pressed into my palm and spread across my face and arms.

"Gabe—"

"It's my turn to decide," I said. "If it happened, or not. You had yours."

She shut her eyes, absorbing the rebuke as if it were a blow, without raising a hand to protect herself.

"I just need some time," I said, more gently. "I need to see Alejandra." I went into the bedroom to get my knapsack, abandoning her half-made breakfast.

She offered to give me the car, but I didn't want to leave her stranded. She offered to drive me to Montevideo, but I couldn't bear to spend four hours in the car with her. I asked her to drop me in Castillos, where I caught the bus to Montevideo. I tried not to be cruel. She wanted to know what I planned to do. I told her I didn't know. I told her I needed to think. I promised I would be there at Abuela's when she drove back on Friday, that I'd help roast the piglet and spend *la Nochebuena* with the family. As planned.

18

I was dreaming another memory, and in this one, I was nestled in the protective shell of my mother's belly. There was a war raging outside, a woman's screams, but I felt safe there, in the belly, in the memory, in the dream. I thought it was Mom who woke me, Lili leaning over me with her hand on my shoulder, waking me from a nightmare like she had done when I was a small boy.

But it wasn't Lili. It was Abuela, in her gray housedress. Abuela, who wasn't the touching type, standing next to the narrow bed that had been her daughter's, with a comforting hand on my shoulder. I was lying on top of the blanket in T-shirt and boxers, curled into a fetal position, drenched in sweat. I glanced at the clock. It was four in the afternoon. The TV in the living room was blasting one of the telenovelas Abuela never admitted to watching. Alejandra was expecting me to meet her at the lab in two hours.

I sat up, and Abuela's comforting hand fell away, the creepy feeling from the dream swooping down to perch on my shoulder in its place. I'd gotten back from the estancia, called Alejandra, taken a cool shower, dropped onto the bed for a quick nap, and, apparently, fallen into a deep sleep. I needed another shower.

"You sounded like a werewolf," Abuela said. She said she hadn't even realized I was back until she came downstairs to watch TV and heard strange cries issuing from my room. "I thought you were coming back with Lili on Friday."

I told her I'd taken the bus. That Mom was getting on my nerves. That I couldn't wait to see Alejandra. She nodded and rewarded me with one of her half smiles. Yes, Alejandra was worth yearning for. Yes, Lili was irritating. "She'll be here for Christmas Eve," I assured her, because I knew she was not as ambivalent as she sounded. Because I pitied Mom. Because I was so deeply attached to both of them in ways that I was, at that moment, too confused to fathom.

It was too late for lunch and too early for dinner, but we heated up one of the stews Elsa had left in the refrigerator and ate together, not talking much. She commented on my array of cuts and scratches and mosquito bites, and I told her I'd spent the night climbing around in the marsh tracking a rare bird. The half lies and omissions came so easily, I had the feeling they were true, that they became true the moment they issued from my mouth—that I could reinvent the bizarre events of the past twenty-four hours without repercussion. If my birth certificate said I was Lili and Keith's son, then I was Lili and Keith's son. History was not facts, it was something we could construe. Wasn't that what Lili had done? Why mess with it now?

Whatever I did, or did not do, I realized immediately that I would never tell Abuela that I was not her grandson. That was the first clear mark in the blank sand of my annulled self. A decision.

"Abuela," I said. "You're not planning to die, are you?"

"Of course I am."

"When?"

"Sometime in the new millennium."

"That's a long window of time. And by your count, at least a year away. Maybe you should eat more."

She chuckled and fixed me in her gaze as she lifted a spoonful of garbanzos and veal from bowl to mouth.

* * *

I took a bus up Rivera and got off in Centro, then walked the rest of the way, moving numbly through the afternoon pedestrian traffic. I hadn't read a paper in days, and I joined the front-page loiterers at a news kiosk, trying to think about anything but what I would do. Or not do. Jorge Batlle wouldn't be inaugurated until March, and Uruguayan politics seemed to have gone into hibernation in the meantime. There was an open trade agreement with Mexico. Brazil's financial crisis was getting worse. More victims from the mudslides in Venezuela. Juan Gelman's open letter to President Sanguinetti had triggered an avalanche of attention from writers around the world. Protests by unpaid government employees in Argentina . . . I moved away from the kiosk.

The Gelman story had been in the news off and on since October, when *La República* published the letter, and I hadn't thought much about it—but now it sprang from the page as if it had been placed there just for me. Juan Gelman was a prominent Argentinian poet whose son and pregnant daughter-in-law had been sequestered by the military in 1976. The remains of his son were found by a forensic team in Buenos Aires a decade later—tortured and shot in the back of the neck. Now Gelman had evidence that his daughter-in-law had been transferred to a prison in Montevideo, where her baby had been born and stolen away from her, and he wanted Sanguinetti to open an investigation to determine the fate of his disappeared daughter-in-law and grandchild. Sanguinetti had claimed—also in an open letter—that there was no evidence the daughter-in-law had been in Uruguay, that investigating such events twenty-three years after the fact was too difficult, and that stolen babies were an Argentinian problem.

Was that what I was? A stolen baby? Stolen from whom, by whom? From the grandparents who never knew I existed? From the half-sister who didn't remember me? Did I even exist? Gelman knew his grandchild had been stolen, but everyone was certain that I had never been born, that Eva had died while pregnant. Shot through the belly, Rubèn said.

Maldad. The word Lili had used, trying to fathom her Argentinian captors, *la lógica de la maldad.* "Evil" was the English word that came to mind. A word, an absolute, that saw little traffic in my areligious family, that was relegated to stories and movie theaters, to *Lord of the Rings* and *Star Wars* and *Batman,* or to the oft-ridiculed and reviled Ronald Reagan, who liked to call the Soviet Union the "Evil Empire." But now it seemed to be everywhere, this evil, floating around in the mundane lives of my reputed family. Stealing a baby from its mother was evil. Torture was surely evil. Murder was evil. And Lili? Could Lili be evil? Had she stolen a baby? Or rescued an orphan?

Was I cursed or lucky? I walked through the now-familiar streets of Montevideo's *barrio* Cordón and thought of the huge stranger of a metropolis across the river, where I had, apparently, been born. Perhaps there were grandparents there, aunts and uncles and cousins. Did I even know my father's last name? Something English, Lili had mentioned it—Davies, that was it. William Gabriel Davies. I wondered what would happen if I tried to set the record straight—get an Argentinian passport, give up my American one, change my surname. Probably it would be impossible. Probably no one would even believe I existed, unless I took a DNA test and tracked down a relative of Davies.

Even angry and confused as I was, I found it impossible to think Lili was evil. Misguided, delusional, disturbed, annoying . . . but not evil. I tried to imagine her young, sick, terrified, and alone. Her baby stillborn, her best friend tortured and, finally, assassinated. Eva entrusted me to her. The *milicos* gave her a birth certificate and US passport for me, listed her and Keith as parents, Montevideo as my place of birth—the US government must have been complicit. I remembered what I'd read in the lipstick book, about the CIA training the military. What if Lili had refused to take me? Who knows where I would have ended up. And once she was back in the US, with an official birth certificate and no witness, would anyone have believed that I wasn't her son? Did I believe her now? Could she have made the whole thing up, read the Gelman story and invented a version for herself and Eva? But why? If there could be a logic to evil, then surely insanity must also have some rationale. But I could no more believe such a depth of insanity in the woman who had raised me than I could believe that she was evil.

I tapped on the open door to Alejandra's office and stepped inside. She was alone, sitting at the computer, and she immediately stopped typing and turned to greet me, bathing me in her most radiant smile.

"I'm writing a paper on the rice bugs," she said, gesturing at the text on her screen.

The smile had the same effect it always did. *Me encantó.* I leaned down and kissed her long and hard, invading her mouth, a hand resting on the back of her chair, another down the front of her blouse and bra, and when I finally pulled away, she laughed and told me to slow down, but her expression was tender and ingenuous, and I knew she was pleased by the vehemence of the kiss. She looked, I thought, like a woman in love—even sitting there in front of a computer, happily writing a paper about microbes in mud. I retrieved her absentee officemate's chair, sat down next to her, and peered at the text on the screen. She was writing a paper in English, but the scientific lingo was so incomprehensible I could hardly follow it, let alone help her edit it.

She furrowed her brow, noticing the cuts on my face. "Is that all from yesterday? I didn't realize you got so cut up."

"I went back out there after dark. Ran through the reeds too fast." I told her I'd found the chicks, that they all seemed to be alive, though I couldn't be sure because I'd only heard them. She was excited, wanted to go back after Christmas and try to find them. She had already given Eduardo the nest. He was photographing and describing it, and then he was going to prepare the samples and archive the nest and some feathers with the natural history museum. It was a grand collaborative effort: Alejandra would extract, replicate, and purify the DNA, which they would send to New Zealand, where Eduardo's colleague would sequence the fragments and compare them to the others he'd analyzed from the Rallidae family. She handed me a photocopy of a phylogenetic tree he'd given her, two sheets of paper taped together along one end. It looked like the ones she did for her bugs, but, she told me, it was based on morphological traits and biological observations as well as genes. She'd been surprised at the extent to which avian systematics were in disarray. Genetic analysis introduced order to the study of microbial life and paved the way to recognition of its diversity in terms of function and chemistry. But it opened up can after can of worms in the old and venerable field of ornithology—Eduardo hadn't been exaggerating about that.

He'd penciled in the English common names of six North American species on the Rallidae tree for my sake, but I only knew two of them from California. Several genera seemed to have been merged without actually changing the species names, so that the *Rallus* genus included some species that were named as if they had originally been in separate genera. The common names were even more screwed up, with some *Laterallus* being called crakes and others, like the Black Rail, rails—and the Spanish names were even worse. All I understood about the branching was that wherever there was a fork, there was a common ancestor and members from each branch would have some common traits or gene sequences. It was hard to see where *gordoni* might fit in. To my thinking, our rails had traits of both the *Rallus* and *Laterallus* genera, but the two genera were far apart in the diagram. Eduardo had penciled in "¿¿¿*gordoni*???" off to the side, parallel with the cluster of *Laterallus* species, but he hadn't tried to connect it to anything else.

"Wasn't Gordon your grandfather's first name?" Alejandra said. "Shouldn't you call it *Laterallus haynesi*?"

That was, in fact, the tradition. Stellar's Jay, Brewer's Blackbird, Cooper's Hawk—all named after distinguished explorers and naturalists. I'd never paid a lot of attention to scientific names, but it seemed it really wasn't uncommon at all to just tack a Latin ending on to a proper name.

"How about the plural?" Alejandra said, smiling. "*Haynesorum*. Then it would be named after both of you!"

I shook my head, unsure how to feel about my claim to the name Haynes, let alone preserving it for posterity by giving it to a bird species. If you wanted to memorialize a person, you would use the last name. But that had not been my intent. The rails owed their identity, maybe even their survival, to the connection between Grandpa Gordon and me, and I'd named them after that connection—not for the dedicated birder and environmentalist Gordon Derek Haynes, but for time spent with a man I knew as Grandpa Gordon. The name Haynes was irrelevant in more ways than one.

"It has to be Gordon," I said simply, laying the diagram out across the desk. "*Laterallus gordoni*, or *Rallus gordoni*, or *Pardirallus gordoni* . . . Gordon's Rail, Gordon's Crake, *Gallineta gordon*, *Burrito gordon*, whatever it turns out to be." What had been a mindless sentimental gesture was now another considered fact to engrave in the blank sand of my non-self: I would not have been slushing around in the badlands of the Quiroga estancia looking for birds, would not have learned to bird or care about birds, would not, in all likelihood, be the nature-loving fool I appeared, still, to be, without Grandpa Gordon.

The issue of names was still a fantasy, in any case, because Eduardo was unsure if they would have enough data to officially name the rails. If you analyzed and compared the right gene sequences, he'd said, they could help you track the relationships and identify the sister species and common ancestors. But you had to know where to look, who to compare with whom. I thought of his story about the African shrike that had never been seen again and was surely long dead—of that single lonely bird, which had either been an unusual individual of a plentiful species, or a hybrid of two closely related species, or the last of its kind. "What about the individuals?" I asked Alejandra.

"Individual what?"

"The individual rails. The male and female, the chicks. They must have different genes, just like we do. To us, they look the same, but they're different enough that they recognize each other."

"Oh. Sure." She gestured at the diagram. "Each of the branches has billions of individual leaves, but they don't really matter to the branch—unless there are too few of them, in which case the branch dies and breaks off."

I turned Eduardo's diagram on its side, so that the branches pointed upwards. It looked more like a lopsided, multi-tiered candelabra than a tree. I picked up a pencil and drew in a branch for *gordoni*. The split that produced the *Rallus* genus was one of the first shown and its only common ancestor with the *Laterallus* species appeared to be near the base of the tree, so that's where I connected my *gordoni* branch. Then I started sketching in the individual leaves at the end of the branch. I glanced up at Alejandra, who was watching me draw, a bemused smile lifting the corners of her lips. I drew five little leaf buds and three fully formed leaves, making each of them a subtly different size and shape.

"There are eight leaves on the *gordoni* branch," I said. "Five chicks"—I indicated the five buds with the end of my pencil—"and three adults." I pointed to the leaves.

"Three?" She looked from my drawing to my face. "You saw another adult? How could you tell it apart from the others? Could you tell if it was male or female?"

"I just heard it. I didn't see any of them, but they were calling simultaneously, and it was clear there were three."

"That's fantastic! Though it doesn't exactly get *gordoni* off the endangered list. Especially since they're all living in one endangered little patch of marsh."

"Eduardo says the babies might leave, scatter about the region. I don't know. They never seem to fly more than a few yards at a time, and they'd have to go pretty far to find another bit of marsh like that. But he says rail movements can be baffling. They fly at night, end up in places you wouldn't expect them."

"I hope I get to see them." She paused. "I wonder if it's been there all summer. That third adult. Why you never noticed it before."

"Same reason I only noticed one at first. Probably the same reason no one has ever recorded this species before." I examined her face in the scientific glare of neon lights—the endearing black fuzz along her hairline, the smooth bronze of her cheek, the fine nose with its tiny, understated crook at the top . . . Not a single freckle. "They seem to be nocturnal," I said, turning back to the diagram, doodling around its edges, adding little tufts of reeds and black rail silhouettes. "We've only ever heard them around sunset, but that was just the start of things. They're active in the dead of night—another useful detail for Eduardo's classification."

"What, did you spend the whole night out there? Set up a tent or something?"

"Not exactly." I set down the pencil and stood up, returning my chair to its place at the officemate's desk and then leaning against the edge of it, putting a bit of distance between us. "I had a fight with Lili," I said, watching her expression shift from curious, to puzzled, to concerned—the smile contracting, eyes narrowing, brow converging. If there was one trait we had in common, it was the excessive black eyebrows, a typical Uruguayan—or Spanish, or Italian—feature that I'd always thought of as "Quirogan," since they clearly didn't come from Keith's side of the family. She was waiting for me to go on.

I told her I'd been so upset by our argument that I'd dashed out of the house and ended up in the marsh, where I waited out the night on the little island near the nest.

"That's why your face is all mangled," she said. "You're lucky you didn't get lost, or stuck in the quicksand. What in the world did you fight with Lili about?"

But I couldn't tell her. Not yet, not then. I felt as if I'd lost my past, and if I lost the future as well I feared I would disappear altogether, shrink into a zero-dimensional point with no mass or extent in time or space, no corporeal presence. I shook my head. "I'll explain later," I said, and she nodded and didn't ask again.

We made love that night in her soft double bed, my family's secrets piled up around us, if not between us. They weren't *my* secrets, I thought. They were inherited artifacts, as useless and annoying as the pink slippers Abuela had saved when we cleaned out the porthole room. The knowledge that Alejandra was my half-sister didn't seem to bother my body—maybe for lack of physical evidence, of common morphological traits beyond those that defined our species. Or maybe because I'd never had a sister and didn't understand what it meant, why our love should be taboo.

Ironically, it was *only* when I was with Alejandra that I felt genuine and whole, at ease in body and mind. When I was alone or with the family, I felt like a Hermit Crab that had inhabited an empty shell, a species with little substance of its own, specialized in dissimulation, in the lie by omission. I was masquerading as Gabriel Haynes Quiroga, caring about the people and things he was supposed to care about, doing the things he was supposed to do, but each morning I'd awaken and find myself confronted anew with the knowledge that I wasn't really the man we all thought I was and I should probably do something about it. I had no idea, however, what that something might be. So I went about the business of preparing for Christmas as if it were just like any other Uruguayan Christmas of my childhood—except, of course, that Dad was missing. And I hadn't had Christmas in Uruguay for six years. And my childhood memories were clearly unreliable.

Christmas as I remembered it had been a casual, but indispensable, Quiroga family event. We had gathered for dinner on *la Nochebuena*, and exchanged small presents, and talked on the phone to Rubén, and set off fireworks on the Rambla. Dad, who was as good as Elsa at normalizing Quiroga relations, had always loved Uruguayan Christmas—the food, the beach, the fireworks, the self-conscious secularization (the official name, which no one used, was *Día de la Familia*), and the lack of commercialization, which only seemed to have arrived in the past few years. It was only now that I realized how important Keith and I had been for this family event, which was not, it seemed, as indispensable as I'd imagined: the years Lili and her *dos rubios* were not in Montevideo, Abuela had apparently skipped the whole affair and Juan Luis and Elsa had gone to Elsa's parents' house.

This year, with Rubén and Lili and me all in Montevideo, there was no question that we would gather at Abuela's house and go through the motions of Christmas, despite the missing older *rubio*. It was still terribly hot and humid, and I headed to the beach in the morning, like Dad and I used to do. I swam myself to exhaustion in the muddy water, going as far out toward the open sea as I dared, and then I sat on the sand watching the beach fill with kids and balls and fathers, until the sun got too high and my mega-applications of sunblock could no longer save me from frying. When I got back to the house, it was already suffused with the perfume of jasmine sprigs and Elsa's indefatigable good cheer. She was in the kitchen making mayonnaise for the *ensalada Rusa*, Abuela was shuffling about the dining room making scrooge remarks about superstitious Catholic holidays, Juan Luis was out back cleaning out the *parrillero*, which hadn't been used in three years—all painfully in keeping with my childhood memories and jarringly banal after the melodrama of the past few days.

I took a cool shower and then I sat myself down on my bed in the prow of the ship to wrap the presents I had collected up—a calendar of photos that the architecture students had been selling to fund their graduation tour to Europe, early tickets to the best *carnaval* concerts at Teatro de Verano, a bottle of *butiá* fruit liqueur I'd picked up at a roadside stand outside Rocha, an electric Crock-Pot I'd bought at the kitchen store in El Shopping, a handmade stuffed pig and a ceramic hair clip from the Tristán Narvaja market . . . I wrapped them in sheets of old newspaper with red and green ribbon the way Lili had taught me, curled the ribbon with the edge of the scissors, and wrote the names of my putative family across the newsprint in red magic marker. *Para Abuela, para Rubén, Juan Luis, Elsa, Alejandra . . .* I was on automatic pilot, piling the wrapped gifts up at the end of the bed, until I got to the sweater I'd picked out for Lili and suddenly started bawling like a four-year-old. It was made of local, hand-dyed wool, a thick knit in a rainbow of rust colors, and I'd bought it at Manos del Uruguay, an artisans' cooperative something like the co-op of dairies that made Conaprole ice cream. I had been looking forward to giving it to her, and now, as I rolled the sweater up in its sheet of newsprint, tied a ribbon around it, and wrote "for Lili" on the side, I was raging with childish disappointment that this small pleasure had been thwarted— that life would not behave the way it should, that parents could not be taken for granted, that I was not who I'd thought I was, and the family Christmas I remembered with such unequivocal happiness had morphed into a complex pageant of betrayal and dissimulation.

By the time I finished wrapping presents and reclaimed my composure enough to brave exposure to the Quirogas, Lili had arrived with her bounty from the estancia. She was in the kitchen with Elsa, slicing up her first harvest of melons, the two of them trying to sing along with Rubén, who was ensconced on Abuela's stool with his guitar. He was playing Uruguayan Christmas songs I'd never heard, *canto popular* from the fifties and sixties that bore no resemblance to the pepped-up versions of "Jingle Bells" and "Feliz Navidad" that accosted you when you walked into El Shopping. Lili was more lively than I'd seen her in weeks, but I couldn't tell if it was just the same bright masquerade she'd always used as a cover, or if she actually felt relieved to have come clean with me. Whatever the case, I could hardly stand to be in the same room with her. I felt entirely estranged, more distant from her than I could ever have imagined feeling when I was growing up.

I spent the rest of the afternoon out back tending the *asado* and drinking beer with Juan Luis. It was way too hot to be hanging around a fire, but then, that was Christmas in Uruguay, shirtless and sweaty and eating too much heavy meat—though I couldn't remember ever roasting a whole suckling pig. Lili had come with a pile of wood and Santiago's *lechón*, which seemed to require a higher culinary art than the usual *asado*. She and Juan had done the hard part, flattening the carcass and covering it with marinade, so that all we had to do for the next few hours was feed the fire and brush the piglet with more marinade. But we hung around anyway, watching it cook and fussing with the coals, arranging them in precise patterns beneath the grill, trying to mirror the thickness of the meat on the various parts of the carcass.

Juan was unusually loquacious, chatting about the estancia and his rice enterprise, suddenly as earnest and exuberant as his wife, though he would surely put a cap on it if I told him that. He was aiming to fill the pond in July so he could form the dikes and plant as soon as things warmed up, hopefully by September. I told him about my subsidy idea. Compared to Juan's carefully calculated plans, my idea was a farfetched pipedream and I expected him to shoot it down before it even got off the ground. But he listened carefully, and when I was done he told me that if I could find any way, subsidy or otherwise, to make buying water from the big canal affordable—and if Caruso cooperated—he would certainly do it. He even said he had some other ideas for maintaining the flow of water into the marsh, but they involved experimenting with the rice culture and he didn't want to risk it the first year or two.

It was almost nine by the time Juan and I wrestled the *lechón* onto a slab of wood, arranged grilled *zapallitos* and baby potatoes around it, and paraded into the dining room. We wanted to set it down as the centerpiece in the middle of the table, but Abuela wouldn't let us. She had objected when Elsa took all the old china and silver out of the cabinet, but now she guarded the elaborately set table as if it had been her idea, and we had to set our plank on the kitchen counter. Juan carved up the meat, and we were about to sit down to dinner, when the doorbell rang. I went to answer it, expecting Gonzalo or one of the *tía abuelas*—but the guest I opened the door to was absolutely unexpected, if not exactly uninvited.

He had a red fleece Santa hat perched on his thinning hair, a bag full of presents tossed over his shoulder, and a shit-eating grin on his freckled face, like a kid reveling in his own surprise. For a moment, crushed in my father's bear hug, I felt like my old self again, pleased and vaguely relieved to see him. He'd booked a last-minute flight and emailed Juan and Elsa, arriving at their apartment in the morning—but Elsa whooped when we walked into the dining room now, as if she too was surprised. Patricia presented little Emilia, who imitated her grandmother, whooping and then laughing in two-year-old manic style. No one thought to introduce Rubén, who smiled amiably and offered a hand and a brotherly pat on the shoulder to the *yanqui* ex-brother-in-law who he knew, at most, as a voice on the telephone in distant California. Abuela let him engulf her in a hug, and when he released her the expression on her face was nothing short of triumphant, her lips stretched in a smile that threatened to break her personal smile barrier. *"Menos mal,"* she said, turning to look at Lili as if she thought Keith's arrival meant the undoing of their divorce. But Lili's eyes were on me, and when I met them—briefly, glancingly—I knew, without a doubt, that in at least one thing she had not been lying: Dad did not know I wasn't his son. And something else: she still loved him. He embraced her, carefully, like a bear caressing a honeybee, and I turned quickly away.

It must happen all the time, I thought, placing myself between Juan Luis and Dad at the table, as far from Lili as I could get. Mothers who keep their kids in the dark about their origins, women who betray their men, children who never knew they were adopted. Would it be more comprehensible, forgivable even, if Alejandra didn't exist, if I hadn't fallen in love with her? But in that case, would Lili have even told me? Do you hate your mother for betraying you with lies about your origins, love your father any less when you find out he's not your father? I looked around the table. And the rest of them? *Mi tía y mis tíos, mi prima Patricia. Abuela.* Did I love them any less? I turned the question around. I was a cowbird raised in a vireo's nest: if they knew the favorite *nieto y sobrino* was the child of the reviled and beloved terrorist and martyr Eva Paden, would they love him less?

My own pleasure in Dad's surprise visit was quickly overshadowed by the realization of just how complicated and Quiroganized our uncomplicated relationship had become. I listened to him entertaining his ex-in-laws in his broken Spanish, and I could not imagine telling him I was not his son, throwing his sense of his life and family into even further disarray than Lili had already thrown it. My heart twisted around itself with confusion and rage as I realized that I was no longer an innocent bystander to the secrets and betrayals that undermined his marriage, not even their unwitting cause: Lili had now made me responsible for her secrets, complicit in her betrayal.

The Quirogas were all disconcertingly civil and well behaved in Dad's presence. It was like having a foreign ambassador to dinner, and for a few hours we looked like a model of family harmony. I managed to scuttle through the evening in my Hermit Crab's shell, stuffing myself with *lechón* and Elsa's *ensalada rusa*, as expected, and Lili was dissembling so well she seemed almost happy. Dad made small talk about California politics and weather, but mostly he kept everyone else talking with his questions, as if he too was an expatriate newly returned and hungry for news. He asked about the election, which Rubén and Juan Luis explained politely and relatively objectively, and about the estancia, which we told him about in chorus, our parallel passions resonating, for a brief moment, like the notes of a single chord—Juan with his rice, Lili with her sustainable vegetables, Rubén with his pet Ñandú and random acts of craftsmanship, Gabriel with his birds.

I described the marsh, waxing poetic about its avian wonders, describing the rails as the first and the last of their kind, an ambivalent Adam and Eve. I guess I reminded Dad of his own dead father—he was thrilled that I wanted to name the rail species *gordoni*—and he listened attentively, providing a sort of validation that piqued everyone else's interest in ways I hadn't been able to do myself. Juan interrupted to tell him about my drawings, describing them in more detail than I myself remembered them, and Lili took it upon herself to tell Dad about the job Eduardo had offered me.

"He makes it sound like paradise," Rubén said. "But the truth of the matter is, it's a quagmire of mosquitoes and mud."

Dad laughed. "My father used to drag Gabe around to places like that all the time when he was small. It's in his blood."

I told them how Alejandra and I had picked our way around the quicksand and climbed through the brush like monkeys to steal the nest for DNA analysis, how I'd refused to let them trap or shoot one of the rails.

"Only a woman in love would follow you out there," Rubén said.

"Only a *biologist* would follow me out there."

"Well," Dad said, "for a discovery like that. A new species . . ."

"An endangered species," I said, glancing at Juan.

"They're going to get married this year," Abuela said suddenly, and everyone turned to look at her. "Before I die," she added.

Rubén started cracking up. "Bravo, Mamá! A Quiroga-Paden liaison! That's just what we need in this family. Finally."

"Abuela," I said, rolling a pea from the *ensalada rusa* across my plate. "You're not going to die this year. And Alejandra and I have no immediate plans to get married." I glanced across the table and had the sensation that the blood rising into my flaming cheeks had drained directly from Lili's face, as if we were connected by a long umbilical cord—a physical connection that, I reminded myself, had never actually existed between us.

"I knew there was a girl!" Keith was beaming. "Are you going to tell me about her, Gabe, or should I ask Lili?"

"You can ask me," Rubén said. "This biologist who follows him into the most godforsaken swamp you've ever seen happens to be a dark-eyed, ringlet-headed beauty, the daughter of—"

"Rubén, will you do me the favor of shutting up?" I got up to refill the meat platter, though it was still half full. "I'll tell you about her later, Dad." I'd wanted to tell him about Alejandra in private, introduce them—show her off. But I wasn't about to discuss her in front of the assembled Quirogas, with all their assorted baggage from the past.

Dad picked up my cue and changed the subject, and somehow, I managed to get through the rest of my twenty-third Christmas Eve on earth without breaking down again. In fact, as the evening wore on, I had the sense that I was truly mastering the art of dissimulation, feeling cooler and more implacable, matching Dad's good cheer in kind, staying away from the wine, and playing my role as the good-natured *hijo, nieto, sobrino, y primo*, even as I tried to sort through the implications of Lili's revelations for each of those relationships. I watched Lili open her sweater from Manos del Uruguay—watched the smile break across her face, which had regained its color, watched her pull it over her head and model it, Dad nodding his approval and Elsa congratulating me on the choice. But when Lili tried to thank me, I turned away, as if it were some other son who had selected it for her. I opened the presents that Patricia piled at my feet—including a laptop computer from my famously generous father—thanked everyone profusely, and sat down on the floor to help Emilia turn an empty box into a house for her new stuffed pig. When everyone except Abuela and Lili migrated over to Juan and Elsa's apartment, I joined the fun, crowding onto their small terrace to watch the fireworks erupt across the city and light the sparklers Dad had bought. And all the while, I was mapping my relations, trying to come up with an algorithm to determine who I should and should not tell, generating a spreadsheet with columns for name, action, timing, consequences, and the list of others who would need to know if I told that person—as if I could distribute my lost and found identities to each according to their needs. But by the time I loaded my drunk *tío* Rubén into the truck and drove back to Abuela's house and fell into bed, all my algorithms had failed and the only clear entries in my spreadsheet were Abuela and Alejandra, with "no" and "yes" in the action column.

19

Polvo. Dust. A thin gray layer of it peeled free and floated down in front of the book spines as I felt along the top shelf for the bag of letters I'd stashed there. It was the morning of New Year's Eve, the cusp of the millennium, and I had been thinking about time. I watched the mass of dust linger on the air like a molted feather, trying to find a word to distinguish it from the dust that blows across the desert floor, or puffs up around your boots when you shuffle along a dry Sierra trail in summer. Indoor dirt was all it was, the stuff that escapes notice until you open the blinds and see the dust motes hanging in a ray of sun, waiting to settle on some overlooked object in a house you thought was clean. A forgotten collection of seashells, an old doll on a dresser, the worn suitcase in the attic, these outdated architecture books in the prow of Abuela's house . . . Layers and layers of dust, like time incarnate. I batted the gray feather I'd dislodged into the trashcan in the corner, unsure whether the dust transformed these prosaic objects into important historic relics, or just bore witness to their irrelevance.

I opened the plastic bag and took out the bundle of letters. They were dust-free, protected by Rubén's leather suitcase all these years and, I suspected, not infrequent handling. I fingered the withered ribbon and riffled the frayed edges of the envelopes, sifting briefly, warily, through the stories I'd heard about the girl who had written the letters with her hand and worn the ribbon in her hair. A labyrinth of paradox. Lili's best friend.

Abuela's favorite. The girl who read philosophy. Who wanted to be an architect for the poor. Revolutionary. Terrorist. Rubén's love of a lifetime. Femme fatale. Doting young mother. Victim of unthinkable brutality. Ghost. The woman who gave birth to me.

When Rubén first described Eva's adolescent "*soliloquios políticos*," I'd been curious, but the idea of reading them now made me squeamish. I slipped the bundle back into the plastic bag and set it on top of the towel and clothes in my knapsack. Dad had left for California the day before, and Alejandra and I had made plans to forgo—or escape—our families' festivities and welcome the new millennium in anonymous splendor, away from the city. It was my idea to escape, but Alejandra had decided where to go and arranged the details. She had a friend who owned a vacation *cabaña* we could use, in some sleepy little beach town about an hour's drive out of Montevideo. I'd promised her I would teach her to bodysurf. And I'd promised myself I would give her Rubén's letters and tell her everything the various members of the Quiroga family had told me about Eva. And Lili. And us.

I'd tell her in the new year, in neutral territory. Far from the Quirogas and Silvas—far from Dad, who had seemed so innocently happy to see his ex-wife that I hadn't had the heart to tell him anything. He'd driven out to the estancia with her and spent two days ingratiating himself with Angelito and getting indoctrinated in the finer points of a sustainable vegetable farm in the middle of the Uruguayan grasslands. I couldn't remember him doing much of anything in the garden when I was a kid, but when Alejandra and I showed up, we found him out hoeing the lettuce fields with Lili. They were getting on so well, and Dad waxed so enthusiastic about everything—the vegetables and the windmill and the new thatch roof, the nightly *asados* and the long green vistas—that I could almost imagine them reconciling and living out there together in their old age. I'd promised Dad we'd take him birding in the marsh, and Lili, after months of apparent apathy, suddenly decided to take an interest in the estancia's birdlife and join us. I was suspicious of her motives, but she was, in fact, as attentive as Dad was, the two of them shuffling along in the ill-fitting rubber boots I'd bought for Rubén and Juan, admiring the *Chajá* family and the *Celestón* and the *Sietecolores*, following us unquestioningly into the reed bed, waiting patiently as Alejandra and I stopped to collect samples, and mumbling appreciatively as I named all the odd and beautiful avian characters that were on display at the pond. The rails were nowhere in evidence that day, which disappointed Alejandra—Eduardo had said we might not hear from them again until the next mating season—but Dad and Lili were impressed nonetheless. They weren't birders, but they had been fully indoctrinated by Grandpa and didn't need cuddly mammals or a thousand waterfalls to recognize the marsh as the sort of place he would have fought to preserve, mosquitoes and quicksand notwithstanding.

Dad and Alejandra had taken to each other immediately, just as I'd hoped. I could sense his pleasure that I'd found someone so interesting, smart, and solid. I saw him trying to share that parental gratification with Lili, leaning over to whisper in her ear as they watched us collect samples and take measurements, oblivious to the tension between Lili and me, to Lili's awkwardness with Alejandra and uncharacteristic disquiet about our sleeping arrangements. By the time we drove Dad to the airport and said goodbye—by the time he'd admonished me to write him more emails on my new laptop and kissed Alejandra on the cheek and swallowed her in a bear hug and left us standing outside the security check waving as he disappeared into the borderless maw between Uruguay and North America—there was a solid "no" entry in his column on my spreadsheet. I thought I'd long ceased to care what they did, and yet I found myself wondering if he had slept with Lili or stayed in Rubén's room as assigned, my mind spawning fantasies of reconciliation like it used to do when they first split up, when I was still their son. I could not, would not, tell Dad I wasn't his progeny. Lili would have to do that. Or not. And he would have to forgive her. Or not.

We had the sweetest New Year's Eve I could possibly have imagined. I wanted that for Alejandra, for us—this night, this perfect night—before we finally had to confront our families' ghosts and my past. The *cabaña* was a two-room wooden box tucked in among the dunes at the edge of the village, built of unpainted eucalyptus and perched on wooden posts stuck in the sand, as transient as the dunes themselves. It had a red sheet-metal roof, and everything inside was painted in shades of red and yellow, so that you had the feeling you were sleeping inside a sunset. There was a small deck with a red hammock where we curled up for a nap, and a cinder-block *parrillero* where we grilled the fish we'd bought fresh in the village. At midnight, we took our bottle of champagne and the four rockets Dad had given me out to the edge of the dunes. There were isolated displays of fireworks like ours up and down the coast, but we were alone on our stretch of beach, and after we'd launched the rockets and toasted the new millennium, we spent an hour drinking the rest of the champagne and trying to slide down the dunes. It was a moonless night and we kept losing and finding each other in the dark, stumbling around the dunes and into each other's arms, making love in the warm sand, drunk, exhausted, happy. I was worried about the next day, about how Alejandra would cope with what I had to tell her. But in those perfect moments, as we found our way back to the *cabaña* and ate a watermelon by candlelight at the yellow table and fell into bed together, I could not believe that any secret from the past could change—that anything could change—who we were together.

The sun streaming through the crimson curtain rousted us in the new year. We packed a bag with towels and *mate* and buttered rolls and headed back to the beach. Still drowsy and in no hurry to eat or swim, we strolled along the tideline, skimming our bare feet over the wet sand, squinting into the morning sun. It was easier to talk that way, while we were walking, our eyes down on the sand, not facing each other. I started with Abuela's stories. Then Rubén's. I told her they'd dumped their stories on me, and she needed to hear them. I told her that secrets were poisonous, that I wanted her to know everything that I knew.

As soon as I mentioned Eva's name, I could feel Alejandra receding from me. She dropped hold of my hand, and I sensed her rolling back into herself, like the water at our feet sliding back into the Atlantic. She let me go on with my monologue until I got to the part about Rubén and Eva reuniting in Buenos Aires after she was born, and then she suddenly stopped walking and interrupted me. "*¿Qué haces?*" she said, and I turned back to face her.

What was I doing? Did I even know what I was doing?

"Why are you polluting our new millennium with these rotten old stories?" She looked like a bewildered little girl, standing there in an ill-fitting orange sundress that she'd pulled on over her bikini, one strap fallen down off her shoulder. It was something her friend had left in the *cabaña*, a part of its inside-out sunset, but it looked out of place in the white glare of morning sun.

I shook my head, morose. The sweetest New Year's imaginable, and I was about to sprinkle the ambrosia with arsenic. I wanted to stop. Leave the ghosts in their shadows. Bury the secret, give it back to Lili, forget it, retrieve the lies that had created me and go on as we were, into our own future, whatever its risks and uncertainties. I wanted not to tell her. It was possible, it was still possible.

I reached out and slid the strap back into place on her shoulder. I planted a kiss on the spot between her eyes where her brows had converged in a half-puzzled, half-peeved little crease. "We have to reckon with the ghosts," I said. Firmly, as if I did, in fact, know what I was doing. "Or they'll never leave us in peace." I had spent two weeks understanding this. Planning what I would tell her. I tilted her face upward and kissed her again, delicately, on the lips, trying to pull her back to me. Then I took her hand and led her up to the dry sand, where I made her sit down next to me. I handed her the thermos and her *mate*, but she just set them aside and sat there playing with the sand in front of her, waiting obediently for me to say whatever it was I felt I needed to say.

I told her Lili's story, holding back the goriest details and resenting Lili anew for loosing them on me, for making me into the steward of horror. I kept my eyes on the water as I talked, but when I got to the part about Alejandra's fourth birthday, I paused and turned to look at her, worried that I might trigger some kind of repressed traumatic memory, and that I really wouldn't know what to do then.

She was sitting with her legs folded back at an impossible angle, scooping up handful after handful of sand and watching the grains run through her fingers, her face shielded by the cool bronze facade it acquired whenever anyone talked about Eva.

I turned back toward the sea and tracked an approaching swell, imagining myself suspended in its curl, in those seconds of vertigo before you knew if you would catch it rushing into shore or be left sliding down its chilly backside like a forgotten bit of flotsam. We were beyond the river's wide maw here, and the waves were bigger than in Montevideo, the water bluer. I told her the rest of the story. The part where I was the main character. I explained carefully that I'd never had even the remotest suspicion that Lili and Keith weren't my parents. That Lili had told no one. I talked and talked, and then I stopped and waited, watching a flock of terns banking and diving above the waves, fishing. Species unfamiliar.

"I don't remember," she said finally. "I don't remember being four. Mamá. I don't know if what I remember is her or her photo."

Her voice was just a murmur in the crash of waves and the cries of terns, but the sound of it filled me with relief. Those violent moments, at least, hadn't embedded themselves in her memory.

"I don't remember the feel of her. Her touch, the look of her. But I remember this word, 'Mamá.' I remember using it, saying it, the taste of it. And Papá, I must have called my stepfather Papá, I must have, because why else would I remember that? My grandparents talked about my father, but he was always Natalio or *tu padre*, never Papá."

She had stopped piling up sand, but was still staring down at her hands. I wanted her to look up at me, wanted to comfort her somehow, but she just kept releasing her small memories, her gaze turned inward, as if I was irrelevant. Or invisible, erased.

"I used to pretend that my baby doll was a boy. My grandmother tried to explain that it was a girl doll, because it had a pink girl-baby dress. But I insisted. She liked to tell that story. I could never say why my doll should be a boy. It just was.

"I only heard much later that Eva was pregnant when they killed her.

"*Un hermano*," she whispered, as if testing the words, her voice infused with a wonder and tenderness that made me fear she'd rather have a long-lost brother than the confused lover kneeling in the sand next to her. Lovers, after all, were replaceable.

"*Medio*," I said then, and she turned, startled, to look at me. "Half-brother."

She shifted in the sand, demolishing the little pile she'd accumulated, and her eyes wandered over the surface of my face, searching my features, I knew, for some reflection of her own—a reflex that I also knew would yield no result.

"If you're a clone of Eva," I ventured, "I must take after my father."

I held perfectly still as she reached out and brushed a sandy finger down the bridge of my nose and along the line of my lip—

and then quickly retrieved her hand as if it had acted without her consent.

"William Davies," she said. "*El rubio.* That's what everyone called him. From a British family. That's all I know, from hearsay. I only have one photo, from their marriage. Black and white."

"William Gabriel Davies." The name stumbled through my lips and landed between us like a pile of bricks. I looked away, down the beach toward the village, where a couple of families had appeared and were setting up an umbrella. "Eva named me after him. Lili says she and Dad had chosen Jonathan for their baby, and they fought when she got back and he found out she'd registered my birth as Gabriel Jonathan Haynes Quiroga. She told him it was in memory of a friend who was murdered with Eva—" I let out a dry cough of a laugh. "*El rubio.* That's what the Quirogas like to call Keith and me. *Los dos rubios.*"

"The argument you had with Lili. Before Christmas. When you spent the night in the marsh. This was it?"

I glanced over at her and she met my eyes now, her eyebrows folding like a hawk's wings before a dive, as if I had finally come into focus. "I was enraged," I said. "Lost, obliterated. My whole life, my existence, a lie. I don't know why she didn't tell me, how she could not have told Dad—"

"She didn't want it to rule your lives." Alejandra interrupted me, her voice emerging from its stunned murmur, caustic with irony. "Eva's ghost haunting you like it haunted everyone else here. Didn't want to waste her life protesting, bitter, walking with placards."

"She thinks we shouldn't be together," I said carefully, turning back to the waves, not looking at her. "You and I. That's the only reason she told me now." I was ready to prove Lili wrong, lay out my evidence—but Alejandra's calm was dissolving in nervous, hysterical, screeching laughter.

"Incest?" she shrieked. "Is that what we have been doing?"

The word dropped like a noose around my throat, a word I'd dismissed both intellectually and emotionally, but now it choked off everything I'd planned to say, and all that came out was a bellow of brute denial. "No! No. We didn't even know—"

"*You* knew!" We were facing each other now, Alejandra rising up on her knees, me sitting back on my heels, our eyes at a level.

"It's not incest," I said. "It's not. Incest doesn't mean—this." I gestured helplessly at the space between us, trying to round up my words. "We didn't know each other as children. We didn't know our— You hardly remember Eva, I never knew her. The only memories we share are the ones we've created ourselves, as adults—"

"*We*, Gabriel? Where is this 'we'? You've known this for two weeks? And you don't tell me? You keep sleeping with me?" She had exploded like a river blasting through a dam, an Alejandra I'd never seen, knee to knee with me in the sand, flooding me with her rage. "You fuck your sister without telling her she's your sister?"

"You're not my sister! You don't *look* like a sister, you don't *feel* like a sister—"

"Who said you get to decide that? Maybe *I* want my brother to be my brother. Maybe *I* feel like a sister."

"But you don't—"

"How do you know that? How could I even know what I feel if I didn't know what I didn't know, what you knew?"

I reached out to touch her face as she stumbled over her words, my palm against her cheek, and it was only when she flinched and pushed my hand away that I began to understand what I'd done, blindly, selfishly, idiotically. That I'd betrayed her. That no matter what I felt, the facts, the scientific facts of who we were to each other had changed in the moment they were revealed to me. And I'd gone on as we were, *as we were*, without sharing those facts. Without asking how she felt about them.

"Alejandra, I'm telling you, now. That's what this is." She had turned away again, deflating into the sand, her legs folded under her. I focused on the frolicking terns, now chased by two thieving gulls, and tried to explain what I couldn't explain. The shock, the grief, the confusion—everything, I realized, she herself was now feeling. The days of denial, uncertainty about Lili's sanity. My spreadsheet of relations, my fears. For her, for me. The terror of losing this last trace of myself, our future, of being erased. I had no excuse for my behavior, but as I retraced my actions of the past two weeks, I could not see how I could have done other than what I did. I could not have told her before this moment, and if I had stayed away from her, I could never have gotten to this moment, and she knew as well as I what that meant when it came to our love, when it came to sex. If that was the issue. Was that the issue? Even as I said it, I realized that what had seemed so helplessly, unquestionably natural and self-evident to me, the inherent seductive, corporeal reality of our love, might, in fact, be the question, one of the many questions—not only for the rest of the world, which I didn't care about, but for Alejandra. And I was sorry, I told her I was sorry, but now she knew, I was telling her.

"We're trapped in their putrid past," she said bitterly. "In this shitty little patch of Uruguayan quicksand. Even *mi querido yanqui*."

"Are we?" I moved around in front of her, blocking her view of the ocean, my fists curled against my thighs. I tried to find my way back to the script I'd set, the logic I'd worked out for myself over the past two weeks. "Alejandra, we're only related by Lili's deranged memory. That's all."

"Genes," she said, staring at me, or through me. "We're related by genes." Her voice had returned to normal and she seemed to cool down as she did the calculation in her head. "Twenty-five percent. Chances are, we overlap by twenty-five percent of the part of our genomes that distinguish us as individuals—

the part that makes us separate leaves in your rendition of a phy-logenetic tree. On average. It's like dealing a hand of shuffled cards, could be more overlap, could be less, but that's the average."

"People used to marry their cousins all the time," I said. "Charles and Emma Darwin were cousins. They had ten kids." I'd done my homework.

"The average for cousins would only be 12.5 percent."

"So what? It only matters if we have kids." I made an effort to master my tone, to sound like I was sure of what I was saying. "We could adopt. There are too many people in the world any-way, who says we have to make new ones? Or we could have our DNA tested, like *Laterallus gordoni*. I looked on the Internet. There are companies that do that. Genetic counseling. They can check for problems." I watched her face, calm now, but inscruta-ble. "I only ever thought about kids since I met you. It's like kids are hardwired into love, being in love. But we don't have to have kids. We don't even have to get married, but—but I want to be with you forever."

"If you want to be with someone forever, you don't lie. You don't keep 'poisonous secrets' to yourself. You, of all peo-ple, should know that." She rose in one supple, heartbreakingly graceful movement, and walked across the burning sand toward the tideline.

I swallowed all my arguments and defenses and followed her, mute, into the water, waiting for her to decide what to do with this most toxic of secrets. She was still wearing the orange sundress, but she waded in up to her waist, stopping in the mid-dle of the whitewater. I worried she would get knocked over and I wanted to tell her to move back from the impact zone, or go farther out where she could duck under the waves, but I just fol-lowed her and stood vigil a few feet away, keeping my eye on the approaching breakers, watching her brace herself against each frothing onslaught, wishing I could be teaching her to bodysurf. Waiting for her to decide what she felt. If I was brother, or lover, or neither. A man who embodied the very history she yearned to be free of—and yet was himself unmoored, bereft of history, of self. I was still waiting when she walked out of the water and back to the cabaña, my face on fire with sunburn. Love was more difficult to calculate than genetic probabilities.

We changed into dry clothes, and I handed her a glass of orange juice and waited while she drank it, and then I dug the bundle of letters out of my knapsack and set it on the yellow table, where it looked, with its red velvet bow, like part of the cabaña's kitschy sunset décor. She'd hardly said five words since we left the beach, and she listened in silence as I told her how Rubén had entrusted the letters to my care, how I'd been uncertain if she would want them. She picked up the bundle and lifted it to her face to sniff, as if acting on some primal instinct, and the next thing I knew, she was shaking with sobs, collapsing accordion-like toward the floor. I caught her before she went down, set the letters back on the table, and sank into a chair with Alejandra folded into a quaking ball in my lap, wrapping myself around her as tightly as I could, terrified that this miraculous planet of a woman would undergo some sort of tectonic rearrangement.

I have no idea how long we sat like that before the shaking stilled and she climbed out of my lap. She went to the kitchen sink and splashed water on her face, blew her nose on a paper towel, and turned back to me, and I was reassured when I saw that she looked the same, red-eyed and drained, but unchanged. She retrieved the roll of paper towels and handed it to me. I hadn't realized I'd been crying too, but my face was wet and my nose was dripping.

"It smells like her," she said, sitting down across from me, her voice normal, calm. "Like Mamá."

I leaned over the table and sniffed at the bundle, but all I could smell was a hint of musty old leather, probably from Rubén's suitcase. I shook my head. "Rubén says she sprinkled her letters with her perfume. He smells it also. Some kind of ultra-sensitive physical memory."

"They're love letters, then?"

"He called them *soliloquios políticos*."

"Sprinkled with perfume?"

I shrugged and turned up my hands. "I guess it was all mixed up. Politics, love. He says she was clever, that they're full of puns and metaphors. Some are from after she took up with Natalio, maybe even later, after you were born. He thought you might want to read them."

She reached over and tugged at the end of the ribbon with one hand until the bow fell open. "And you?" she said, glancing at me.

"He doesn't know about me."

"Of course, but—do you want to read them?"

"No," I said immediately. "They weren't written for me."

"They weren't written for me either." She picked up a letter from the top of the pile, slipped it out of its envelope, and unfolded it. She couldn't have read half a page before she stopped and looked up at me. "What if you went back to California?" she said.

"I don't want to go back to California. Not without you."

"If you had no choice. And we wrote letters to each other."

"We'd probably write emails," I said, thinking of my new laptop.

"Same difference."

"Emails are worse than letters. You don't think about them. You're definitely not writing for posterity."

"Eva wasn't writing letters for posterity. She wasn't writing for her daughter. She was writing for Rubén."

"Who knows. She was writing for Rubén. He kept them for posterity. Maybe he thought they were important. History."

"He kept them for himself," Alejandra said. "And he's still alive."

I thought about Rubén holding the letters, lifting them to his face to inhale their elusive perfume, the perfume that sent Alejandra into convulsions of grief, the perfume I couldn't detect. I thought about dust again. Its adherence to unwanted objects. How much you needed before you had history. The lack of dust on the letters.

"Doesn't he have kids?" Alejandra asked.

I nodded. "Two daughters. I've never met them, but I think the youngest is at college in New York."

We sat there looking at each other across the table, and then Alejandra refolded the letter in her hand, slipped it back in its envelope, and handed it to me. I set it back on top of the pile and retied the red ribbon. We would give the letters back to Rubén. Unread.

EPILOGUE

I don't think I was writing for posterity when I started writing this story, at least not consciously. I was writing for myself, the way I used to draw birds, before other people got interested. I wanted a record of Gabriel Haynes Quiroga's observations from those months before the millennium turned, wanted to make an artifact of them, something I could hold in my hand or put on a shelf to gather dust. A record of discovery. It took me nearly two years to realize I wanted—needed—to do that. We were in California then, recently arrived. Fall of 2001.

Alejandra's grandfather had died in May, leaving her free to take the postdoctoral fellowship she'd been offered at UC Davis. Eduardo's *Historias ilustradas de aves uruguayas* was about to go to press, and I had plans to sign up for a master's course in scientific illustration the following summer. In the meantime, I'd landed a job with a state-funded project that was monitoring the effects of habitat destruction and climate change on waterbirds in the Central Valley. Alejandra had a whole team of microbial ecologists to work with, and I was either out in the field counting birds, or inputting data and helping a programmer develop an experimental GIS program that would generate time-based maps of species distributions. The valley itself was a flat agricultural wasteland with little oases of wetlands, but we liked our jobs, and the Sierras were only a couple hours away. That's where we were on September 11, blissfully oblivious, camped on the shore of a nameless little lake at eleven thousand feet. That's also where our son was conceived, two days later.

I'd wanted to introduce Alejandra to a better side of California, so I'd planned a backpacking trip as soon as we arrived, before we settled into our apartment and started work. We hiked in on the steep east side, and Alejandra, who had never seen a real mountain before, loved every second of it: the physical challenge of the hike, sleeping under stars that were denser and brighter than any she'd ever seen, the startling granite vistas, the complete absence of human presence when I led her off-trail. She said it felt like a fundamental revelation, like discovering a new physical dimension.

It wasn't something we'd planned, Alejandra getting pregnant then. We hadn't yet decided if we wanted kids, had been too busy and caught up in our lives together to even lay the groundwork for that decision. There were new genetic tests we could do, but they were expensive—and neither of us was eager to expose the old film of Lili's memory to the bright light of science until we had to. It was a low-probability case, Alejandra said when she missed her period, something to do with having changed pill prescriptions the month before—not supposed to happen. But she also claimed she knew exactly when it happened.

The day she saw her first Bald Eagles. An afternoon skinny-dipping in our little lake, leaping into the icy water and laying ourselves out to dry in the alpine sun, smooth glacier-carved granite against our skin, the eagles appearing like two avian voyeurs above us. We'd pulled on our clothes and stayed there into the evening, watching them scoop fish out of the lake, a juvenile in second- or third-year plumage and a white-headed adult, both of them born wild, their legs unbanded and wings unmarked by any human hand. They'd returned the next evening, and the one after, and I'd imagined they were father and son out fishing together, though, of course, I couldn't tell if they were related, couldn't even tell their gender. Somehow, those two eagles have become part of the founding myth of our little family, of our son's conception and of our own small revelations—Alejandra comprehending wilderness for the first time, me accepting its loss, embracing my role as a cartographer of adaptation.

When we came out of the mountains that September, it was clear that even in the hemisphere of "*la tontería ecológica*," even in California, no one beyond a handful of scientists was going to be talking about the loss of wilderness, or adaptation to habitat loss, or even climate change anytime soon. It's a paradigm shift, Alejandra said when we heard Rubén's ménage of messages on the answering machine in our new apartment—*the collapse of capitalism! divine retribution!* yanqui *hegemony in decline! are you okay? where* are *you?* It was as if the continents had been flipped upside down, she said, the south watching the north combust. She herself watched the past-blind, nationalist US politics unfold with the voyeuristic fascination of a tourist—unaware, at first, that she had a US citizen growing in her womb. And I, who had spent the first months of our acquaintance watching the Uruguayan elections unfold with equal fascination, began translating the images and memories from those months into words and arranging them into sentences and paragraphs that I wrote down in my sketchpad.

The present was crowding out both past and future, and I felt the need to record this bit of personal past that wasn't yet and might never be history—to create some depth perception in a one-dimensional world where words like "evil" and "heroic" were suddenly so overused and abused they were ironed flat of meaning. I hoped my own words would evoke meaning in the same magical way that my sketches evoked the three-dimensional forms of live birds, but I erased as much as I wrote, until the rough surface of the pages looked as frayed and worn as the knees of my old jeans. Not long after Alejandra announced that she was pregnant, I started typing everything into the computer, where it was easier to rearrange, or delete, whole sentences and paragraphs. Writing this story has not, as it turns out, been as straightforward as drawing a semblance of a bird or noting down a bunch of field marks. It's taken me nearly three years to make my way through it—three years in which my son breathed his first breath, took his first steps, and uttered his first Spanglish words.

We didn't plan Águila's conception, but his gestation was meticulously orchestrated. As soon as Alejandra realized she was pregnant, we submitted blood samples for the most detailed genetic test we could find. It didn't show much, except that we have a 21 percent gene overlap—at the low end for half-siblings, but enough to substantiate Lili's story and make us worry about the risks for our baby. Alejandra scheduled every form of prenatal testing possible, and we agreed that if they revealed a significant probability that our gene overlap would limit the child's prospects, she would have an abortion. I don't know what we would have done if the tests revealed an unrelated problem in our baby, but we didn't have to confront either decision. We were lucky, Alejandra and I. We, as individuals, escaped the trap of the past. Two tiny leaves among the billions on our overly vigorous branch of the phylogenetic tree. Now, three. We chose the lies we could live with and, unlike Lili, we've made our peace with them.

Operación Cóndor. That's what they called the international ring of state-sponsored terror that Eva and Lili and Willy Davies fell victim to. Along with Juan Gelman's granddaughter, who'd been raised by an Uruguayan policeman and his wife, and the middle-aged Uruguayan woman I just read about, who survived the tortures and, after a twenty-year search, found out that her son was raised by *milicos* in Argentina. And many, many others, whose stories I haven't followed. It's written down in books, now, dramatized in movies . . . and forgotten again. Is it history? I watch the news reports of torture at Guantanamo and Abu

Ghraib, listen to the US government's defense of it, and wonder about the logics of evil, its many dimensions. They say Bush and Rumsfeld ordered it. That Kissinger was complicit in Operation Condor, that the CIA trained the Uruguayan *milicos*. I suppose it was named for the *Cóndor andino. Vultur gryphus*. Larger and even more imposing than the California Condor, with a range running the length of the Andes, throughout western South America. But whoever construed Nature's most magnificent vulture as a mascot for terror didn't do his homework, because *Vultur gryphus* never comes anywhere near Buenos Aires, or Montevideo, or São Paulo.

It was Águila's birth that finally healed the fracture in my relationship with Mom—though not, I fear, the deeper, long-ossified fractures in her own psyche. I was surprised, but I didn't protest, when Alejandra said she wanted Lili to accompany Águila's birth. I was even more surprised when Lili agreed, abandoning Angelito and the chickens to Rubén's care and jumping on a flight to San Francisco as if she had just been saving her pennies and waiting for our invitation. In the sleepless euphoria of our baby's birth and first month of life, with Mom installed in the little workroom that would eventually be his bedroom, and Dad popping in to visit every weekend—the two of them slipping off to fight and seduce each other like old times, even though Dad now had a girlfriend—I felt, for the first time in nearly two years, completely at ease in my family, surrounded by the flotsam of love, remorse, sarcasm, and sardonic humor that my upbringing, if not my birthright, had made me privilege to. And at the focal point of it all, my baby son, who has an inde-fatigably amiable disposition that Keith and Lili claim mirrors that of his father as a baby. He was and is the family darling, and already, by the tender age of eighteen months, the happy beneficiary of that most coveted of Quiroga family commodi-ties: Celia's esteem.

We brought Águila to Uruguay for the first time last Christmas, and like a cat gravitating to the most disinterested human in the room, he immediately latched on to Abuela. He had only just begun to talk in complete sentences and Abuela is not one to gush over children, but the two of them were inseparable, toddling around the house counting things and carrying on a mysterious conversation that no one else could understand. The day before we left, Abuela took me aside and told me that Águila had "The Gift," that it was a privilege to recognize it so early and we should nurture it. I couldn't quite imagine extrasensory perception being one of my son's many gifts, but I never argued with Abuela and wasn't about to start. We were standing by the window in the living room, and she took hold of my forearm to make sure she had my attention, tilting her face up to fix me in her gaze. "Two thousand three is my year," she whispered, tightening her grip on my arm and holding my eye until tears started rolling down my cheeks and I nodded in acquiescence.

So we said goodbye last year in earnest, Abuela and I. She died in May, letting Lili care for her during her last weeks—a comfort for Mom, I guess, if not for Abuela. It's not something Mom and I ever talk about, but I'm glad Abuela never knew that Águila and I were Eva's offspring. That her own grandchild had been stillborn in an Argentinian torture center, and her daughter never trusted her love enough to tell her. Whether these were lies or benign omissions, I've gotten so used to living with them that I can almost comprehend Lili and the creation lies that formed and ultimately ruptured her own little family.

Occasionally, I worry that Alejandra and I have betrayed Eva's ghost—and William's and Natalio's—with our secret. But for the moment, it's the living I'm concerned with. They've left me alone for the day, sitting at Abuela's old dining room table, trying to finish this story that has been so long in the telling, trying to get it right, the saddest part, the tragedy—the part that truly matters. Alejandra is off with friends, Rubén at the estancia, Juan Luis at work. We spent most of our three-week vacation at the estancia, and Elsa thinks Águila has been deprived of sand castles and good ice cream, so she and Lili took him to the beach and to the La Cigale shop on the Rambla, which has managed to survive the latest economic crisis. They've decided to rent the house, but they haven't made much progress cleaning it out. Lili wants to sort through item by item, Juan wants to sweep everything into a moving van and pack it off to the estancia to store in the barn, and Rubén has slated the barn for other purposes and wants to hold an estate sale: as if in homage to Abuela's own principles of salvage, no one dares to throw anything away.

Someday, we will have to make a decision about what to tell Águila, about which lies and omissions really matter. As I sit here squinting at my laptop screen, surrounded by half-packed boxes, the glare of the January sun flooding through open blinds and violating the gloom of Abuela's old house, I imagine Águila sorting through our things the way Mom and Juan Luis and Rubén have been sorting through Abuela's. I picture him coming upon this manuscript, blowing the dust from its surface and trying to decide what to do with it. He'll wonder if he should throw it away or retire it to a corner of his bookshelf with the old photo albums, if he is meant to read it, if he wants to—how deeply he really wants to know his father. I wasn't writing for posterity when I started this little memoir. I certainly wasn't thinking of my son. If I had been, I might have told the story differently, indeed, I probably would have censored and revised these pages into nonexistence. Even now, as it dawns on me that I want Águila to read this story someday—maybe *because* I imagine him reading it—I worry that the melodrama and violence of our family history may eclipse the miracle of the *Perdurallus gordoni* discovery. And the tragedy of its loss.

* * *

The Quiroga family has navigated comfortably through the economic crises of the last few years. No one is getting rich, but even with the ever-fickle Uruguayan economy in shreds and Juan slated to lose his ministry job when the Frente takes power in March, the Quirogas are doing okay. Juan even voted for Tabaré this time, along with a lot of Colorados who held Batlle and his cronies responsible for the lack of financial regulation that left Uruguay so susceptible to Argentina's banking crisis. The economy is supposedly picking up—with help from the IMF, which now owns the future—though you wouldn't know it from a walk through the city. Montevideo is a phantom of its end-of-millennium self, a phantom of a phantom, as sad and abandoned as Abuela's empty house. The Quiroga estancia, on the other hand, is thriving, this year's flood notwithstanding.

Lili's vegetable farm is a particularly bounteous subsistence operation, which Rubén has started to capitalize on. He refurbished half the barn with two rooms and a bathroom, and he's started advertising on a website for "ecotourism," billing the estancia as a sort of dude ranch that offers vegetable gardening workshops and birdwatching tours, instead of horses and cows. Last year, to my surprise, they attracted two birding couples from Boston. Flying from the US to Uruguay in the age of global warming doesn't seem particularly "ecological," and there are lots of more beautiful, exotic places to bird, but the Bostonians were charmed by the whole experience—the English-speaking dynamo who grew and cooked the meals, the guitar-strumming tenor, the spoiled El-Trigal-eating pet Ñandú, and, not least, the mosquito-infested wild marsh, which one of Eduardo's students led them into.

In the end, it was Juan's own plan that allowed him to grow rice without drying out the marsh. My efforts to obtain water subsidies led to naught, but Juan developed a system that, instead of inundating the fields in a half-foot of water for two months of the summer, covers them with a thin lens at crucial times and leaves a steady flow from the pond into the marsh. He says it's cutting-edge agricultural science that has only been tested on a couple experimental fields in Europe, but it's given him good crops for three years, and his organic rice has turned out to be relatively immune to the price fluctuations that plague the other growers. He might even come through this year's flood relatively unscathed. But I can't say as much for all of the estancia's inhabitants.

The species report for *Perdurallus gordoni* appeared in the May 2001 issue of *The Auk*, but the Committee of South American Birds has yet to decide whether to accept it as a new species and genus. As predicted, there was a hullabaloo about naming it without a type specimen, especially since it turned out to be a new genus with only one branch and, as far as we knew, only a handful of tiny leaves. Still, when the species description was published, we celebrated.

That first spring, our pair had rebuilt a larger, more deluxe version of their nest in the same place, a virtual rail mansion that they've reused for three years running now, even though Eduardo said rails don't usually reuse their nests. They produced four chicks that year, and six the following. We don't know how many eggs they were sitting this year. In the summer of 2001, Eduardo's students braved a night in the marsh and managed to record my mysterious third adult. *Burrito Perdido Gordon.* Gordon's Lost Rail. That's the genus name we came up with, *Perdurallus.* Because the chicks invariably disappear shortly after fledging. Eduardo thinks they disperse, that they go out in search of other hidden pockets of marsh to the east and north. He spotted an almost mature juvenile in the Bañados de India Muerta in the fall of 2001, and we all got excited—but it hasn't been seen since. That is the only *Perdurallus gordoni* that has ever been seen or heard anywhere outside the Quiroga marsh. But until the flood this spring, our pair—or trio, because for all we knew they had some kind of love triangle going—was cranking out babies and we could hope that at least some of them found homes and survived. We were optimistic.

In another time, the flood might have been your garden-variety local natural disaster. There was a freak storm, torrential rains at a time of year when the streams and canals were already full. Caruso's canal overflowed its banks and the dike on Juan's pond broke, sending water sweeping across the rice fields. Caruso lost a newly planted crop, and Juan had to delay planting for weeks and still isn't sure if his crop will mature. The house and Mom's vegetables and orchard were saved by the tilt of the land, but when Juan's dike broke, water flooded into the marsh that he'd so diligently guarded from desiccation, and all the low-lying nests in the reed bed and around the pond were washed out. It was early in the season, and Eduardo, whose student had been monitoring the nesting birds, says all except the *Pollona Azul* and the *gordoni* have rebuilt. The *Pollona Azul* are still hanging around the pond, and no one is worried about them anyway. But our rails, who had already been sitting eggs for at least two weeks, have not been seen or heard since the flood. Their beautiful nest is gone, ramp and all, the bush where it was a random tangle of branches.

Águila can't pronounce "lost" yet, or *perdido*. "Doden Wost Wail" is what he gamely calls the mythical little birds I spent the last two weeks searching for. Eduardo and his student had already been out there four or five times since September, playing the rail recordings, to no avail. I thought maybe they were just hiding, bereaving the loss of their nest and family in the making, and I searched for them afternoons, evenings, mornings, often with Águila strapped to my back. Alejandra complained about the mosquito repellent and said he would be happier chasing Angelito or helping Lili plant lettuce seeds than slogging around with his morose father. I spent a night out there by myself, since we know now they're only active at night when they're not nesting. Hoping in vain I would hear their forlorn trills.

Maybe they stuck with the nest and drowned. Maybe they wandered off in search of their progeny. Maybe there is still a lone bird in there, gone mute with loneliness. Maybe our trio would have been eaten by a fox or died of old age this year even without the floods, maybe there are dozens, even hundreds, of Gordon's Lost Rails living incognito in some other remnant of marsh on the far side of the continent. And maybe they're truly, irretrievably gone—not lost in the world the way we hoped when we named them, but lost to the world, *perdido para el mundo.* That is what we think now, Eduardo and I and his colleagues. A shrunken and diminished habitat, after decades of draining marshes. A freak storm of the sort caused by altering the earth's atmosphere, a century of human development and profiteering in buried carbon. Millions of years of slow, painstaking, idiosyncratic evolution. Lost. Another statistic for the mass extinction.

We did our individual bests. Alejandra likes to remind me of that. She likes to point out small successes, the ones I myself have shown her—the Bald Eagles that graced our son's conception, the Peregrine Falcons, the reestablished tidal marsh in Point Reyes, the migrant bird refuge that one of the Central Valley rice growers in our bird monitoring project agreed to . . . the 134 avian species still living happily ever after in the Quiroga marsh, along with who knows what in the way of little invertebrates that no one has ever looked for. But staying optimistic is no easy task when you've set your heart on telling the truth. My intuition, my naturalist's empathetic moral sense, tells me in no uncertain terms that we failed the *Perdurallus,* one species to another, that they were unwitting minor characters in a human story, doomed by human history in the same way our own children are—but without *Homo sapiens'* capacity for adaptation. Without awareness.

I'm going to save this file on a disc now, and then I'm going to delete it from my laptop so I won't be tempted to change it. Alejandra suggested that when we get back to Davis I have it printed and bound together with my old bird journal from 1999—she has always loved that journal, and it's just languishing on a shelf in our workroom. I like that idea. I'll store it properly then, in the old leather suitcase I found in Abuela's garage, neatly bound and dust-free. When Águila is old enough—twenty-three, say, or eighteen, or maybe even fifteen—I'll open the suitcase, take it out, and lay it in his hands. This thing I've made. It's our legacy, after all, a natural history of loss, a map of lacunae, passed down from the great-grandfather whose genes he doesn't carry and the missing grandparents we haven't acknowledged. His father's longing and empathy for the last nuances of a nature he'll never know, tempered by his mother's science, the strange comfort of her biogeochemical perspective, of adaptive microbes and geologic time. Is it perverse to want your child to love what is already lost, to know longing? Am I wishing pain on my son? I don't think so. I'm wishing beauty on him. A naturalist's sensibility. Dangerous idealism. Cynical hope.

ACKNOWLEDGMENTS

I owe my own birder gene to my cousin David Gaines, the much-loved naturalist—and real-life instigator of the movement to save Mono Lake and the California Gull—who taught me to bird when I was a kid. David didn't live to see this book take flight, but his spirit inhabits every page.

The rail that Gabriel discovers is fictional, as is the Quiroga family estancia and its marsh. All of the other birds and animals described have been observed in their corresponding regional habitats. Since Gabe started birding in Uruguay in 1999, any number of wonderful field guides of Uruguayan birds have been published, in addition to a new edition of the Narosky guide that he uses. Similarly, the details of Alejandra's research are fictionalized, but plausible and based on actual research projects and the state of knowledge at the end of the 1990s.

Many, many people supported the creation of this novel in many ways, over the many years, and in the many places that I worked on it. My small writers group in Northern California has accompanied it through all its drafts and interruptions, even as I wandered around the globe: Sean Swift, Ray Holley, and—above and beyond our group meetings—Jean Hegland contributed smart readings, group brainstorming, tough love, and encouragement that were essential to this creation.

I want to thank Dr. Ignacio Porzecanski for sharing his knowledge of Uruguay's eastern wetlands and environmental issues, arranging for me to tag along with PROBIDES staff in their field work, and, not least, for his wry humor, encouragement, and hospitality during my first years of researching this book. I'm grateful to Juan Manuel Pérez Ferreira for welcoming me to his estancia, teaching me to drink whiskey, and letting me pick his brain about rice farming, Uruguayan style. Drs. Silvana Tarlera Robles and Ana Fernández Scavino opened their lab to me at the Universidad de la República, explained their work in detail, and took me along on their sample collection excursions. Thanks are due as well to Dr. Santiago Claramunt for catching a number of inadvertent mistakes in the bird descriptions and science. In Rocha, I'm indebted to Elsa Niell for her friendship, hospitality, introductions to local *estancieros*, and help with practical logistics.

In Montevideo, these dear friends shared their stories, answered my naive questions, regaled me with their various versions of Uruguayan politics, and, not least, offered housing and a space to write when things were most precarious: thank you, Graciela Martinez, Aurora Sopeña, Giselle Petrides, Nancy Umpierrez, Pepe Chau, and Sofia Gil Turnes. Special thanks to Graciela for loaning me her apartment and for her astute reading of the final draft; to Nancy for her somewhat suspect Uruguayan sayings; to Aurora for psychological insights; to Giselle for her political histories; to Pepe for always checking up on me; and to Sofia for bringing us all together, in absentia. The loft of Pepe's printing shop, replete with offset press and solvent fumes, takes the prize as the most inspired writer's garret I've ever inhabited.

During the years this book was on hold, I met Dr. Mandy Joye, and her knowledge and love of microbial ecology influenced the way I thought about Alejandra's bugs. I'm grateful to the Hanse-Wissenschaftskolleg (Institute of Advanced Study), which brought us together, and to Mandy for her comments on a draft of *Accidentals* so many years later. Thanks are also due the University of Bremen and the Volkswagen Foundation for funding the Fiction Meets Science program, which kept me employed and allowed me flexibility to work on this book when I ended up staying on in Germany. I'm also grateful for the support—both practical and emotional—provided by my sister and brother-in-law, Kathie Gaines and Ray Welch, and my friend

Monica Larenas as I worked through the final edits in California.

Without the faith, perseverance, and professionalism of my wonderful literary agent, Pamela Malpas, *Accidentals* would never have found its way into the hands of the talented and dedicated team at Torrey House Press, Kirsten Johanna Allen, Anne Terashima, Rachel Davis, and Kathleen Metcalf.

ABOUT THE AUTHOR

Susan M. Gaines is the author of the novel *Carbon Dreams* and of the science narrative, *Echoes of Life: What Fossil Molecules Reveal About Earth History*. Her short stories have appeared in numerous literary journals anthologies; they have been nominated for two Pushcart Prizes and been selected for the *Best of the West*. Gaines's fiction is informed by a youth spent hiking and birding California's mountains and coastline, and by her education in chemistry and oceanography. She is the recipient of an Art in Science Fellowship at the Hanse Institute for Advanced Study, as well as the 2018 Suffrage Science Award. Currently at work on another novel, Gaines divides her time between her native California, Uruguay, and Germany, where she co-directs the Fiction Meets Science research and fellowship program.

TORREY HOUSE PRESS

Voices for the Land

The economy is a wholly owned subsidiary of the environment, not the other way around.
— Senator Gaylord Nelson, founder of Earth Day

Torrey House Press is an independent nonprofit publisher promoting environmental conservation through literature. We believe that culture is changed through conversation and that lively, contemporary literature is the cutting edge of social change. We strive to identify exceptional writers, nurture their work, and engage the widest possible audience; to publish diverse voices with transformative stories that illuminate important facets of our ever-changing planet; to develop literary resources for the conservation movement, educating and entertaining readers, inspiring action.

Visit www.torreyhouse.org for reading group discussion guides, author interviews, and more.

As a 501(c)(3) nonprofit publisher, our work is made possible by the generous donations from readers like you.

Torrey House Press is supported by the National Endowment for the Arts, Back of Beyond Books, the King's English Bookshop, Jeff and Heather Adams, the Jeffrey S. and Helen H. Cardon Foundation, the Grant B. Culley Jr. Foundation, Jerome Cooney and Laura Storjohann, Heidi Dexter and David Gens, Kirtly Parker Jones, Suzanne Bounous, Diana Allison, the Utah Division of Arts & Museums, and Salt Lake County Zoo, Arts & Parks. Our thanks to individual donors, subscribers, and the Torrey House Press board of directors for their valued support.

Join the Torrey House Press family and give today at www.torreyhouse.org/give.